GAYLE WILSON
THE INQUISITOR

ISBN-13: 978-0-7783-2320-4
ISBN-10:   0-7783-2320-X

THE INQUISITOR

Copyright © 2006 by Mona Gay Thomas.

www.MIRABooks.com

Printed in U.S.A.

Praise for GAYLE WILSON

"Gayle Wilson will go far in romantic suspense. Her books have that special 'edge' that lifts them out of the ordinary. They're always tautly written, a treasure trove of action, suspense and richly drawn characters."
—*New York Times* bestselling author Linda Howard

"An exhilarating continual action thriller that never slows down."
—*TheBestReviews.com* on *Double Blind*

"Wilson gives her readers just what they want: more thrilling adventure and heart-wrenching suspense.... Inspiring. Wilson is destined to become one of the suspense genre's brightest stars."
—*Romantic Times BOOKclub,* 4 ½ stars, on *Wednesday's Child*

"Gayle Wilson pulls out all the stops to give her readers a thrilling chilling read that will give you goose bumps in the night."
—*ReadertoReader.com* on *In Plain Sight*

"Writing like this is a rare treat."
—*Gothic Journal*

"Rich historical detail, intriguing mystery, romance that touches the heart and lingers in the mind. These are elements that keep me waiting impatiently for Gayle Wilson's next book."
—*USA TODAY* bestselling author BJ James

Also by GAYLE WILSON

DOUBLE BLIND
WEDNESDAY'S CHILD
IN PLAIN SIGHT

And watch for the newest novel from
GAYLE WILSON

BOGEYMAN

Available December 2006

To Dianne, Mary, Charlotte, Joy, Katsy, Becki
and my mom for sticking with me throughout
this incredible journey and for reading them all.
I love you!

Prologue

She had been a gift. Something that had fallen into his lap without any effort on his part. Surprisingly, she'd proven to be more satisfying than most of the others, all of whom had been carefully selected after weeks of study.

It hadn't been time to begin thinking about the next one. By now he was conscious of the smallest sign of that, even those he had once thought bore no relationship to his needs.

A sense of anxiety that increased day by day until it became an urgency he could no longer ignore. The sensation that something wasn't right in the pleasant world he inhabited. Those were inevitably followed by an indefinable feeling that things were slipping out of control. Then finally came the rage that still shocked him with its intensity.

None of that had occurred. Not this time.

Yet when he'd seen her standing on the street corner in the rain, strands of dark hair plastered against those alabaster cheeks, the compulsion to take her and make her his had been overwhelming. Irresistible.

This wasn't the way things were supposed to be done. Not his normal attention to detail. But in this instance, he had no regrets that he had given in. His impulsive decision seemed to have worked out. And apparently no one was even looking for her.

Which meant there was no need to hurry, he thought with a degree of anticipation beyond any he could remember. He literally had all the time in the world.

Time for him. And for her.

A gift, he thought again, brushing a stray tendril of hair off her cheek.

When it was dry, her hair had demonstrated an unexpected tendency to curl. Something he would never have guessed from the way it had appeared that afternoon.

He smiled at the memory. She had looked like a bedraggled puppy, lost in the storm. Her face had lit up when he'd stopped the car, opened the passenger-side window, and leaned across the seat.

Do you need any help?

There had been no hesitation on her part. No fear. She had immediately stuck her head and shoulders inside the vehicle in response.

Only directions.

By then, despite what his intellect screamed at him, it had been far too late to provide those and drive away. He'd seen her smile. He'd seen those big, brown eyes and under them the mascara she'd applied to her lower lashes smudged from the rain.

He'd taken care of that imperfection, of course. As soon as he'd gotten her to a safe place, he had painstakingly cleaned off her makeup, leaving her skin smooth and bare as a baby's.

Innocent.

Except she wasn't. None of them were. No matter what they said, none of them were free from the stain. None were pure. Especially not the ones who pretended to be once they understood.

She hadn't pretended. She'd been defiant. Angry. Profane.

He had found he liked her that way. It had broken the monotony of fear and pleading.

In contrast to the others she'd been... Sassy, as his grandmother would have said.

Sassy. He liked the word, too, now that he'd remembered it. He tasted the syllables in his mouth as he whispered them against her ear.

The perfect word. Perfect for her. And she, in turn, was perfect for him. His lovely, defiant unexpected gift.

"Time to wake up."

Although he hated it, he had to keep her drugged on the chance that she might, by some miracle, free herself and get away. That had never happened before—and it never would. Not as careful as he was.

That was his nightmare, however. That one of them might escape and tell everyone about the things he'd done.

Those were only for the two of them. For them to share. As they would share this.

Her lashes fluttered, telling him she was almost awake. He had timed it to the minute. All he had to do was to wait while the drug wore off. And when it had...

Although he had not been conscious of his needs when he'd taken her, he knew them now. They surged through his body with an inexorable force, driving the ebb and flow of his emotions.

He touched her face, again relishing its smoothness. Devoid of the foundation she'd been wearing, her skin was that of a child. Even to the faint sweep of color that now overlay those perfect cheekbones. Another sign, if he had needed one, that she was conscious.

"I know you're awake," he said, bending close again to whisper the words into her ear.

Her hair moved against his lips, its softness stirred by his breath. Without raising his head, he turned, so that her face was in profile, as he watched the slow, sleepy lift of her lashes.

With the drug, she would be confused. They always were, no matter how many times he'd come to them.

He had watched the sequence of that confusion perhaps a hundred times and never tired of it. First, she would try to think where she was. To separate dream from reality. Nightmare from truth.

Then, in one fell swoop, it would happen. She would remember. She would remember everything.

And she would know.

The knowledge would suddenly be there in those wide, dark eyes. If he weren't careful, he would miss it.

He straightened to smile down on her. Her eyes, slightly glazed, appeared to be focused on the ceiling above her head. She had probably memorized its every crack and imperfection. They, too, would help clear her disorientation. And in a few seconds—

She turned, her head rolling on the hard mattress until she was at last looking at him. Although he was smiling, it didn't reassure her. But of course, they were too far along for her to have any delusions left.

Not his sweet, sassy drowning puppy.

She knew. She knew exactly what he was. And she knew what was going to happen to her. It was all there in the beautiful dark orbs locked on his face.

Her eyes widened, even as they stared up into his. They were no longer defiant, however. He had seen to that.

The only thing in them now were the questions neither of them yet had answers for.

When will this be over?
When will you let me go?
When, dear God, will you finally let me die?

One

"One more question, Dr. Kincaid. If you don't mind."

The damp December air had seeped through the multiple layers of clothing Jenna had donned in preparation for this interview. The station had insisted the clip be filmed in front of the mall, so that its steady stream of Christmas shoppers would be visible behind them. Although Jenna acknowledged it was an appropriate backdrop for a segment on holiday depression, that didn't mean she was enjoying the setting.

As the largest mental health practice in the greater Birmingham area, Carlisle, Levitt and Connor was called on throughout the year to furnish speakers for a variety of informational workshops as well as for interviews on local news programs and talk shows. Those requests were unusually heavy this time of year, so the psychologists and psychiatrists on staff rotated the responsibility. Tonight had been her turn to be the public face of the practice.

Normally Jenna didn't mind her thirty seconds in the spotlight. The visibility brought in new clients, which was beneficial to everyone. Sometimes they asked for an appointment with whichever of the group they'd seen on television or heard on the radio. And at this particular time of the year, it was never a bad thing to have increased billing.

"Of course," she said, smiling at the young man who looked all of eighteen. She suspected he might be one of the station's interns. Either that or the passage of another year had made her more aware of her own age in comparison.

At thirty-four she'd accomplished most of the goals she'd set for herself. At least, she amended, the professional ones.

There was plenty of time for the rest. Something she'd been telling herself for the last five years.

"This afternoon the police department conceded that the murders of Sandra Reynolds, Margaret DeSpain and Callie Morgan were the work of one killer," the reporter said. "What can you tell us about the person who might have perpetrated those crimes?"

Jenna hadn't yet heard that the police had issued that statement. Of course, she'd been seeing patients up until she'd left the office. Even if she *had* known, she wouldn't have been prepared to comment publicly on those murders. This was outside the scope of the subject matter she'd agreed to, as well as outside any area of expertise she might claim.

She allowed the smile she'd been holding for the camera to fade, considering the topic that had just been introduced. She took a breath as she tried to decide the best way to handle the kid's question before settling on simply telling the truth.

"I'm really not in any position to answer that. Not only have the details of those crimes not been made public, I'm *not* a profiler. Forensic psychology is a very specialized field, one I have little training for."

The reporter's mouth had tightened as she talked. A dull flush climbed up his neck and into his cheeks. It was obvious he felt her answer was either deliberately nonresponsive or, worse, a slam at his interviewing skills.

"I realize that," he said quickly. "I wasn't speaking in the particular. Just tell our viewers in general what makes a psychopath like this tick."

From his standpoint, the amended question was a good recovery. From hers, it left her as much under the gun as the previous one.

Other than the courses in abnormal psychology she'd taught as a grad assistant, Jenna hadn't had much occasion to think in depth about the kind of sociopath who enjoyed torturing and then killing women. And it was evident from the few details that had been released about the condition of the three bodies that this one found great pleasure in the suffering of his victims.

"From what I've read," she said, choosing her words carefully, "this killer doesn't appear to be psychotic. He's apparently very well organized, selecting his victims with care and carrying out the murders while leaving behind little forensic evidence that might help the police."

"He's killed three people, and you're saying he isn't crazy?" The reporter's tone was mocking, allowing his skepticism of that full rein.

"He's clearly a sociopath, but…" Jenna hesitated, thinking how difficult it was to use appropriate terminology when the public had such clear, if erroneous, notions of what words like *crazy, insane* and *psychotic* meant. "The killer's obviously incapable of feeling compassion for his victims, no matter how much they suffer, but if you met him in a social or professional environment, you might not notice anything out of the ordinary. Other than possibly thinking how charming he is."

"Which would help him in getting his victims to trust him."

"Unfortunately. Although he's clearly manipulative, he may also be very personable and articulate."

"So what creates someone like our charming sociopath?"

"No one really knows. The current thinking is that biological factors may play a role, some genetic predisposition if you will. There's no doubt, however, that the majority of these people were also the victims of childhood abuse—either physical or emotional or a combination of the two. Some case studies done on serial killers reveal that mistreatment was both prolonged and severe. It isn't hard to understand how a child subjected to isolation, a lack of affection, physical and mental domination, or actual physical abuse might become an adult who lacks the ability to feel normal empathy for his fellow human beings."

"Surely you're not suggesting that every abused child grows up to be a Ted Bundy."

"Actually, a very small percentage do. However, it *is* a common background for those we've had the opportunity to study in depth. Unfortunately, we can never know which children will emerge from those situations to become sociopaths. Or more importantly, which of those sociopaths will go on to kill."

"Because they've been trained in inflicting pain early on?"

"Pain. Domination. They desperately need to be in charge, possibly because as children they had so little control over what was happening to them."

"You sound as if you have some sympathy for them, Dr. Kincaid."

"I have sympathy for any child who's abused. They're helpless to prevent what's being done to them, often by the very people who should be their protectors."

"I meant that you seem to feel sympathy for the sociopaths they eventually become."

As a psychologist who had read study after study detailing the horrors of the abuses she'd just spoken about, Jenna supposed that was true. Certainly in the abstract. In light of what had been made public about what had been done to the murdered women...

"Not all sociopaths kill," she said again. "When they do, they must, of course, be subject to the laws that govern the rest of us. Once they've killed, it's unlikely they'll stop on their own. Before that can happen, they have to be apprehended. I hope the police find something to help them very soon, some piece of evidence that will lead them back to the murderer. Or that someone who knows something about those crimes will come forward with the information."

"So...you're saying he's definitely going to kill again."

And Merry Christmas to all, Jenna thought, realizing the trap she'd fallen into.

Still, there was very little that could be said in response to that question except the brutal reality. Despite the fact that hearing it was likely to inflame fears that had been rampant in the community even before today's announcement, she really had no choice.

This was something else the killer would feed off of. Not only would the murders themselves give him a sense of power, so would the media attention they'd attracted, such as this interview, and the terror it would create.

She should have cut this kid off without answering his original question. Since she hadn't, she could in good conscience now do nothing less than tell the truth.

"If he's not caught. It may not be here. Not if the police get too close to discovering who he is, but...even if they do, he won't stop killing. Not until he's finally been taken into custody."

"Or until he's dead."

Sean Murphy had already put his finger over the off button on the remote, when something made him hesitate. The reporter was busy closing out the segment, probably reiterating what the female psychologist had said. Nothing of what he was babbling about registered.

Sean was focused instead on the woman standing beside the interviewer, her hand clutching the collar of her coat as if trying to keep out the cold. It was clearly a defensive gesture.

An unconscious one? Or was it possible she was aware of how closely she matched the profile of the killer's victims?

That was unlikely, he decided, since the local cops hadn't yet publicly connected the latest three to the others. Maybe he should warn Dr. Jenna Kincaid that she met almost every one of the criteria the task force had put together over the course of the past four years of their investigation.

Late twenties or early thirties, Sean assessed. Tall and slender, with dark hair and eyes. Even her clothing, professional rather than provocative, followed the pattern the bastard had established with his first murder, which they now believed had been more than seven years ago.

His gaze having followed the line of the long navy coat down to the low-heeled boots she wore, Sean raised his eyes once more to the psychologist's face. Her features were striking but not classically beautiful.

She wouldn't draw every masculine eye, he acknowledged, but she'd find her share of admirers. The bone structure underlying that clear olive skin was too anatomically perfect not to attract attention. The discriminating would recognize it would be just that perfect when she was eighty.

And you've always considered yourself discriminating.

The image he'd been studying was suddenly replaced by an advertisement for a local car dealer. Sean punched the button, shutting off the television, before tossing the remote down on the bed.

He walked across his motel room toward its wall of glass, where he pushed aside the draperies to look out onto the interstate that paralleled the wide right-of-way just across the parking lot. The scene he encountered was depressingly winter-dreary, although the climate was generally mild.

The weather would make the killer's hunting easier. More people outdoors than in the northern cities. Not that the bastard ever seemed to have a problem finding victims.

Maybe what Dr. Kincaid said was right. Maybe he was so charming the women made it easy for him.

He would have had to be something special to charm Makaela. His sister had been nobody's fool. And unfortunately she'd had a lot of experience with phonies.

Apparently not enough to see through whatever ploy her murderer had used to persuade her to go with him.

Sean put his palm against the glass, using its coldness to fight the fury that flooded his brain whenever he thought of the things that had been done to his sister. They could still bring him wide awake, sweat pouring off his body, as he struggled against the nightmare images of what she'd suffered.

The press in Detroit were the ones who'd christened her murderer "the Inquisitor," a name horrifyingly appropriate. Too soon the people in this town would learn what the others had about the maniac in their midst.

Unless the bodies were too decomposed to make them obvious, as the first two here had been, most law enforcement agencies now recognized those signature mutilations. The special agent on the FBI's task force, the one who'd put Sean onto the Birmingham murders, had recognized them as soon as he'd read the description of the last victim.

Now that the locals had connected the three, they would be forced to take the next step and admit that these killings were part of a series, which, through the efforts of the Bureau, had been linked and credited to one man.

An unimaginably cruel and sadistic madman.

The cops here would add whatever information they had managed to uncover to the profile that was slowly, but relentlessly, being built. And when it was complete...

Sean's hand closed into a fist that he slammed into the glass. The window shuddered in its frame, although the blow had not been particularly hard. It hadn't been done in anger. It had been measured. Like a gavel pounded against a judge's bench. Or a hammer driving a nail.

The last one in your coffin, you bastard. And as God is my witness, I'll be the one who'll put it there.

Long after the television screen had gone dark, he couldn't get the psychologist out of his mind. After a while, he stopped trying, allowing her image to fill his head.

She'd been so perfect he had wondered—briefly—if the cops had put her up to that interview. After mentally reviewing the clip, something he was able to do with almost complete fidelity, as if he were watching a replay, he decided that what he'd seen hadn't been a performance.

Her slight hesitancy and the care with which she'd worded her opinions made him believe she had really been speaking off the cuff. The expression on her face, although quickly controlled, had made it obvious that the reporter's question about the murders had caught her off guard.

That's what you get for trusting the media, my dear.

He smiled as he raised the wine he'd bought on his way home in a semitoast before he brought the glass to his lips. He grimaced slightly at the taste before setting it back on the coffee table.

He had thought the merlot would make the evening more

enjoyable, easing his disappointment about how quickly the locals had tied these three victims together. Now that they had, he knew it would be only a matter of hours before they made the connection to the others.

His intent was always to break the pattern so that wouldn't happen. But if he were able to succeed in that, then what would be the point of the entire exercise? Old habits die hard, he admitted with a smile.

As some of them had, fighting the sweet release of death until the very end.

At that thought, somewhere deep inside his body was a wave of sexual pleasure, so sharp, so pure, it literally stole his breath. He closed his eyes, allowing himself to relish both the feeling and the memories that had provoked it.

Instead of the faces of the women whose suffering at his hands had induced that remembrance, the image of Jenna Kincaid clutching her coat against the cruel invasion of the cold as she wept for the child he had been again formed behind his lids.

They're helpless to prevent what is being done to them, often by the very people who should be their protectors.

It was rare that someone was able to articulate so clearly, so precisely, the nature of the injustice he'd suffered. That she had done so without knowing anything about him.

She was obviously someone of value. Someone he should get to know. Someone he should allow to know him.

Not like the others, of course. She was above all that. Just as he would be when he was with her.

She, unlike the rest, understood what drove him. Interacting with someone who could comprehend that on an intellectual level was a luxury he hadn't allowed himself in a very long time.

Simply another kind of indulgence, perhaps, but one whose time had definitely come.

Two

The sound of her door being flung open brought Jenna's eyes up. The secretary she shared with three other therapists was aware that she used the last ten minutes of the hour to make notes on the session that had just ended. Why she would interrupt—

Except it wasn't Sheila. Not *just* Sheila, she amended. Her secretary was looking at her over the broad shoulders of the man who seemed to fill the opening.

"I'm sorry, Dr. Kincaid," she said. "I tried to tell him—"

"We need to talk."

The intruder offered no apology for the interruption. The curt sentence had been more of a command than a request. Whatever his problem—and Jenna wasn't using that terminology in the sense of something that needed treatment—she didn't have the time or the inclination to deal with it today.

"I'm sorry. You'll need to make an appointment—"

"How much?"

"I beg your pardon."

"How much is it going to cost to talk to you? What I have to say won't take an hour, but I'm willing to pay for one if that's what it will take to get you to listen."

As if to prove his point, he took his wallet out of the back pocket of his jeans. Behind him, Sheila pantomimed dialing and then bringing a phone to her ear, brows raised in inquiry.

Jenna shook her head, the movement slight enough that she hoped it wouldn't be noticed by the man now in the process of opening his billfold. She was unwilling to call the police until she knew more about what was going on.

The guy didn't look deranged. Actually…

Actually he looked pretty normal, if you thought normal was six-foot-something of solid muscle enclosed in black chamois and denim. He was carrying nothing in his hands, and the worn jeans hugged his narrow hips too tightly to conceal a weapon. He was also clean-shaven, although there was a hint of a five o'clock shadow on the lean cheeks.

The black hair was so closely cropped it couldn't possibly become disarranged, which might have given her some indication of his mental state. The fact that it had so recently been trimmed seemed a point in his favor. People who had really "lost it" weren't usually concerned with personal grooming.

His eyes, however, were the most compelling argument that there was nothing seriously out of whack in his psyche. They were a clear, piercing blue, the color startling against his tanned skin and ebony hair.

And right now they were focused on her face as he calmly waited for her answer, wallet open, long, dark fingers poised to pluck from it whatever amount she named. Still evaluating him, as she would any patient, Jenna noticed that his nails were neatly trimmed, the hands themselves completely masculine, fingers square despite their length.

"Hundred and fifty?" he asked. "That do it?"

She blinked, breaking the spell he had cast. "I'm sorry. I'm completely booked this afternoon, as I'm sure my secretary told you. If this is an emergency, I can try to work you in early tomorrow—"

"Lady, I'm here in an attempt to save your life. And I'm even willing to pay for the opportunity. All you have to do is tell me how much."

He strode across the room, stopping when he reached her desk. Her gaze had followed him, her chin automatically lifting as he approached, until she was looking up into those ice-blue eyes.

Above the right, a dark brow arched. "One seventy-five? Two hundred? Obviously I'm not up on the going rate for... *therapy.*"

Jenna's lips were still parted from her uncompleted sentence. Despite the obvious sarcasm, she closed them, glancing back at Sheila with a slight shake of her head to indicate she was willing to see him.

The secretary's mouth opened, probably to protest the decision, but then she snapped it shut. She reached for the knob of the door, pulling it closed behind her as she returned to her office.

Jenna wasn't sure Sheila still wouldn't place that call to the police, despite the fact it had been vetoed. She also wasn't sure she wouldn't be relieved if she did.

She looked back at the man who had invaded her office and now seemed to fill it. He, too, had watched the secretary's departure. He turned back as Jenna refocused on his face. There was something in his gaze that looked like approval.

Because she'd been crazy enough to let him stay?

Or maybe he was pleased at the ease with which he'd gotten his way. Something he seemed far too accustomed to doing.

"You can put your money away, Mr.…?"

"Murphy. Sean Murphy."

Although she waited, he didn't offer to elaborate on the information, so she went back to the salient part of what he'd told her. "You said you're here in an attempt to 'save my life.' I'm not sure what that means, but given how serious it sounds, I'm willing to listen. You have…" She glanced at her watch to make her point. "Exactly ten minutes before my next appointment."

He held her eyes, maybe assessing how serious she was about the timeframe she'd just given him. After a few seconds, he closed his wallet. He struggled to push it back into his pocket, verifying her initial assessment about the tightness of his jeans.

Now, if only she'd been equally correct in gauging his mental state…

"I saw your interview yesterday."

Something shifted in the bottom of Jenna's stomach, cold and hard and a little frightening. She swallowed, determined not to display any outward sign of that sudden anxiety.

"The one on holiday stress?"

"Must have missed that part. What I saw was you giving your *professional* opinion about the man who killed three women here."

"I tried to make it clear to the reporter that serial killers don't fall within my area of expertise—" she began, choosing her words with care.

"What you made *clear,* Dr. Kincaid, was that you thought the poor, mistreated son of a bitch just couldn't help himself."

The apprehension Jenna had felt was suddenly replaced by anger, most of it self-directed. She had known she should have cut the reporter off when he'd started that line of questioning. Instead, she'd been too conscious of the public-relations aspect of the interview. If she'd seemed uncooperative, that might well have been the only part of the segment to be aired.

And what if it were?

Of course, it was easy to sit here now, without the red light of the camera focused on her face, and know what she should have done. She'd made a mistake, but she didn't deserve to be chastised for it by someone who obviously had his own agenda.

"I never said that. I never said anything *like* that."

"Close enough. And as a psychologist, you had to know he'd feed off your remarks."

She had thought something similar yesterday. Not that the killer would "feed off" her comment about sociopaths being the products of abuse, but that he would delight in hearing *anyone* talk about the murders. Just as he would relish the increased terror that kind of interview would bring within the community.

"He's *already* feeding off the media frenzy," she said, refusing to allow this jackass to intimidate her. "I doubt anything I said yesterday is going to add to his enjoyment."

Since the police had announced the connection between the homicides, not only had the local media been all over the story, the twenty-four-hour cable news stations were carrying it as well. It seemed that the killer had now been linked to several murders in other parts of the country.

Jenna hadn't had time to do more than glance at the lead story in the morning paper. That had been enough to let her know this was going to remain at the top of the front page until this killer was caught. Or until things got so hot for him here that he moved on to another location.

Which was essentially all she'd said yesterday, she reiterated mentally. Actually, there was *nothing* she'd said that wasn't completely accurate.

She had talked about the interview to Paul Carlisle, the founder of the practice, as soon as she'd gotten to work. That's when she'd discovered that the station had replayed the part about the murderer on both the late-night news and again this morning, although they hadn't bothered to repeat the rest of the interview.

Maybe Sean Murphy had seen one of those broadcasts. In any case, there was nothing she needed to apologize for, she decided. No matter what he thought.

"You really don't have a clue, do you?"

"I'm *sorry?*" Her voice rose on the last word.

"You tell someone who likes torturing women that he's just some poor abused kid who isn't responsible for what he's done—"

"I never said that. I never said anything *like* that."

"Yeah? Well, you can bet that's what he heard."

"And who made you the expert on what he heard?"

"A long and intimate acquaintance."

Her analytical mind took over, replaying his words. "Are you saying...you *know* him? You know who he is?"

"I know *what* he is. And I know what he does. Apparently a lot better method of 'knowing' him than whatever crap you were spouting."

Jenna stood so abruptly that her desk chair rolled back and hit the wall behind her. "We're through here."

She reached across the desk to punch the button on the intercom. If he didn't leave, she'd tell her secretary to do what she had wanted to when he'd first barged in.

"You're exactly his type, you know."

Startled by the change in tone, Jenna looked up, her finger stopped in midair. There was no longer any trace of approval in his eyes. They were cold. And very angry.

"What the hell is that supposed to mean?"

"You can look it up when the locals finally get their act together. Dark hair. Dark eyes. Tall. Slender. And not a prostitute or a waitress among them."

The trepidation she'd felt when he said he'd come to save

her life stirred in her stomach again. Today's front page had featured pictures of the local victims. And the description he'd just given fit them all.

"I don't know that he's ever done a psychologist," Sean Murphy went on, seeming to relish the impact his words were having, "but I've got a feeling he'd be interested."

"In *me?* Are you suggesting that the killer would be interested in *me?*"

"Since you're out there telling the world what a poor, misunderstood bastard he is."

She didn't bother to refute the accusation again. He had decided that's what she'd said. There was probably nothing she could do to dissuade him from his perception.

And what if he's right? What if that's what the killer heard, too?

Which would be a hell of an assumption. First, that the murderer had even heard the interview. And second, that he'd misinterpreted her words exactly as this arrogant SOB had.

"Thank you for your concern," she said, working to keep any emotion out of the conventional words. It was obvious Sean Murphy had come here to frighten her. She wasn't about to give him the satisfaction of knowing he'd succeeded.

As soon as he was out of here, she would call the police and tell them what he'd said. That business about having a long and intimate acquaintance with the killer would probably be of interest to them.

"Believe me, Dr. Kincaid, concern for you isn't what brought me. Since you didn't seem to have any idea what you'd done, however, I *did* feel a certain moral obligation to warn you."

"Then consider that your 'moral obligation' has been fulfilled. I *assure* you I feel duly warned."

As she said the last, she again reached for the intercom button, hoping he'd take that as a hint that they were done. Instead of turning toward the door as she'd hoped, he stood there, directly across from her desk, his eyes once more assessing.

"He's smart," he said as if she hadn't spoken. "And he'll be in no hurry. He never is. A couple of months. Maybe more. Actually, it could be any time. Any time *he* chooses."

"Thank you." She held his eyes without letting her own reveal any reaction to the threat. And she now had no doubt that's what it was. "I'll be sure to remember that."

For the first time a tilt at the corners disturbed the thin line of his lips. The smile seemed to soften the spare planes of his face, although it held not one iota of amusement.

"There *is* one thing he doesn't know," he added. "Something that may work to your advantage."

Maybe he *was* disturbed. Maybe those signs of normality she'd noted didn't mean jack shit.

"And what is that, Mr. Murphy?"

"That I'm every bit as patient as he is. When you see him, you might want to tell him that."

The bite of the cold outside air was welcome after the overheated interior of the office building. Sean stood a moment in front of its double glass doors, staring unseeingly across at the lot where he'd parked the rented SUV.

Guilt had reared its ugly head even before he'd turned on his heel and walked out of Jenna Kincaid's office. It hadn't abated during the short ride down on the elevator.

He'd done what he'd come here to do. He'd frightened her so that the next time some reporter stuck a mike under her nose, she'd think twice before she made excuses for a murderer. And he couldn't quite figure out why he felt like such an asshole.

Maybe because of what was in her eyes when you told her some sadistic bastard was going to torture and kill her? How the hell did you think she'd react?

Actually, he'd been surprised at how well she'd dealt with everything he'd thrown at her. He'd been so furious about the garbage she'd spewed during that interview, he hadn't really stopped to think about her reaction.

He had been brutally—unforgivably—direct about the possibility that if the killer had heard her sympathetic explanation for his behavior, she would have attracted the attention of the last man on earth whose attention she would want. Despite his threat, Jenna Kincaid had kept her poise.

Only in her eyes had he seen any evidence of the fear he'd deliberately tried to create. And remembering what had been in them, he felt even more like a bastard.

He jammed his fists into the pockets of his leather jacket and started down the steps. After years of operating in hostile environments, he automatically scanned the parking lot, looking for anything out of the ordinary.

Like someone staking out the place where she worked?

He'd meant the question to be mocking. As the thought formed, however, Sean acknowledged that if the Inquisitor had seen that interview, he'd know exactly where she worked by now.

That clip had been replayed at least three times. And after the official announcement from the cops yesterday, the bastard would have been glued to every newscast, hoping to catch any publicity his actions had generated.

He would have seen Dr. Kincaid's pity party for him, all right. And by now, almost twenty-four hours later, he would undoubtedly know *all* about her.

Telling himself that wasn't his problem, Sean punched the key lock remote as he approached the SUV. Although it was only a little after four, the halogen lights in the lot had already come on, glinting off the vehicle's black surface.

It would probably be completely dark before Jenna Kincaid came out of her office. Certainly before she got back to her apartment.

Even if the killer had become interested because of what she'd said, it was probably too early to worry about her being followed. The Inquisitor would undoubtedly do his stalking electronically first. Maybe visit the library and check out microfiche from the local papers.

It might be weeks before he started tracking her physically. Or anyone else, Sean amended, attempting to reassure himself. At this late date, the killer wouldn't break his normal pattern. Not unless something happened to interrupt the cycle.

Like finding a woman who expressed sympathy for him? One who also satisfied every other criteria of his sick hunt?

Sean realized he was standing beside the SUV, the remote in his hand still pointed at the lock. He opened the door, sliding into the cold leather seat. He inserted the key into the ignition, but for some reason his fingers hesitated before they completed the act of turning it.

His eyes lifted to the rearview mirror. Reflected there were the double doors through which he'd just exited.

He had no idea if Jenna Kincaid normally came out that way. No idea if there was a separate parking lot for the staff. Those were things he hadn't thought he had any need to know.

Now he knew he was wrong.

He didn't like dealing with feelings. He was far more comfortable with facts. Things he could see and hear. Prove or disprove. What he felt now fell into none of those categories.

The hair on the back of his neck had begun to rise, a phenomenon he'd experienced more than once in his career. On a street in Somalia. Before an ambush in Afghanistan. While his unit had been searching an underground bunker in Iraq, which they knew was very probably booby-trapped.

Every time, the premonition that something dangerous was at hand had proved to be accurate. And he'd never told anyone about any of them.

What he felt now was that same gut-level surety. Inexplicable. And yet undeniable.

The bastard was here. Close enough that if he had known where to look, he could have seen him. Close enough that Sean could feel the strength of his evil deep in the most primitive part of his brain.

The realization that he'd been right about the danger Jenna Kincaid was in was no comfort for the guilt he'd been feeling. He closed his eyes, seeing Makaela's face as it had looked when they'd pulled out that stainless-steel drawer in the morgue in Detroit. After a fraction of a second he destroyed that nightmare image to replace it with the face of the woman he'd left inside the building behind him.

A woman he now knew with absolute gut-certainty he could use to finally get the man who'd flayed his sister alive.

Three

Jenna saw her four o'clock, operating on autopilot. She was unable to concentrate on what her patient said because the words of the man who had supposedly come to warn her echoed and reechoed in her head.

I don't know that he's ever done a psychologist, but I have a feeling he'd be interested.

That had so obviously been an attempt to frighten her that she was furious with herself for allowing him to succeed. She'd said nothing that was sympathetic to the killer in that interview. No one could have sympathy for someone who did what he did. Whatever her visitor's agenda—

A long and intimate acquaintance...

Despite the man's boast, she hadn't placed a call to the police after he'd left. She couldn't formulate a logical reason why she hadn't. There had just been something about him that had made her believe he wasn't involved in the murders.

Just like every woman who opened the door to Albert Di-Salvo believed he couldn't be the Strangler.

She closed the folder in which she'd been attempting to add notations. That was as pointless as trying to get what had happened an hour ago out of her head, but surely she could put it into perspective. Hundreds of people had talked publicly about those three murders, both on the air and in the newspaper. Was the killer going to come after each of them?

Or maybe only the ones who fit the victim profile.

She realized that her hands were trembling. Just as they had been when Murphy walked out of her office.

That had been mostly the result of anger. If there was any consolation to be taken in how she'd conducted herself, it would be that she hadn't given in to the tears she'd been on the edge of. Growing up, she'd always had a tendency to cry when she got really mad, a trait she thought she'd conquered long ago.

If she wanted to indulge that childish propensity, it would have to wait until she reached the privacy of her own home. Which couldn't be soon enough, she decided.

She picked up the phone and punched in Sheila's extension. "I'm leaving for the day. Any change in tomorrow's schedule I should know about?"

"Nothing really. Staff meeting at nine. After that you've got a full slate of appointments. It *is* that time of the year," the secretary said, her tone sympathetic.

That was something they would talk about in tomorrow morning's meeting. Everyone was feeling the double stress of the holidays and the murders. She had overheard a couple of the other therapists talking about an increase in requests for appointments, even from their regulars.

"Try to fight off the least desperate," she said aloud.

Sheila laughed. "Will do. Have a good night."

Yeah, right. "Thanks, Sheila."

She hung up and then looked at the folders stacked on the left-hand side of her desk. With the meeting in the morning, it was unlikely she'd have time to look over the files of the patients she'd be seeing during the day. Still, she wasn't willing to stay late to review them. If she tried, she'd probably be unable to keep her mind on what she was reading.

She was going home instead and breaking open the bottle of Jack Daniel's she'd bought to make sauce for the bread pudding she was to take to her mother's on Christmas Day. Maybe that would help her sleep. If not, it would certainly be good company while she didn't.

The staff parking deck was relatively full for this late in the afternoon, which was also a reflection of the season. Jenna had ridden down in the elevator with a couple of other staff members. Their cars had been closer to the building, so that she was now making her way to the outer perimeter of the deck alone.

The sound of her footsteps echoed off the concrete roof, seeming louder than they should. She realized as she approached the place where she'd parked this morning that the security light for this section was out, leaving the area in shadows.

She actually hesitated before she managed to control her uneasiness and continue toward her Accord. She punched the remote, the resulting beep and blinking lights reassuring in their normalcy.

Everything here was as it should be, she told herself. This was the building where she worked. The deck where she parked her car every single day. She mentally reiterated each phrase, a deliberate litany of the ordinary.

She didn't relax, however, until she'd opened the driver's side door and slid behind the wheel. As soon as she hit the autolock, the tension that had built as she'd crossed the deck released, leaving her drained.

Her eyes flicked to the rearview mirror and then she turned and looked into her backseat. Something she'd never done before in her life. It was empty, of course.

And just what in hell were you expecting to be there?

Disgusted that she'd given in to her paranoia, she jammed the key into the ignition and turned it. The dependable engine roared to life, its sound magnified by the low ceiling of the garage.

Looking over her right shoulder, she eased past Paul Carlisle's Porsche, which had been pulled in beside her car at a slight angle. She cleared its back fender, but just barely, congratulating herself as she completed the maneuver, and aligned her car so that it pointed toward the exit.

She glanced down to shift into Drive when a tap on her window brought her head around so quickly she felt the strain in her neck. Her heart began to pound before she recognized the founder of the practice standing beside her car. She pushed the button that would lower the window, determined to keep any trace of that reaction out of her voice and expression.

"What is it?"

"Just wanted to check on you," Paul said. "I meant to get down to your office this afternoon, but you know what they say about good intentions."

She nodded, unsure what this was about.

"You okay?" Paul asked, his brow slightly furrowed as he leaned forward, peering into the car.

"Just tired and stressed. Like everyone else this time of year."

"The thought of having to make the annual holiday pilgrimage to visit the folks in Douglasville has me thinking seriously about some good mood-altering pharmaceuticals."

Although Paul had smiled at his own slightly twisted brand of humor, she knew there was a certain level of truth to what he'd just said. He'd often joked that he had gone into psychiatry because of the practice he'd already had with his extremely dysfunctional family.

"I don't suppose you'd be willing to share your stash?" she asked, answering his grin.

"You're not still worried about that interview, are you?"

It was the perfect opportunity to tell him about the man who'd burst into her office. For some reason she didn't; maybe it was the same ambiguity in her feelings about Sean Murphy that had prevented her from calling the police.

"As long as you don't feel I said something I shouldn't—"

"Nothing but the truth. If it makes one woman more cautious or one cop more diligent, that's a good thing."

She nodded again, hoping those would be the only consequences. Again the idea of unburdening herself to Paul brushed through her mind. Before she could, he smiled.

"We're going to talk about all this tomorrow morning."

"All *this?*"

Did he intend to warn the others to be wary of getting ambushed during interviews? Or maybe to keep their opinions to themselves if they were asked about the murders? She would be uncomfortable with his issuing either of those admonitions. As if he were urging the others to learn from her mistakes.

"If these homicides go on much longer," Paul continued, "we're going to have some serious fallout. People are naturally nervous just knowing there's a serial killer in the area, and that stress is going to build with each subsequent murder."

"Do you know..." Jenna hesitated, unsure she wanted an answer to the question she'd been about to ask. It was probably better to be informed, however, than to continue to operate in the dark. "Do you have any idea how long that might be? I mean, have the police given any kind of timetable...?"

The question ground to a halt. It seemed inappropriate somehow, with three women already savaged, to be wondering when they should expect the next victim to surface.

"One of the cable networks said he goes months between acts. Apparently he's a meticulous planner. That's one thing that's made it hard for the authorities to get a handle on him."

The matter-of-fact answer wasn't comforting. Of course, Paul had no reason to suspect she might *need* comfort. And unless she told him…

"Anyway, glad you're feeling better," he said. "Don't let the local yahoos get you down. If they were any good, they wouldn't be stuck in this market."

She laughed. "No, I won't. I just didn't want to say anything that might embarrass the practice."

"I don't think you could ever do that, Jenna. You did fine, especially considering you had no way of knowing what was coming."

She'd explained to him that she hadn't heard the announcement from the police. If she had, she might have been more prepared.

"Thanks. I really appreciate that."

"Only the truth. Just like what you said." He stepped back but kept his fingers wrapped over the opening in the door where the glass disappeared. "Okay then, I'll see you in the morning."

He tapped the knuckles of both hands on the window frame before he turned to walk to his car. As he opened the door of the Porsche, he glanced back at her. Although it was too dark to see his face, she imagined that same furrow forming again as he wondered why she was still sitting there.

She raised her left hand, palm toward him. He acknowledged the gesture with an answering wave.

She let her hand fall to the button that raised the window. As it slid up, she put the car into Drive and pressed down on the accelerator. The Honda responded, moving toward the ramp.

She exited the parking deck, turning to the right, which took her around the front of the building. A couple of patients hurried across the crosswalk that led from the main entrance to the public lot, causing her to slow.

As she waited for them to clear the street, her eyes considered the line of cars they were heading toward. Almost in the center of it, directly in front of the crosswalk, was a black SUV, with someone sitting in the driver's seat.

Although it was too dark to determine the man's coloring, there was something eerily familiar about the shape of his head. Something that created a trickle of alarm.

She strained to see through the twilight gloom. As the people who'd been crossing the street passed by the SUV, the man inside turned to look at them. His profile was backlit by the halogen lamp on the main road.

Not only was that close-cropped head familiar, she realized, so was the outline of his nose. She'd noticed it when he'd been in her office. Almost aquiline, it was marred by a slight ridge, indicating that at some time in the past, it had been broken.

A horn sounded behind her, one short tap. She looked into the rearview mirror, recognizing the distinct headlights of the Porsche. Caught up in the realization that the man who'd warned her about being a target of the killer was parked in front of the building, she hadn't even been aware of the Paul's approach.

With a last glance at the SUV, she pressed the gas, driving through the crosswalk and on toward the highway. As she did, she tried to decide whether that information tipped the scales in favor of calling the police.

To tell them what? That a man who believed she might be a target of the killer had come to warn her? That he'd been parked outside her building more than an hour after he'd issued that warning?

Neither fact made him a murderer. With all the tips and prank calls she knew would be flooding the hotline the cops had set up, that information would only peg her as another kook coming out of the woodwork.

She glanced in the mirror again, trying to decide if the SUV had pulled out behind her. There was definitely another car behind Paul's, but the Porsche's lights were too bright for her to be able to tell anything about its size, much less the make. Maybe when she made the turn out of the office park, she would be able to see the vehicle more clearly.

With that thought, she looked up at the traffic light, which had already turned green. Trying to avoid having Paul blow at her again, she accelerated rapidly, directing the Honda out onto 280.

Merging into the heavy afternoon traffic took a few seconds of complete concentration. By the time she was able to check her mirror again, the Porsche's headlights were right behind her. The reflection of the crowded intersection beyond them appeared as simply a mass of lights and cars. It was impossible to determine if the one that had followed Paul around the office building had already made the turn.

The line of traffic ahead began to move. Forced to focus on the normal rush hour stop-and-go of the busy thoroughfare, a major artery on this side of town, Jenna was unable to check behind her very frequently. In none of those quick surveys was she able to identify a black SUV.

She took a breath, again trying to put things into perspective. Although she was sure Sean Murphy had been sitting in that SUV, she couldn't prove he'd been waiting for her. And she couldn't be sure he'd followed her away from the office park.

All she was sure of right now was that she was becoming paranoid. She'd let some stranger rattle her so badly that she was looking over her shoulder, imagining that someone was stalking her.

She'd bought into the hysteria that had been growing in this town since the suggestion was first made that the three local murders might be connected. Now that they had been officially, the nutcases were starting to surface.

Including the one who'd shown up at your door today.

She often told patients that their fears had only the power they gave them. Right now she was giving far too much credence to one man's opinion. Even if the killer *had* heard what she'd said, the idea that it would cause him to target her was so far-fetched she should refuse to spend another second worrying about it.

She was approaching the intersection where she would exit onto the road that would eventually take her up the crest of the mountain to her apartment. She concentrated on the promise of a long, hot bath, followed by a stiff drink and some mindless television.

She wouldn't watch the news. She would put this negative merry-go-round out of her mind and get on with her life. She was no more likely to be a target than any other dark-haired woman in Birmingham. And she couldn't even venture a guess how many of those there might be.

Jenna slowed for the red light, glancing to her left to check for oncoming traffic before she made her turn. As she waited for a couple of cars to clear the intersection, she unthinkingly allowed her gaze to drift to a car pulling up beside hers.

Her recognition of its driver was instantaneous. Although she couldn't see their color, she could feel the intensity of those blue eyes. Fear jolted through her chest, as powerful as if Sean Murphy had pointed a gun at her.

He nodded before he turned to look out his windshield. Apparently the light had changed in the seconds he'd held her gaze because he put the SUV into motion immediately, moving past her car and on through the intersection. Paralyzed by a combination of disbelief and dismay, she watched until his taillights became indistinguishable in the string of red that stretched out in front of her.

At some point she became aware of the blare of horns behind her, their cacophony not nearly so patient as Paul's quick honk had been. Hurriedly she made the turn, hands trembling on the wheel.

Only when she had reached the peace of the narrow street that led to the apartment complex overlooking the city did she begin to calm down. As the noise of traffic faded behind her, so did the burst of terror she'd felt when the SUV had eased up beside her.

Coincidence, she told herself. Even if it weren't, it would have been easy enough for him to find out her home address. She was listed in the phone book as J. Kincaid, not exactly a reach for anyone of normal intelligence. And obviously not the smartest decision she'd ever made.

That listing had been done before she'd finished her Ph.D. and gone into practice. Although it could be rectified—and it would—it was too late to do anything about it in this case.

Too late. The words had a finality to them she didn't like. Or want to accept. She would call in the morning and get her number unlisted in the next book. Right now…

Right now she was home. And there had been no headlights coming up the street behind her.

She pulled into one of the vacant parking places in front of her unit and turned off the engine. Music drifted out into the night from inside one of the apartments. Mannheim Steamroller. One of their Christmas albums.

Peace on Earth.

Except not tonight. Despite the Jack Daniel's and the long, hot bath she'd promised herself, Jenna knew she wouldn't be able to sleep.

Everything would run through her head like a videotape on high speed. All she'd read or heard about the murders. The descriptions of the victims. What Sean Murphy had said.

Those were the things that would reverberate over and over again. The accusation that she'd fed the killer's fantasy of his own importance. That she'd been sympathetic. The troubling claim that she fit the victim profile.

She took a breath, knowing none of this was getting her anywhere. She needed to get inside, lock the door and try to forget it all. There was nothing else she could do tonight.

As with most of the other things she'd worried about during her life, this would all look better in the morning. She'd have that talk with Paul and get his advice, which she'd always found to be both reasoned and knowledgeable. Until then...

Until then she would do her best to put Sean Murphy's words out of her head, refusing to give them—or him—any more control over her life.

Four

"We've seen the tip of this iceberg in the questions that were thrown at Jenna. We should all be prepared to be asked about that same kind of information concerning serial killers, particularly this one. Background, psychological profile, predictions. We'll be questioned by the media and by whomever we're standing beside at the next Christmas party. And we damn well better be prepared to answer them."

Although Paul hadn't looked in her direction, the fact that he'd prefaced his admonition with a mention of her interview made Jenna feel that his comments had been directed at her. Responding that way was just what she'd thought yesterday—paranoid. She was simply the first to be ambushed. It could have happened to any one of them.

And would any of the others have come across as being sympathetic to a serial killer?

The fact that she'd gotten so little sleep last night wasn't helping her put this into perspective. She shouldn't be so worried about the opinion of one man. And as far as she knew, that was all Sean Murphy's warning amounted to.

"Unless someone has something else…?" Paul waited,

allowing the silence to build. "Okay, then, I guess it's back to the salt mines. Have a good day. Or at least try to."

People began to rise from the table, the casters on the heavy leather chairs moving silently over the thick carpet of the conference room. Several people began conversations with those seated around them. Not one of them met her eyes or tried to include her.

Although that isolation could certainly be attributed to a normal give-and-take among colleagues or even to her proximity to the head of the table where Paul was still standing, it felt to Jenna as if something else were going on. Some kind of censure, perhaps, for the way she'd handled herself?

She pretended to be occupied with gathering up her notes and putting them into her briefcase. When she finished, she bent to pick up her purse. She straightened to find Paul watching her.

"Sheila said you had a visitor yesterday."

She shouldn't be surprised that her secretary had told someone what had happened. And gossip traveled as quickly in this office as in any other. She should have anticipated that and talked to Paul about it herself. Since she hadn't...

"Some kook with an ax to grind," she said, trying to remember how much of the conversation Sheila might have heard.

Nothing more than Murphy's opening salvo, she decided. That in itself had been revealing enough.

"Narrow the field," Paul suggested. "What kind of kook?"

"He'd seen the interview I did and wanted to berate me for being sympathetic to the killer."

"Is that all?"

She hesitated, wondering if she wanted to give more validity to the man's warning by mentioning it. She waited until a couple of people had moved away from where she and Paul were standing before continuing. She didn't want an audience.

Beth Goldberg, the member of the staff Jenna was closest

to, had stopped behind Paul, her brows raised. She was obviously wondering what was going on, and knowing Beth, also wondering if she needed rescuing.

Jenna tilted her head toward the door. A gesture of dismissal that Beth immediately recognized.

When the rest of the staff had also eddied toward the exit, she turned back to meet Paul's gaze. He had propped his hip on the edge of the conference table, obviously prepared to wait until she spilled her guts.

Maybe that wasn't such a bad idea. If she suddenly disappeared, she wanted someone to be looking for her.

And why in the world would you suddenly "disappear"? Stop buying into Murphy's mind games.

"He claimed I was a match for the police profile of the victims."

She realized that she'd managed to surprise Paul. The head of the practice was seldom at a loss for words, but the silence after her statement stretched for several seconds.

"I didn't know they'd issued one."

"Neither did I. Apparently, someone has. Maybe the FBI. Maybe it's based on the murders he's committed in other locations. I don't think the police here are talking about it yet, but…" She took a breath, reluctant to put reality into words. "The pictures on TV this morning…" The images she'd worked so hard to dismiss last night were again in her head. "He could be right, Paul. They all had dark hair. And they were career women, not street people or prostitutes—"

"Stop it." Paul took her elbow and shook it.

She hadn't even realized she'd crossed her arms over her body. Or that her voice had risen as she'd repeated the things Sean Murphy had said to her yesterday.

"Just stop it," Paul repeated, sliding his hand comfortingly up her arm until it rested on the top of her shoulder.

Despite the fact that the room was now deserted, he leaned nearer and lowered his voice. "First of all, we need to talk to the police. If there *is* anything to this profile business, we'll deal with it. He could have been making that up, you know. You said he was a kook. Maybe he saw you on TV and decided to have some fun at your expense."

"That's not how I read him. I know that's what I called him, but..." Unconsciously she shook her head. "He seemed serious. Deadly serious. He clearly didn't like what I said in the interview, but I think his warning about the profile was genuine."

That's why it had bothered her so much. Whether the guy was right or not, he had believed what he said. And if he were as well informed as he appeared to be, then...

"I think I'd like to talk to the police," she said, the words out almost before she realized she'd made the decision.

Paul nodded encouragingly, as if she were a patient who'd just made a breakthrough, before he released her shoulder and again took her arm. "Then let's make the call and set it up."

Jenna had told everything to the officer who'd taken her statement. What had happened in her office. That she believed Murphy had been waiting for her to leave the building last night. About his car pulling up beside her as she'd prepared to make her turn.

The policeman had barely seemed interested, making her decide halfway through that she'd wasted the afternoon. None of the murders had been committed in the jurisdiction of the small police department where her office was located. When he'd called, however, Paul had been told to send her there.

The three separate law enforcement agencies where the three bodies had been found were only taking calls that directly related to the murders. Whoever Paul had talked to obviously hadn't believed that her call did, so she'd ended up telling her story to someone who didn't seem to know any more about what was going on with the investigation than she did.

She'd attempted to remedy her own lack of knowledge as soon as she'd gotten home. Paul had insisted she have Sheila clear her schedule for the entire afternoon, so when she'd left the police station, she hadn't returned to the office. Instead she'd picked up both the morning and evening newspapers and read every word they contained about the case.

Tonight's had included a lot more information on the previous murders, as well as the FBI's psychological profile of the killer. There was nothing in it she hadn't already suspected. Maybe this wasn't her field, but the fact that this guy had killed so often and still avoided detection gave plenty of clues as to the kind of person he was.

Exactly the kind Murphy had described. *Smart. And in no hurry.*

As for the victims…

The photos in the paper were grainy and too dark to distinguish details. Still, it was clear that the facts he'd laid out before her yesterday afternoon concerning the type of women the killer was attracted to were essentially correct. And if he was right about that—

It didn't mean he was right about the murderer coming after her. To think that he would feel a compulsion to kill her because he'd seen her on television…

Talking about him. Dissecting him.

Jenna straightened, as if backing away from that double row of black-and-white pictures. When she did, she realized her back was stiff from the hours spent leaning over the coffee table where she'd spread out the newspapers.

With one hand pressed against her spine she reached down with the other and picked up the plate with her half-eaten sandwich. As she did, she glanced toward the front windows and saw that in her haste to read the news, she'd forgotten to close the blinds.

She must have reached over and turned on the lamp at the end of the couch at some point, but she hadn't consciously realized it had gotten dark outside. She looked at her watch as she set the plate back on the coffee table and walked across to pull the cord. It was already after six.

Without thinking, she looked down at the next section of the complex, which stretched out across the mountain perhaps a hundred feet below her own. Her gaze had already traced across the cars parked behind those units, most of them familiar, when she noticed the black SUV in the row almost directly across from her apartment.

There were thousands of big, dark SUVs in this upscale neighborhood. She would swear that this one, however, had someone sitting in the driver's seat. Someone—

She quickly stepped away from the window, hardly able to believe what she was thinking. Could Sean Murphy be sitting out there watching her apartment? Hoping she'd come out?

The policeman who had taken her story this afternoon had told her that if she had any more trouble with the man who'd come to her office she should call them. Paul had told her the same thing.

But what if it wasn't him out there? What if she was seeing dangers where they didn't exist?

She turned to look at the phone on the table at the end of the couch. And then her eyes flicked back to the newspapers still spread out over the coffee table.

Although the reporters had been careful about what details they'd released, there had been enough of them to leave no doubt the murdered women had suffered horrifically. Had one of them been suspicious and not called the cops because she didn't want to make a fool of herself?

Jenna walked across the room and picked up the phone. She hesitated another second or two before she punched in 911.

As she waited through the rings, she looked back toward the window, but from this angle she couldn't see the line of cars.

"Jefferson County 911," a woman answered. "What's your emergency?"

"I talked to the Mountain Brook Police today about a man who's been harassing me. I think he's outside my apartment."

"He's at your door, ma'am?"

"I think he's parked across the parking lot."

"You *think?* Can you see him?"

"I can see someone sitting in a car that looks like his."

"And what's he doing, ma'am?"

"He's just sitting there. I think he's watching my apartment."

There was a long silence. Although the dispatcher's voice had been expressionless, the questions themselves had become more telling.

"The officer I spoke to this afternoon told me to call if he bothered me again." Jenna fought the urge to slam down the phone in the face of the almost palpable disbelief.

"Did you get a restraining order, ma'am?"

"Nobody suggested that. Do I need one?"

"Well, it would require him to stay so many feet away from you or your property. If you don't have one, and if he isn't bothering you…"

The dispatcher let the sentence trail, but it was obvious what the woman was suggesting. The police weren't going to do anything. Not until Murphy did.

"You *do* know there's a serial killer on the loose?" Jenna asked, no longer bothering to hide her own frustration.

"Yes, ma'am. Most of the officers in this area are working on some aspect of those murders."

Again, although there had been only politeness in her voice, the dispatcher had made her point. Jenna could only commend whoever had trained her.

"Ma'am, if you *really* feel you're in danger…" Again the dispatcher's words were allowed to trail.

Did she? Did she believe Sean Murphy was the murderer the police were seeking? Did she believe he was out there in the parking lot because he intended to kill her?

"Thanks," she said, pushing the off button with her thumb.

If she got the police out here, what were they going to do? Tell Murphy to move on? He wasn't doing anything except sitting in his car. Even she was forced to acknowledge that.

Carrying the phone with her, she walked to the window again. This time she made no attempt to hide the fact that she was looking out it.

Nothing had changed during her conversation with the dispatcher. The SUV was parked in the same place, the security lights shining down on its top.

Her eyes focused on the interior. That's when she realized she'd been wrong. Something *had* changed. There was no one in the car now.

She scanned the parking lot. Although the people who lived in this complex usually came and went throughout the evening, not a single soul was outside now. Even the curtains on the lighted units across the way were drawn, shielding their inhabitants from the night.

Maybe she'd been wrong. Maybe one of them had been sitting in his car. Listening to the ending of a song. Or to one of the popular sports discussion shows. Finishing a conversation on their cell phone.

There were a dozen legitimate reasons for someone to be sitting in their car.

Jenna almost dropped the phone when it shrilled, vibrating in her hand. She lifted it, holding it out in front of her as she waited for the number to appear on the caller ID display.

It wasn't one she recognized, but that didn't mean anything. Maybe someone from work who'd heard about what had happened was checking on her. Or maybe the dispatcher had decided to pass her call on to the police after all.

When the phone rang a second time, she punched the talk button, bringing the receiver to her ear. "Hello?"

"Should I be expecting a visit from the cops?"

There was no doubt in her mind who was on the line. The same deep voice. The same nearly unidentifiable accent.

"Any minute now."

"You don't lie worth a damn, Dr. Kincaid. I would think that someone with your training would be much better at that."

"I'm not lying."

He laughed, sounding genuinely amused. That should probably have unnerved her as much as seeing him sitting outside her building had. It made her angry instead.

"What do you want from me?" she demanded.

"Absolutely nothing, I assure you. Not one thing."

"Then why are you out there?"

"Out where?"

He wasn't going to admit what they both knew. He had parked across from her apartment so he could watch her.

"I'm sorry you thought I was sympathetic to him." If placating the man would put an end to this nonsense, Jenna was more than willing to do that. "Nothing could be further from the truth. He's vicious and sadistic, and believe me, I want him caught as much as anybody in this town."

"It's good to hear we're in agreement."

"Look, I've said I'm sorry for the way I came across. I don't know what else you want me to say—"

"I told you. I don't want a thing from you, Dr. Kincaid."

"Then why are you outside my apartment? Why did you wait for me to come out of the office last night? What kind of game are you playing?"

"I'm *not* your concern, Dr. Kincaid. Believe me, I don't intend you any harm."

"Then stop stalking me."

"Legally, what I'm doing—"

"Don't talk to me about 'legally.' You followed me. You're outside my apartment. You're calling me. If that isn't stalking—" She stopped the tirade because she knew she was giving him what he wanted. Control. "Just go away and leave me the hell alone."

The catch in her voice on the last word made her furious. The day she let this bastard make her cry—

"Did you read those papers, Dr. Kincaid?"

He must have been parked out there when she'd arrived this afternoon, the newspapers under her arm. She had been so focused on getting inside and devouring them that she'd never thought to check out the parking lot. Of course, that wasn't part of her normal homecoming routine. It would be from now on.

"I read them," she answered.

"Then you know what I told you yesterday is true."

About how well she fit the profile? "I don't think—"

"Good," he interrupted. "Don't think. Just close your blinds, lock your doors and stay inside."

"What does that mean?"

"It means that if I were a woman in this town who looked so much like the rest of them, that's what I'd do. It's what other women all over this town are doing right now. I'm suggesting you join them."

Jenna tried to come up with a response, but she couldn't find words to express how his advice made her feel. Angry, of course. Yet fearful, too. And furious with herself that with a few words he could make her feel that way.

"Leave me *alone*." Her voice was soft, but she allowed the emotion she felt into her tone, something she rarely did.

"I know you won't believe me, but that really would be your worst nightmare. You do exactly what I tell you, and I promise nothing is going to happen to you."

Jenna opened her mouth to respond, but the click on the other end of the line told her it was too late. He'd had the last word, just as he'd intended.

Frozen in shock by what had just transpired, she realized she was standing with the phone still pressed against her ear and her mouth open. She closed it, swallowing her fury, and lowered the phone. She pushed the off button as she took a deep breath, trying to think.

She wasn't going back through 911. And she for damn sure wasn't going to talk to the Mountain Brook police again. She was going straight to the task force instead and demand that she be allowed to meet with one of the detectives working the case.

At the very least, Sean Murphy had some kind of fixation with the killer. And at the worst…

She'd get the restraining order the dispatcher had mentioned. Something that would keep him off the grounds of her apartment complex and away from her office as well.

Paul knew a lot of people in this town. He would help her figure out whom she should call. Then, if this bastard pulled this same stunt tomorrow night—

The police would deal with him, and she wouldn't have to. Never again.

And right now, that's really all she wanted.

Five

"I saw the segment you did for Channel 47 on holiday depression. I confess that it struck a little too close to home. Especially the part about feeling let down that things don't live up to your expectations."

Despite Paul's undoubtedly kind intentions in insisting she take yesterday afternoon off, it had made today a scheduling nightmare. And when Sheila had asked her this morning, Jenna had reluctantly given the okay for a new patient to be added to the end of her already full appointment calendar.

After less than five minutes spent with John Nolan, she was wishing she'd put him off until another day. Nothing he'd told her so far seemed to warrant the urgency he'd expressed when he'd called the office.

He had asked for her by name, however, and more importantly, he'd specifically mentioned the television interview. That had set off a few alarms. Enough that she had decided to work him in, just to see what kind of read she got.

Even before he'd arrived, she had discarded as ridiculous the idea that a serial killer would be brazen enough to show up at her office. Calls like Nolan's resulted from most of the interviews the staff gave. Add that to the increased demand for counseling brought on by the pressures of the season, and there was nothing unusual about the guy's request for an immediate appointment.

She'd already been booked solid the rest of the week with the makeups from yesterday and her regular patients, many of whom also had trouble dealing with the holidays. If she hadn't agreed to see him today, Nolan would have been forced to wait until after the New Year, which Sheila said he really didn't want to do.

"That's something that's extremely common," she said, trying to sound interested. "Not only with Christmas, but with any occasion we look forward to with a lot of anticipation. Is this something you experienced last year?"

"Last year. Every year I can remember. It seems that nothing I do is quite good enough."

"For your family? Or for yourself?"

"Both, I suppose. It just doesn't seem to matter how much I plan or how hard I work, things…unravel. And there's nothing I can do about it."

"And that makes you feel…?" She hesitated, allowing him an opportunity to fill in the blank she'd left.

His lips pursed slightly as he looked down at his hands. They were well shaped, the nails clean and neatly trimmed.

On the paperwork John Nolan had filled out, he'd written self-employed. He hadn't put anything in the section on insurance or in the one that asked for his occupation. Which meant he could be anything, she supposed, from a writer to a day trader.

Nor had she been able to glean much about either his education or financial status from his appearance. The maroon V-necked sweater, which he wore over a white button-down collar dress shirt and the khaki trousers were too generic to offer much socioeconomic information.

His hair, light brown and slightly sun-glazed, appeared to have been freshly cut, although it was a little longer than she normally found attractive. And yet he was, she admitted. Very attractive.

Just as she reached that conclusion, he glanced up, meeting her eyes. His were hazel, tending more toward green than brown. They widened as he realized she'd been watching him.

"So how does that make you feel?" she prodded.

"Inadequate."

Her smile widened. "The human condition. At least for most of us. Do you want to talk specifics? Something particular that happened last Christmas?"

"Not really. Suffice it to say that I again fell short. And they let me know about it."

"Your family," she clarified.

"My mother in particular. She's always been hard to please. I know I should be used to it by now, but for some reason I always think that this time I've found something she'll have to approve of."

"So this is a pattern that's been repeated over and over, no matter what you give her."

"Implying she's the problem and not me?"

His question was a little too glib, but perhaps he'd done some reading on the subject. Many people did these days, especially with the proliferation of mental health information on the Web.

"Is that a possibility?" she asked, her tone neutral.

"More than a possibility. It's almost certainly the case."

"Then if you recognize that…" Again she hesitated, waiting for him to draw the obvious conclusion.

"I should be able to do something about it. You're right, of course. And believe me, I've tried. I still manage to end up feeling as if I've failed. Her. *And* myself."

"Then maybe the first step in changing your feelings is to acknowledge that no matter what you do or how much trouble you go to, you probably aren't going to please her. That should lower your expectation to a more reasonable level."

"It sounds simple, but… Look, I'm a grown man. I'll be the first to admit that she shouldn't have that much power over me. Not enough to spoil one holiday after another."

"She's your mother. Most of us were raised to care about pleasing our parents. Just not, I hope, to the detriment of our own well-being. You mentioned that my comments during the interview about holiday depression had struck a chord. Do you think that what you've felt over the years might be classified as depression?"

"I don't know. I guess one person's depression is another person's excuse for a stiff drink and a good dinner."

Not too far off the mark, Jenna thought with an inward smile. Not that depression wasn't real and serious, but to some people, anytime they felt disappointment or sadness about something, even if those feelings were justified by the situation, that qualified in their minds as depression. John Nolan seemed to have a more realistic attitude.

"Is that what you do? Indulge yourself to make up for how she makes you feel?"

"Occasionally. After hearing you talk, I realized the mistake I make every year is in still having any expectation of pleasing her."

"So will that help with the stress this year?"

"It should. But then, I *am* here."

"Taking steps to deal with your feelings is definitely a move in the right direction. So what do you think you need to do next in order to feel better?"

"What do *you* think, Dr. Kincaid? That *is* why I came, you know. To hear your advice."

Again, something about the exchange seemed contrived. It was all too pat.

Of course, some patients didn't want to give voice to the obvious conclusions. They wanted to have them spelled out, so that they became more like directives. Since Nolan's mother was obviously controlling if not domineering, perhaps he needed that kind of instruction.

"All right. Other than on gift-giving occasions, what kind of relationship do you have with your mother?"

"Distant," he said with a laugh. "Both physically and emotionally. That's by choice, by the way. Probably by both our choices."

"And she doesn't want a closer relationship?"

"If she does, she's never given any indication of it."

Which was strange, considering the apparent power play at Christmas. Still...

"Then if you're both comfortable with not seeing one another, why not mail her presents to her. That way she can't express any overt disappointment in them. Not any that will be up close and personal."

"She's the only family I have. I'd feel terrible not flying out there for the holidays."

"And how would that be different from how you feel now?"

He laughed, and Jenna gave him points for acknowledging the absurdity of the caveat he'd just offered. Actually, she liked him better for the laughter.

Still, she'd begun to feel that he was a little old to be so thoroughly manipulated by his mother and perhaps less than truthful about why he was here. Somewhere in the back of her mind was a sliver of uneasiness.

"Maybe I'd just feel more guilty."

"Or *maybe* you'd feel more in control," she suggested.

"You said it doesn't matter what you give her. This year send her an expensive bouquet of roses and then go out and have that good dinner, knowing that you've done the best you can. If she doesn't like your gift, you haven't lost anything. Except the experience of watching her disapproval."

"Do you really think something like that will work?"

"I think if you tell yourself this Christmas is going to be different, it will be. Call her and tell her you aren't going to be able to make it this year. Send the flowers. Then tell yourself that you've done your part, and if she doesn't like them, that's her problem."

"She *is* my mother."

"Yes, she is. And ultimately it's *your* choice as to how much control you're going to allow her."

His eyes again dropped to his hands. "You're right, of course. I know that. It isn't easy to change the dynamics of a relationship as it's existed all your life."

"You want to or you wouldn't be here."

"I think I believed that you would just give me something to make me feel better about myself."

"I thought I was," Jenna said, smiling at him when he looked up. "You thought I'd give you some medication."

"I did, but… If I may, I'd like some time to think about what you've said."

"Of course."

"And I can call you again if I want to talk?"

"Call my secretary and ask for an appointment. I have to warn you, though. I may not be able to fit you in so quickly."

"I know. And I appreciate that you saw me today. I didn't expect it, to tell the truth. Not with what you said about how many people have problems this time of year."

"That's why we try to see anyone who needs us."

He nodded, and then he stood. Jenna rose as he extended

his hand. She took it and was surprised to find his handshake firm, his palm slightly callused. Of course, a couple of sessions a week at a gym could explain that.

"Thank you," he said earnestly.

"You're welcome. Call again if you want to talk more."

"I will."

He released her hand, stepping away from the desk. He had almost reached the door before he turned back, nodding once more before he went through it.

Jenna blew out a breath, before sinking back into her chair. She should write up her notes on the session, but instead she pushed the folder that held John Nolan's paperwork to the middle of her desk.

She crossed her arms over her chest and exhaled again, this one audible in the silence of her office. All she wanted to do now…

…*was to have a stiff drink and a good dinner.*

Maybe her last patient was a better therapist than she was. She picked up the phone and punched Sheila's extension.

"I'm gone," she said when the secretary answered. "Nothing at eight tomorrow, right?"

"And a cancellation at nine. You're in luck."

"Thanks, Sheila. Hold that thought."

"I will, believe me. See you tomorrow."

Jenna put the phone down and pushed her chair away from the desk. As she did, she turned to look out the expanse of glass behind her. Although she was an hour later than usual leaving, for some reason she was surprised to find that night had fallen with seasonal suddenness.

The anxiety she'd managed to hold at bay most of the day bubbled up again. She was no longer able to distinguish between the unease caused by the general hysteria that gripped the city and that created by her personal nemesis. All she knew was that she hadn't had time to take care of the restraining order, and that she now faced the prospect of returning to her apartment to find him waiting for her again.

She thought about giving in and driving out to spend the night at her parents' home. Only the knowledge of how isolated that big, empty house was made her decide that going back to her own apartment was the lesser of two evils. And if Sean Murphy *was* there again—

She would call the police. And this time she would keep calling until someone paid attention.

Head lowered against the wind, Jenna hurried across the parking deck, the sound of her heels echoing off the concrete. She had deliberately parked nearer the building this morning.

A good idea, she decided, since the staff lot was practically deserted. Of course, this close to Christmas everyone was eager to get away from the office as quickly as they could to take care of the hundred and one things that still needed to be done in preparation for the holiday.

She was going to have to learn to say no to additional appointments at the end of an already full day. It wasn't good for her or for the client.

Tonight she had felt her patience unraveling as John Nolan droned on and on about not being able to please his mother. Normally that kind of thing wouldn't have bothered her, but she'd had to fight the urge to tell him to get a grip.

Maybe that's what she should have done, she thought as she fumbled in her bag to retrieve her keys. She had already punched the unlock command before she looked up.

The driver's side of the dark blue Accord was directly in front of her. In the accumulation of road splatter from the last few rainy days, someone had written "Help me" on its side.

The *H* began on the left side of the door, the other letters tracking neatly across its length. She stopped, reading the words twice to make sure they said what she thought they did.

Help me? Why would someone write "Help me" on her car?

She glanced at the three remaining automobiles on this level. None of them bore a similar message.

Some kind of prank? Except this was a monitored area, used only by the staff. And they gained access to it with a card.

She was sure the words hadn't been there this morning. Given their position, she would definitely have noticed.

"Something wrong?"

She turned to find Gary Evers, one of the other psychologists on staff, watching her. She shook her head, embarrassed to admit she'd been stopped in her tracks by some words scrawled in the road dirt on the side of her car.

"Just trying to figure out who's been leaving me messages," she said, nodding toward the Honda.

Gary looked at the door and then back at her. "*Help* me? The tradition where I come from is 'wash me.'"

Jenna tried to remember where Gary was from, but all she knew was that it wasn't anywhere in the South. Of course, the tradition here was the same as the one he'd quoted.

"That *would* make more sense."

"Maybe it's a message from someone who feels he can't afford your services." Gary's smile invited her to share his amusement.

For some reason, she couldn't see the humor in the situation. Maybe it was the result of the long hours she'd put in today. Or—more likely—the result of everything that had happened during the last three. Of second-guessing her own actions and reactions. Just as she was now.

Was this a staff member's idea of a joke because she'd come across as sympathetic to the killer? Or had it been written in anger by someone else, someone who had taken her research-based explanation about the forces that created such a monster as a defense of his actions.

Someone like Sean Murphy?

However the words had been meant, she could find nothing the least bit amusing about them. "I don't think that's the proper avenue for someone seeking pro bono therapy. Or for a co-worker having a laugh at my expense."

"You think someone *here* did that?" Gary's eyes again touched on the scrawl.

"It *is* a secure lot."

"Yeah, but…" Realizing she'd been serious, Gary shook his head. His smile had been replaced by a slightly quizzical expression. "You want me to wipe it off?"

Realizing that she was making herself ridiculous, Jenna forced a smile. "I have to get the car washed, anyway. Maybe that was the intent."

"To get you to wash your car?" His tone had lightened in response to hers. "Think Paul's been out here nosing around?"

Although Carlisle was a stickler for having the staff present their best faces to the world at all times, the thought of him prowling the parking deck looking for dirty cars was also ridiculous. Pointing that out was obviously Gary's intent.

"If not Paul, then somebody," she said. "I get the message."

Gary laughed. "I'll let you know tomorrow if I've got a similar inscription on mine. You sure you're okay?"

"I'm fine. Just tired. I'm going home to a long, hot bath and a tall drink." Something that was getting to be a habit. "I have no idea why this…" She stopped, refusing to admit how much the writing had bothered her.

"Everybody's on edge right now. With good reason. God, you weren't thinking—" He stopped, realizing that was exactly what she'd been thinking. "Look, this is somebody's idea of a joke. A stupid one, granted, but... You can't really think *he* did this."

"I think maybe someone who was angered or annoyed by what I said in the interview decided to mock what I do."

"Why would anyone have been angered by your interview?"

"Did you hear it?"

"Just the part about the killer."

The clip they'd played over and over. The one without her take on holiday depression.

"Did *you* think I came across as sympathetic?"

"You came across as a professional discussing someone who's obviously mentally ill. And doing it in a reasoned manner."

"And if you weren't a psychologist? How would it have come across to you then?"

His hesitation was slight, but it was enough. "Look, I don't—"

"That's what I was afraid of," Jenna said, her words strained and flat. "Thanks for trying, though."

"You can't let yourself be held hostage to the morons of the world. If you do, then they win. You said nothing wrong, Jenna. Believe me, nobody here thinks so."

That at least sounded genuine. It didn't explain the writing on her car, but it did make her feel marginally better about who might have put it there.

"You want me to follow you home?" Gary asked.

"I appreciate the offer, but I have a couple of things to pick up on the way. I'll be fine. Really."

"Everybody's feeling the pressure. I honestly don't mind following you, even on your round of errands. We could stop and grab a bite to eat. Or get a head start on that drink you mentioned."

She was a little surprised by the offer. Although Gary had

been a member of the practice for well over a year, she'd gotten no vibes that he found her attractive.

Maybe he didn't. Maybe he was being kind because it was obvious she'd been upset by the message. She was reading more into the gesture than it warranted.

"That's really very sweet, but…maybe I can get a rain check. Some night when we haven't both been working late."

"You got it."

Jenna couldn't tell if he was relieved or disappointed. As he made the agreement, he'd stepped forward, reaching for the door handle of the Honda.

She realized that she hadn't punched the remote. The accompanying beep when she did echoed through the nearly empty deck, just as her footsteps had.

Gary opened her door, and she slipped into the seat, using the excuse of fastening her seat belt to delay looking up at him. When she did, he was peering down into the car, his lips slightly pursed.

"Lock your doors."

"You think—"

"I think I'd tell any woman in this city the same thing right now. Better safe than sorry."

Unsure how to respond, she nodded. "I will."

"Be careful," he added, closing the door. He put the tips of the fingers of his right hand against the glass for a moment before he straightened, allowing her room to back out.

She inserted the key and started the engine. Then she looked out through the window to smile at him again. Before she put the car into Reverse, she lifted her hand and waved.

He didn't return the gesture, but he stood watching as she headed toward the exit. When she looked back, just before she began the descent to the lower level, he was still standing in the same spot. And he was still watching her.

Six

Sean came awake with a start, neck muscles straining as his head jerked up off the pillow. His breath rasped in and out of his lungs as if he'd run a race.

He had. One he'd lost a long time ago. One at which he would never get a second chance.

Not unless you counted this.

He stretched his eyes wide in an attempt to wipe away the last of the dream. The motel-beige walls and plastic-backed floral draperies, which he had pulled across the window in order to sleep, helped to orient him.

He remembered where he was. And he knew why he was here.

The nightmare he'd just had was the same one he'd experienced over and over in the years since Makaela's disappearance. Although he was painfully aware of how his sister had died, the dream never played out to that end. He always awoke before it could, his body drenched in sweat and his heart beating as if it would tear its way out of his chest. Today had been no different.

He closed his eyes again, waiting for the pump of blood to

slow. He hadn't experienced the terror of the dream in a long time, but he knew he shouldn't be surprised it had happened now.

He was closer to Makaela's murderer than he'd ever been before. He knew that with a certainty for which he could offer no rational explanation. He simply knew it.

Just as he had known outside Jenna Kincaid's office two nights ago that the man he sought was also there. So near he could feel his evil. Could sense it in the air around him.

This was a smaller city than the ones the killer had chosen before. A limited population spread over a relatively contained geographic area, bound by the narrow valley that ran between the two mountain ridges in which the original settlement had been made.

Not only was the hunting ground here more contained, thanks to the friend Sean had made on the FBI task force, he'd gotten in on this spurt of homicides early. While the bastard was feeling invincible. Maybe this time…

Feeling his expectations rise to a level experience had taught him was premature, Sean released a slow breath, deliberately focusing on his plans for today. One step at a time. He had learned long ago that was the best way to keep the images from the dream, as well as those that represented the fulfillment of his quest, out of his consciousness.

After a moment, he held his wrist up so that despite the artificially darkened room, he could see the hands of his watch. It was 3:30 p.m. Which meant he would have time to shower and shave and maybe get something to eat before Jenna Kincaid left the office.

It would all get easier once he'd completed his move into the vacant unit in the building below hers, which might take place as early as tomorrow. The apartment he'd chosen wasn't directly across from hers, but it did have a view of both the front entrance and the expanse of glass in Jenna's living room.

He could only imagine how she would react when she discovered he was there. As much as he'd like to, there was probably no way to prevent her from finding out, which would almost certainly mean a confrontation with the local cops.

He wasn't overly concerned about that. He had his own resources within the law enforcement community, people who would be willing to speak to the locals on his behalf.

And he wasn't breaking any laws. Not by moving into an empty apartment. Nor would he be by sitting outside in the parking lot.

From now on, he was going to keep a very low profile. The only way he had any chance of finding the man he'd come here to kill was to fade into the background of Jenna Kincaid's world, so that when the real stalking began, the man he was hunting would never know that he, too, was being stalked.

"Hey, sport. Whatcha doing?"

"Watching Wiggles," Ryan said.

His nephew's voice was so soft Sean had to strain to hear the words. If he hadn't already known the probable answer, he wouldn't have been able to decipher it.

Sean had long ago learned to keep his feelings about the boy's choice of TV shows and books to himself. The kid didn't need criticism, not of any kind. Especially not from him.

His day-care teachers all praised Ryan's sweet nature and gentle disposition, assuring Sean that his nephew would eventually grow out of his shyness. Of course, none of them knew the kids' backgrounds. He had figured that the fewer people who knew about Makaela's murder, the better.

"You have a good day at school?"

"Uh-huh."

"Not much longer now," Sean said, allowing his voice to rise teasingly at the end.

"Till Christmas?"

"That's right. You getting excited?"

"Are you coming home?"

Sean swallowed the lump that hopeful question created. He knew he was their security blanket. Knew and accepted that that was his role. They were his family. And he was theirs. Literally all they had.

The problem was that he had also undertaken another role. One he took just as seriously. One he was far more suited to than playing mama and daddy to a couple of youngsters.

"As soon as I can," he said, being careful not to make any promises he couldn't keep.

"Before Christmas?"

"I don't know, Scout. I hope so."

"I got you something. Me and Cathy."

"Yeah?"

"Something good. You're gonna like it."

"I know I will."

"Cathy don't think we're getting a puppy, but I asked Santa."

They'd been over the dog thing a dozen times. Ryan had been told over and over again that it wasn't possible. The lease didn't allow it. Besides, it was hard enough to get someone good to live in and take care of the kids while he was away. If the job required cleaning up after a non-housebroken animal in the bargain—

"Uncle Sean?"

"I'm here. Look, we talked about the puppy. Maybe next summer. If we can find a house with a fenced-in yard—"

"That's what she said."

"Well, she's right. I explained all that."

"I still asked Santa. That's okay, isn't it?"

Sean closed his eyes, wishing he weren't several hundred miles away. Wishing he had answers for that kind of question.

Wishing most of all that this wasn't the kind of fucked-up world where somebody could murder a little boy's mother.

Makaela would have known how to respond to that wishful tone. She would probably have been able to juggle a full-time job and a puppy. When all he seemed able to manage—

"Uncle Sean? You still there?"

"Yeah. It's okay to ask Santa, Scout, just as long as you're prepared for him saying no."

"Like when you pray."

"What?"

"That's what Maria says. It's okay to pray for something, but that don't mean you're gonna get it."

"Doesn't mean," Sean corrected.

"Doesn't mean you're gonna get it. Santa's like that, too?"

"Something like that."

"But sometimes you do."

Get what you pray for, Sean thought, automatically filling in the missing syntax. "Sometimes."

"I wish you were home."

"Me, too."

"You want to talk to Cathy?"

"Sure. You be good, now. Mind Maria."

Maria Alvarez had been a godsend. She was older than he'd been looking for, but she had become the grandmother the kids had never had. Despite her references, when he'd first hired her, Sean had thought about setting up one of those home-surveillance cameras. It had quickly become apparent by the way the children responded to her that wouldn't be necessary.

"Hey, Uncle Sean."

"Hey, Princess. How are you?"

"Fine. How are you?"

Where Ryan was withdrawn, Cathy was the proverbial

chatterbox. She never met a stranger, something that occasionally gave him nightmares, too. Only, her radar seemed pretty good in detecting the good guys from the bad.

The same thing you thought about Makaela.

"Missing you guys. Wishing I was home," he said aloud. That was the truth. There was no need to prevaricate.

"Maria and I are making a fruitcake."

Visions of the brick-shaped, perennial butt of holiday jokes flashed through his mind. "Yeah? Sounds good."

"My job is measuring out the fruit."

As far as Sean was concerned, the word *fruit* when used in conjunction with fruitcake was a misnomer. The artificially colored bits of red-and-green gunk it usually contained bore no resemblance to the real stuff.

"Your grandma used to make fruitcakes."

The memory was just suddenly there in his head. Unexpected. And unwanted.

"Really? Cool. Did Mama help?"

"Yeah," he said, fighting the rush of memories that had accompanied the first. "Yeah, she did."

That was the problem with allowing any of them in. It opened the door to the rest. The ones he had fully intended never to think about again. Another reason the interview Jenna Kincaid had given had bothered him.

"We'll save you a piece, but you have to promise that you'll be home in time for Christmas."

He swallowed, fighting two sets of emotions. Determined to give in to neither.

"I can't promise that, Princess. I told you."

"But you'll try, won't you? Ryan really wants you to be here. He needs you to. He's started all that stuff about wanting a puppy again."

"I know. He told me. You keep talking to him, okay? Make

him understand that… That now just isn't the best time for something like that."

"I will. He's just a baby."

The gulf between Cathy's seven-going-on-thirty maturity and Ryan's immature four-almost-five seemed immeasurably wide. At least it was better than it had been three years ago when family services had handed the kids off to him.

He'd had no idea what to say to a four-year-old who had just lost her mother in the most brutal way imaginable. And no clue in hell what to do with a two-year-old.

That initial panic had, in the intervening years, given way to more normal concerns like whether or not he was providing all the right things for them. Child-care issues. Keeping up with vaccinations and checkups. Just getting them to bed at a reasonable hour sometimes seemed Herculean.

At least it had before he'd found Maria. And if it all worked out here…

He destroyed the thought, realizing how far from those concerns the one he was currently embarked upon was. How foreign to his problems with childcare.

"Gotta go," he said, glancing at his watch again.

It was already four-thirty. With traffic, making it to Jenna Kincaid's office before five would be a close-run thing. And it would mean doing without dinner again.

"But you'll think about it, won't you?" Cathy said, bringing his attention back.

"The puppy?"

"No, I know we can't have a dog. Getting home before Christmas. You'll try, won't you?"

"I told you the last time. It just depends on how things go down here."

"In Birmingham."

"That's right."

"That's where that killer is, right?"

The question caught at Sean's gut, twisting it. He hesitated, wondering if someone could possibly have said something to the little girl about those deaths here.

"Who told you that?"

"I saw it on the news. Maria turned it off, but they said 'Birmingham.' I'm pretty sure."

"And it worried you?"

"Yeah. A little."

"Nothing's going to happen to me, Princess. You can quit worrying about that."

There was silence on the other end. It lasted long enough that he felt that same squeeze of dread in his belly.

"You hear me, Princess. I'm taking care of business down here, and then I'll be home. I swear to you."

"Okay."

"You take care of your brother. And save some of that cake for me."

"Okay."

The usually bubbly voice was still subdued. Sean closed his eyes, trying to find words that would comfort a child whose world had already been destroyed once.

"Have I ever lied to you?" he demanded.

"No," she said softly. "At least I don't think so."

"What does that mean?"

"Is it him?"

"What him?"

The question was too harsh. He'd guarded them against everything he could possibly think of and still she'd somehow learned what had happened.

"The man who killed Mama."

There was no way he could deal with this. Not from this distance. Not over the phone.

"I don't know."

"But you think so. That's why you went down there, isn't it?"

"I thought I could help the cops."

"Because of what you know about Mama?"

"That's right."

His heart rate was beginning to slow. Maybe she'd known all along. Even at four, not much had gotten by her. And he had no idea what the social workers had told her before he'd gotten stateside. He'd never asked, and she hadn't volunteered the information.

"You promise that's why you went."

"I promise."

There was no response. The silence stretched until he wondered if she'd hung up.

"Princess? You okay?"

"I'm okay. But…I really think that even if you haven't finished helping them, you need to come home for Christmas. For Ryan's sake. Tell them everything you know as soon as you can, okay?"

"Just as soon as I can," Sean promised. "Mind Maria, now. Tell her to give you a kiss for me."

"I will. I love you."

"I love you, too. Talk to you soon."

"Bye, Uncle Sean."

"Bye, sweetheart."

The line went dead before he was forced to tell another lie. He punched the off button on the cell and closed it to stick it back into his jacket pocket.

Tell them everything you know as soon as you can….

If only it were that simple. That clean. A collaborative effort between him and the local cops.

He knew what was likely to happen instead. Despite the

fact that the guy had murdered at least fourteen women, Sean would be arrested if he so much as touched him.

Jenna Kincaid was his ace in the hole. No one could possibly object to his killing the bastard in order to protect a prospective victim. All he had to do was to wait until the Inquisitor made his move against the psychologist, as he was now convinced he would. Then he could avenge Makaela's murder under the guise of preventing another one.

There would be a couple of people on the national task force who would know what he'd done, but he could trust them to be pragmatic about the guy's death. One less maniac on the loose. One less murderer to lose sleep over. And one less victim's photograph to pin on their whiteboard.

No one who had seen those pictures was going to come after the guy who'd put an end to this monster. Nobody involved in the manhunt was going to grieve for that bastard's death. That was the one absolute certainty he had had going into this.

It was the one he intended to cling to until this was over and he headed back to Michigan to buy a puppy for a little boy and to prove to a little girl that he still had never lied to her.

Seven

It was cold. It was dark. And it was beginning to rain.

Jenna knew she was being ridiculous again, but the knowledge of how irrational this was didn't stop her from pulling into the service station three blocks from her office, which offered a free car wash when you filled up your tank.

She had planned to do exactly that, but when she pulled next to the pumps, she noticed a windshield squeegee and a roll of paper towels sitting in the middle of them. Nearby was a container of soapy water. With those, she could clean the writing off her car while her gas was pumping.

That method also had the advantage of getting her home and out of the cold more quickly. Something that at this point weighed heavily in its favor.

She stepped out of the car, her shoulders hunched against the assault of the wind and rain. She swiped her card and at the prompt lifted the nozzle. As she turned to stick it into her tank, out of the corner of her eye, she caught a glimpse of a black SUV pulling onto the service road she'd taken to get to the station.

She watched as it drove by and into the lot of the upscale

supermarket next door. The nozzle still in her hand, she continued to track its progress as the driver maneuvered the vehicle into a parking space. The taillights winked off. Although she waited, eyes straining at the distance, no one emerged from the car.

Jenna started as a horn blasted at close range. Her eyes jumped from the car she'd been watching to the pickup that had pulled up behind her at the pumps. The driver rolled down the window and stuck his head out.

"You gonna get gas or not, lady? I gotta pick up my kid at basketball practice."

In an unthinking response to that demand, she began once more to direct the nozzle she held toward the opening of her tank. As she did, the writing on the side of her car seemed to leap out at her.

Help me. Sean Murphy's idea of a practical joke? An attempt to make her believe the killer had sent her a message?

It seemed to fit with all the rest. His contention that she'd been sympathetic to a murderer. His attempt to terrorize her by telling her she matched the victim profile. Even his mocking phone call last night.

This had gone far enough, she decided. Too damn far.

She turned, slamming the nozzle back into its niche on the body of the pump. She opened the car door and climbed behind the wheel. She started the engine and then maneuvered around the rear end of the car in the line in front of her.

The man behind her yelled something through his open window, but his words were lost in the wind and growing distance between them. Her total concentration was on the SUV in the next lot.

It was parked near the main entrance of the grocery store, where the shoppers who were coming in and out walked right by it. At this time of the evening, the place was crowded because of the deli-bakery this market was noted for. Since it was on her way home, she had often stopped here to pick up something for supper.

In addition to the people coming in and out of the store, the lot was well-lit and patrolled by a security cart. If she was determined to confront Murphy, this was probably as safe a place as she could find. Undoubtedly safer than the deserted lot of her apartment complex last night.

As she approached the SUV, she realized that the nearest open space was in the next row over and three or four slots down. Only when she'd pulled in and turned the key, killing the motor, did doubt about the wisdom of her actions resurface.

Despite her initial assessment in her office that day, there was really no way to know if Murphy was dangerous. He was certainly out of line in following her. And if he had written those words on her car—

Remembering the chill she'd felt when she'd seen them— obviously the effect he'd been trying for—she grabbed the keys from the ignition and climbed out. She hit the remote to lock the car and dropped the key ring into the pocket of her coat.

As she walked toward the SUV, she expected him to peel out of the parking place in an attempt to avoid her. The vehicle didn't move, however, not even when she crossed in front— clearly visible through the windshield—to get to the driver's side.

She glanced up long enough to verify that Sean Murphy was watching her approach. Before she could knock on the driver's side window as she'd intended, he opened his door, forcing her to step back against the car parked beside him.

In the light of the halogen lamp, he seemed to loom above her. She fought panic caused by the sudden realization that this was probably not the smartest thing she'd ever done.

She had deliberately provoked this confrontation. It was too late to back out now. Besides, the best defense…

"What the hell do you think you're doing?"

She sounded like a broken record. They'd had this conversation last night. Obviously, it had gotten her nowhere.

"Stopping to pick up something for dinner." His voice was conversational, in contrast to the shrillness of hers.

"And you were going to do that without getting out of the car."

"Actually, I was listening to something on the radio." He inclined his head toward the open door. From inside the SUV came the sound of a country song.

"Are you honestly going to tell me that you aren't following me?"

"I believe I was here first. Are you sure you aren't following *me,* Dr. Kincaid?"

The amusement in his voice produced the same reaction it had last night. Jenna couldn't remember ever striking anyone in her life. She couldn't even remember wanting to. But she wanted to hit him.

"I was at the service station when I saw you drive by and then park over here. You didn't get out of the car. You didn't go inside. It's pretty obvious you were just waiting for me to finish getting gas."

"The last time I checked this was a free country. I told you. I stopped by to pick up something for dinner. I'm in the process of moving and cooking's difficult right now. Somebody recommended this place, so I thought I'd give it a shot."

She didn't believe him. Nor did she believe his story about listening to whatever was on the radio.

"I'm going to get a restraining order against you."

"That's your prerogative. Just be warned they may want you to demonstrate I've actually done something I need to be restrained from doing. Something illegal. You should probably be prepared for that."

"How about storming into my office?"

"I offered to pay for your time. And I left as soon I said what I had to say. Which, if you remember, was a warning that you *might* be in danger. And I haven't been back."

"You followed me home."

"I drove down a public thoroughfare at the same time you did. You turned off. I went straight. That hardly constitutes 'following' you."

"And last night? At the complex? How do you explain that you were sitting out in the parking lot looking in my window?"

"I told you. I'm moving."

It was so unexpected, so thoroughly brazen, that it took a moment before the implication registered. "Moving *where?*"

"There are several units available. Have you been satisfied with the management? They seem nice enough, but you never really know until you've lived somewhere—"

"Are you saying that you're moving into *my* building?"

"I couldn't afford anything on the crest. Just into the complex itself."

The audacity left her breathless. Renting one of those units not only meant that he'd be living practically next door to her, it effectively destroyed her claim that he'd been spying on her when he'd been parked across the street last night. He could say that he had simply been checking out the place before signing a lease.

"You can't do that."

"As of tomorrow, I can."

Tomorrow was the fifteenth. Her own lease ran from midmonth to midmonth, so it was possible he was telling the truth.

"Why?"

"I'm a good neighbor, Dr. Kincaid. I swear you won't even know I'm around."

"And I guess I can expect more of what you did today."

There was a beat of silence. Given his glibness in answering every other question she'd thrown at him, she was surprised he didn't have a ready response for this one.

"And what was that?"

"Don't play dumb with me. You wrote on my car."

His mouth opened, and then he closed it to shake his head. She thought she heard a breath of laughter, but it was cut off so quickly she couldn't be sure.

"Believe it or not, I don't write on cars. I haven't since I was twelve. Something interesting?"

"What?"

"Whatever was written on your car."

"Not to me."

She couldn't make a dent in that wall of supremely confident male arrogance. He mocked both her anger and her threats, treating her as if she were some hysterical female who just didn't get it. Not the killer. And certainly not him.

Despite everything, her impression was still that they were not one and the same. She wasn't afraid of this man. No matter what he said, she knew he'd been following her. And yet standing within two feet of him, she had no sense of danger.

That wasn't the result of any logical thought process, because it couldn't be. It was strong and instinctive, however, and she was practiced enough in making that kind of evaluation that she respected this one.

"I'd still like to know what it said," he repeated, the mockery carefully controlled.

At this point she could see no reason not to tell him. Actually, she found that she wanted to tell him, which implied, as incredible as it seemed, that she believed he *hadn't* written those words.

"It said 'Help me.'"

A crease formed between his brows. "Somebody wrote 'Help me' on your car? While it was in the staff parking deck?"

She had wondered if he knew where she parked, and he'd just admitted he did. Would he have made that admission if he'd been the one who'd written that message? Or was he clever enough to make it so she would wonder?

"Could have been a patient," he offered as she tried to decide the answer to those questions.

"Patients don't have access to the area."

He smiled, the first expression of amusement that seemed free of mockery. It softened the harsh features, making them…appealing, she realized. Almost handsome.

"You think that's funny?"

"The naiveté of it. I assume there are elevators from the building to the deck."

There were, of course. They all used them.

"There are probably service elevators as well," he went on. "Maintenance. You have security?"

"Of course."

"Full-time on every level."

She knew there were security people. She saw them periodically. She'd never concerned herself with where or how often they patrolled. She'd never before needed to.

"We're a mental-health care practice, not a missile site."

"Then you probably shouldn't be surprised that people wander in and out of your parking deck. Those who work there do it legitimately. Patients may do it because they get onto the wrong elevator or get off on the wrong floor."

Obviously someone had gotten past whatever system was

in place. And despite the big deal she'd just made of the writing, it was possible that, as Gary had suggested, it had been intended as a joke.

One of the other staff members? Even Gary, she realized. Just a little therapist-to-therapist humor.

"You've made your point," she conceded stiffly.

"I don't need you to 'help *me*,' Dr. Kincaid. Maybe you should narrow your suspect list down to someone who does."

She thought briefly of her new patient. She couldn't imagine John Nolan in that role, however. She couldn't imagine any of the people she'd seen seeking out her car to write on it.

"My patients have more effective ways to express their needs. I assure you they take advantage of them."

"I wasn't thinking of a patient. I was thinking of someone who might believe you understand the demons that drive him."

Had Sean Murphy written those words on her car so that he could at some point make this suggestion? Another twist on the refrain he'd introduced when he'd burst into her office?

"And what makes you think *he* wants to be helped? As I said in the interview you keep quoting to me, this isn't my field, but it's my impression that people like him enjoy what they do. They don't want to be helped because in their view of the world they don't see anything wrong with the mission they're on."

"Maybe he believes you feel the same way."

"I'm not going to dignify that with a response. A person would have to be insane not to think what he's doing is wrong."

"I didn't say that you think that. I said maybe he *believes* you do. Or maybe he wants to find out what you think."

"About him?"

"Of course. He's the absolute center of his own world. He doesn't care what you think about anything else."

"So how would writing on my car tell him that?"

"Maybe he was watching you. Studying your reaction."

It was a possibility she didn't want in her mind. Now that he'd put it there, she knew it would be hard to dislodge.

"The only person I *know* is watching me is you."

"Then maybe you'd better look again. I'm not the one you need to worry about, Dr. Kincaid," he said. "You can believe that or not, but the quicker you understand it, the quicker you can start dealing with reality."

"With *your* version of reality."

"If I'm right, if he *is* watching you, it's with a purpose. While you're talking to the cops about that restraining order, you be sure you mention what happened with your car. Ask for Lieutenant Ray Bingham. Tell him I sent you."

That advice was the last thing she'd expected from him. It threw her, making her question the assumptions she'd made. All except the purely instinctive one.

"Are you…?" She hesitated, unsure what kind of law enforcement he might be. Obviously not local, which left… "FBI?"

"My interest in this is personal. That doesn't mean that I don't know what I'm talking about. You tell the cops about your car."

If he were trying to scare her, he'd succeeded. Of course, he'd done that from the moment he'd walked into her office.

He leaned into the interior of the SUV to cut off the engine. The music that had provided a backdrop for their conversation ended abruptly, leaving in its wake a silence she felt she should fill.

Before she had come up with anything, he closed the door, hitting the remote to lock it.

"What are you doing?" she asked.

"I'm going inside to get something for dinner. Don't let me keep you."

As neat a dismissal as any she'd ever made with a patient reluctant to end a session. He nodded before he brushed past her. She watched, lips parted on the last word she'd again not gotten to deliver, as he made his way toward the well-lit entrance to the market. He never looked back, but she didn't move until he disappeared inside.

She was no closer to a resolution. Not about the message. And not about him.

All she knew was that Sean Murphy wasn't averse to her talking to the cops about him. Not if it accomplished the task he'd given her.

And right now, doing that didn't seem nearly as foolish as it might have half an hour ago.

Eight

This time Sean had no idea what had awakened him. Not until the phone rang again.

Not his cell, he realized, but the room phone. Since he'd had no idea where he'd be staying until he'd gotten into Birmingham, he couldn't imagine who could be calling him at this number. The cops? With a warning or a re-straining order?

Except he hadn't told Jenna Kincaid the name of the motel. So how could the locals have tracked him down?

They couldn't, he concluded. Not without a time-consuming process of elimination he doubted they had the interest or the manpower to carry out right now. Not in the middle of a multiple-homicide investigation, one that required coordination with all the other law enforcement agencies looking for this killer.

The phone rang again, interrupting that speculation. Without sitting up, he reached over and picked up the receiver, putting it to his ear. "Hello?"

A strange emptiness seemed to fill the line, more threatening than any silence should be. Sean pushed up to prop on one elbow, straining to hear something. The sound of breathing. Background noise. Even static, which would at least tell him the line was engaged.

Normally, by this time he would have returned the receiver to the cradle, deciding the caller had dialed a wrong number. For some reason he didn't do that. Nor did he repeat his greeting. He waited instead, the hair on the back of his neck beginning to lift.

And finally into that disturbing stillness came a sound, so faint that at first he couldn't begin to guess what caused it. As he listened, the noise grew in volume. Still elusive. Still unidentifiable, at least until it assumed a pattern. A rhythm.

Breathing. Someone was breathing into the phone.

His mind considered and then rejected all the variations on the heavy-breathing theme. The quality of this was different. It wasn't sexual. It was as far from sexual as he could imagine anything being.

Suddenly, in the background, he heard another noise. Although indistinct, it sounded like the creak a door might make as it was opened. His guess was strengthened by the more solid click that seemed to represent a reclosing.

The intake of breath that followed was clearer, louder than anything that had gone before. And then the words came, a stream of them. An outpouring.

Soft, seemingly mindless, the same phrases were repeated over and over. They grew in agitation and volume until he could finally distinguish the words.

"Please. Please. Please. Don't. Please. Please don't. Please. Please don't hurt me anymore."

Only with the last sentence did he understand. Although he'd heard the expression "blood ran cold" all his life, he now knew it was a physiological process. Something that could literally happen.

He should have been prepared, then, for what came next. He wasn't. Not even after all the pleading.

The scream seemed to echo and reecho inside his skull, growing to a crescendo that had nothing to do with the sound transmitted through the receiver. He listened, too horrified to slam it down, while the cry shattered the emotional distance it had taken him three years to put between himself and his sister's death.

Despite Makaela's courage, despite what he knew would have been her resolve not to give the bastard the satisfaction, this is what her suffering would have come to. That desperate begging. Followed inevitably by an unbearable agony. And then, finally, by the knowledge that there was no hope. No escape.

Nothing but death. Devoutly wished for. Deliberately denied.

Rage, as overpowering as his initial horror had been, flooded his body. He opened his mouth to give voice to that fury. Before he could, a click in his ear, followed by the dial tone, destroyed the sounds he'd heard as well as any opportunity to respond to them.

Stunned by the speed with which it had all happened, for endless seconds he was unable to breathe, much less formulate a plan of action. Then, determined to break through that paralysis, he punched the O on the dial pad, waiting through the three long rings it took for the motel operator to answer.

"Front desk."

"A call just came through to my room. I need to know where it originated."

"A phone call, sir?"

"That's right. I need to know the number it came from."

"I'm sorry, but we don't have the capability to provide you with that information."

"What do you *mean* you don't have the capability? Everybody has caller ID. Where the hell did the call you just put through come from?"

"I'm sorry, sir." The cheeriness had been shattered by his profanity, but the operator managed to hold on to her customer-service politeness. "We don't subscribe to that service. We so seldom have any call for—"

"Long distance?"

"I'm sorry?"

"Was it a local or a long distance call?" His voice had risen with each unanswered question.

"Sir, I've told you—"

"Get me the Birmingham Police Department. Lieutenant Ray Bingham. And don't you fucking A tell me you don't have the capability to do that."

"Makaela O'Brien was the killer's eighth identified victim," Lieutenant Ray Bingham told her. "She was thirty-six years old when she died. A single mother. She left two children behind, a four-year-old girl and a two-year-old boy. Sean Murphy is her brother, older by…" Bingham glanced down at the folder he'd been reading from. "By two years. Her *big* brother," he added, his voice softened by the realization.

Jenna wondered if that played a role in Murphy's quest. The fact that for most of his childhood he had probably been expected to take care of his little sister.

Or maybe that wouldn't have made a difference. He struck her as a man who would make any sacrifice necessary to protect his own. And if he couldn't, as one who would try to avenge them.

"And he's here to find his sister's murderer?" she asked aloud.

Although he appeared to be in his late thirties, Bingham

was going bald. Rather than giving in to the loss gracefully, at some point he'd made the decision to beat nature at her own game, and shaved his head. Before he answered her question, he put his hands behind that dark, well-shaped head, his fingers interlocked.

"That's what the man says."

"You don't believe him?"

"I don't have any reason to *disbelieve* him. Murphy has friends on the national task force who speak very highly of him. And he not only identified himself almost as soon as he got here, he gave us information that hadn't yet filtered down through the official pipeline."

"Because you hadn't associated the murders here with the others."

"You'd think that'd be easy, wouldn't you? Everybody does. Why the hell didn't the cops see what was going on? In case you might be wondering the same thing, Callie Morgan's murder was the hundred-and-twelfth homicide in the metropolitan area this year. We don't automatically assume any of them are connected. And I can't ever remember having a serial killer operating in this area. Not during my years on the force. Not in my memory."

"If you don't believe he's here to discover the identity of his sister's killer, then…"

"Murphy, you mean?"

With the detective's question, Jenna realized that, while her mind had still been occupied with the information he'd provided about her "stalker," the detective had moved on to the difficulties this case presented for the local police departments. Her preoccupation with Sean Murphy was something she had just as soon Bingham *not* notice, but there were still questions she needed answered. "What other reason would he have for coming here?"

"Maybe he's writing a book. Been known to happen. Usually not with relatives, but…" The broad shoulders under the white dress shirt lifted. "It's always possible."

With a killer like this, one gaining national notoriety now that the FBI had figured out that those deaths were connected to one person, writing this story might be a very lucrative endeavor. She just couldn't imagine Sean Murphy in that role.

"Maybe he wants you to help him," Bingham went on.

"Me?"

"Maybe that's why he's following you. You certainly have the credentials."

"That isn't something I'd be interested in doing."

Not in a hundred years. Despite her training, she knew she didn't have the stomach for that kind of research. She couldn't believe Sean would be interested in that, either. Whatever he was here for, it wasn't to collect material for a book that would exploit his sister's death.

Which brought her full circle. Back to the question of why he was in Birmingham. And more importantly, why he was following her.

"He told me I fit the victim profile."

Still leaning back in his chair, the detective looked at her across the desk. "Yeah? So do thousands of other women. From what I've seen of the profile, it isn't all that specific."

Dark hair and eyes. Tall. Not a prostitute.

"Murphy said that the killer would be attracted to me because of the interview I did. Do you think that's possible?"

"Sorry, I didn't see it. But again, you aren't the only local woman who's given interviews."

"He thought that in the course of mine I came across as… sympathetic to the killer."

She was aware that she sounded defensive. Of course,

when you've been told the same thing over and over, you begin to wonder if it could be true.

"Are you?"

"No one could be. Not if they know what he's done."

"Then I wouldn't worry too much about whatever Murphy thinks. The important thing would be whether or not the killer felt the same way."

Something else Sean told her. That the Inquisitor would have been watching the news—something she actually agreed with. And that he would have interpreted her statements exactly as Murphy had. "What if he did?"

Without unlacing his hands, Bingham brought them down over his head. When they were in front of his face, he pushed the joined fingers forward, popping a couple of knuckles. Then he put his palms flat on his desk to lean toward her.

"We don't have any idea what sets this guy off, Dr. Kincaid. Much less what makes him go after a particular victim. I haven't seen anything from the FBI that suggests he chooses those any differently from the way most serial killers do—at random and based on opportunity. There's nothing in the official profile to indicate he's ever done anything other than that. And believe me, during the past forty-eight hours, I've read all of the material the Bureau has collected."

The dark eyes held on her face, as if willing her to believe him. It wasn't that she didn't want to. It was just that she was aware that even the FBI didn't claim profiling was an exact science.

She knew that much of it was guesswork, pure and simple. Highly educated perhaps, but still guesswork.

"Do I think he's watching the local news?" the lieutenant went on, apparently viewing her silence as acceptance. "Without a doubt. Did he see *your* interview? Chances are, given his ego, he did. Does that mean he's gonna choose you for his next victim? In my opinion, highly unlikely."

Although the information was intended to be comforting, Jenna found she needed more than the detective's opinion. After all, that's what Sean Murphy had offered. For all she knew, his might even be better than Bingham's.

"Why it is unlikely?"

"Because that isn't his pattern. It's been less than two weeks since the Morgan woman's body was found. And we got lucky in that somebody stumbled on it quickly. He's not even *thinking* about the next one. He's too busy glorying in his success."

"Specifically what does that mean? 'Glorying in his success.' In police terms, I mean."

"Reliving the act. Handling whatever he took from her. Looking at it. Maybe revisiting the location where he killed her. Only we don't have any idea where that is right now."

"He takes souvenirs?"

That information was something she hadn't read in the papers, although she should have assumed it would be the case. It was certainly the norm.

"Yeah, but don't ask me what. That's one of the things the feds have put the lid on. No release of information concerning his trophies."

The phone on the desk between them rang. Bingham shrugged apologetically, and reached out with one large, beautifully manicured hand to grab the receiver. "Gotta answer this. It's the hotline."

Hotline? For the investigation?

"Bingham."

He said nothing else for perhaps twenty seconds. His eyes found her face, however, as he listened.

"Tape," he said, his tone confident.

He listened again, his gaze falling to a pencil on his desk as he did. He picked it up with his free hand, but rather than taking notes, he turned it over and over, bouncing the eraser and then the lead against the blotter.

"It isn't time. It's only been two weeks since Callie Morgan. He'll still be able to control his impulses. He isn't gonna risk another snatch until he has to."

The motion of the pencil stopped, the big hand stilling as he listened to whatever had been said in response.

"She's sitting in my office right now." The dark eyes lifted to Jenna's face.

He listened again. A long time. Although Jenna couldn't distinguish any of the words, whoever was on the other end of the line was now talking loudly enough that she could hear the sound of his voice, even from across the desk.

"I'll tell her." Bingham hung up the phone, steepling his fingers before he lowered them to lie in the center of his desk. "Our mutual friend."

"Murphy?"

"Someone called his hotel room. Some kind of harassment."

She's sitting in my office right now. Which seemed to indicate that Sean had implicated her in some way.

"Whatever he just suggested, I didn't call him. I have no idea where he's staying."

"According to him, no one does. Don't worry. You aren't a suspect. The call came in minutes ago. While you were here."

"Reporters can be remarkably resourceful, especially when the story is as big as this one. If they found out Murphy's connection to the case…"

"That's an angle I hadn't thought of," Bingham said. "I think Murphy did some interviews when he came home to identify his sister's body. He thinks this is our boy."

Our boy. For a moment, Jenna didn't understand what the detective meant. And when she did—

"The Inquisitor? But…" She shook her head, trying to make sense of that. "Why would he call Sean Murphy?"

"There was something he wanted him to hear."

The lieutenant had said "tape." She'd been thinking of duct tape, which the papers said had been used to bind the victims. The word could have referred to an audiotape as well, she realized belatedly. The chill she'd felt when Dingham had mentioned souvenirs was back.

"What?"

Bingham exhaled, his mouth rounded and his cheeks slightly inflated. "You sure you want to hear this?"

She wasn't. Despite having driven downtown after work today to talk to someone on the task force, she had now discovered she didn't want to know any more about the murders than she had to.

Of course, if she were involved, as Murphy suggested, she had no choice but to be informed. Like it or not.

"Maybe I ought to," she conceded.

"Murphy thinks that what he heard was another victim."

"*Another* victim?" Bingham made no response, letting her work it out on her own. "You said it was too soon."

"That's why I think it's a tape."

"Are you saying that he *recorded…?*"

She stopped, unable to articulate her realization of what the killer must have recorded. And then, armed with that tape, he'd called the brother of one of the women he'd tortured to death to make him listen.

Jenna swallowed the vomit that crawled into her throat. There was no reason to be shocked at that cruelty. It was far *less* diabolical than what he did to his victims.

"Do you think… Could it possibly have been his sister?"

"That crossed my mind. Murphy apparently hasn't considered that possibility yet. Maybe he can't afford to. He believes that what he was listening to was live."

The word lay between them, grotesquely inappropriate. Obscene. Just as the actions it described.

"That denial is a form of self-protection."

Bingham shrugged. "Can you blame him?"

She couldn't. No one could. Not given the circumstances.

Still, based on her impressions of Sean Murphy from the few meetings they'd had, he was bright enough that at some point he was going to figure out that what she'd suggested was a possibility. Especially since the lieutenant had already planted the seed that what he'd listened to had been on tape.

It was only a small step from that to the next horror. The kind of step someone close to one of the victims couldn't help but make. Probably in those dark, lonely hours after midnight.

"There *is* another possibility," she said.

The dark eyes widened, questioning. "Yeah?"

"That it might have been someone's idea of a prank. There are people who are capable of doing something like that."

"I've met a few. But…" Bingham shook his head. "That isn't something you're going to convince Murphy of."

"Something like that would be easy enough to fake. And given what he knows about the murders, the power of suggestion would be extremely effective. It would go a long way toward convincing him that what he was hearing was authentic."

"Murphy wouldn't be easy to fool. Not with his background."

She had asked Sean if he were law enforcement, and he'd denied it. She couldn't think of anything else that would give him the expertise to make that kind of distinction.

"What kind of background?"

"According to the guy on the task force who vouched for him, Murphy was career military. Some kind of elite special forces unit. The agent who told me wouldn't go into detail, but I got the impression that whatever his specialty was, Murphy's seen *and* heard his share of people dying."

It fit. The air of danger she'd sensed at their first meeting. Even his arrogance.

"Retired?"

According to Bingham, Sean would have had been thirty-eight when his sister was murdered. It was possible that, if he'd enlisted young enough, he'd already put in his twenty.

"Guess he didn't figure he had much choice saddled with the kids and all. Despite them, catching this guy has become a personal vendetta for him. And somebody in Washington took the trouble to cue him in early on this one."

Vendetta. Sean Murphy might not have been able to protect his sister, but apparently he was determined to bring the man responsible for her death to justice. And suddenly, the reality of what he was doing hit her.

Sean Murphy believed every word he'd told her. He really believed that because of the interview she'd given, she had become the target of the same man who had murdered his sister.

And because of that, he also believed that all he'd have to do to find Makaela's killer was to follow her.

Nine

He was exhausted. And at the same time he was elated.

There had been few times in his life when he had felt so completely in control. Of the woman he'd found. Of Murphy. And his ability to manipulate both simultaneously...

He smoothed the sweat-drenched hair away from her face. Delicately he touched a drop of blood at the corner of her eyelid with his thumb, removing it with precision and yet with the gentleness of a mother's touch.

He smiled at the analogy, thinking how apt it was. Then he put his thumb to his mouth, sucking her blood from his skin.

The elation he'd felt only seconds ago was already beginning to fade. He knew from experience that it would eventually give way to melancholia, an old-fashioned word that reflected the emptiness he felt when they were gone.

Of course, there was nothing to say he had to give her up yet. As incredible as it seemed, there had still been no bulletin about this one. Apparently nobody was looking for her.

Perhaps there was no one to report that she was missing. Which would mean no one cared where she was. Or who she was with.

His eyes considered the backpack she'd been carrying. He had thrown it into the corner of the room when he'd carried her inside. With the drugs and restraints, he'd had no reason to fear she'd be able to reach it. And no reason to believe there was anything inside that might help her escape or do him harm if she did.

She hadn't been the type to carry a weapon. Far too trusting, he thought, as he left the cooling body and crossed to where her bag lay.

He stooped, balancing on the balls of his feet while he unzipped it. He lifted the strap, allowing the contents to spill out onto the floor.

With his free hand, he sorted through the textbooks and notebooks. Other than an unopened package of gum and a billfold, that was all the backpack had contained.

A student. Which perhaps explained why no one had reported her missing. Maybe she didn't live in a dorm. Or have a roommate. Or maybe she was the kind who didn't come home every night, so that her absence during the last three days had gone unnoticed.

Eventually, someone—family or friends—would realize they hadn't seen or heard from her. Or the school would begin to check because she had missed so many classes. How long it would take for either of those to happen was anyone's guess.

He opened the wallet, exposing a debit card, a student ID and several plastic pockets filled with pictures. All of the people in the photographs were young. And they were beautiful, he realized as he studied the snapshots. Both the girls and the boys. Fresh-faced and eager. Full of life.

As he thought that, he flipped to a picture of the woman who lay dead across the room. Obviously it had been taken at a dance or a pageant because she was wearing an evening gown. Not a dance, he decided, because she was alone. He lifted the picture, bringing it closer to his eyes.

Her hair had been considerably longer when this was taken, and she had worn it in a different style. It was also a different color, he discovered, turning the photo to catch the light. It was much fairer than it appeared now, especially when it was wet. As it had been the afternoon he'd found her.

Revulsion at her deception sliced through him, destroying the last trace of exhilaration he'd felt at her death. How could he know that *this* wasn't the real color of her hair? How could he ever know that *he* wasn't the one she'd deceived?

He closed the billfold, tossing it down among the scattered books. She was a whore and a liar, who deserved nothing less than what she'd gotten.

But he, too, bore part of the blame for the fact that he'd wasted his time on her. He hadn't followed the plan, so he had also gotten what he deserved.

She'd been a test, sent to try him. And he had failed. He hadn't had enough resolve to stick to the things he knew kept him safe. Preparation before he set everything into motion. Attention to detail. Taking his time to make sure that nothing escaped his due diligence.

From now on, he swore, that's what he would do. This time he had allowed himself to be sidetracked, but that wouldn't happen again.

Not when he had so many other things that needed his attention. Murphy. Jenna Kincaid. He had almost forgotten her in the distraction this one had provided.

And that's all this had been. A foolish distraction. A failure of purpose. Something he should have guarded against.

Which was exactly what *she* would have told him. Except she wouldn't have been so forgiving of his mistake. Another of her lessons that he'd forgotten. And as always, he knew he would be punished for it.

Perhaps that's why Murphy had been allowed to get so close. A punishment for his distraction.

If so, that could be easily remedied now that he was again focused on what needed to be done. Actually, he'd already begun the process earlier this evening.

He wondered how Sergeant Murphy had enjoyed his phone call. Only a tiny foretaste of what was to come, but after all, the man deserved something for his devotion to his dead sister, misplaced as it was.

As for the threats he'd made... Something special, he thought. And he knew just what that should be.

Jenna stood in the outer hallway of the police station. She hadn't told Bingham what she planned to do. It was none of his business, but she suspected he wouldn't see it that way.

She shifted her weight, leaning back against the tile wall, her arms wrapped around her body for warmth. A surge of cold came in every time someone opened one of the glass front doors, but she didn't dare move. From where she was standing, she could see the steps that led up to the entrance. If Sean Murphy came in this way, she couldn't miss him.

She glanced at her watch, surprised to find it was only a little past six. It had been full dark when she'd arrived, but then, they were approaching the shortest day of the year.

If she hadn't decided to come downtown, she would probably be just getting to her apartment. And if Murphy intended to keep an eye on her, as she now believed he had been during the last few days, then he might be carrying out this same vigil there.

She straightened, pushing away from the wall to walk over to the front doors. She looked through them onto the parking lot. She had pulled her car into a spot in the first row, an area illuminated by both the lights on the building and those of the lot. And there were probably a dozen security cameras in place around the perimeter as well.

All she had to do was walk down those steps, get into her car and go home. There was no guarantee the man she was waiting for would show up here tonight, no matter what Bingham thought. Even if he did, what she had to tell him could—and probably should—wait until they were both less emotionally drained.

As she paced back to the wall, the description Bingham had given of the call Sean received echoed in her head. Despite what she'd told herself as she considered the security provisions in place here, it reinforced the reality that nowhere in this town was safe.

Not for her. Not if Murphy was right.

She could surrender to that fear, letting it hold her hostage and keep her from her normal activities. Or she could continue to go about her business, wary of anything that seemed out of the ordinary.

Or she could pursue a third option. The one that had her standing in this drafty hallway, subjected to the curiosity of everyone who entered the building.

A rush of cold air made her raise her eyes to the doorway she was supposed to be watching. Sean Murphy stood in the entrance, his right hand holding one of the glass doors open.

His eyes held hers for a few heartbeats, and then he stepped inside, allowing the door to close behind him. As she tried to decide how to frame the question she'd been waiting to ask, he closed the distance between them.

He moved with the same athletic grace she'd noticed in her office. And her chin lifted so that, despite the height difference between them, her eyes maintained contact with his.

He searched her face before he asked, "You talked to Bingham?"

"I'm sorry."

Sorry his sister had been one of the killer's victims. Sorry for the experience he'd just gone through. Sorry that every conclusion she'd come to about his actions had been wrong.

"You don't owe me an apology. If anything—" He stopped, his gaze focusing on the door of Bingham's office. "He told you."

"About your sister?" she guessed, nodding.

His attention came back to her. For the first time she noticed how exhausted he looked. His eyes were rimmed with red, shadows like old bruises below them.

"I'm sorry," she said again. "I didn't have any idea."

He nodded, lips set, eyes no longer making contact with hers. The angle of his head as he looked past her emphasized the stubble on his cheeks. With his coloring, he would probably have to shave twice a day to avoid it. Something he obviously wouldn't have taken time to do tonight.

"Look," he began, turning back to face her, "there's no doubt now that I was right."

She shook her head, unwilling to accept the only interpretation which made sense of that. "Right about what?"

He drew a breath, deep enough that it lifted his shoulders. His lips parted, but before he could say anything, the front doors opened, letting in another rush of frigid air.

A couple of uniformed cops manhandled a struggling teen through them. Although it was the blast of cold that had attracted her gaze, the fight the kid was putting up, along with the profanities he yelled, kept it there.

Like watching a train wreck, she thought.

"Come on," Sean said, putting his hand under her elbow to turn her away from the door and back toward Bingham's office.

Despite the fact that she was wearing both a sweater and coat, she was aware of the strength of the fingers wrapped around her arm. She walked beside him, their bodies almost touching, too conscious of his nearness. So near she could smell the faint, not unpleasant scent of damp wool and the soap he'd recently showered with.

To her surprise, he guided her past Bingham's office and into another hallway, one that ran at right angles to the hall where she'd been waiting. Arrows on the wall pointed to an interview room and a break room. There were rest room symbols there as well, with their own directional arrows.

Sean stopped as they rounded the corner, releasing her arm. Not only were they sheltered from the cold, the noise level back here was considerably less, creating a sense of privacy she wasn't sure she welcomed.

Evidently it encouraged the completion of the revelation he'd begun out in the main hallway. He wasted no time in laying it out for her again. "I know now that I was right about him being attracted to you."

As good an opening as she was likely to get. "Actually, that's what I wanted to talk to you about."

"You were waiting to talk to me about…him?"

Maybe he'd thought she'd wanted to offer condolences about his sister. That would be a logical assumption, considering what her first words had been.

"You came here to find him, didn't you?"

He hesitated, obviously trying to think how to answer. Wondering, maybe, if Bingham had put her up to asking.

"You're here because he killed your sister," she went on. "And because the police haven't been able to stop him."

"I'm here to help in any way I can," he said, seeming to choose his words with care. "I've been following the investigation since the task force was formed. The national task force. I came down here because I thought I could provide the cops with some background—"

"If that's what you told Bingham, that's fine," she interrupted. "I don't care. You can tell them anything you want. But…that *isn't* why you're here. You and I both know that, so just don't lie to *me,* okay? I don't give a damn who else you feel you have to lie to, but don't lie to me."

After the display of temper in her office, she expected him to get angry. To deny her accusation. To walk away. To do *something*.

For a long time he did nothing. Then he nodded, a single abrupt motion.

She gave him credit for the intelligence that had obviously led to that quick agreement. What she'd said had been logical and reasoned. He'd recognized that so there had been no argument. And no denial.

"You've been following me because you believe he is. You think he's chosen me, and because of that, so have you. You intend to use *me* to get to *him*."

Again he said nothing, his eyes locked on hers.

"That's what this is all about, isn't it? Not about looking out for me. You *want* him to come after me. That's what you've been hoping for from the beginning."

"I warned you."

She laughed, the sound bitter. "And that makes it all right? You warned me, and now I'm on my own. 'Hey, lady, there's a guy who wants to slice and dice you like he did my sister. And oh, if you don't mind, I want to watch you just in case I might be able to grab him when he comes to do that.'"

She hadn't known how furious she was until she began to give voice to the realization she'd made in Bingham's office. Furious that Sean Murphy had been using her. More furious that some innocent comment she'd made might really have triggered something in a sociopath's brain that had set him after her.

Pain so powerful it was almost a physical force appeared in the depths of those clear blue eyes. Then, with ruthless control, it was replaced by an answering fury. "You better hope I'm watching," he said, each word a carefully enunci-ated threat, "because it's for damn sure nobody else will be."

She had a right to her anger. She had been used. Still, what she'd just said to this man, who knew, perhaps better than anyone other than the FBI, how vicious an animal stalked her, had been unforgivable. Seeing its impact made her regret that she'd opened her mouth.

"If you're convinced I'm a target—"

"I wasn't. Not until tonight. After tonight—" He stopped, taking another breath so deep it, too, was visible.

After tonight. And what had happened tonight…

"The phone call? *That* convinced you?"

The anguish he'd controlled was back in his eyes. She wondered if he had just reached the point Bingham believed he would inevitably come to. Had he begun to wonder if the screams he'd heard could have been those of his sister?

"There's no other way he could have known I'm here."

"No *other* way? What does that mean?"

"No other way except that he saw me following you. How else could he know?"

"He saw *you* because…he was trailing *me?* Is that what you're suggesting?"

"You have a better explanation?"

She didn't, but she didn't want to admit that because it ter-rified her. "Maybe he's figured out *your* pattern."

"My pattern?"

"You show up wherever he's operating. Don't you think he's smart enough to figure that out by now?"

"Except I haven't. I was in Detroit where my sister was killed. And then not again until now. Not until this one."

"But…you worked with the task force," she said, trying to remember what Bingham had told her.

"I talked to them. Because of Makaela, I had some credibility. In any case, they were willing to meet with me."

The "credibility" he had just mentioned might also have come from his background. Even the detective had seemed impressed with that.

"Then why now? Why here?"

"Because they were in on this one early. And because someone at the Bureau was willing to call me."

If he really hadn't been on the scene of the murders before, then he was probably right. The only thing that would have attracted the killer's attention to him was the fact he'd been following her. And in order for the killer to know that…

"He's been following me," she said softly.

Sean didn't respond. Not verbally. But she could tell from his expression that's what he believed.

"I didn't do anything wrong," she said, clinging to the truth she'd reiterated over and over. She'd given an interview that was supposed to deal with holiday depression. In response to an unexpected question, she'd made some general statement about sociopaths. How could that have caused a murderer to come after her?

She could appeal to the police for protection. With the entire city to watch, and without any kind of proof…

Of course, there was the writing on her car. Sean was the one who'd suggested she tell the cops about it. Not that it had done any good.

They hadn't taken it seriously. No one had. Even Gary had thought the message was a joke.

"So you're it? You're my only hope?"

He didn't react to the sarcasm. At least not with anger. Another emotion moved behind those blue eyes instead, but she didn't know him well enough to be able to identify it.

"Look—"

"Then do it right," she interrupted. "I'll make it worth your while."

His eyes narrowed. He tilted his head, as if unsure of what he'd just heard. "What?"

"I'll pay you. To protect me. That way we both get what we want."

The side-to-side motion of his head had begun before she finished. His mouth opened, as if he intended to argue, and then he closed it.

She could almost see him thinking. If he were as bright as she thought, he would arrive at the conclusion she just had.

They wanted the same thing. He wanted to catch the man who had killed his sister. And if the Inquisitor really was stalking her, she wanted someone to stop him. Why they shouldn't be working together—

"You want to *hire* me to protect you?"

"All I'm suggesting is that it's to our mutual benefit to work together. And that I'm willing to pay you *very* well to do what you planned to do all along."

Ten

Sean tried to think of something discouraging to tell her. Something that would make the arrangements she'd just suggested ridiculous. Only, there wasn't anything.

He *had* been keeping an eye on her in the hope the killer was stalking her. This afternoon he'd been given proof that what he had hoped for was a reality.

So why wasn't he jumping on her proposal with the eagerness it deserved? She was offering him access to her every move and asking nothing in return.

If the killer had come after her while Sean had her under surveillance, he would have intervened. He would never have let Makaela's murderer do to another woman what he'd done to her. Not if it was in his power to prevent it.

Besides, he hadn't started this with the intent of getting proof to convict this bastard. If he found him, there would be no need for a trial.

"If he knew I was watching you 24/7, it might drive him off."

He didn't really believe it was that simple. Just as he didn't believe that the killer's victims were chosen at random.

For what it was worth, that the Inquisitor wasn't strictly opportunistic was a conclusion the task force had also come to. They hadn't gone public with that belief on the theory that it might make local law enforcement less vigilant, something nobody wanted.

"So that I'd no longer be a target? Forgive me if I say that, from my perspective," Jenna said, "that wouldn't be a bad thing."

At least she was honest. Besides, the bastard already knew he was here. It was a given, then, that he also knew he'd been following her.

"It's obvious he doesn't care if you know he spotted you," she went on. "He would never have called you if he did."

"He wouldn't have been able to resist. There's a certain one-upsmanship that the FBI mentions in its profile. He thinks he's smarter than everyone else."

"He's smart enough to have eluded everyone for this long."

"A lot of that's been luck. The locals not knowing what they were dealing with until it was too late. No database of organized knowledge about him. All of which has now changed."

"And his own intelligence," she reiterated stubbornly. "Don't sell him short."

"Is that your *professional* opinion, Doctor?"

It pissed him off that she was telling him how to think about Makaela's killer. He'd spent weeks studying every particle of information about those murders that he could get his hands on. Months working his way into the confidence of the people on the task force, the people who had the expertise Jenna Kincaid had admitted she didn't possess. Now, after reading the local papers, she was pretending to be some kind of expert on what this guy was, as well as on what he was likely to do in any situation.

"*Absolutely* a professional opinion. Mine *and* the Bureau's.

According to them, he's highly organized. Careful. Methodical. Repetitious. And because of that, he's gotten away with fourteen murders in the past seven years."

"Fourteen that we know of," he corrected.

"All the more reason to credit him with having a very good brain."

"I don't 'credit' him with anything." He repeated her word, mocking it.

"Then you won't get him. Not if you refuse to treat him with the respect his intellect deserves."

"What he deserves—"

"Nobody's arguing that he's a Boy Scout. You can believe he's as evil as you want because he *is*. All I'm saying is that you discount his intelligence at *your* peril." Her pupils dilated suddenly, her mouth remaining open after the last word.

He could read in her face the realization she'd just made. Whatever mistakes he made in dealing with the Inquisitor would not be at *his* peril, but at *hers*.

If he agreed to do what she'd asked, that's what he'd be risking. Not just his chance at avenging Makaela's death, but the life of another woman.

A woman who, in spite of his intentions, had become real to him. Too real. Someone he'd talked to. Someone who, despite everything he'd said that first day, he'd come to respect.

She had guts. Enough to challenge him at every turn, even before she had known who he was or what he was doing. As she had when he'd called her. And last night in the parking lot.

The question was: Did she have the courage to undertake the game she was proposing? It was one thing to acknowledge intellectually that a killer was out to get you, to "slice and dice" you, as she had so graphically phrased it.

It was something very different to deal on a daily basis with the idea on a visceral level. To admit to the possibility that someone really wanted to torture you to death. To make you scream in endless, mindless agony.

Just as the woman he'd listened to tonight had screamed.

He had almost forgotten why he'd come down to the police station. There was another victim out there. Another woman in that madman's hands. As he stood here bargaining with Jenna Kincaid for *her* safety, that woman, whoever she was, was suffering the same brutal torture his sister had. The rage he'd felt when he viewed Makaela's body roared through him, as powerful, and as painful, as it had been then.

"I need to talk to Bingham," he said, turning away.

She put her hand on his arm to stop him. "You haven't answered my question."

"Sorry. That's not why I came. That's not what I do."

"Protecting someone? But you could, couldn't you?" For the first time there was a note of pleading in her voice. "You think you have the skills to stop him. A man who's murdered all those people."

That wasn't a matter of "belief." He *knew* he had those skills. Just as he knew from experience that he could kill.

Especially this man.

"Yes."

"The same skills required to protect someone."

"Look, I can't guarantee—"

"I understand that. Believe me. If he *is* targeting me…" She took a breath, allowing the sentence to trail. When she began again, it was something different. "All I'm asking is that you try. I'll pay whatever you want, including expenses."

It wasn't something he even had to think about. He had prepared for this mission, and that had included making sure he had the resources to carry it out. He didn't need—or want—her money.

"There are some things that aren't for sale, Dr. Kincaid. And some people."

He could tell from the change in her expression that she knew she'd made a mistake. Apparently she was a good enough therapist to realize she shouldn't have offered him money. Not for *anything* connected to his sister's murder.

Unfortunately, she wasn't good enough to know that the next incentive she tried wasn't going to be any more successful.

"Then I'll get that restraining order," she said. "You may have friends on the task force, but this is my town. I've lived here all my life. I have friends, too. Some of them very well connected. I promise you I'll do everything in my power to keep you away from me. I'll lie if I have to so that the police will offer me around-the-clock protection from him. But it will effectively be from you as well."

As threats went, this one wasn't all that impressive. In this situation, the locals would be spread too thin to provide twenty-four-hour surveillance, no matter who she knew.

He could still keep an eye on her, even if the cops beefed up their patrols around her apartment. If she got some judge to sign an order to make him keep his distance, he wouldn't obey it. And this time she'd never know he was there.

Just as she would never have known if he hadn't felt obligated to tell her that she'd made herself a target. As he had acknowledged before, that was a mistake.

"If you'll give me your word that you'll do the best you can to protect me," she said, her voice persuasive, "then I'll help you get what you want. I'll help you get your sister's murderer."

"Makaela. Her name was Makaela."

"Makaela," she repeated. "I'll help you. Just please…do this. For me. And for Makaela."

She was using his sister's death to try and get what she

wanted. That should have made him more determined than ever to do this his way.

Still, he couldn't deny that on some level she had gotten to him. Maybe because he really believed he was the best hope she had. Maybe the only hope.

He would wonder later what he would have told her if his cell hadn't rung. Restraining his inclination to curse the interruption, he took the phone out of his jacket pocket and flipped open the case. It was halfway to his ear when he remembered the phone call this afternoon.

The bastard couldn't have this number.

Of course, he would never have imagined that the killer could track him to the hotel where he was staying, either.

If you hadn't given yourself away by approaching Jenna Kincaid, he wouldn't have.

Forcing his hand to complete the motion it had begun, he pressed the phone to his ear. He waited a couple of seconds, making sure he could trust his voice to pronounce the necessary word without trembling. "Hello."

"Ray Bingham, Sergeant Murphy. Where are you?"

"About fifteen feet from your office."

"Then I'll open the door for you."

The connection was broken, leaving him once more with the sound of a dial tone in his ear. He lowered the cell, closing it before he shoved it into his pocket.

"Bingham?" Jenna asked.

"He got impatient."

For a moment neither of them said anything, the intensity of the conversation they had before the interruption seeming to weigh on them both. She didn't ask him again, and because he'd had no good answer, he chose not to return to the question.

"I thought you were coming in to see me, Sergeant Murphy."

They turned to find the detective watching them from the

end of the hall. He looked confused, but neither of them offered an explanation for what they'd been doing out here.

Almost unconsciously Sean glanced down at her again. In the last few seconds she had somehow managed to regain her composure.

Her eyes met his unflinchingly. At least they weren't pleading with him to save her life anymore. And before they could, he stepped past her, walking toward the place where Ray Bingham waited.

"You should probably hear this, too, Dr. Kincaid," the detective said.

Sean's expression must have revealed his frustration over that invitation. As he approached, Bingham said under his breath, "She's gonna hear it soon enough, anyway."

Sean didn't look back to see if she was following. He walked to the open door of the detective's office and sat down in the leather chair on the other side of the cluttered desk.

Bingham closed the door as soon as his second guest came through. Then he grabbed a straight-back chair from against the wall and placed it beside the one Sean was sitting in. He indicated with a gesture that Jenna should take it.

Jenna's eyes again met Sean's before she did, but he couldn't read what was in them. All he knew was that he didn't want to describe the phone call that had brought him here in front of her. The experience was too raw. And too personal.

He had thought he'd come to terms with the manner of Makaela's dying. Not with the fact that she was dead, of course. Or that someone had taken her life in the most brutal way possible.

Only with the fact that it was over and done, and that there was nothing he could do to bring her back. All he could do was take out the bastard who had murdered her.

And keep him from ever doing that again to another woman.

That had always been part of what drove him. Not just his sister's death, but the determination not to let her murderer do to another family what he had done to theirs.

So why in hell did you refuse Jenna Kincaid's plea that you do exactly that?

"We just got a call," Bingham said. "A twenty-year-old student at UAB, Carol Cummings, has been reported missing. She was supposed to attend a study session for a group project on Tuesday and never showed up. A friend got concerned because it wasn't like to her let her classmates down. The friend went to Cummings's apartment several times and couldn't get anybody to answer the door.

"She finally checked with some of the girl's teachers and found out Cummings hadn't been in class all week. Nobody can remember seeing her since last weekend. Long story short, the friend alerted the administration, who called the girl's parents. They've filed a missing person's report."

The knot in Sean's gut was back. The one that formed whenever he learned there had been another victim.

Despite the detective's conviction that the sounds he'd heard during this afternoon's phone call had been taped, he had known then what he was listening to. He just hadn't had a name or a face for this one. Now he knew at least one of those.

"That doesn't necessarily mean something's happened to her, you understand," Bingham went on, as if he were trying to convince himself. "At that age, there are a lot of things that could explain somebody ditching a few classes. She may have hooked up with someone last weekend and decided to go out of town with him—"

"Dark hair, dark eyes?"

The detective's mouth snapped shut with Sean's brusque interruption. His lips tightened before they pursed. When he opened them again, he didn't deny the reality of what Sean had asked. "Yes to both."

"Son of a *bitch*."

There was silence in the room after his uncharacteristic outburst. The uncomfortable kind that says nobody wants to talk about the subject under discussion. Yeah, well, neither did he.

"Where's the last place she was seen?" he asked, deliberately breaking it. None of them could afford to indulge in that sensibility.

"Five Points South," Bingham said. "She and a friend had gone to Dave's from the library. The friend had to leave for a date. Carol stayed, saying she'd catch a ride with someone going back downtown."

"You said it's too soon," Jenna said. "You said he would still be enjoying the success of the last one."

"That's why I believe this isn't connected. It doesn't fit the pattern."

"As we know it," Sean said.

"Meaning?"

"That all we have on some of the victims is an approximate time of death. Some of the bodies were too decomposed when they were discovered to tell us much."

"Callie Morgan's was found two weeks ago. And according to the coroner, she'd been dead for less than four days. I don't think anything we know about this guy indicates that he kills this frequently."

"Sometimes…" Jenna began, and then stopped, her eyes meeting Sean's. She hesitated, licking her lips before she continued. "As I said at the start, this really isn't my field, but… Sometimes whatever compels them grows stronger as they achieve success. Like someone addicted to a drug, they need more and more to reach the high they crave. What worked in the beginning doesn't satisfy them as it once did.

For some killers, that means more brutality or a great humiliation of the victim. A better posing of the body. For others… For others it may mean that they just need to kill more frequently."

"Then God help us all," Bingham said, "if any of what you just said is true of this one."

Eleven

The police cruiser had followed Jenna back to her apartment. Although she doubted it had been part of their instructions, the two young cops had even come inside with her. They'd walked through the rooms, opening closet and shower doors and checking under the bed.

The precautions should have made her feel safe. Instead, as soon as she'd watched them get back into their car, it made her realize exactly how alone and defenseless she was.

Despite the fact that Sean had admitted to Bingham that he believed the call he'd received this afternoon was a result of the killer having seen him with Jenna, the detective hadn't been willing to assign three shifts of officers to her protection. Not when every available person was needed in the now desperate search for Carol Cummings.

Jenna understood the logic of his decision. She even recognized, at least intellectually, the moral correctness of it. After all, there was no real evidence to back up Sean Murphy's theory. The two words scrawled in the road dirt on the side of her car could have been written by anyone. And Sean's claim that the only way the killer could have known he was in town was if he, too, had been following Jenna had not been convincing to Bingham.

Now, as the taillights of the patrol car disappeared down the sloping drive below her apartment, the fear she'd fought for three days lay like a weight in the bottom of her stomach. Unconsciously she wrapped her arms around her body in an attempt to regain the sense of security that had always been a part of her life.

She wondered if she would ever again feel completely safe. Certainly not until the killer was caught.

And based on law enforcement's track record thus far, Sean Murphy seemed to represent the best chance of that happening.

Was he somewhere out there in the darkness? Watching her apartment, perhaps from the one he'd just rented?

Her eyes focused on the lighted windows of the complex below, the lives of its inhabitants shielded by drawn blinds and curtains. The black SUV she'd come to know so well wasn't in the lineup of automobiles parked in front of them.

Although Sean hadn't agreed to the deal she'd offered, that didn't mean he wasn't maintaining his surveillance. As far as she knew, she still represented his best opportunity to find the man who'd murdered Makaela. And despite the fact that she'd gone to the police to complain about what he'd been doing, she would feel enormously better right now if she could be absolutely certain he hadn't given up on that.

Sighing, she reached up and pulled the drapes across her windows, shutting out the night. Then she walked across the living room to turn on the lamp beside the couch.

The newspapers she'd perused so carefully yesterday were still stacked on the coffee table. She bundled them up and headed toward the kitchen and the tall metal garbage can that sat beside the back door. When she had dumped them inside, she checked the dead bolt and the chain. Both were fastened.

Tomorrow she would call and see how quickly she could get a security system installed. Even if no one knew right now how the killer approached his victims, she needed to establish some kind of sanctuary, somewhere she could feel safe. Other than her office, this was where she spent the majority of her time.

She turned away from the door to face the empty kitchen. She should eat something, but the thought of food was slightly nauseating.

Anxiety, she conceded, which wouldn't be helped by an empty stomach. Especially since she'd skipped breakfast and grabbed a candy bar out of the machine in lieu of lunch.

Tiredly she pushed her hair away from her face with the spread fingers of both hands, trying to formulate a plan that would make the endless hours of the night manageable. Something she could get through with her sanity intact.

First she should fix something to eat that wouldn't literally make her sick. Watch the news while she ate it. Then take a long, hot bath and a couple of aspirin and find something in her to-be-read pile that would take her mind off the events of the day.

She walked over to the side-by-side refrigerator and opened the freezer half. Although it was well stocked with microwave dinners, there was nothing there that looked remotely appetizing.

Closing the door, she opened the refrigerator side. The first things she spotted were a couple of foil-wrapped baked potatoes she'd brought home from the local seafood place where she and her parents had had dinner Monday night. They had been leaving the following morning for a ten-day cruise and had wanted to say goodbye.

After briefly considering the time span between then and now, she began laying items out on the counter—one of the potatoes, a package of shredded cheese, a jar of bacon bits and the sour cream. At some point in the process the thought of a hot, twice-baked potato became appetizing. Until she turned back to the shelves to locate the butter.

Next to its glass dish sat a small white box. A thin red ribbon, the width used to trim lingerie or baby clothes, was tied in a simple bow on top.

Although the package appeared innocuous enough—innocent, even—there was nothing about it that was the least bit familiar. She knew she hadn't put what looked like a gift into her refrigerator.

She reached for it and then hesitated, her hand hovering in front of the box. She tried to think if this could be something her mother had had with her on Tuesday that had somehow gotten included in the sack with the baked potatoes.

Potatoes Jenna had taken out and set on this shelf herself. And she damn well knew she hadn't put that box beside them.

Maybe it was a present. Something her mom had intended as a surprise?

Except her parents hadn't come back to her apartment that evening. Her mother had been in a hurry to get home.

So who had put this box here? And when?

After the confrontation with Sean Murphy last night, she'd been so angry that the thought of cooking hadn't entered her head. She'd eaten ice cream straight from the container, standing over the sink while she finished it off.

She couldn't remember opening the fridge at all except to take the fudge ripple out of the freezer side. Then, after tossing and turning most of the night, she'd overslept, so that she hadn't had time for her usual minimal breakfast.

Actually, the last time she could swear she'd opened the refrigerator side of the unit was Monday night when she'd stuck those two potatoes inside. Four days ago. And as far as she knew, no one else had been inside the apartment in that time.

As far as she knew…

She took a step back, leaving the door open. Again she crossed her arms over her chest, as she considered the box.

It was obviously gift wrapped, only there was no occasion to celebrate. None that she was aware of.

Sean's idea of a practical joke? If so, to what purpose? If he wanted to prove to her that someone could enter her apartment

The resident manager had a key. Was it possible someone had asked him to deliver this?

And put it into her refrigerator?

Hardly a request a normal person would consider granting. And Jerry Rogers was as normal as they came.

Her mother was the only other person who had a key. Before she opened that box, she was at least going to check with her mom to see if she left it. If she hadn't, then she was going to call Lieutenant Bingham and demand that he get someone over here, no matter how busy they were.

And I'm sure he'll consider the fact that there's a box tied in red ribbon in your fridge far more important than Carol Cummings's life.

She turned toward the phone, only to realize that if she *did* call her mother, what it would entail. She would either not understand why Jenna was making such a big deal out of this, or worse, if Jenna explained what that was going on, she and her dad would be on the next plane home. They'd probably demand that she move back home, at least until this was all over.

Which, as unbelievable as it seemed, sounded incredibly appealing right now.

If you were fifteen.

Which she wasn't. She was a grown woman. A professional therapist with a Ph.D. in psychology. Someone who should know how to deal with anxiety and fear.

She wasn't going to become one of the idiot females who, according to the cops who had checked out her apartment, were flooding the hotline to report that the killer had taken their cat to torture. Or that he parked every night at the end of their street and if the cops would just come out and pick him up—

That kind of panic-induced fear gave the bastard the feelings of power and control he craved. Power over the citizens of an entire city, who were seeing bogeymen everywhere.

Just like you.

It's a box, for God's sake. And despite your not being able to figure out how it got here, there's probably a perfectly rational explanation for it.

Gingerly, as if she expected the thing to explode, Jenna reached in and picked it up, holding it with her thumb and middle finger. She was surprised at how light the thing was.

Empty? Anything was possible, although the idea of someone taking the trouble to break into her apartment and put an empty box, wrapped as a gift, into her refrigerator was more bizarre than someone choosing this way to give her a gift.

She set the package on the kitchen counter. Only then did she realize she shouldn't have touched it at all. Not without gloves.

The idea that this might somehow be connected to the murders was a thought she'd deliberately tried to push to the back of her mind. Now it was like the proverbial elephant in the living room.

If she acknowledged that this might be evidence in the investigation, she would have to acknowledge the possibility that the killer was the one who put it there.

Which would mean that he had been here, inside her apartment.

It was a thought that terrified her, despite the search the

two cops had mounted before they'd left. She closed her eyes, taking a breath to try to steady her racing heart.

She didn't want to do this. She didn't want to open the damn box. She didn't want to *know* what was inside.

Yet, *not* to open it would make her the same kind of person she'd just ridiculed. The kind who imagined a murderer lurking around every corner.

Except if you were a dark-eyed, dark-haired woman in this town right now, that probably wasn't a bad supposition. Especially if someone who claims to know the killer "intimately" believes you are his next victim.

According to him, Sean Murphy was the expert. The one who'd talked to the people on the national task force and studied all the material available. The one who claimed he wanted to catch his sister's murderer, no matter what it took.

Then why the hell wouldn't he be interested in this?

Without allowing herself time to reason her way out of the impulse, she walked back into the living room and picked up the phone. She punched up the caller ID list, looking for the number from which Sean had called her two nights ago.

It was the fourth one on the list, right after two calls from her mother and one from Paul, which had come in just a little while before she'd gotten home tonight. He hadn't left a message, but she would call him back, anyway. He was probably wondering how the interview with the police had gone.

With Sean's number highlighted, she punched Redial, waiting through four long rings before he answered. She was a little surprised at how familiar his voice seemed. Familiar and comforting. Unbelievably comforting right now, considering the terms on which they'd parted.

"Someone left a box in my refrigerator."

Five or six seconds of silence ticked by before he asked the obvious question. "What kind of box?"

His tone sounded conversational. At least it contained none of the near-hysteria that had gripped her.

The fact that it didn't helped her gather some composure. She didn't intend to let him know how badly this had shaken her.

Not unless he makes me beg for his help.

"White. Small. Tied with a red satin ribbon."

Another silence, this one perhaps even longer than the first. "How small?"

"Maybe…two by three inches. Maybe less. It looks like the kind of box department stores put jewelry in."

"Maybe you have a secret admirer." There had been no attempt to lighten his tone, despite the fact that the words would seem to call for that.

"That's what I'm afraid of."

Sean made no pretense of not understanding. "Call the police."

"And what if it's a present from my mother? A chocolate-dipped strawberry or something."

"Do you think that's what it is?"

She had never really believed, not even when she'd been frantically searching for an explanation—any explanation other than the one she couldn't bear to face—that her mother had put this package there without telling her about it. "No."

Let him draw his own conclusions, she thought. If he were as dedicated to tracking down his sister's killer as he'd claimed, then surely it would be to his advantage to check this out. If he didn't—

"You touch it?"

Sean's question interrupted her attempt to justify her belief that he'd come over here. Surely he wouldn't let his obvious anger over her offer of money keep him from wanting to investigate something that might be tied to Makaela's death.

"Only to take it out of the fridge. I know now that I shouldn't have, but…I kept thinking there had to be some logical explanation."

"You come up with one?"

"If I had, believe *me,* I wouldn't be calling you."

"Back door. Five minutes."

The line went dead, abruptly enough that she blinked at the sound of the dial tone. Apparently when Sean Murphy decided something, he didn't waste any time in putting that decision into action.

Sergeant Murphy, she amended, remembering what Bingham had called him.

It made sense that he wouldn't be an officer. Not with that oversize chip on his shoulder about his background.

Despite that, she wasn't surprised that he was accustomed to command. She would be willing to bet he was tough as nails with the men who served under him. And that they respected him for it.

She put the phone down before she walked across to make sure, for the third time, that the dead bolt on the front door was thrown. Then she headed back to the kitchen to wait for the man who had promised, against her expectations of his refusal, to help her.

Twelve

One of the dumber stunts he'd ever pulled, Sean acknowledged as he made his way through the shadows at the back of the units situated on the crest of Red Mountain.

These apartments, including Jenna's, were not only the largest and most luxurious within the prestigious complex, they occupied the premier location as well, a spectacular view of the city spread out in front of them. Positioned as they were, however, their back patios edged a steep and rocky incline, meaning there wasn't a lot of room to maneuver covertly.

All it would take would be for someone to look out as he crossed beneath a back deck or for some dog to raise the alarm. Given the state of hysteria rampant among the occupants of the area, someone might very well shoot first and ask questions later. After all, this was a state known for its high percentage of gun ownership.

The trek would be worth the risk if it kept the man he believed would even now be watching Jenna's apartment from spotting him. Maybe worrying about that was a case of trying to close the barn door after the horse had escaped, but he had no other choice. Not if he were to have any chance of taking the killer unaware.

And he was still convinced Jenna Kincaid represented the best way to do that. If the box she'd called him about was connected to the murders—as far-fetched as that seemed—then he'd have proof beyond any shadow of doubt that he was right.

In that case, the moral dilemma would be in deciding whether or not to send her straight to Bingham with whatever the killer had left. If he did, the detective would know she was being stalked. There would be no more arguments from the police about not having enough manpower to offer her protection.

And if they do, you lose your best chance of catching Makaela's killer.

He closed his mind to the implications, concentrating on making it to Jenna's apartment with enough stealth to escape detection. Even if no one took a potshot at him, they still might pick up the phone and dial 911. Although a resident might normally be hesitant to make that call, he would bet no one would think twice about doing it tonight.

Since the back doors weren't marked, at least not in any way he could see, he'd begun counting from the end apartment. If he made a mistake and knocked on the wrong door, he'd probably give someone a heart attack. Considering the terrain, it was doubtful the inhabitants of these particular luxury units ever had back-door visitors.

Hoping he'd counted right, he crossed the neat brick patio behind what he believed was A-12. Wrought-iron furniture, in some kind of aged-metal finish, had been set among carefully landscaped terraces. A fountain and the small pond it fed were empty in a concession to the cold. The rest of the year they would provide a soothing backdrop to a peaceful retreat.

Almost unconsciously he compared this to the backyard of the rental house where he lived. Its trampled patch of yard

contained a secondhand swing set and a turtle sandbox. If he
had needed anything else to remind him of the gap between
Jenna Kincaid's life and his...

And why the hell would you even be thinking about that?

Angry for allowing himself to be sidetracked—even momentarily—from what he'd come down here to do, he rapped
once on the solid wood of her back door. Before he could
bring his hand back to strike again, it opened.

Jenna was wearing the same clothes she'd worn at the police station. Her eyes were wide and dark in a face that was
a couple of shades paler than it had been the last time he'd
seen her. So much so that he wondered if, despite having
called him, she might already have opened the box to discover
what he suspected would be inside.

He pushed his way in, conscious of her nearness as they
literally brushed shoulders. The same sexual awareness he'd
experienced when he'd taken her arm at the precinct tightened his groin.

Not the time nor the place, he told himself, just as he had
then. *And certainly not the woman.*

The admonition had as little effect on his physical response
to her as it had then. Despite the increasingly obvious gap
between their circumstances, he'd been attracted to Jenna
Kincaid from the moment he'd first seen her.

*That would be Dr. Kincaid to you, Murphy. Why can't you
get that through your thick Irish skull?*

Even if he hadn't undertaken a mission that demanded
every bit of experience and skill he possessed, thinking about
the differences between them, and wondering how he could
ever bridge them, should be discouragement enough. No
matter how strong his attraction.

Despite the fact he was more than a little rough around the
edges, he'd never had trouble making a connection with any

woman he wanted. His reluctance to try with *Dr. Kincaid* was more the result of his realization that even if she was, by some stretch of the imagination, interested as well, he wasn't sure he could keep her interested.

With the strength of the sexual pull he felt, that was a chance he wasn't willing to take. Not now. Not with everything else going on.

He watched as she closed the door, engaging the dead bolt and then replacing the security chain. When she turned, he could sense her tension, vibrating beneath the surface of her composure like a tuning fork that had been struck. It was obvious she was holding herself together by sheer willpower.

Grudgingly, he admitted he was impressed. Most women would have been hysterical by now.

Another mark in her favor. Not that she gave a damn whether or not he was handing those out.

However well she was handling this, she was only a distraction to what he'd come here to do. "Where is it?"

The harshness of his tone reflected the dichotomy of his feelings. Thankfully, she'd have no way of knowing that.

"On the counter." She looked past him, lifting her chin in that direction.

He turned and realized the box was exactly as she'd described it over the phone. The red satin ribbon, tied neatly into a bow on top, gleamed invitingly in the glare from the light above the sink.

In spite of its innocent appearance, the same anxiety he had sensed in Jenna flared within his chest. If this had been left by Makaela's killer, then no matter how macabre its contents, it was a link to his sister.

To her death. And to her suffering.

He wondered if Jenna was aware of the trophies that had been taken from each of the bodies. She must have been, he realized, or she would have opened this by now. If not, she would have had no reason to suspect the box was anything other than what it appeared.

"Could be a Christmas present."

His suggestion had been an attempt to delay the inevitable. Right now he was no more eager to untie that ribbon than Jenna obviously had been.

"In my *refrigerator?*"

"Something perishable."

Which was, of course, exactly what he feared.

The sense of dread that thought evoked nauseated him, but there seemed to be no other reason to put this where it had been found. He jerked his mind away from the possibility he'd been considering.

There was really no point in speculating on what the package contained. Either he opened it and found out, or he called the cops. Either way, he would know soon enough. And so would she. Probably before either of them really wanted to.

"Any idea how long it's been there?"

"The last time I can remember opening the door was Monday night. I think I would have seen it if it had been there then."

But she wasn't certain. So any time since Monday. And in actuality, maybe sometime before. Of course, if this were what he believed it was, given the timing of the Cummings girl's disappearance...

He resisted the urge to relieve his growing tension by expelling several quick breaths through his pursed lips. That was what he always did before his unit went into action. A stress-release mechanism that was both habit and talisman.

Of course, the woman beside him would probably think he'd lost his mind. Again, he questioned himself angrily, *What the hell would it matter if she did?*

Surprisingly, he discovered it did. Despite the almost

constant animosity between them, he didn't want to look like a fool in front of Jenna Kincaid.

The sensation was so foreign to his normal attitude about women that it took him a moment to identify what he was feeling. Another to understand why.

That was surprising, too, although it probably shouldn't have been. Jenna Kincaid was a desirable woman. One who, despite his initial impression, was both smart and courageous. Two qualities he'd learned to value in his life.

He pulled his eyes away from hers to look back at the box. It wasn't going away, no matter how long he delayed.

"Gloves?"

"What?"

"You have any gloves? Plastic ones, preferably."

"I think…" She started forward and then stopped as if reluctant to get closer to the box. "I think there are some under the sink. The maid uses them."

The maid. She was definitely the kind who would have one, he thought with a touch of bitterness. Anybody who could afford this apartment would.

And just as his mother hadn't to the people she'd worked for, Dr. Kincaid's hired help didn't seem to have a name. Just "the maid."

"Would you get them, please?"

He understood why she didn't want to. If she hadn't made the comment about who used the gloves, he would have retrieved them himself.

But she had. And so he didn't. A petty revenge that he acknowledged.

She glanced at him again, a quick look under her lashes, before she refocused on the other side of the room. Her lips tightened, but she didn't argue.

She crossed the ceramic tile floor, her heels clicking in the apartment's well-insulated stillness. She didn't look at the counter where the box sat, but homed in on the cabinet under the sink. She opened it and located what he'd asked for by spinning a carousel that held cleaning supplies, neat and well ordered—probably the job of "the maid." Then she turned, holding a pair of yellow plastic gloves out to him.

Once more she'd passed the challenge. And had made him feel like a jackass in the process. All without saying a word.

He walked over and took the gloves from her hand. As he did, his fingers grazed hers. The same jolt of awareness was back again. Stronger than before.

This hadn't been part of the plan. Sometimes nature, however, in the guise of testosterone, trumped intellect and intent. Even his.

"Thanks," he said brusquely, an attempt to destroy this very different kind of tension.

Her eyes were still wide and dark, but now there was a flush of color along her cheekbones. Seeing it, his arousal strengthened.

It was pretty obvious by her blush that she knew exactly what he was experiencing. Women usually did.

Neither of them had time for this, even if they had the inclination. And he didn't know that she did. He only knew that he shouldn't.

Jenna Kincaid was his ace in the hole. And if he allowed himself to become involved with her…

Mentally backing away from the possibility, he deliberately broke the contact between them by turning to look at the beribboned box. The bow was a simple one, tied like a child's shoelace. The kind that could be undone by pulling on one side.

There were no visible wires. No tape. No oily stains that might indicate plastic explosives.

It still looked exactly like what his first impression of it had been. A gift. One obviously intended for Jenna. And all he had to do to find out what was inside was to pull the end of that narrow ribbon.

"Step back."

"What?" Her tone was sharply questioning.

"Step away from the counter."

"You think it's going to *explode?*"

"No."

"Then why—"

"Because I said so."

She laughed, the sound short. "Sorry. You're going to have to do better than that. That one hasn't worked since I was five."

"Okay. How about I want to check out what's inside without having you looking over my shoulder while I do it?"

"This is *my* apartment. And *that*—" she nodded again toward the box "—was left inside my refrigerator. Because of that, I'm going to assume it's something that was intended for me. At least for me to see."

The last phrase had been less confident. Maybe she had begun to figure out some of the possibilities. After all, she was a psychologist. Despite her initial disclaimer, she knew more than the average person would about serial killers.

"Suit yourself."

He laid one of the pair of gloves she'd handed him on the counter and then tried to slip his right hand into the other. Whoever the maid was, her hands were obviously a hell of a lot smaller than his. He turned the cuff back until he could insert his fingers into the openings designed for them.

Then, expelling one long breath, he reached over and, taking the end of the ribbon between his gloved thumb and index finger, tugged on it. The satin slipped free of its knot, the other side falling onto the counter.

He carefully laid the end he'd pulled down, straightening

it with one finger as he considered his next move. Although he didn't look back, he was aware that in spite of his injunction, Jenna was leaning forward, putting herself into position to look into the box when he opened it.

Realizing that he'd forgotten to breathe during the past few seconds, he took another breath, this one slightly unsteady. Then, before he had time to change his mind, he reached out with the same two fingers he'd used to untie the ribbon. Still holding his breath, he gripped the lid and lifted it up and away from the box.

Thirteen

As soon as he'd lifted the lid an inch or two, Sean made a sound. One Jenna couldn't begin to identify. One she wasn't sure she wanted to.

Despite the sense of horror that had grown the closer he'd come to revealing the contents of the box, she had instinctively taken a step forward. And then another. Moving closer until she was standing so near she could hear him breathing.

Air ratcheted in and out of his lungs, the inhalations ragged. Ugly.

Gathering what courage she had left, she peered around his shoulder. Compared to what her imagination had suggested might lie on the square of cotton wool, what she saw there was anticlimactic. A gold ring, its styling antique and its dark red, heart-shaped stone clouded with age or dirt, was centered on the pristine white liner of the box.

For a few seconds she thought it might really have been intended as a present. Of course, there was no one in her life right now who would give her something like this. Not as a token of a romantic relationship, which was what it looked like.

Since she'd never seen the ring before, she knew it didn't belong to anyone in her family, which seemed to indicate…

"Why would he put that in my refrigerator?"

She didn't want to accept the obvious answer to her question. That he had taken the ring off Carol Cummings's hand and sent it to her as a warning that she was next.

Sean dropped the lid down over the box, hiding what it contained. As he straightened, his shoulder brushed her cheek.

She immediately stepped back, increasing the distance between them. Despite her response, she admitted that she wouldn't have minded remaining that close to him.

He exuded strength. He had from the first day, despite his obvious anger.

Her sense that he was in command, both of himself and the situation, was something she needed as her own world spiraled out of control. That was the same reaction that had sent her scrambling into her parents' bed when, as a child, she'd been unsettled by a nightmare.

What was happening right now *was* a nightmare. One Sean wanted to bring to an end as much as she did. The difference between them was that he possessed the skills to make that happen.

She didn't. And she knew it.

"He needed to make sure you were the one who found it," Sean said. "Putting it there was the surest way to guarantee that."

The cops, who had finished their cursory examination of the apartment only minutes before, wouldn't have opened the refrigerator door. And if the maid had, she would have assumed it was a gift.

Jenna had to wonder if the killer had also chosen the refrigerator because he wanted her to think exactly what she had thought. That whatever was in the box required preservation.

A stupid assumption, perhaps, but one she'd made all the same. And it had both terrified and horrified her.

"What's the ring supposed to mean?"

For a long time there no answer from the man still standing in front of her. He took another breath, but he still didn't say a word.

"Sean?" Jenna realized this was the first time she'd called him by his given name.

The fact that she'd asked him to come when she found the box instead of the police would make a mockery of calling him anything else. For whatever it was worth, they were in this together, inextricably bound until it was resolved.

He turned so that, for the first time since he'd lifted the lid, she saw his face. It had gone gray beneath the tan.

Only then did she realize what she should have known immediately. *She* wasn't the one who was supposed to recognize that ring. *He* was.

She was simply the conduit through which it had been conveyed. As the killer intended her to be. He had known all along that when she found it, she would call Sean rather than Bingham.

The nausea that had eased with her identification of the object in the box, something far less grisly than she had prepared herself to see, churned through her stomach again. How could he have been sure what she would do when even she hadn't known? Not until her hand had closed around the phone.

"It's Makaela's," she said. Not a question, but a conclusion. The only one that made sense.

"It belonged to my grandmother. Makaela always wanted it, even as a child. My mother finally gave it to her on her twentieth birthday."

"And the killer took it when…" She hesitated, unable to say the words.

They would make what had happened to Sean's sister too real. Too close.

Makaela's murderer had slipped this ring off her finger, obviously as one of his trophies. An object he would touch and feel and look at over and over again in order to re-create the pleasure her suffering and death had given him.

"I looked for it when I cleared out the house. I thought maybe she'd lost it. Pawned it. She would have done that if she'd had to. It would have been for a good reason—to feed the kids or pay the rent—but she would have done it. And she would have gotten it back as soon as she could. I even looked for a ticket. Checked with a couple of nearby shops." He shook his head, the movement small. Almost regretful. "I guess I could have asked the kids if she'd been wearing it, but they were still babies. I didn't want them to ever think about what might have happened to it. Somewhere inside, I think I always knew."

Other than the tirade in her office, what he'd just said represented the largest number of words she'd heard him string together at one time. That he was willing to share this much of his anguish over his sister's death was undoubtedly the result of shock.

That would be natural, considering what he'd just discovered. And that meant, as much as she wanted to deny her own admission, it was up to her to think clearly right now.

"We need to call Bingham," she said. "There may be trace evidence—"

"There won't be. There never has been. Not on any of the bodies. No fibers. No hair. No prints."

"He's human. He makes mistakes. Or…he will eventually," she hedged, knowing Sean was right, at least about the ring.

This wasn't something that had been left behind, overlooked at a crime scene. The killer had given it to them. And he was smart enough, and careful enough, to make sure there was nothing on it or the box that could lead the police back to him.

"It doesn't matter," she argued. "We still have to let the police know."

"This isn't about them."

"What?"

"This is between me and him. That's the way he wants it."

"I don't care *what* he wants. I don't even care what *you* want. I'm calling Bingham."

She turned to put her intent into action. Before she had taken a step, Sean's hand shot out, long hard fingers closing around her wrist.

Shocked, she looked up into his face again. His features were drawn, his skin still almost devoid of color.

"It's a challenge."

It's a challenge... From the killer? He was challenging Sean? To what? Some kind of duel? A duel of wits? With more victims as the stake?

"I don't care what he's doing," she said again, twisting her arm in a vain attempt to free her wrist. "We *have* to call the police. We have to tell them about that." She glanced back at the box sitting innocently on her counter, its red ribbon gleaming beneath it.

"That ring belongs to my family."

"I'm sure they'll give it back when all this is over."

"It won't *be* over. Not if they're allowed to stop me. And if you're determined to do that—"

Had he finally crossed the line between desire and obsession? Enough had happened that she couldn't blame him if he had. Burying his sister. Seeing to the disposal of her house and her possessions. And dear God, seeing to her children as well.

It would be impossible for Sean to distance himself from the trauma of his sister's death and its painfully intimate connection to this ring. Someone else needed to objectively examine the evidence the killer had provided. Not as something personal, but as something that might be valuable in building a case against him. Only the detectives would be able to do that.

"You're hurting me," she said, holding his gaze.

He blinked, the blaze of anger she'd seen in his eyes suddenly clearing. He freed her wrist, stepping back as he did.

"I'm sorry."

"We *have* to call Bingham, Sean. We don't have a choice. We have to tell the police about this."

"What do you think they're going to do?"

"Examine it, for one thing."

"You read the papers. Has there ever been any evidence?"

"You can't just assume—"

"He *put* this here. Do you think he would take any kind of risk, even the most minute one, that would lead them back to him? *Think,* damn it."

She had. And she'd already reached that same conclusion. So why was she arguing the point?

"What do *you* want to do with it?"

"I want to find out what comes next."

"What comes next?"

"Everything he does has a purpose. He put Makaela's ring here for a reason. What do *you* think that was?"

"To frighten me. To prove he can get into my apartment. To taunt *you.*"

She had added the last defiantly. She knew that's what Sean thought. Obviously, he was right. The ring would have been meaningless to her. Only to Makaela's brother would it have any significance.

When he didn't respond, she added the other conclusion she'd come to. "And to show me he can anticipate what I'll do."

"Anticipate?"

"When I found the box, I didn't call the cops. I called you. He knew that's what I'd do."

"He *hoped* that's what you'd do."

"What's the difference? He was right."

"He isn't omniscient. Don't give him more credit than he deserves."

Omniscient. All-knowing. She realized she was surprised at his use of the word. Surprised Sean would know it, much less use it correctly.

Because he isn't an "officer and a gentleman"? Or because he doesn't have the same education you do?

It was the kind of snobbery she had always professed to hate. Yet in Sean's case she'd bought into it.

"Isn't that what *you've* been saying?" she challenged. "That there's no need to call the police because he won't have left any evidence on the ring or on the box?"

"Acknowledging that he's careful is a hell of a long way from believing he can read minds."

"I don't, but you can't deny he seems to be very good at reading people."

Something about her comment had resonated. She could see its impact in his eyes, although he didn't respond directly. And what he said instead—

"You wanted something from me."

"What?"

"Tonight. At the precinct. You asked me for something. I'm asking for something in exchange. Quid pro quo."

She had asked him to protect her. Not just to watch her in hopes of catching his sister's murderer, but to guard her from him. Apparently he was prepared to do what she'd asked, but on the condition that she not call the police about the ring.

"Why?"

"I told you. This is personal."

He had said before that it was a challenge. Issued by the killer. And directed at him.

"Then why didn't he leave the ring in your refrigerator?"

"He wants to prove he can do both."

"I don't understand."

It was if she were in the middle of a game whose rules she didn't understand. Or a game where there *were* no rules.

"He wants to prove he can take you, like he took Makaela. And that it won't make any difference whether I'm watching you or not."

Her first inclination was to think what she'd thought before. He'd lost all perspective about his sister's murderer. Grief, anger, the need for revenge had combined to unhinge him.

Still, there was something about the explanation he'd just given that had a kind of perverted logic. Especially when she remembered the phone call he'd received.

If the killer wanted someone to know about the Cummings girl, why not make that call to the cops? Better yet, to a local reporter, any one of whom would have given the story the widest possible coverage?

He hadn't. He'd placed the call instead to the brother of a woman he'd killed almost three years ago. Someone who wasn't a cop. Someone who couldn't give him the publicity he craved.

There had to be a reason for his choice. A twisted one. Or maybe the word she'd used before. *Perverted.* But there *would* be a reason.

She knew enough about organized killers—the FBI classification into which the Inquisitor fell—to know that very little they did was by chance. As she had told the interviewer, the man Sean sought wasn't insane. He was cruel and cunning and ruthless, but he wasn't mad, no matter how bizarre the scenario of the ring appeared.

Was it possible Sean was right? That this *had* been a challenge to him? And if so, what did that mean for her?

"So…now you're *offering* to protect me?" she asked.

"Every second of every day. And every night."

She opened her mouth to argue there was no need for that. She closed it again with the realization that the same man who had tortured and killed at least fourteen women had been inside her apartment. Inside this very room.

"And what do you get in exchange?"

"You say nothing to Bingham or anyone else about that." He inclined his head toward the box.

He had offered to give her what she'd asked for. And she should have jumped at it. But something else was going on. He was playing her. There was something…

"The ring would make them take the threat against me seriously. If he saw it, Bingham would have to admit I'm in danger."

The detective had downplayed that idea this afternoon, and because she had wanted desperately to believe he was right, Jenna had let him get away with it. Now she had the proof she hadn't had then.

"Maybe," Sean agreed. "I guess that would depend on your definition of 'seriously.'"

An overextended police department, currently engaged in a life-and-death hunt for a missing girl. Or a battle-hardened soldier with a thirst for revenge.

Her intellect screamed that there wasn't a choice. Call the cops. They were the professionals. Let them put guards around her apartment. Or, better yet, out at her parents' house, with its state-of-the-art security system.

That was the kind of protection anyone with half a brain would opt for. The thing that made the most sense.

It wasn't the option her gut was telling her to go with. Not as she looked into the ice-blue eyes of a man who wanted nothing more than to catch the killer who had taken his sister's life. Given an opportunity, Jenna knew that nothing would prevent Sean Murphy from attaining that goal.

"I swear to you he won't get by me," he said, his voice low and intense. "He won't do to you what I listened to him doing to Carol Cummings. What I saw he did to Makaela. I promise I won't let him, Jenna. I won't let him take you. I swear that to you on my sister's soul."

She had always been someone who followed her head rather than her heart, refusing to let her emotions overrule her common sense. There was nothing logical about letting Sean's fervor and determination outweigh every other consideration.

"I can't," she whispered. "I really wish I could help you, but… This is my life we're talking about."

"They can't keep you safe."

"Please don't say that. It isn't true, and it isn't fair."

He held her eyes, evaluating. For the first time she let him see in them her fear and desperation. Surely, since he'd seen his sister's body, he could understand the risk he was asking her to take. She expected him to argue against her decision. To point out its flaws. To make more promises.

What he said instead threw her.

"Without me, the ring means nothing."

"What?"

"I never reported that it was missing. I wasn't sure it was. Even after I'd finished cleaning out the house, I couldn't be sure Makaela hadn't let the ring go long before her death."

"What are you saying?"

She knew, of course, but she couldn't believe he would do this. Despite her refusal to go along with what he wanted, she had trusted him. She had almost come to think of him as a friend. Someone who was on her side. And now…

"The ring isn't in any police report. There is nothing but my word to connect it to my sister."

"You just *told* me—"

"But I won't tell them. You call Bingham, and I'll swear I've never seen it before. That I was never here. That I don't have any idea what you're talking about."

"That's insane."

"Maybe. And maybe it isn't 'fair.'" He mocked the word she'd used. "Neither was having to tell a four-year-old that her mother isn't ever coming home again. Any belief I ever had that anything in life is *fair* ended three years ago. I'll do whatever it takes to get my chance at this guy. Even if that means walking out that door and taking my sister's ring with me.

"If that's your choice, Dr. Kincaid, maybe you'll get lucky. Maybe he'll change his mind. For your sake, I hope he does. But for my sake—and for Makaela's—I'm going to assume that he won't."

Fourteen

What Sean saw in Jenna's eyes made him despise himself. She looked as if she'd been stabbed in the back by someone she'd trusted.

Except I never asked you to trust me. I never made you any promise except this one. And if it comes with a price tag attached, you're old enough to know that's the way the world works. You get what you want, and so do I.

What he wanted, what he had wanted for nearly three years, was a chance to go one-on-one with the bastard who had tortured his sister to death. Nothing had changed about that—nothing ever would—despite the pain he saw in her eyes.

"All right."

After the anger of their last exchange, Jenna's capitulation had been a little too quiet. Too submissive.

"So we do this my way?"

He wasn't sure why he needed her to put it into words. Maybe because he felt like a bastard for pushing her to this point. Why not go all the way?

"You've seen to that, haven't you?"

He had. That had been his intent since he'd opened the box. Not to leave her any other option but to depend on him for protection. And in doing so, give him access to his sister's murderer.

"Then let's get out of here."

"What?"

"He's probably got a key to this place. He may have used it to provide other surprises you haven't discovered yet."

Her pupils dilated, the black expanding into the circle of brown that surrounded them. That was something she hadn't considered. Something she didn't want to think about. Neither did he.

"Where do we go?"

"I don't know. I'll figure that out when we're out of here."

"For how long?"

"As long as it takes."

There was no use trying to guess at a timeline. That wasn't anything they could control.

"I'd better pack."

He had expected that. Just as he anticipated that she'd want to continue to go in to work.

She hadn't yet figured out that unless she wanted to make this easy for the Inquisitor, her life was about to change completely. And only if he was successful would it ever go back to the way it had been before.

"Lead the way." He made a mocking flourish with his hand toward the front of the apartment.

She took a breath, obviously as a prelude to arguing that she was perfectly capable of packing her own bag. And then she apparently remembered what he'd just said.

…*other surprises you haven't discovered yet.* It was enough to put an end to any thought she had of objecting.

She closed her mouth and nodded. As soon as she started toward the door of the kitchen, he reached out and picked up the box that contained Makaela's ring. He slipped it into the inside pocket of his jacket.

Despite the lie he'd just told, if this were found in her apartment, the police would put two and two together. Then the hunt they'd frantically begun this afternoon would widen to include another missing woman.

He'd started to follow her across the kitchen when the doorbell rang. The melodic tones seemed more fitted to a mansion than an apartment, even one as expensive as this.

It took only a moment for him to recover from its unexpectedness. He sprinted after Jenna, grabbing her arm before she could enter the living room.

"You expecting someone?"

She shook her head. "My parents are out of town. And the people I know don't usually drop in without calling."

This could be anything, Sean told himself. Delivery. Wrong address. The cops.

If Bingham had changed his mind because of the Cummings girl's disappearance, they might have staked out Jenna's apartment, which meant it was possible they'd seen him come in through the back. That was a complication he didn't want to deal with tonight. Not after the lie he'd told her about Makaela's ring.

"Stay here."

He crossed the room, his steps making no sound on the thick carpet, and put his eye to the peephole. Not the cops, he realized with a surge of relief. At least not uniformed ones.

The guy standing outside appeared to be waiting patiently for someone to answer the bell. He was half turned, looking at the panorama of city lights spread out below the apartments.

With his hand, Sean gestured Jenna forward. Then he moved aside, allowing her to assume his place at the peephole.

She looked out and then quickly straightened. She mouthed, "Co-worker."

He raised his brows, questioning, but she shook her head, shrugging her shoulders at the same time. Her bewilderment as to why her unexpected guest was here appeared genuine.

Sean stepped to the side of the door, jerking his chin toward the knob. After a moment she obeyed, sliding the chain out of its slot and then turning the dead bolt. She hesitated before her fingers closed around the knob, glanced at him as if for confirmation.

He gave her a nod of encouragement. After taking a deep breath, she opened the door.

"Gary? What are you doing here?"

Her voice held just the right note. Of course, if Sean had read her correctly, she really had been surprised to have this guy turn up on her doorstep.

Especially tonight. Maybe "Gary's" motives were entirely innocent, but his being here right now seemed to be a hell of a coincidence.

"Paul had a charity thing. He tried to reach you and couldn't, so he asked me to check on you. He wanted to be sure you got home okay."

"He asked you to come by?"

There was a slight hesitation, followed by a laugh. Even to Sean's straining ears, the sound of the guy's laughter seemed slightly embarrassed. As did the explanation that followed.

"I think he meant for me to call. I'm the one who thought coming in person might be a better idea."

It was clear from what Sean could see of Jenna's profile that she wasn't quite sure how to respond. After a moment she said, "Well, as you can see, I'm here. And I'm fine."

"I think Paul felt that with everything that's gone on this week and with the news this afternoon about the disappearance of the student from UAB, you might find the prospect of the weekend... I don't know. Intimidating, maybe."

"Intimidating?"

"The thought of spending so many hours alone. He just wanted you to know that he's concerned. We all are. And that any one of us is only a phone call away."

"That's very kind."

There was another slightly awkward pause. Sean was willing the guy to just finish whatever he'd come to say and get the hell out of here.

"So how did things go with the police?" the man on the other side of the door asked, instead.

"They don't feel I'm in any danger. They reminded me that lots of people have commented publicly on the killer. It would be impossible for him to target all of us. I think I just let things...get under my skin."

"That's perfectly understandable. Considering. I wanted to apologize if I came across as unsympathetic about the message on your car—"

"And that was one of them," Jenna said with a laugh.

"I'm sorry?"

"Things I let bother me when I shouldn't have. You were right. That was probably someone's idea of a joke. It certainly wasn't anything to get upset about. I just need to step back and put everything into perspective."

"If you need help doing that..."

"What you said yesterday was really helpful. I just wasn't in the mood to hear it. Not then."

"Everybody needs a sounding board occasionally. Even those of us who do this stuff for a living. Everybody in this city is on edge right now. With good reason."

"I couldn't believe it when I heard another woman was missing. Not so soon."

"The police seem to be pretty far off in their estimate of how frequently this guy is going to strike. Makes you wonder what else they've gotten wrong."

It seemed a strange thing to say if you'd come to comfort a person who was feeling threatened. Especially coming from someone who was trained in dealing with people under stress.

Judging by her hesitation in responding, Jenna, too, seemed taken aback. Apparently the guy picked up on that.

"I'm sure they're doing all they can," he added quickly. "It's just…frustrating."

"I really think they are. But, believe me, I *do* appreciate your and Paul's concern."

"Okay, then. I'll guess I'll see you on Monday."

"I'll tell Paul you came by."

"It's okay. I promised to call him after I tracked you down."

"Tell him I'm fine. And thanks again."

"You're very welcome. You take care, now."

Although that sounded like a farewell, Jenna didn't close the door. Apparently she was watching the guy leave. Maybe that was considered polite behavior down here. It wouldn't be in Michigan. Not this time of year.

After an eternity, he heard a car start out front. Jenna waited until the sound of its engine had faded down the drive before she finally closed the door. Then she took time to turn the dead bolt and to slip the chain back into its slot before she turned her head to look at him.

"You think your boss really sent him?"

"He must have. That would be too easy to check out."

"What do you know about the guy?"

"Not a lot. He joined the practice a couple of years ago. Maybe a little less."

Well before the last murders in San Diego.

"Although we all see a pretty wide variety of patients," she went on, "Gary's specialty is posttraumatic stress disorder."

"Where's he from?"

Jenna shook her head. "He probably told me at some time, but I honestly don't remember."

"From the lack of a discernible accent, I'd guess the Midwest."

"That's possible. I can find out on Monday if it's important. You're surely not thinking…"

"Why not?" he asked when she hesitated.

"Because Carlisle, Levitt and Connor hired him. He's definitely credentialed. Paul would have verified that. So would the insurance carrier. And he undoubtedly came highly recommended as well. The practice is extremely selective. It can afford to be."

"You wouldn't be biased about that."

"Maybe. But I also know Paul. We're only as good as our reputation. And that's something he guards closely."

"What kind of relationship do you have with him?"

"With Paul?"

"With the guy who just left."

"Other than a few general, semiprofessional conversations, I don't think I've exchanged more than two dozen words with Gary Evers. Until yesterday."

"When you talked to him about your car." That was obvious from the conversation he'd overheard.

"He saw me looking at the writing. It was probably obvious I was bothered. He suggested I was reading more into it than I should."

"How about your relationship with your boss? Isn't it unusual that he'd be checking up on you on a weekend?"

"Technically, Paul isn't my boss."

"Yeah?"

"I tend to think of him in those terms, as well, but…that's not how a group practice is supposed to work. But to answer your question, I would classify my relationship with him as excellent. Professional. Mutually respectful. He's let me know that he values my work and that he's glad I'm a member of the staff. And he's encouraged me all along to tell the police about everything that happened. He hasn't made me feel as if I were overreacting to anything."

She hadn't said it directly, but then she didn't have to. She had drawn a contrast between the two men and their responses.

"You like him?"

"Paul? Very much. Probably more this week than at any time I've worked for him. Of course, we've interacted on a more personal level than ever before."

"And Gary?"

"Up until yesterday, I would have said that I didn't have a basis for feeling anything at all about him."

"And after tonight?"

"I guess that it was thoughtful he'd come over personally to see about me."

"That didn't seem strange to you at all."

"That a co-worker would be concerned enough to do that? Not really. Should it have?"

The question had that same frosty attitude she'd adopted that first day in his office. As if she were talking to someone who didn't quite understand the way her world worked.

"With what's going on in this town right now, what kind of guy would be crazy enough to show up unannounced at a woman's door? Especially when he knows that woman believes she's being stalked."

"I'm not sure he knows that."

"Me, neither. Still… It's a good question. One I'd like to put to 'Gary.'"

She smiled at his emphasis on the name. "In any case, you've earned your keep already."

"What's that supposed to mean?"

She must have read his tone. "I'm just trying to say—badly, I'll admit—that I'm glad you were here. Thank you."

"We're operating on my terms now."

"*Your* terms?"

"You aren't hiring me. You aren't paying me. And you damn sure aren't running the show."

He could tell by the flash of anger in her eyes that she wanted to protest, if not his conditions, his expression of them. She was the kind of woman who was used to being in charge. Of her life. Of her practice. Of her world.

What he needed her to understand was that she was no longer in control of any of those. The sooner she understood, the easier his mission would become.

Fifteen

"**I** need to pick up my things from the motel," Sean said as he navigated the winding drive from the complex.

He drove with the same sure confidence he brought to everything he did, Jenna thought. To every movement. Every decision.

Maybe that came from years of commanding men, but she would be willing to bet that much of it was inherent in his personality. He obviously had no problem taking charge. If he ever second-guessed himself, she'd seen no evidence of it.

It had been his decision to take his SUV and leave her Honda in its usual place in front of the apartment. He had even guided her out the back and down the slope to the parking lot rather than going out through the front door.

When he'd arrived in response to her call, he'd left the SUV at the front of the apartments one level down from the crest. Despite that precaution, he had taken time to visually check the area before they'd even approached it. She wasn't sure whether to be reassured by his diligence or worried by the paranoia it seemed evidence of.

Maybe having to identify your sister's body did that to you.

"I thought you said you were moving today."

That had obviously been a ploy to make her back away from calling the police. One she'd fallen for.

"The unit wasn't ready."

"Were you seriously going to rent an apartment here?"

"Why not? There were six available when I called. I took the one closest to yours. Now I'm wondering who took the others."

She thought about that, deciding she needed him to put that cryptic pronouncement into some kind of context. "You think he might be moving in here, too?"

She'd tried to keep her tone light, but the truth was the suggestion he'd just made had shaken her. It still did, even though they were leaving the lights of the complex behind.

"The manager showed me the vacant apartment using a passkey."

"So?"

"I wonder if he does that for everyone. And I wonder if he's still got it."

"The passkey?"

"The killer's been inside your apartment. There was no evidence he broke in. Sounds like a key to me."

"One he 'borrowed' from the resident manager."

Coldness settled in the pit of her stomach. The thought of the man who'd tortured those women walking through her rooms, examining her things, maybe touching them, sickened her.

"I'm not saying he knew about it. I'd be curious to know if one is missing."

"Why not ask?"

"I plan to."

She let the silence build for several seconds before she returned to her initial concern. "Do you really think it's possible he might try to move in here?"

"We still don't know how he makes his approach to the victims. Friendly neighbor is as good a hypothesis as any. Or someone who needs help moving in. Maybe because he's got a broken arm."

That had been one of Ted Bundy's methods which was obviously where Sean had gotten the idea. Of course, that didn't mean he wasn't right about the Inquisitor. Still, Bundy had used the scenario over and over again, changing his act to fit the situation, even in locations where he'd killed before.

Despite knowing that, she knew instinctively she, too, would probably have rushed to the aid of anyone with some visible handicap. To move furniture. Open an apartment door. Fix a flat. The possibilities were endless.

"Or he might already be living there," Sean said. "Provided he's wealthy enough."

He had glanced into the rearview mirror, checking the traffic behind them. Before he looked back at the road, he met her eyes.

"Those apartments are close to the office. That's why I chose them."

"Right. That and the view."

The sarcasm had been clear. And it bothered her.

She'd never spent a lot of time thinking about the privileges she'd grown up with. Her friends had all come from similar backgrounds. She realized that most of her personal contacts, other than those she had with her patients, had been limited to people from the same socioeconomic group. Even the men she'd dated.

And they'd never included anyone like Sean Murphy.

"I'm sorry to say there's not much of a view from my room," he said. "For obvious reasons, however, you're still going to have to come in."

While she'd been thinking about her social circle, Sean had left the interstate and was now pulling into the lot of one of the inexpensive motels that dotted this exchange. Though only a couple of exits removed from the area where she lived, this represented one of the seedier sections of the city. A place she would have advised a visitor to avoid.

Although neat and well kept, it was obvious by the cars parked in front that the motel's clientele wasn't affluent. Sean's rented SUV was one of the more expensive vehicles in the lot.

"This is it," he said, stopping in front of a room on the bottom floor of the two-story structure. He shut off the motor and turned to her again. "Not the Hilton."

She wasn't sure how to answer that. Especially since she'd been thinking something very similar. And feeling guilty about it.

"I never believed you came to town for the amenities. Or for the view."

"It's got a coffeepot. That's the only 'amenity' that's ever mattered to me."

"I don't know. Hot water's high on my list. Other than that…"

She let the sentence trail. If Sean wanted to win "Whose accommodations are the worst," she'd play along. She wasn't going to apologize for her home, no matter how he had tried to make her feel.

Without answering, he opened his door and stepped out of the car. She watched as he made the now familiar scan of the area.

She couldn't imagine that he really believed the killer would try to snatch her in a place this open, but she couldn't fault him for his diligence. Not given the stakes.

She'd been waiting for him to give her some kind of signal that it was okay to get out. Instead he walked around the front of the SUV to open the door for her.

It was the kind of old-fashioned courtesy she'd been raised

to expect. And she realized with another flood of guilt that she'd been surprised he'd done something that she would have taken for granted from any other man of her acquaintance.

He held out his hand. After a slight hesitation, one she hoped he had been unaware of, she put hers into his. Hard and slightly callused, his fingers closed around hers with a strength that created a shiver of awareness in her lower body. A sensation that was definitely sexual in nature.

Hiding that unexpected bit of self-discovery by looking at the door to his room rather than at him, she released his hand. Despite the cold, it seemed she could still feel his fingers, warm and supportive, around hers. She couldn't remember the last time a man's touch had so completely disconcerted her.

Only a few minutes ago she'd been thinking of him as someone outside her realm of experience. Alien to who she was. And then she had reacted to him on the most primitive level at which a man and woman could connect.

Apparently unaware of her reaction, he put his hand around her elbow. Maybe the gesture was intended to urge her forward, since her realization of her attraction to him had literally stopped her in her tracks. Or maybe it was again the same kind of gesture any of her other escorts would have made to help her safely onto the curb.

No matter his motive, she reacted, not so much to his hand on her arm as to her acknowledgment of how fully aware she was of it. And of him.

She pulled her elbow sharply forward, removing it from his grip. Although it hadn't been the message she'd intended to send, she realized belatedly there was no way what she'd done could be construed as anything other than rejection. Of his touch and his solicitude.

Sean made no comment, stepping past her to lead the way

to the door of his room. As he did, he began to struggle to remove his wallet from the back pocket of his jeans, causing a flashback to that afternoon in her office.

Almost the first thing she'd noticed about him was how well he filled out that nearly threadbare denim. Her training had told her then her awareness of that was clearly sexual in nature. So why had her response to the feel of his hand on her arm taken her by surprise?

Because he'd been a blank slate the first time they'd met? And now…

Now she knew enough to know he *was* outside the realm of her experience. And enough to fear her inability to deal with the things that set him apart from the other men she'd known.

Still trying to cope with what had just happened, she watched the movements of those long brown fingers as they slipped the key card into its slot and then turned the handle. Sean pushed open the door and, holding it, stood within the frame waiting for her to enter the room.

In order to do that, she would have to pass very close to him. She started forward, edging toward the other side of the doorway.

As she brushed by, she was once more conscious of his size. Not only his height, but the width of his shoulders and muscled chest. Something else she'd noticed during that first encounter. Something she had almost forgotten in the animosity of their next few meetings.

Those had generated a very different kind of heat because she had decided by then that he was the enemy. Now she knew he wasn't—

"This won't take but a minute," he said.

Leaving her standing just inside the door, which had closed behind her, Sean walked across the room to drag a duffel bag from the top of the closet. He tossed it onto the bed, and then, as she watched, he began to take things out of the drawers of the dresser. Methodically he rolled each item of clothing— underwear, jeans, T-shirts—and stuffed them inside the canvas bag. He worked with an efficient rhythm, emptying the drawers in a matter of minutes.

When he was done, he moved over to the closet, sliding open the mirrored door. A few shirts and a couple of pairs of khaki pants hung on the motel's wooden hangers. He lifted all of them off the rack and repeated the process he'd used on the rest of his clothing, filling the bag.

"The other stuff is in the bathroom."

She wasn't sure why he'd bothered with the explanation. He barely glanced at her before he disappeared inside the other room.

Leaving her alone in what was essentially his bedroom.

Her eyes automatically tracked back to the duffel bag. She could hear the occasional clinking noise, indicating that he was cleaning off the counter.

As she listened, she was aware of the queen-size bed that suddenly seemed to dominate the room. She couldn't remember the last time she'd been in a motel room with a man. College, maybe. Spring break.

If so, the natural tension created by the situation had probably been eased by having had too much to drink. Or by a long friendship. But this…

She was acting like she was eighteen and had come here for a one-night stand. The last thing on Sean Murphy's mind was having a physical relationship with her. As far as he was concerned, their connection was for one purpose and one purpose only. To bring down the man who had killed his sister.

"I think that's everything."

His comment brought her gaze up. Sean was standing just

outside the door to the bathroom. There was no doubt in her mind that he'd been watching her. And for the few vital seconds it mattered, she couldn't think of a response because she knew that what she'd been thinking was probably written on her face.

"You okay?"

"Of course," she said, trying to gather her composure.

He nodded, still holding her eyes. "I *did* warn you, you know."

Stupidly, she didn't have a clue what he was talking about. "About what?"

"Shall we say the inelegance of the establishment?"

"Coffeepot. Hot water. A bed. What else could anyone need?"

There was a hint of amusement within the clear blue eyes. His lips twitched, but instead of answering, he walked across and pushed the black Dopp kit he'd held in his hands into the duffel bag. Then, with what seemed to be a single motion, he zipped it and hoisted the strap onto his shoulder.

"Ready?"

For some idiotic reason, she wanted to suggest that he might want to look under the bed. Take another glance into the bathroom. Check the shower enclosure. All the things she did as a matter of course when she was ready to check out of a hotel. Apparently he didn't feel the need for any of those activities.

"Of course."

He gestured toward the door, and since she was still hovering in the same spot she'd occupied the entire time she'd been in the room, she was much nearer to it than he was. She turned and took the three steps that would take her there, opening the door to the cold.

She stepped across the threshold, her eyes focusing on the SUV parked almost directly in front of the room. In the light from the motel's security lights, its black hood gleamed as if newly waxed.

Sitting in the middle of its dark expanse was a small white box, identical to the one she'd found in her refrigerator, even down to the narrow red ribbon neatly tied into a bow.

Sixteen

Jenna stopped so abruptly that Sean walked into her. Dislodged by the contact, the heavy duffel slipped off his shoulder, slamming her in the back.

"What the hell?" Before the words were out of his mouth, he saw what had stopped her in her tracks.

He still had the key card in his hand, retrieved from the top of the dresser where he'd laid it when he'd come into the room. He grabbed Jenna's arm, pulling her back toward the door.

As he did, he dropped the bag, hurrying to reinsert the card in the lock. The sudden flood of adrenaline made his hands tremble as he tried to fit it into the narrow slot.

Using every ounce of willpower acquired during years under fire, he controlled the vibration, finally managing to slide the key in. As soon as the light blinked, he turned the handle, literally shoving Jenna into the room.

Then he bent to grab the strap of the duffel. He threw it in, too, before he dived inside. Once there, he turned the dead bolt and slammed the safety hook down over its knob.

Only then did he take time to breathe. And to consider all the implications of what had just happened.

The bastard was out there in the darkness. Taunting him.

He'd recognized that back at Jenna's apartment. The box she'd found had been a message to him. Obviously, so was the one outside.

Because of the contents of the other, the killer had believed he would be compelled to take the couple of steps necessary to reach out and snatch it off the SUV. In those seconds, he would have been vulnerable. A visible target.

And so would Jenna.

It was that realization that had driven him back into the room. Now that he knew she was safe…

He bent, unzipping his bag. Because he was hurrying, it took a few seconds to locate the Glock he'd stowed inside. He took the weapon out, pulling back the slide to chamber a round.

"What are you doing?"

"Stay here," he ordered as he headed toward the door.

Before he could get it unbolted, Jenna was at his side. She wrapped both hands around his wrist, pulling his hand away from the lock.

"Stop it. What do you think you're doing?"

"Don't you understand?" He took time to glance down at her, reading confusion in her eyes. "He's out there. Maybe if I'm lucky—"

"You're going after him with a *gun?*"

He ripped his arm from her hold and threw the hook off the knob. He reached down to unfasten the dead bolt, but she grabbed his wrist again.

"Call the police, Sean."

"He won't be here when they arrive."

"You can't do this—"

He wrenched his arm away, managing this time to get the door unlocked. Jenna made another attempt to stop him, but furious with the delay she was causing, he pushed her away with his forearm.

Although he hadn't meant for it to happen, he had shoved her hard enough that she stumbled back against the foot of bed. Although she didn't fall, he could see shock in her eyes that he had treated her so roughly.

He didn't have time for apologies. Only instructions. The kind that would save her life.

"Don't come outside. Lock the door as soon as I'm out. *All* the locks. And no matter what happens, no matter what you hear, don't open it. Not until I tell you to."

She didn't respond, neither to agree to his instructions nor to rail again against what he was doing. Instead, her eyes, full of hurt, held his.

You would have been hurt a lot worse if I wasn't doing this.

The attempt to justify what he'd done didn't work. Ignoring the flood of regret he couldn't do anything about, he eased open the door.

The security lights made the parking lot almost as bright as day. Which was their purpose. For his, darkness would have been preferable.

Of course, he'd made this kind of hunt in the daylight as well as at night. This was *his* territory. *His* field of expertise.

Let's see how you like being hunted, you bastard. And by someone who's got the ability to fight back.

He slipped through the door, pulling it shut behind him. Despite what had just happened between them, he knew Jenna would do exactly as he'd told her. She was too smart to do anything else.

The box with its red ribbon was still on his hood, illuminated by the halogen light above it. It was possible the killer had left as soon as he'd placed it there, but Sean didn't believe that.

The bastard would be all too eager to watch the outcome of his latest stunt. That meant he'd be hiding someplace where he'd have a clear view of the SUV and the entrance to the room.

His back to the door, weapon held out in front of him, Sean surveyed the parking lot before his gaze moved to the field that lay between the motel and the interstate. Although the security lights didn't illuminate every part of it, the grass had been closely mown before the winter had killed it.

The only way someone could be watching from out there—without taking a chance on being seen—would be if they were lying down. The man he sought wouldn't do that. He was too much an egotist. Too convinced of his own power.

And he was definitely here.

As he had that day outside Jenna's office, Sean could feel him. He could feel the son of a bitch's eyes focused on him as he waited, gun extended, trying to figure out where he could be hiding.

Somewhere with an unobstructed view of this area. Somewhere he could observe without being seen.

One of the parked cars?

His gaze swept along those on his right and then to his left. There was no one in any of the nearby vehicles. Anyone seated in those farther down the walkway wouldn't be able to see enough to satisfy what he believed to be the intent of this exercise.

Suddenly, as his visual survey reached the end of the walkway on his left, he saw what he'd missed before. The back and the front sections of the complex extended beyond the sides. In the front, that extra space was occupied by a restaurant. In the back, a block of four rooms, two stories of them, jutted into the parking lot, perpendicular to the wing his room was in. The view from the lower story of that extension would be blocked by parked cars, but from the rooms on that second floor—

He examined their windows. The first was brightly lit, its drapes pulled back to reveal the interior. A child sat on one of the double beds watching television. Sean could see light flickering from its screen.

The next two were also occupied, as evidenced by the lights on inside. The black-out curtains had been drawn across their windows. It was impossible to tell if someone was holding the edge of the drapes away from the glass to see out, but the interior lights argued against it. They would make it much more difficult to see outside.

As he rejected those rooms, too, his gaze moved on to the last. The one on the end of the extension. No cars were parked in the spaces below it. And no light edged around the plastic-backed drapes. All that was visible was the exterior door preceded by an expanse of black glass.

His eyes flicked back to the room beside it. Despite the fact that the lights were on behind it, there was something about the quality of the glass itself that was different from that of the last room. When he examined it again, he knew why.

The drapes had not been drawn over the last window. There was nothing between its glass and the darkened interior of the room.

Was the killer sitting in that darkness? Was he watching as Sean stood here, weapon drawn? Could he feel his eyes probing his hiding place?

The possibility that he might be was enough to set him off. Instead of cutting across the parking lot, Sean ran along the sidewalk, hugging the building.

He was aware of the doors and windows he passed, mostly because of the alternating pattern of light and noise, but he was unconcerned about them. If any of the occupants heard the sound of running footsteps and glanced out to see a man with a gun, it couldn't matter. Not at this point.

Instead of worrying about someone calling the cops, he was trying to figure out how was he going to get to the man in that last room. As he'd just ordered Jenna to do, the killer would have every lock secured. And the doors here were solid enough that Sean wouldn't be able to physically break it down. Not even to get to the man who'd murdered Makaela.

His mind offered a dozen solutions as he ran, each considered and then rejected as unworkable. He could try firing into the mechanism or shooting off the knob. Although that would quickly bring the cops, the chance of it actually working on a door like these was slim. They were designed to prevent that kind of attack. As was the bulletproof glass in the windows.

As soon as the thought formed, he questioned it. A precaution that would make sense, but was it true? Was that part of the building code in Alabama? Somehow he doubted it. Especially not for a place like this.

By now he'd reached the stairs to the second level of that back wing. The sound of his feet pounding up their concrete risers echoed in the enclosed stairwell, loud enough that he wondered if the bastard could hear them.

Rounding the top of the stairs, he approached the room where the child had been watching television. This close to his goal, Sean automatically slowed, trying to think through what had pretty much been, up to this point, gut reaction.

As he passed by the window of the first room, the boy looked up. His eyes widened as he took in the gun. Before Sean had cleared the length of its glass, the kid had begun to yell, his words indistinguishable.

Ignoring him, Sean kept moving, but more cautiously now. Even if the boy's parents called the cops, this would be over before they arrived. He would already have accomplished the mission that had brought him here.

And if you're wrong? If someone perfectly innocent is

sleeping inside that room? Another child. A woman like Makaela. Or Jenna.

Again he slowed, passing the next-to-last window, one of the two with the drapes drawn. He stopped when he reached the span of wall between it and the room that was his destination.

He leaned back against the bricks, allowing his breathing to ease. Trying to decide how best to deal with the window just ahead.

If he intended to knock, rather than simply start shooting, he would have to cross in front of it in order to reach the door. If his prey was inside, and if he'd been watching to gauge Sean's reaction to his "gift," he would also have watched his progress to this point. He would already know Sean was out here. And he would know he had a gun.

Was the killer similarly armed? Knives had always been his weapon of choice, but maybe that only applied when his victim was tied down and helpless. What was going on now was so far outside the killer's pattern that all bets were off.

From out on the interstate came the wail of a siren, drawing Sean's gaze across the expanse of winter-dead grass beside the right-of-way. After his sprint along the walkway, gun clearly visible to any guest looking out the window of his room, he expected to see a couple of patrol cars heading for the exit to the motel.

Instead, he saw an ambulance, lights flashing, traveling in the opposite direction. Its siren quickly faded in the distance, leaving him once more to consider the best way to proceed.

While his mind raced through the alternatives, his eyes once more swept across the patch of open ground that sloped downward from the highway. The action was unconscious. So much so that his attention had already refocused on the room at the end of the second-story walkway when something snapped it back to the right-of-way.

He scanned the area again, trying to find whatever it was that had triggered the sense there was something out of place. Something he should have noted. Something—

The anomaly was obvious, now that he was looking for it. In the center of the pale grass of that open field, just before it began its climb to the roadbed, was a patch of darkness.

Not shadow. It was too intense for that. And besides, there was no object out there to cast it.

A rock the road-construction crew hadn't bothered to move? When they had moved all the others, leaving perfectly level ground for the state's mowing machines?

Maybe a puddle left from the recent rains. That was the most convincing theory, especially since the light from the highway above created a sheen on the black surface. Almost as if it were—

Plastic. Black plastic bag. Garbage bag.

As soon as the words formed in his brain, he knew that was what he was seeing. Despite the distance, he could tell it was the right size and shape.

The fact that it *had* shape, something that made it distinct from the flat, featureless grass that surrounded it, made him know the bag wasn't empty.

Trash, he told himself, fighting the rush of bile into the back of his throat. Someone had thrown garbage off the interstate. Maybe they'd stopped up there in the middle of the night and tossed the bag over the rail.

He pulled his eyes away from the black plastic to focus on the end of the walkway in front of him. Two steps and he would stand before the plateglass window of the last room. Another and he would be at its door.

He had no choice but to look into the window before he did that. If he saw anything that made him doubt his theory about the occupant of that room—

Putting his head against the wall behind him, Sean took a couple of deep breaths, blowing them out silently between pursed lips. He took one more, holding it. Filling his lungs in preparation for his assault.

Then he lowered his head, looking out once more at the grassy knoll. The bag was still there, gleaming in the light of the halogen lamps as cars continued to whip by above it.

The only way he would ever have seen it was if he came up here. Stood in this exact spot. Waited outside this room.

To prove that theory, he took a couple of steps back, moving in front of the window with the drawn drapes. The end of the walkway and its metal railing now blocked his view of the area where the bag lay.

This time he put his head back against the glass and closed his eyes. He was completely unaware at that moment that the room behind him was occupied.

One after another, he allowed the series of painful realizations into his brain. This had been part of the killer's plan. He'd intended for Sean to come here.

Not because there was anyone in that last room. That had been a lure. Something to make him react in a certain way, just like the box on the hood of his car.

And he had done exactly what the killer had expected him to. He knew now that he'd been led up here because he was supposed to see what lay in that empty field beyond the parking lot.

To see it and to know what it was. And finally, to understand why it had been left there.

The ultimate taunt. The thing that would bring back the most painful of all the memories associated with Makaela's death.

In that black bag, identical to the one into which the Inquisitor had stuffed his sister, was another body.

That of the girl whose screams he had listened to? If so, Carol Cummings was finally at peace. Something he knew that the family who had loved her would never know again.

Seventeen

"You were right," Bingham said. "It's the Cummings girl. How the hell he managed to get the body down here without somebody seeing him..."

"Middle of the night." Sean forced the words past the constriction in his throat as he watched the technicians work over the body. "Maybe he approached the spot from the motel rather than the interstate. Less likely to be seen doing it that way."

Unwilling to wait until morning to examine the area around the girl's corpse, the cops had set up floodlights, along with the customary yellow tape. In the damp cold the three of them were standing just beyond its perimeter on the edge of the motel parking lot.

Jenna had said almost nothing since the detective's arrival. She stood beside Sean now, her right arm wrapped across her chest, left hand holding the collar of her jacket against her neck. Occasionally a tremor ran through her frame. A couple had been strong enough that, although their bodies weren't touching, Sean had become aware of them.

He wondered if she was conscious that that was the same

position she'd assumed during the television interview. He had classified it then as defensive. It still was.

And why not? He'd been telling her for three days that she would be next. Now Carol Cummings was dead, and his warning must weigh even more heavily on her.

Especially since she's watching the forensic examination of the last victim's body.

As soon as he'd given in to his conviction about what the bag in the right-of-way contained, he'd gone back to his room to notify the police, a decision that had not been prompted solely by concern for Jenna. After all, as he had believed she would all along, she'd stayed inside, every lock on the door secure. He had listened to her unfasten them after he'd identified himself. As unfamiliar as the feeling had been, he'd admitted while he waited that he'd come back rather than using his cell because he wanted to be with someone while he made that call.

He didn't know what his face had revealed when Jenna opened the door. Whatever it was made her step forward as soon as he was inside and put her arms around his body.

There had been nothing sexual about the embrace. It offered comfort. Acknowledgment, perhaps, that he wasn't in this alone. Remarkably, he'd welcomed both.

His left arm, the one not occupied with holding the Glock, had automatically closed around her, cradling her warmth against the black, aching coldness in the center of his chest. He had released her as soon as she'd moved, leaning back to look up at him.

It had been a close-run thing. He had wanted to bury his head against her shoulder instead. To take solace in the fact that she was warm. And alive.

"What happened?" Her eyes searched his face.

"I need to call the cops." A brief reprieve before the inevitable moment when she would have to know.

"Did you kill him?"

"Did you want me to? That wasn't the impression I got."

"What I *want* is for you to help the police stop him."

"Something they haven't been able to do. Not after seven years and five different locations. With that track record, I don't have a lot of hope they're going to."

He wasn't feeling particularly forgiving toward the law enforcement community's incompetence right now. If he was right, lying in that grass outside was the latest in the cops' long string of failures.

There had been too many of those since this had started. Maybe Jenna still had faith in their abilities. He no longer did. And he wasn't going to pretend.

"Maybe—"

He cut off whatever defense of them she intended to make. "I think he's dumped Carol Cummings out there."

It took a moment for her to absorb what he'd said. When she had, she shook her head, the denial obviously not related to the information, but the girl's death.

"I need to call Bingham." He'd pushed past her toward the phone on the nightstand, leaving her to cope with the news.

Despite the comfort he'd willingly taken from having her body against his, he'd had no consolation to offer. He had felt drained of every human emotion. Empty. Eviscerated.

The feeling hadn't eased in the hour or so since he'd made the call. He was just relieved he wasn't the one who would tell the girl's family that their daughter was never going to come home again. That she'd never marry. Or give them grandchildren. Or care for them in their old age.

Carol Cummings would never do any of those things because some psychopath had stolen her life. And there was nothing anyone could do to get it back for her.

Not even if they caught him. Not even if they executed him.

All the cops could hope to do now was keep him from butchering someone else. So far they hadn't been able to accomplish that.

"They'll check it out," Bingham said, obviously a reply to his comment about the killer using the motel lot as a staging ground for dumping the body. "From our initial observation it's clear he didn't drive a car out there. They haven't even found footprints. Not yet."

Which would argue that he'd rolled the body down the incline from the highway, Sean thought, his eyes following what would have been the track of its descent. And if he had, someone must have seen him. Or seen something.

"Any idea how long she's been there?" He wondered how closely they could pinpoint the time the body had been placed in the field. And whether it would matter.

"Not yet." Bingham glanced at him before his gaze returned to the spotlighted scene beneath the shadow of one of the city's major thoroughfares.

"If he dumped her from the road, somebody had to have seen something."

"Yeah? They didn't anywhere else. Unless we get luckier than anyone else has..."

There had been no trace evidence found on any of the victims. Or on the bags into which they'd been stuffed.

Garbage.

That was exactly how he treated them. As if they were so much garbage. Something to dispose of in empty fields or abandoned houses or, as in Makaela's case, on the side of a country road.

As soon as the forensics team had arrived, they'd split the top portion of the bag to verify that its contents were what they all expected. Now a photographer was taking pictures of the body and its surroundings.

Despite the portable spotlights, he was using a flash, which allowed Sean to track his movements around the dark shape on the ground. From the multiple flashes, it was obvious he intended to capture every inch of plastic, every blade of grass, as well as the girl's face and body.

That was one thing he wouldn't have to remember about this one, Sean thought. He had seen the autopsy photographs they'd taken of Makaela, although that had been long after her death. Eyelids sliced off, her vacant eyes had reflected a horror he tried not to let himself think about.

"If you can," he advised Bingham, "keep those away from her family."

"What?"

"The photographs. They'll have enough to deal with without seeing the pictures."

"I wish to hell *I* didn't have to," Bingham said. "Son of a bitch," he added, his tone bitter. "Every freaking cop in the metro area is out looking for that girl, and he dumps her in plain sight of a major artery. This ain't his usual method of disposal, by the way."

He wondered how long it would take Bingham to come to the conclusion he had. That the Cummings girl had been put here for *him* to find.

"Overconfidence," he said aloud.

The bastard had plenty of reason for that. The cops were no closer now than they had been on the day when they'd finally realized the connection between the murders.

"Maybe," Bingham said musingly. "Still…"

In the sudden silence, Jenna turned her head, looking at Sean rather than at the technicians working the body. He held his breath, expecting her to mention the boxes to the detective. He ignored her, and after a moment she seemed to refocus her attention on the activity out on the right-of-way.

"Makes no sense, actually," Bingham went on. "Rural county. Lots of places he could have dumped that body. Places where we wouldn't have found it for weeks. Maybe months. So why drop her in our laps? Especially this late in the game?"

"We learned from the guy in Wichita that patterns don't always hold. Maybe he needed to get rid of this one quickly."

Bingham laughed. "Because we were so hot on his tail?"

"Maybe you were and didn't know it," Sean said, deliberately refusing to look at the cop.

He liked Bingham. And he knew that as far as the police would be concerned, he wasn't playing fair. A feeling that would certainly be the opinion of the public, as well. If they found out.

"Hot on his tail? Yeah, well, you're right. If we are, I don't know it. All I know is that after fourteen murders this guy breaks his pattern to lay a victim out in the middle of a field below one of the busiest intersections in the state. And right in front of your motel room, too. Now, there's a hell of a coincidence for you, Sergeant Murphy," the lieutenant added softly. "Even to an ignorant black cop from a backward city like this."

"Obviously, he knows I'm here." Denial would make Bingham more suspicious. "That isn't a coincidence."

"So he hands you a body? Like a gift? How'd you happen to see it, by the way?" Bingham turned, checking out the windows of the motel behind them. "The way the land lies and with that fence," he said, looking back at the right-of-way. "Parked cars between. I purely don't know how you could see that bag out there. Not from your room."

Sean had known the question would eventually be asked, if not by Bingham, then by someone on the national task force. He had, however, hoped to avoid it tonight. He hadn't had time before the cops arrived to figure out from what other vantage points, if any, he might have been able to see the body.

"You want to show me where you were when you spotted it?"

"Second floor," Sean said, deciding that the less elaboration he made the less likely he was to be tripped up.

"Dr. Kincaid with you?"

"She was still in my room."

Bingham's gaze moved to Jenna, but she didn't look at him. "So you're up on the second floor…doing what?"

"Looking for an ice machine."

"You two gonna have a drink? In your motel room?"

"I don't think that's any of your business."

Jenna's voice was cool. Just as it had been the day he'd walked into her office, so furious with the suggestions she'd made in that interview he'd allowed himself to be blinded to any other consideration by his desire to confront her.

He knew that didn't mean she would be on his side if this came down to a demand from the cops for cooperation. If she told them about the boxes he'd intercepted—

"This is a murder investigation, Dr. Kincaid." Bingham's normal drawl had been sharpened, apparently to reflect the seriousness with which he took his responsibility. "That means *everything's* my business."

"You know exactly what happened to that girl. And you know who did it. The fact that Sean and I might have been having a drink in his room couldn't possibly have any bearing on either."

"I just didn't realize y'all had gotten so close. Seemed a little strange. Almost as strange as our boy choosing this location to unload his latest victim."

"You were right about that," Sean said.

"About her being a gift to you? Why do you think that is?"

"He knows why I'm here." He'd made his intentions clear in those interviews in Detroit.

"So he's kicking sand in your face."

"It's his idea of a taunt."

"Pretty sick one if you ask me."

"Well, he's a sick SOB. Everybody knows that by now. *Almost* everybody."

The gibe was stupid. So far Jenna had held the line, supporting what he'd said. Why risk her cooperation?

"I never said he wasn't sick," she said.

"Just not crazy."

"He knows exactly what he's doing. You of all people should know that."

It was enough to make him turn to meet her eyes. Like her voice when she'd chided Bingham for his suggestion, they were cold.

"All I tried to do was point out that he isn't insane," she went on. "Not by any legal definition."

"You have an opinion, Dr. Kincaid, about why he's suddenly changing the methods that have worked for him in the past?"

Despite Bingham's question, Sean didn't break the contact he'd established with Jenna. He held it as the silence stretched.

"Maybe because you aren't getting any closer," she said, finally looking at the lieutenant.

"What does that mean? As far as the change, I mean."

"The police aren't a challenge anymore. Neither is the FBI. The game is only exciting if the stakes are high. You aren't raising them, so he is."

"He's *trying* to make it easier for us to catch him? Is that what you're suggesting?"

"I'm suggesting he's trying to make it more interesting. If that means that he needs to take risks he hasn't taken before, then apparently... Apparently, he's now willing to do that."

"Let me get this straight. We're not challenging him, so now he's decided to concentrate on someone who has." He nodded in Sean's direction. "And since that someone is th guy you're getting cozy with in cheap motel rooms, doesn' that worry you a little bit? You know, I didn't really take wha you said this afternoon seriously, but now I'm not so sure Maybe the Inquisitor _is_ interested in you, Dr. Kincaid. An now that he's freed up his schedule, so to speak—"

"If you're trying to scare me, Lieutenant, you're succeeding.'

"Then why do I still get the feeling something's going o here that I don't know about? Like maybe why you were look ing out at the right-of-way from the second floor when there' an ice machine in that alcove right there." Bingham turne again, looking back toward the motel.

Sean didn't bother to mimic the motion. He knew what wa coming. A knowledge that had nothing to do with premoni tions and far more to do with what he'd learned about th woman at his side.

She still trusted the guys with the badges and the camera and the collection kits. At least more than she trusted him.

"If you don't tell him, I will," Jenna said.

He couldn't have cued it better if they'd all had a scrip The detective's reaction was on page as well.

"You been keeping something from me, Sergeant Murphy' Something that has a bearing on my case? Something that' got to do with that little girl who's lying dead out there?"

Without any comment, Sean reached into his jacket pocke and removed the box he'd taken off the hood of the SUV. H held it out, but Bingham didn't reach for it.

"Now, what the _hell_ is that?"

"Another present. It was left on the hood of my car. It' from the same source as that one," Sean said, raising his gaz to the spotlit scene in front of them.

"Why?"

"To make me go looking for him. And find her."

Bingham thought about it, apparently accepting the explanation as the truth. "You open it?"

Sean shook his head.

"There was another box," Jenna said. "Earlier. Just like that. It was left at my apartment. In the refrigerator."

"The *refrigerator?*"

Sean knew the instant the implication hit the detective. It was there in his eyes, and then quickly masked by a display of what appeared to be genuine fury.

"What do you two think you're doing? Playing Mr. And Mrs. North? You got that one, too?" Bingham demanded, looking from one of them to the other.

Jenna had begun to shake her head when Sean took the first box out of the other pocket. "My sister's ring."

There was a subtle change in the detective's eyes, some of the anger fading. "She was wearing it?"

"Apparently. I never knew what had happened to it."

"Shit." None of them said anything for perhaps ten seconds, and then Bingham added, "Sorry, Dr. Kincaid. And you swear you ain't opened that one?" He nodded toward the box still tied with ribbon.

Sean shook his head again.

Bingham turned to yell over his shoulder at one of the technicians. "Crawley. Bring a bag. Got something for y'all."

He looked back at Sean as the man began to trot across the dead grass. "I'm gonna say this once, and I'd better never have to say it again. You mess with my investigation from here on in, and I'll lock you up. I don't care who you are or who you know or what the bastard did to your sister. This is my case. I'm in charge, and you need to get that through your head. You understand me, Sergeant Murphy?"

Sean nodded for the third time. He'd been yelled at plenty of times and by men more experienced at humiliation than

Bingham. Besides, the lieutenant was right. Sean should have given him the box from the hood of the car.

The only reason he hadn't was because he knew if he did, then the other would come out. The one that had been left in Jenna's apartment. And they would use that one to take her out of his hands. If they did that, his chances of doing what he had come down here to do were diminished.

"Take that to the lab," Bingham said to the tech who'd arrived. "It's from the murderer."

The man held out a plastic bag, allowing Sean to drop the box inside before he sealed it.

"Might as well take the other one, too," the detective said. "It's been opened, but do whatever you can." He watched as the process was repeated. "And while I'm at it, I think you folks better join me downtown for a little debriefing session. I want to hear all about what you've been up to tonight. Besides, a few hours spent giving statements will keep you out of my hair. And theirs," he said, glancing back at the forensics team. "And if it doesn't, then I damn sure know what will."

Eighteen

"Quite a layout," Sean said, his gaze considering the high-ceiling rooms that were visible from the oversized foyer.

Jenna realized that she should have anticipated how he would view her parents' house. The street-smart bravado that he wore like a badge of honor had been warning enough.

At the time she'd mentioned coming here, however, she'd been more concerned with issues of safety and the sense of sanctuary this place had always provided than with worrying about how he'd react to it. Now she knew that the gulf that stretched between her background and his had just gotten wider. And at a time when she didn't need any more barriers between them.

"My grandfather built this long before labor costs made building places like this prohibitive."

"Yeah?"

That single syllable managed to convey his disdain both for her specious argument and the wealth of her ancestors. She wondered again about his background, something he hadn't shared.

And he won't. Not as long as things keep happening to point up the differences between it and yours.

"If you're hungry—" she began, only to be cut off.

"You said there's a security system."

She thought briefly about pleading hunger or exhaustion, both of which were very real after the events of last night and the hours they'd spent down at the police station. But she had a feeling that after Bingham's scathing lecture on staying out of the way of the investigation, Sean would have little tolerance for anyone else trying to tell him what to do.

"The windows and doors are wired. If they're tampered with after the system is set, an alarm goes off," she explained, gesturing toward the control panel on the foyer wall.

As soon as they'd entered, she had punched in the code that prevented that from happening. Then she'd automatically rearmed the system. Living out so far from police protection had made security concerns routine for the entire family while she was growing up. Entering the front door today had triggered those familiar responses.

"Which sounds where?"

"The security company. Vanguard. At least it used to be. They call first to verify that the alarm wasn't accidentally triggered. Which happened often enough when we were kids. If they receive no response or a negative, they notify the police."

"Which ones?"

Sean had evidently picked up on the jumble of jurisdictions in the area. She thought a minute, trying to remember what her father had told her about recent efforts to annex this upscale, and as yet unincorporated area, into one of the local municipalities. Something she believed had failed.

"It should still be Shelby County Sheriff's Department."

"How about the upstairs windows? They wired, too?"

"Actually…" She didn't know, she realized. She'd always

assumed they were, but given the stakes, making that kind of assumption could be both foolish and dangerous. "I don't know."

"Should be easy enough to find out."

He made a sweeping gesture with his hand toward the staircase at the far end of the foyer. Carpeted in cream, the stairs led to a landing where they split before continuing upward to the second floor. Each side led to a separate wing. One of those had traditionally been designated for the children's rooms; the other, for the adults.

Jenna bent to grasp the handle of the suitcase she had also carried into the house, preparing to lead the way up to the familiar living quarters at the top of the stairs. Sean, who had yet to set his bag down, followed her as she climbed.

Without any conscious decision, she turned to the right as she reached the landing. Toward the wing that contained her rooms, as well as her brother's and three guest suites.

Her parents' domain, which occupied the other half of the second floor, included separate bedrooms and baths for each, as well as a large sitting room and her father's office. Despite the fact that they were gone, it would have felt like an invasion of their privacy to bring a stranger into that space.

Since Jenna hadn't lived in this house in more than ten years, except for two rare summers when she hadn't been in school, giving Sean a tour of the other bedrooms didn't seem too personal. Not until he followed her into the one where she'd slept throughout her childhood and adolescence.

His blatant masculinity seemed out of place among the girlish accoutrements of the room. She hadn't noticed its color scheme or furnishings in years, so familiar they no longer made any impression at all. Now she tried to view them through his eyes, realizing how much the room revealed about the years she'd lived in this house.

He didn't comment on any of it. Not the shelves filled with

dressage ribbons and trophies. Nor the framed certificates she'd won for school achievements, long forgotten by everyone but her mom. Not even the photographs that chronicled every phase of her growing up.

Although his gaze had lingered for a few seconds on those, instead of asking about them—or about anything else—Sean walked over to the window and examined it, taking care not to touch the glass or the frame. "These are wired. Basement?"

"I'm sorry?"

"Is there a basement?"

"Of course. A garage and storage areas are down there."

"Want to show me?"

"Look—"

He turned. One brow arched, seeming to mock her attempt to question his request. "Yeah?"

"I just—" She stopped, shaking her head. "If you're having second thoughts…"

Maybe he was afraid she was going to throw herself into his arms again. If so, he didn't need to worry.

She no longer bothered to deny that she was physically attracted to him. She had been from the moment she'd seen him—at least before he'd opened his mouth to chastise her.

Still, her reaction last night to having him safely back inside the motel room wasn't anything she was likely to repeat. The stress of that moment had destroyed her inhibitions. Now that she was aware of how strong her attraction was—

Sean's words interrupted that self-castigation. "I haven't. I just need to see the house. All of it."

"Why?" Maybe it was a dumb question, but she wasn't sure what the point of this was. Not as tired as they both were.

"Because I need to find a way to breech its defenses."

She laughed, shaking her head at the archaic terminology before she realized that he was serious. Deadly serious.

And why shouldn't he be? Sean knew better than anyone what kind of maniac they was dealing with.

An intimate knowledge, he had said. And now, having watched the forensics team work over Carol Cummings's mutilated body, she understood what he had known all along.

"You want to let me in on the joke? Believe me, I could use a good laugh."

"Sorry," she said quickly. "That was...nerves. A sense of disbelief, maybe. It's hard for me to fathom that someone would consider breaking into my parents' home. And even harder to believe—"

Despite her conviction that Sean was right about the Inquisitor's intent toward her, she couldn't bring herself to put it into words. It was like something out of a movie. A novel by Stephen King.

It was not the stuff of real life. Not hers. It couldn't be. And especially not here, the place she had always considered to be the securest haven in her very safe world.

Even as those thoughts formed, Sean was moving. He crossed the room to take her by the shoulders. He shook her once, hard enough that her head snapped back. His eyes bored down into hers, his lips compressed so tightly they appeared colorless.

"You damn well better believe it," he said, every word like a blow. "You'd better think about it every minute of the day. Because the first time you let down your guard, he's going to be there. And he isn't going to care how much money or influence your granddaddy had. He's going to treat you like he treated all the others. If you don't remember that, every waking minute, even in your dreams, then you're going to end up like they did."

Too shocked to respond, she simply stared up into his face. It was ruthless. Implacable. Just what she had wanted him to be when she'd begged him to protect her.

She had thought then that his eyes were cold. Now they were blue flame. Like looking into the heart of a fire.

She could feel the heat of his fingers through the thin knit of her sweater. His hands gripped her upper arms so hard they would leave marks on her skin.

Even though that force was being used to remind her of the danger she faced, she celebrated their strength. He was strong enough to do what she had asked of him. Skilled enough. And looking into his eyes, she knew he was cold-blooded enough.

Finally she nodded. Sean released her so suddenly she had to take a step back to keep her balance. The anger that had caused his voice to shake hadn't yet disappeared from the lean features.

She licked lips gone dry and attempted to make some coherent response to his warning. "I won't forget. It's just…" Despite her resolve not to call attention to them, she glanced at all the mementos of an ideal childhood. "This is my parents' *home*," she said, trying to make him understand what that meant to her.

"Which only makes you more vulnerable. You feel that because you're here, you're safe. You always have been. What you have to remember now is that you're not. Not here. Not anywhere. Not until he's dead."

She nodded again, compelled by his surety to accept as truth something she wanted to deny.

"As long as you remember that," he went on, seeming not to expect an answer, "this is as good a place as any to make a stand."

The military terminology again seemed out of place. As if they were playing G.I. Joe. This time she felt no inclination to laugh.

"You know the house better than he ever could. And I'll learn it. Every inch of it. So that when he shows up…" Sean let the sentence trail, but it was clear what he expected to happen.

For the first time the reality of what they were doing sank in. She was bait in the trap Sean Murphy was trying to set. And despite their agreement, protecting her wasn't—and never would be—his primary goal.

Jenna had fixed a family-size frozen lasagna dinner she'd found in her parents' well-stocked freezer. Although her stomach had been empty enough that at one point during their tour of the premises, she'd become light-headed, she had been unable to eat more than a few bites of the food piled on her plate.

Whatever Sean was feeling after the events of the last twenty-four hours, he'd eaten with the steady concentration of a man shoveling coal into a furnace, although the glass of wine she'd poured and placed beside his plate had remained untouched.

"More?" she offered.

"I'm fine, thanks."

Her eyes fell to the congealing mass of pasta and meat sauce on her plate. She prodded it with her fork, trying not to think about the approaching night. A primitive, unreasoning fear of the darkness, the same terror that had made her ancestors huddle around the fire in the center of the cave, had begun as soon as the sun sank, painting shadows over the familiar scene beyond the breakfast-room windows.

"For what it's worth," Sean said, bringing her gaze up, fork frozen in midmotion. "He's going to be busy with other things tonight."

There was only one "he" in the world they shared. What Sean meant by "other things," however…

"The Cummings girl's death is still fresh," he said. "The excitement it caused very new. All he's going to want to do right now is savor it. You're the last thing on his mind."

It would be comforting if she could believe that. The problem was she knew better.

"He was enjoying torturing Carol Cummings when he wrote those words on my car."

"You've got no proof that was him."

"You're the one who told me to tell the police. You seemed pretty sure at the time he'd left that message."

"'Help me?' You think that's what he wants? For you to say some mumbo jumbo and make him well?"

The flood of anger had as much to do with her exhaustion as with what he'd said. After all, it wouldn't take a genius to figure out Sean's opinion of what she did. He'd made that patently obvious the day he'd barged into her office, wallet open.

"Maybe," she said calmly. "On some level."

He laughed, wiping his mouth before he slid her mother's white linen napkin under the edge of his plate. A tiny smear of sauce remained on the corner of his lips.

For some reason, Jenna couldn't take her eyes off it. Annoyed, she jerked them up to find he'd been watching her.

"Surely, Dr. Kincaid, you haven't bought into the idea that he wants to get caught. To be forced to stop what he's doing. Believe me, he doesn't want to stop. He enjoys it way too much. Making people hurt. Listening to them scream. Life's blood to someone like him."

She had never heard the expression used that way before, but it was apt. In this case, a little too apt.

"I'm a psychologist. I have no illusions about what he is."

"Just some poor, misunderstood son of a bitch whose mama abused him."

"There's little doubt that someone did, given his rage against women. As for the former... I imagine there are a lot of people who understand him very well. Your friends at the Bureau, for example."

"The most important thing about that profile is what it doesn't say."

"What it *doesn't* say?"

"No name. No occupation. No age. Other than the standard stuff about middle-aged white male, the details are few."

"It also says he's organized, with a high IQ."

"He isn't just *organized*. He's meticulous. I told you that."

"Look, I know you're still angry about what I did. I thought if there was the slightest chance—"

"There wasn't. If there was anything to be found on those boxes, he wouldn't have left them."

"I can understand that you'd want to keep the ring, but…" She shook her head, remembering Bingham's face when, just before he'd released them, he'd told them what was in that second box. "The other didn't concern you. Surely Carol Cummings's family deserves—"

His laughter interrupted that platitude, its sound harsh and grating. "You still don't get it, do you? That finger didn't come from the Cummings girl's body. I don't doubt he took one of hers. It's part of his signature. But he wouldn't have left it for me."

It took her too long to make sense of what he'd just said, maybe because she didn't want to. And when she had…

"Makaela? You think that was—"

"Just like the ring. And the phone call. He knows I'm here, and he knows why."

Sean was here to kill him. She had finally understood that last night.

"Then why do you still need me?"

She hadn't meant to ask the question. It seemed self-serving. Cowardly, perhaps.

And who wouldn't be both? Considering the consequences of failure.

"I'm not sure I do. What I *am* sure of is that *you* still need me. His attraction to you hasn't lessened. If anything, the fact that I'm involved with you will have increased it. Nothing would give him more pleasure than to be able to hand me another one of those gift-wrapped boxes."

The few bites of dinner that she'd managed rose to the back of her throat. She closed her lips, swallowing in an attempt to force them down again.

Sean was right. Everything the killer had done had been a jeer and a challenge directed at him. Taking her despite Sean's protection would be the ultimate taunt. And there was nothing in this world the Inquisitor would enjoy more than being able to make it.

Nineteen

Some sound pierced his exhaustion, dragging Sean from the depths of a sleep he hadn't known he'd fallen into. At first, drugged by his almost desperate need for rest, he resisted waking, telling himself that whatever he'd heard was the product of a dream, but he could find no lingering dregs of one in his consciousness. He knew from long experience that the images from his recurring nightmare were always still there when he opened his eyes.

He did that now. For a few seconds he literally had no idea where he was. Then, as memory of the past few days came flooding back, panic followed almost simultaneously.

He was in the sitting room that connected to the huge bedroom belonging to Jenna's mother. He'd insisted that she sleep there, rather than in her old room.

It was the only one of the bedroom areas that had the kind of arrangement he'd wanted. A bed and bath where Jenna could have a degree of privacy. An attached sitting room providing a place where he could sit all night in relative comfort and guard the only entrance to the room where she slept.

Except he hadn't guarded her. He'd fallen asleep, instead. And despite what he'd told her about what the Inquisitor would be doing tonight—

The sound came again. This time he lunged off the brocade love seat, chosen because he'd believed it would be uncomfortable enough to force him to stay upright and awake.

He realized after he'd taken a couple of steps toward the open door of the bedroom that the Glock was, thankfully, still clasped in his right hand. His fingers had automatically curled around the weapon even as he'd scrambled off the couch.

His rush slowed as he approached what seemed to be total darkness in the other room. Despite the lamp on the table beside the sofa, which was now behind him, he couldn't make out anything inside the bedroom. Not the furniture. And certainly not the occupant.

He took a step to the side of the door, putting his back against the sitting room wall as he raised the gun in both hands, the right supporting the left. He held his breath, listening again for whatever he'd heard before.

Someone talking? Examining his impression of the noise, he decided that's exactly what it had been, the words low enough to be indistinguishable.

He hadn't heard the phone ring. So this must be—

Nightmare. And that's what the muttering had sounded like. Someone in the throes of a nightmare.

Despite his conviction, he led with the Glock as he side-stepped around the door frame and then into the darkened room. He made a survey of its interior, his eyes tracking the movement of his weapon as he swung it in a slow arc. As they adjusted to the moonlight filtering in through the drapes, he began to distinguish the shapes of the furniture.

His scan completed, he brought his gaze back to the king-size bed, which had been placed in the center of the room.

Semiautomatic extended, he took another couple of steps, far enough that he could tell Jenna was there.

With that knowledge his heart rate began to slow. He released a breath, drawing air into lungs that seemed to have forgotten how to perform that normal, physiological process on their own.

The sound this time was more prolonged, the words clearer, either by virtue of his nearness or because of their repetition. "No. No, please. Please don't."

He'd done this to her, he realized. And he'd done it deliberately.

He had intended to frighten her badly enough that she wouldn't be tempted to do anything foolish. That she would be on her guard at all times...*even in your dreams*.

"Jenna."

Her name echoed in the stillness. He waited, becoming aware as he did of a subtle fragrance surrounding him.

Not Jenna's perfume. He recognized that by now. Associated it with her presence. Despite the fact that she no longer lived in that trophy-filled room in the other wing, and hadn't in years, the darker, stronger scent she normally wore still lingered there.

This was lighter. Sweeter. Like roses. The old-fashioned kind that had grown in his grandmother's garden. The flash-bulb image of them, drooping in the summer heat, releasing their familiar scent into the heavy air, caught him off guard.

It shouldn't have. Smell was the sense most closely associated with memory. Even now there were certain odors—most of them unpleasant—that sent him instantly back to that dirty, four-room public-housing apartment where he'd grown up.

He'd fought the comparison from the second he'd entered this house. He'd pushed the remembrance of "home" as he knew it out of his head as ruthlessly as he always did all those other memories. Denying them now, he took another step forward.

"Jenna? Wake up. Everything's okay."

Some nearly imperceptible change in the quality of her breathing let him know that she was no longer asleep. After a moment she lifted her torso off the mattress, propping on one elbow to look up at him. He wondered if she even knew who he was, his body silhouetted against the dim light from the other room.

"What is it? What's wrong?"

"You were dreaming."

For a moment, she said nothing. And then, her voice flat, "About him. And her."

"Carol?"

That was possibly the first time he'd said her name. He had tried not to think of her as a person. That would do nothing but weaken him. Something he couldn't afford right now.

Carol Cummings was dead. Just like Makaela. There was no longer anything he could do for either of them. His only concern now was Jenna.

She straightened until she was sitting upright in the bed. With her hand, she pushed the fall of dark hair away from her face. "I think so. I don't really—"

"It was just a dream. Go back to sleep."

The command was abrupt, its tone verging on anger. He was reacting to her vulnerability now as he had when he'd shaken her last night.

She had looked up into his face then as if she'd never seen him before, her eyes full of pain. And the only thing he had wanted to do was to pull her to him. To hold her trembling body against his and whisper promises he had no right to make.

Nothing's going to happen to you as long as I'm here.

He had once made that same vow to Makaela. And he had failed.

He had no right to make that promise to another woman.

Not even to one who brought out all the protective instincts he had believed he'd left behind with his childhood. In the rat-infested slum his family had called home.

"Have you slept?" It sounded as if she really cared.

Or maybe she just wants to know if you're on the job.

He forced that caustic thought into his head in an attempt to erase the other. "Enough."

"I don't think that's possible. They say once you lose sleep, you can't catch up. What time is it?"

He realized he had no idea. It could have been an hour since he'd sat down in the other room, intent on staying awake, or it could as easily have been six or seven.

"Wait. I know. I moved it because the light bothered me." Jenna reached across to the bedside table and turned a clock whose face had been to the wall. The digital display read four-thirteen.

Closer to his last estimate, he realized. And while he'd slept, anything might have happened.

He knew from experience that after a while sleep deprivation caught up with you, no matter how determined you were. He'd been managing on four or five hours for the past several days. If he was going to screw up, as he'd told Jenna, last night was probably the safest time he could have chosen.

"Right now I'm hungrier than I am sleepy," she said, turning back from the clock to look at him again. "As hard as it is to believe, I think I may have slept out."

She'd eaten very little the night before. Not that he could blame her, considering what she'd been through. If she was hungry now, he'd encourage her to eat. Doing without food was no more conducive to clear thinking than doing without sleep.

"I make a decent omelet."

He regretted the offer as soon as the words were out of his mouth. He should have gotten the hell out of here while he had the chance. He should have let her get up and fix her own breakfast and eat it alone.

Preparing a meal for the two of them was a little too much camaraderie for the situation they were in. Despite the fact that he hadn't accepted her money, what they had was essentially a business arrangement. Something he damn well better remember before Ms. Moneybags reminded him again of his place.

"There should be eggs and cheese in the fridge even with Mom out of town," Jenna said. "We can check out the pantry for additions, but I won't make any promises about those."

She reached over to the table beside the bed again, this time to switch on the light. In response to the sudden glare, she raised her hand to shield her eyes.

Backlit and in profile, her breasts strained against the pale blue nightgown she wore. They were fuller than he'd expected them to be from her slim build.

The size to fit into a man's hand.

Unable to pull his eyes away, he saw that her nipples, tautened by the chill of the room or the aftermath of the dream, were clearly visible through the fabric. Whatever it was, it was sheer enough to reveal the dark aureoles surrounding them.

She turned, lowering her hand. For too many telltale seconds his gaze remained focused on the V-shaped neckline of her gown, unconsciously examining the shadowed cleavage revealed by its cut.

Only when the growing tightness in his groin made him realize what he was doing, did he raise his eyes to her face. Hers held on his, as a sweep of color rushed under the smooth skin of her neck and into her cheeks.

"I'll check out the rest of the house while you dress." He forced the words through a throat gone dry and tight.

He turned on his heel and crossed the room, closing the bedroom door behind him. Once safe from what he'd seen in her eyes, he leaned back against the wood, expelling a pent-up breath. The heat that had flared between them was a complication he didn't need. He had come here for one reason and one reason only.

Jenna Kincaid wasn't someone he could have a relationship with. Not a sexual one.

All he wanted from *Dr.* Kincaid, he reminded himself bitterly, was the mutually satisfying arrangement they'd agreed on. Anything other than that—

Thinking that there could *be* anything other than that was the height of stupidity. Or self-delusion.

Their worlds were daylight and dark. As different as that perfumed bedroom behind him was from the projects where he'd grown up. Although their sexual attraction might bridge that gap for a while, it would never destroy it.

That wasn't what he'd come here to destroy. And nothing, not even his growing awareness of Jenna Kincaid as a highly desirable woman, was going to get in his way.

"There's no excuse for what you did last night. You need to understand that this department won't tolerate your interference in our investigation in any way, shape or form."

Sean knew he had no choice but to listen to Ray Bingham's lecture, just as he had last night. After his initial anger had passed, he had acknowledged that it was only by virtue of Bingham's sympathy and good nature that he wasn't in jail. Something he was infinitely grateful for.

"Your guys find anything useful on or in those boxes?"

He had to work to keep any trace of "I told you so" out of the question. If there had been any forensic evidence on the boxes or their contents—other than contact contamination easily identifiable as coming from his jacket pocket or from Jenna's apartment—Bingham would have started this with that news.

"The examination is ongoing."

The cop's clipped tone told Sean all he needed to know. "Meaning the only thing you've established is that the trophy contained in the second box didn't come from the Cummings girl."

Bingham hadn't called it a trophy when he'd told him that. And the detective's voice had held what seemed to be sincere regret for having to tell him what Sean had accepted from the instant he'd seen the package on his hood.

"All we've established so *far,*" Bingham reiterated stubbornly.

"I'd appreciate being informed of whatever you turn up."

"Look, Sergeant Murphy, you've got connections. Some folks I respect speak highly of you. And you've got a record with the army few people can match. I checked. Hell, I even *like* you. None of that changes the fact that you aren't the one investigating this case. Not in any way, shape or form."

A favorite phrase, apparently. Or maybe Bingham was determined to emphasize that Sean wasn't going to be party to whatever the police discovered. Judging by what they'd managed to find out about the Inquisitor so far, that refusal wasn't going to be much of a loss.

"What about the phone call?"

"What?"

"The one he made to my room. You trace that yet?"

"All we know is that it was made from a cell phone."

"And you can't trace the number?"

"We suspect it was one of those with prepaid minutes. The kind you can buy at the Wal-Mart."

"How about the location of the tower?"

"No way to trace that without some starting point."

"What does that mean?"

"You got to have a service to backtrack on. Those phones don't have that. They're virtually untraceable."

The son of a bitch was always one step ahead of technology. Organized and intelligent. Like Jenna had said.

"So you got nothing," Sean said, his voice flat.

"They're still working on the body."

"Which will tell you what the rest of them told you. Time and cause of death. Oh, yeah. And the kind of tools he uses. That never varies. And none of it gets us anywhere."

"Every department in the area—"

"Don't bother blowing smoke up my ass. Save the news releases for the media."

There was a brief silence on the line. When the lieutenant spoke again, to Sean's surprise he obeyed the injunction. "You do understand what those boxes mean, don't you?"

"I understand."

"I know you were convinced that Dr. Kincaid was going to be his next victim, but… Frankly, it looks to me like he's targeting *you*."

"He's playing me."

"*Playing* you?"

"To get me stirred up enough to do something stupid."

To give Bingham credit he didn't say, "Like concealing evidence?" His question was on the money, exactly what Sean had been thinking.

"Like come after him?"

"I think that's what he wants."

"Leaving Dr. Kincaid vulnerable."

"She *is* vulnerable. Whether I'm here or not. I've been trying to make her realize that."

"Maybe you need some help."

"In convincing her? You volunteering?"

"Help in protecting her."

Sean controlled his anger, making sure it wasn't reflected in his voice. "You put a bunch of cops out here, and he's going to target someone else. You'll leave him no choice."

"I doubt Dr. Kincaid would be upset if that happened."

"The good citizens you're supposed to be protecting might be. How many mutilated girls do you think they're going to tolerate? Jenna's the best chance we have of stopping him."

"*Jenna?*"

Sean ignored the question.

Eventually the lieutenant went on. "She agreeable to being bait for your scheme?"

"He chose her. I didn't."

"I'm not so sure about that anymore. *You're* the one who convinced her she was destined to be his next victim. If it's really you he's been after all along, then maybe when you started following her—"

"He was at her office."

"The writing on her car? That what you're talking about? As far as we know right now, that could have been done by anybody. A kid. A patient. Maybe even somebody else's patient. Somebody who was pissed with the therapy they were getting. It may have no relationship to the Inquisitor at all. And as I understand it, that happened *after* you showed up at her office. Maybe it's *you* our boy's following, Sergeant Murphy. Maybe he has been all along. Maybe he didn't even know Jenna Kincaid was alive until you pointed him to her."

When Sean said the killer had been at her office, he hadn't been talking about the message on the car, but he wasn't about to admit that to Bingham. It was possible the detective had experienced one of those episodes of premonition or prescience or whatever the hell the psychic dingbats called it.

If he'd been a street cop for any time at all, it was more

than likely he had. A tightening in your chest when you were on a stakeout and knew something bad was about to go down. The prickle of hair on the back of your neck as you approached the driver's side on a routine traffic stop. The kinds of things old cops and old soldiers never ignore. If they did, they never got to be old cops or old soldiers.

What Sean had felt that night in the visitors' parking lot outside Jenna's practice had been like that. Definitely a warning. As real as any he'd felt in Somalia or Iraq or in half a dozen other places and situations during his twenty.

This one had also been something else. A very real sense that evil was at hand. Cold and black and soulless.

No matter how convinced he was of the reality of what he'd experienced that night, Sean wasn't about to start spouting that kind of crap to Bingham. It would be the final nail in the coffin of whatever credibility he had left.

"Are you saying *I* led him to Jenna?"

Without a convincing argument for why he knew that was wrong, Sean countered with the only thing he had. The anger that suggestion generated.

"I'm saying it's a possibility."

"No, it's not."

"And that since it *is* possible," Bingham went on as if he hadn't spoken, "you owe it to Dr. Kincaid to back off."

"To leave her in your hands."

"At least to give her the choice."

"She made her choice."

Despite the rage simmering beneath the surface, Sean knew that wasn't entirely true. He'd done more than a little arm-twisting to convince Jenna that her best chance for survival lay with him rather than with the overworked cops.

That had been at the time when the police were frantically searching for Carol Cummings. Now that she'd been found—

"I'd like to ask her." Bingham's voice was deceptively soft. "Maybe explain a few things to her at the same time."

"You want to talk to her now? Or you want the number of her cell?"

"So she's still with you."

"She doesn't feel safe anywhere else. Of course, you're welcome to try and convince her otherwise."

"Thanks for permission."

Bingham sounded amused by his offer rather than pissed. That was okay. Sean was pissed enough for both of them.

"Always glad to be of assistance to the law enforcement community." He'd already started to take the phone away from his ear when the cop's next question stopped him.

"So how are the kids? Missing you, I'd bet. Must have been tough on them. Losing their mom. Getting displaced from everything they'd ever known. Finally they get settled into some kind of family security again, and then boom, you're gone."

The rage Sean had worked to control boiled up, closing his throat. The interrogation had been framed in a tone of concern and sympathy, but he had no doubt where this was headed.

"They're in very good hands, but thanks for asking." He didn't bother this time to soften his sarcasm.

"So what happens if you go *permanently* missing? What do you think that's gonna do to them?"

"Why don't you let me worry about that? *And* about Jenna Kincaid. It seems to me like you've got enough on your plate without trying to take care of my niece and nephew."

"Look—"

"Or about a woman you don't believe is a target of the serial killer who's already handed you four bodies. Seems to me *he* might be your primary concern right now. Or maybe these things work differently in this 'backward city.' I guess an 'ignorant black cop' like you knows more about that than me."

Sean heard the profanity before he got the phone away from his ear. As he pushed the off button with his thumb, he couldn't deny the feeling of satisfaction at getting some of his own back with Bingham.

It was stupid. Childish, even. But then so was the guilt trip the head of the local task force had tried to use on him to get him to back off.

Still, he didn't want to make an enemy out of the detective. He didn't need that. Neither of them did.

They had a far more implacable foe they needed to fight. And no matter what Bingham said, Sean still believed that the best way to defeat that foe was through Jenna.

The problem was that every argument the lieutenant had used against that conviction was valid. And persuasive.

Just not quite persuasive enough to make Sean forget everything that was at stake.

Twenty

Jenna had decided to take a shower before she came down. As she'd descended the stairs, she'd heard Sean talking. And since there was no one else in the house, she made the logical assumption that he was carrying on a conversation by phone.

One that had ended when he'd heard her footsteps?

"Was that your cell?"

"Bingham," Sean said without looking up from the egg he was breaking over the side of one of her mother's Royal Doulton bowls.

The guilt she'd felt since she'd told the policeman about the boxes resurfaced. No matter what Sean thought, she knew that telling the truth had been the right thing to do. Especially if it brought them one step closer to the murderer.

"They found something?"

Sean hadn't taken time to shave, and the omnipresent five o'clock shadow was quickly becoming a beard. Despite the hours of sleep he'd gotten last night, his eyes looked almost as exhausted as they had yesterday.

"Yeah. That the trophy didn't come from the Cummings girl."

He had told her that last night. Learning that his suspicion had been confirmed, especially since he had delivered the report in that flat, matter-of-fact manner, was almost as chilling as listening to it as his theory had been then.

"I'm sorry."

He ignored her expression of sympathy, picking up another egg from the carton to crack against the edge of the bowl. He used one hand to break and open the shell, his movements quick and skillful, as if he'd been doing this for years.

"He wants to talk to you, by the way."

"Bingham?" She was disconcerted by the information. A little defensive. "About what?"

"Protection."

She examined the word, not quite sure what the under note she'd heard in Sean's tone signified. "Does that mean you're backing out?"

"Of our deal? I thought maybe you wanted to."

"I told you I'm sorry. I thought that if there was the slightest chance those boxes held a clue—"

"He thinks I may have led him to you."

That took a couple of seconds to interpret as well. The first pronoun was obviously a reference to Bingham, so the second must be—

"The *Inquisitor?*"

"Bingham thinks he may have been watching *me*. And that the only reason he expressed an interest in you is because of mine."

"You're saying he's doing these things because you came to my office? And because you followed me?"

"I'm saying that's what *Bingham* thinks."

"What do *you* think?"

"That he saw your interview that night. And he responded to what you said exactly like I did."

They were back to that. Of course, it shouldn't come as a surprise. Sean's entire premise about the Inquisitor targeting her had been based on the few words she'd said on camera.

"But…Bingham thinks the whole time you thought he was watching me, he was really following you."

"Bingham's a local cop with a whole lot of shit going down and not enough expertise or experience to know what to do about it. Besides, maybe he doesn't know everything you and I do."

"Like what?"

"That they save every newspaper clipping about their work. Pin them on the wall. Make shrines of the more lurid tabloid stories. You *know* he was watching the news that night. *Especially* that night. The day they made the announcement about his accomplishments here. You aren't Bingham. You *have* the expertise. You damn well *know* he saw you."

"Why are you doing this?"

The long brown fingers hesitated before they repeated the journey across the counter to pick up another egg. He cracked it hard enough to make the bowl sing, then adroitly separated the halves with his thumb and ring finger.

"I thought you were hungry."

"Don't play dumb with me, Sean. That may work with the cops, but as you pointed out, I'm not Bingham. This is what I do for a living."

"Analyze people?"

"Analyze their motives for saying the things they say. So now I'm wondering why, after all your arguments to the contrary, you're trying to convince me the killer isn't interested in me."

"Bingham's the one who wants to convince you of that."

"Why? What does it matter to Bingham what I believe? Or who I call on for protection? Right now, I'm just one less woman he has to worry about."

"He thinks that if I walk away from you, he will, too."

If I walk away from you, he will, too.... Again, there was only one interpretation that made sense.

"Because...it's *you* he wants?"

"That's the current thinking downtown."

"Is it what you think?"

His eyes came up, holding hers for perhaps five seconds. Then they dropped again to the eggs he was breaking for a breakfast she could no longer imagine trying to choke down.

"I think he'd get more satisfaction out of doing what he did before."

This wasn't about Carol Cummings's murder. That wasn't what Sean was talking about. This was about Makaela. And what the killer had done before...

"He'd get more satisfaction from destroying someone you should have protected."

He broke another egg, the movement of his hand as steady as it had been with all the others. Whatever he felt about his sister's death had long ago been rigidly encased in the hard-ass persona he wore like a medal.

Or like a shield.

If not for his determination to avenge Makaela's death, even if it cost him his own life, she might have believed he'd come to terms with its trauma. Now she knew that he hadn't.

"You weren't there when it happened," she said, unable to ignore his pain, no matter how skillfully he pretended.

"Wherever I was, wherever she was, she was my responsibility."

"Why?"

"Because she was my sister."

"She was an adult. There comes a time when—"

"Maybe for you. Things didn't work that way in my family." The kind of bond he'd shared with Makaela would have been forged in something other than an ideal family situation. The out-of-proportion responsibility he had felt for his sister was probably the product of a skewed sibling relationship, something beyond a normal big brother attitude.

"So how *did* they work?"

"We looked out for one another."

"Did you? *All* of you? Or was it really only you looking out for Makaela?"

"I'm not one of your patients, Doc. Go peddle your psychobabble to someone who might be inclined to buy it."

"So it's okay for you to play psychiatrist, but *your* psyche's off limits."

"I don't know what you're talking about."

"You told me in no uncertain terms how what I said in that interview would have been interpreted by the man who murdered your sister. If that isn't playing psychiatrist, what is?"

"I read the profile the FBI put together."

"So did I. It seemed pretty run-of-the-mill. A lot of guesswork, which is always the case. And nothing I read made me half as sure about *anything* as it made you. So that makes me wonder if there isn't something else going on here."

"Like what?"

"I don't know. And I'd be willing to bet you won't tell me. Actually, I doubt you've ever told anyone."

"You want to know what makes me tick? Is that it? Hell, there isn't all that much to tell. I grew up in a slum, and I grew up fast. When I was old enough to leave, I did. And I never went back. End of story."

He held her eyes defiantly, clearly waiting for a response. There was literally nothing she could say to that recital. As far as it went, it was more than likely true.

But she knew it wasn't complete. Not by a long shot.

He looked down at the eggs he'd broken and then back up again, meeting her eyes. "Still hungry?"

She shook her head, knowing that whatever the truth behind the man Sean Murphy had become, she wasn't going to learn it by asking questions. Not of him.

"Yeah, well, I guess that's the difference between you and me. I am. You mentioned something about a pantry."

Without answering, she walked across the kitchen and opened the double doors on the far side of the room to reveal shelves loaded as they always were with canned goods and staples. As she stood there, trying to solve the enigma Sean represented, he came up behind her.

She stepped to the side to allow him an unimpeded view of the contents. At the very least there should be canned mushrooms. Those, with the cheese he'd laid out on the counter—

"Call Bingham."

He was standing slightly behind her left shoulder, close enough that his breath stirred her hair. She nodded again.

"He could be right, you know. If I walk away from you now, the Inquisitor might follow me."

"You don't believe that."

"Does it matter?"

"It does to me. We had a bargain. I've kept my end of it. And I expect you to keep yours. You can tell the lieutenant for me that I'm not interested in whatever it is he has to say."

"Tell him yourself. Maybe if it comes from you, he'll believe it."

The day had seemed endless. The local television broadcasts and even the cable news networks were full of Carol Cummings's murder. The police confirmed that she'd been butchered by the same man responsible for the torture and death of the three other Birmingham victims.

During the afternoon, a couple of people from work, including Paul Carlisle, had called Jenna on her cell. He'd confirmed that he had asked Gary to check on her, which seemed to put Sean's concerns about her co-worker's nighttime visit to rest. Still, as a result of his warning, Jenna had told no one other than her boss that she was staying at her parents'.

She'd put off calling Bingham as long as she could, figuring that he'd be dealing with the media most of the day. Finally around four o'clock she'd phoned his office, expecting to be told that they'd take a message and have him call her back. Instead, she was put through at once, as if he had been waiting for her call.

The detective had gone through everything she'd heard from Sean this morning. He had even offered her around-the-clock protection to replace the services of the man he was now convinced the killer was really after.

Jenna had refused. All she had to go on was instinct, and it was telling her, as it had from the beginning, that her best chance for survival lay with Sean. A man who was almost as much a mystery now as the day he'd stormed into her office.

She raised her eyes from the novel she'd been pretending to read to find him watching her. He didn't look away, not even when she closed the book and put it on the table beside her chair.

"I think I'll go up now." She stood and realized that he had risen, too.

Although she hadn't been able to find fault with Sean's manners, she didn't believe they extended to standing whenever a lady did. Which meant—

"You don't have to come," she said quickly.

She didn't want to deal with the sexual tension that had been thick in her mother's bedroom this morning. Something in his eyes then had made her far too aware of the thinness of the silk gown she wore.

Aware, too, that they were alone. Isolated from an outside world that seemed full of danger.

As absurd as it sounded, right now Sean Murphy represented everything she had once believed characterized her life. Safety. And familiarity.

Given her circumstances, it was far too easy to want to cling to both. And far too dangerous.

Not the danger the Inquisitor offered, but an escape from it. An escape back to the sense of security she'd always felt here. The sense of security that Sean gave her now.

"I need to check out the rooms upstairs," he explained.

It was a reminder of reality she could have done without. Now that he'd made it, however, she couldn't deny she'd feel more comfortable if he went upstairs with her.

"Thank you."

"All part of the service."

"Don't," she said softly.

"Don't what?"

"Pretend you're the hired help."

"As I remember, that's what you wanted."

"I thought it was the only way you'd agree. Obviously, I was wrong. Again. Do you want me to apologize for that, too?"

"Why not? You do it so well."

"Apologize?"

"All the social graces."

"And that makes you uncomfortable."

"What it *makes* me—"

For a moment she thought he must have seen or heard something that had made him stop in midsentence. His eyes were still focused on her face, however.

"I know you don't like me—" she began.

"You don't know anything about me. *Especially* not how I feel about you."

The shimmer of sexual awareness she'd felt this morning stirred again. Deep within her body there was a flutter of anticipation. This was what the sparring between them had been leading up to. This was why he'd been on edge all day.

On some level, long before she had admitted it, she'd known that eventually this was going to happen between them. She just hadn't known it would be tonight.

"Then why don't you tell me? Explain it to me so I'll understand exactly what I've done wrong. Or what I've said that's made you so angry."

"I thought you were supposed to be good at your job."

"I *am* good at my job."

"Analyzing motives. That's what you said, right?"

"Among other things. Behaviors themselves, for example."

"As in 'actions speak louder than words.'"

"Because something's a cliché doesn't mean it isn't true."

"And what do you make of my behavior?"

"That you're very confident of your abilities when you're in a situation you understand and can control. It's the things you can't control that make you vulnerable. And angry."

"Isn't that true for everyone?"

"Maybe, but I think with you it's to the extreme. You're absolutely certain that if you can find your sister's murderer, you can kill him. That's why you left the motel room last night. You never even considered calling the cops."

"Did you?"

"Of course."

"Why didn't you?"

"Because I was *also* sure that if you get the chance, you'll kill him."

"And you want me to."

It hadn't been a question, but she answered it, anyway. If

she was asking for the truth from him, it seemed she was obligated to provide that in turn.

"Yes, I do. And if wanting that is a sin, then it's one I can live with."

"Especially since his blood won't be on your hands."

The sarcasm was clear. Biting. The accusation undeniable.

"If I help you, it is."

"And how are you going to help me?"

"I told you. It's what I do."

"You think you can do a better job than the FBI profilers?"

"They don't have a patent on guesswork. And I doubt they know anything about him you don't."

She could read the surprise in his eyes. The important thing was how quickly it was replaced by interest.

Of course with Sean it was always difficult to tell what he was thinking. It was an art he'd perfected long ago, either as part of his military background or earlier. In whatever family situation that had led to the unusual relationship with Makaela.

"You think we can come up with something the cops didn't?"

"I think that working together, we have a chance."

She was aware as she extended the olive branch that the idea of their working together might backfire. That it might turn into the very thing she'd been attempting to avoid in giving them something to think about other than the reality that they were alone in this house.

And the equally undeniable fact that, however their relationship had begun, it had become something neither of them had anticipated. And something neither of them wanted to do anything about.

Twenty-One

"I still think he was abused. Obviously by a woman. Someone close to him. Someone in a position of authority."

"Maybe he just went to Catholic schools."

Jenna looked up from the page of notes she'd jotted down. She expected to find amusement in the blue eyes, but they were cold. Just as they had been last night.

"Did you?"

"As long as my mother could afford it."

"And Makaela?"

"Until high school. Mom saw it as a form of protection for her."

From the neighborhood? Or from someone else? In any case, the theme of protection for his sister was repeated, although Sean didn't seem to realize the significance of its recurrence.

Without commenting on the revelation he'd just made, she wrote "Nuns" on the paper and drew a question mark after it. "Actually, I was thinking about his mother."

"The usual suspect."

She nodded, ignoring his sarcasm as she considered other

possibilities. "It could have been a grandmother. Or an aunt. More rarely a neighbor or a teacher."

"No father around?"

"The most likely scenario, but we can't be sure of that, of course. Not without other evidence." They couldn't get that without the ability to do research, and they couldn't research without somewhere to start. "Was yours?"

"What?"

"You've mentioned your mother and your sister. I just wondered if your dad was around while you were growing up."

"More analysis?"

"Idle curiosity. I don't seem to be coming up with any earth-shattering ideas on him."

She lifted the pad she'd been scribbling on. There really wasn't much new or of value there, she admitted.

"You know the stereotype. It isn't far off the mark."

Stereotype? His *father?* "What stereotype is that?"

"The shiftless, drunken Irishman."

Her heart started to beat faster, but she controlled her face and her voice. "Was he?"

"Most of the time."

She'd resisted the urge to ask the logical question earlier. She didn't resist it now. "Is he the one who abused Makaela?" And then she waited for the explosion.

"Until I was big enough to stop him."

She had thought she might learn something from his reaction, but she'd never expected him to answer. She wasn't quite sure what to say now that he had. "When was that?"

"He was six-five. Two-hundred-seventy, eighty pounds. Even stinking drunk, he managed to kick my ass on a regular basis. Up until I was seventeen."

Given what she'd already figured out about the family dynamics, she would have been willing to bet those beatings had been in response to Sean's intervention in something else that had been going on in that household. That was something she didn't dare ask about.

"So what happened at seventeen?"

"Idle curiosity?" he mocked.

"No, you were right. I want to know what makes you tick."

He laughed. "It's not all that interesting. He was drunk, pounding my mother pretty good, even for a Saturday night. I got in from my shift at the plant in the middle of it. He had her down in the corner of the kitchen, pummeling her head. When I pulled him off, I hit him in the mouth as hard as I could. And by that time it was pretty hard. He stumbled over her feet, fell backward and cracked his skull on the cabinet."

Her years as a therapist should have made her better prepared. Still, the story, told with complete dispassion and by someone she was attracted to, shocked her. "It killed him?"

"Unfortunately not. The cops got involved, however, and he ended up in jail, luckily that time for longer than my mother was in the hospital. When she got out, she finally got up the courage to take Makaela back home to her parents in Michigan."

"You didn't go with them?"

"I went to juvenile detention until I turned eighteen. The judge suggested the army. I took him up on the offer, and the rest, as they say, is history. So now that you know everything there is to know about me, you want to get back to him?"

Everything there is to know. She didn't, of course. But at least now she understood why what she'd said in that stupid interview bothered him so much.

To Sean Murphy, abuse didn't give you a license to hurt. In his case it had produced the opposite effect, making him overprotective toward the sister whose share of those drunken, senseless beatings he'd probably taken for years.

But he hadn't been able to intervene to prevent her death. So now he was trying to do what he saw as the next best thing.

"You have to know—"

"What do *you* know, Doc? I thought that was the question. I thought you were going to figure out who this guy is. Or isn't your guesswork any better than the shrinks' at the Bureau?"

He had shared more of himself than she had any right to expect. And now the door to his past had again been slammed firmly shut. Trying to force it open would accomplish nothing except anger and resentment.

"Your friend on the national task force didn't share any names with you?" She kept her eyes on the notepad as she asked.

"I don't think they have any."

"But they *do* have suspects, don't they? They *have* questioned people."

"'Persons of interest' is the current terminology. As far as I'm aware, none of them have ever panned out."

She pushed the appealing possibility of that kind of short-cut from her mind, trying to concentrate again on what she knew with a degree of certainty, based strictly on the crimes.

"He's white." The victims had been, so that was a given.

"That narrows it to what? A few million?"

"Late thirties or early forties," she continued, ignoring the sarcasm. "He could be a little older, but not much."

"The Feds think he's older, based on the first murders."

According to the FBI, the Inquisitor had butchered his first victim more than seven years ago. Jenna would be willing to bet there had been earlier killings not yet linked to him.

Those would be in his hometown. Or somewhere nearby. And the reason they hadn't been connected to him was because he'd still been perfecting his methodology.

He probably hadn't abducted those women. He'd attacked

and killed them wherever he'd encountered them. And then, after the first few, he had discovered the brief brutality of that wasn't enough to satisfy the rage that drove him.

Based on what she remembered from the classes she'd taught, those victims would probably have been his age or slightly younger, even if his abuser was an older woman. Most serial killers began to kill in their mid- to late twenties. Allowing a window of five years for those earlier, as yet unconnected murders...

"I think they're wrong," she said. "The current victims have all been in their mid-thirties."

"Except for Carol Cummings."

The UAB student had been twenty. She had also been shorter than the others. Slightly overweight. From the photographs on the news, those few extra pounds hadn't made her unattractive.

The girl's death was enough of a variation to be considered as falling outside the pattern. Combined with the fact that he hadn't let the normal time lapse between his victims—

"He didn't plan to take her." As she voiced her sudden realization, she looked up from the pad and straight into Sean's eyes, which narrowed as he thought about what she'd said.

"He didn't stalk her," she went on. "That's why there was such a small gap between Callie Morgan's murder and this."

That should make her feel better about her own situation. It wasn't that the Inquisitor was becoming less controlled— or in profiler terminology, less organized. It was simply that he'd had a stroke of luck with his last victim. And he'd taken advantage of it.

"She fell into his lap," Sean said softly.

"Young enough to think nothing like what happened to the others could ever happen to her. We have to tell Bingham."

"Tell him what? That this one was some kind of accident?"

"It *was*," Jenna emphasized, unsure why he didn't see the importance of that. "She disappeared from Five Points. Where there are *always* people. Someone may have seen him."

"Doing what?"

"Leaving a bar with her. Getting into a car. *His* car."

Only as she said the words did she realize their implication. Even if someone had only seen the car, it would narrow the field of suspects exponentially. Added to the other things they knew, it might be enough to give them some "persons of interest" here.

"He's not that stupid," Sean said decisively.

Could he have been? Would he have taken a chance on someone seeing them together?

"Maybe it didn't seem stupid at the time."

"Being seen with a woman who's going to turn up dead?"

"Maybe he didn't intend to kill her. Not then."

"So that means someone he knew? Or someone who was with him for some other reason?"

"She was a student." Jenna was sure that the Inquisitor was too old to be one, even on an urban campus that catered to people in the work force, but it *was* possible he was connected to the university in some way. "Maybe he's a teacher."

"Still too risky. Maybe more so. Everybody who had any association with the Cummings girl will be questioned. He wouldn't want to be pulled in. Somebody might take a look at where he's been before he came here."

He had probably lied on any application or résumé, but if the cops got interested and began backtracking, that kind of falsification would fall apart very quickly. Sean was right. He was too smart to put himself in that position.

"Then if he didn't know her, why would he take a chance on being seen with her?"

"He picked her up at night."

"At *Five Points?* Too many people. Besides, where was she

between the time she left her friends at the bar and when it got dark? She told them she was going back to campus, so why hang around…what, two or three hours? She said she needed to get back to study."

"It was raining."

"What?"

"The day she disappeared," Sean clarified. "I wanted to take a look at the places where they'd found the bodies. It was raining so hard I had to give it up. I literally couldn't see the ground in front of me."

"He picked her up in the rain." She knew how it must have happened. The area around the fountain deserted except for a lone girl trying to make her way back to her dorm in a storm. "He offered her a ride. Or maybe she asked him for one. And despite Callie Morgan's death, he just couldn't resist. He knew that the chance of anyone being out in that rain, especially as cold as it was… He picked her up, Sean. For once he took a risk. For once he played the odds."

Sean pushed back his chair, the legs sliding noisily across the ceramic tile of the kitchen floor. Startled, she looked up to see him take his cell phone out of his pocket.

"You're calling Bingham?"

"Maybe somebody will remember. *Because* of that rain. Maybe somebody saw something they didn't realize at the time was important. If the cops can remind them—"

He didn't bother to finish the sentence. He punched one of the preset buttons on his cell instead, and then walked over to the breakfast room windows overlooking the pool.

She didn't listen to whatever he told the lieutenant. The theory might come to naught. Even if they were right, maybe no one had been outside that day. Or looking out a window. Maybe the Inquisitor had been as lucky as he'd always been before.

Even if no one had witnessed what happened, she knew

on some level beyond logic she was right. He had picked Carol Cummings up in the rain, and then he'd driven her to wherever he'd killed her. And at some point in that journey she must have known.

Suspicion first. Increasingly frantic questions that had gone unanswered until there was no more room for uncertainty. Or for hope. Finally there would only be room for the terrible reality. That what had been done to the three women whose deaths and mutilations had filled the pages of the local paper for days was about to be done to her.

Jenna lay listening to the rain and watching the minutes and then the hours change on the digital clock. She hadn't bothered turning it to the wall. Its dim light wasn't what kept her awake tonight.

She turned over, pummeling the down pillow in an attempt to fashion it into a more comfortable shape. Even when she had done that, she didn't bother to close her eyes. She knew the images would still be there.

She listened instead, straining to hear the comforting sound of Sean's snores from the adjoining room. If he were asleep, the drum of rain on the roof drowned out any evidence of it. And if he were awake—

Maybe he was struggling as she was to put the scenario they'd created for the Cummings girl's abduction out of his head. Or maybe for him tonight's attempt to enter the mind of the Inquisitor had created other images. Ones that centered around another murder. *Another woman he'd vowed to protect.*

Which brought her full circle to what she'd learned about him tonight. Something else that had made it impossible to calm her restless mind. She kept thinking about what his life had been like. Comparing it to hers. Knowing that as soon as they'd walked into her parents' house, he had done the same.

She pushed up from the mattress, straining to hear any sound from the other side of the door. Even if Sean were sleeping, she'd feel better simply being in the same vicinity. If she were in the sitting room, she would at least be able to hear the reassuring sound of his breathing.

She pushed the covers back, swinging her legs over the edge of the bed. A flash of lightning illuminated the room, revealing for an instant the arrangement of her mother's beloved furnishings.

Tonight nothing felt familiar. It seemed alien and somehow frightening. Which was ridiculous.

Acknowledging that didn't prevent her from stepping onto the floor. She shrugged into the robe she'd laid at the foot of the bed. As thunder followed the lightning that had lit the room, she crossed the thick carpet on bare feet, almost running toward the door.

When she opened it, the low light on the table by the love seat temporarily blinded her. As soon as her vision adjusted, she realized that the sitting room was empty.

Her uneasiness over that discovery was disproportionate to the cause. Sean had gone to the bathroom. Or downstairs to the kitchen. Just because she was alone up here...

Alone. The word reverberated, causing her to wrap her arms around her body as her eyes surveyed the room again, paying special attention to its shadowed corners. As if she thought Sean might be hiding from her.

Which was even more ridiculous than her initial desire for companionship. She was a grown woman. Someone who was supposed to understand how the human mind worked.

Instead, she was fueling her own irrational fears. She took a breath, deliberately trying to quell her sense that something was wrong. "Sean?"

She waited, listening to the sound of the rain. Bathroom,

she thought, moving across the room toward the hall that would lead to her father's suite.

It was dark. Surely if Sean had left the sitting room, he would have turned on a light out here.

She fought against her growing fear, knowing, even as it filled her chest, that there must a perfectly legitimate explanation for his absence. He'd gone downstairs. He'd thought of something he needed to tell Bingham and didn't want to disturb her while he made the call. Or maybe he'd decided to get a good night's sleep in one of the other bedrooms.

Whatever he was doing, it wasn't cause for anxiety. This was her parents' home, with a state-of-the-art security system. That's why they'd ended up here.

And no matter how "organized" the Inquisitor was, he couldn't walk through walls. She was imagining bogeymen where none existed.

Except for the one who'd killed Carol Cummings.

Pushing that thought out of her head, she stepped out into the hall. She turned on the light in her father's bedroom to find its king-size bed still made, the bronze coverlet undisturbed. Although the bathroom door was open, she crossed to look inside. It was also empty.

Downstairs. A phone call or a midnight snack. Something mundane. Something easily explained as soon as she found him. He'd laugh about the fact that she'd been so frantic.

She hurriedly retraced her steps. As she exited the bedroom, heading toward the stairs, she noticed a dim light in the other wing, and suddenly everything fell into place.

If Sean had decided to sleep rather than stand guard, he wouldn't have used her father's bed. Not with three guest rooms only a few feet away. As she approached the top of the staircase, she looked down at the landing and then on to the foyer beyond.

With the rain there was no moonlight coming in the glass

panels on either side of the front door. Judging by the almost total darkness below, there were no lights on the first floor, which negated the possibility that Sean might be in the kitchen.

She raised her eyes, focusing on the light emanating from the other wing. Now certain that she knew where Sean was, she hurriedly crossed in front of the curving wall of windows that separated her parents' suites from the other bedrooms.

As she grew nearer, she could tell that the light was coming from her bedroom. Puzzled because that didn't seem to fit with her theory, her steps began to slow. She thought about calling out again, but because of her confusion, she didn't.

She walked toward the open door instead, stopping just before she reached it. Holding her breath, she leaned forward to look into the room.

Sean was holding one of her old dressage trophies. He appeared to be reading the engraving on its metal tag.

A perfectly logical explanation. Just as she'd told herself. She drew a calming breath and moved forward into the doorway. "What are you doing?"

He spun around, the gun she'd seen him take out of the duffel bag replacing the loving cup as if by some sleight of hand. Knees bent, he held the weapon out in front of him, its muzzle centered on her chest.

For seemingly endless seconds they remained frozen in that silent tableau, their mutual shock holding them motionless. He moved first, straightening out of his crouch as he lowered the gun. His mouth opened and then closed, but he didn't speak.

"I'm sorry," she whispered, realizing how very close he'd come to pulling that trigger.

And if he had, it would have been her fault. A man charged with protecting someone from a monster like the Inquisitor couldn't afford to be taken unawares.

"What the hell do you think you're doing?"

She should have been the one asking that question, considering where she'd found him. Shaken by what had almost happened, she told him the truth instead. "Looking for you."

"Why?"

A legitimate question. And she couldn't think of a single legitimate answer to it.

Because I couldn't sleep. Because I keep thinking about you. And Makaela. And Carol Cummings. And because I don't want to be alone.

She picked the least revealing. "I couldn't sleep. I thought that maybe if you were—"

"If I was what?"

"I thought maybe you were awake, too. When you weren't in the sitting room—" She realized she still didn't know why he'd left. "What are you doing in here?"

She glanced around at the familiar objects, trying to fathom what might have brought him to this room. Surely he hadn't come to look at the awards she'd won in junior high.

Without answering, he laid the gun on the top of her dresser and then bent to pick up the trophy he'd been holding when she'd walked in. In the confusion of that moment, she hadn't even realized he'd dropped it.

He set it back in place before he turned to look at her. She couldn't read whatever was in his eyes. All she knew was that right now they weren't cold. Or angry. If she were forced to characterize what she saw in them—

He was embarrassed, she realized. *Because he'd been snooping and she'd caught him?*

She supposed she should feel annoyed that her privacy had been invaded. But since she hadn't lived in this room in almost a decade, she couldn't drum up any indignation over his presence.

"Idle curiosity."

Just to see what makes you tick.

"About *those?*" She nodded toward the array of loving cups.

He hesitated, and then, with the arrogance she had become accustomed to, he said, "You're the psychologist. You figure it out."

"You were curious about me. But I thought you said you knew all you needed to know the day you came to my office."

He said nothing, still holding her eyes.

"Or is it possible that some of your preconceived ideas haven't turned out to be accurate?"

"You'd love to hear me admit to that, wouldn't you?"

"You bet your sweet ass I would."

His eyes widened, whether at her language or the force of the emotion behind it. One corner of his mouth lifted and was quickly controlled.

"So do I get an apology?" she prodded.

"Is that what you're waiting for? An apology?"

"I believe I deserve one. Don't you?"

For a moment he said nothing. Then he walked toward her until he was standing directly in front of her. The difference in their heights was emphasized by the tilt of her chin as she continued to hold his eyes challengingly.

His seemed to search her face. Finally his lips parted. She held her breath, unable to believe that he was finally going to admit he'd been wrong.

"Deserved or not, this is the only thing I want to give you right now." He lowered his head as he said the words until the last was whispered against her lips.

They, too, had parted because, at some point in the middle of that sentence, she had realized he was about to kiss her. And realized also how very much she wanted him to.

Twenty-Two

Still he waited, giving her the opportunity to protest. To refuse. To step back, breaking the contact between them.

She did none of those things. She shut her eyes instead, anticipating the feel of his lips closing over hers.

When they did, they were nothing like she'd expected. Warm and soft and very sure, they teased along her open mouth, dropping one small kiss after another until she ached for whatever came next. Then, as he finally enfolded her in his arms, his tongue invaded with a demanding expertise that for some reason surprised her.

It shouldn't have, she acknowledged, as he deepened the kiss. There had been no awkwardness in his embrace. No bumped noses. Nothing to detract from the intensity of what was happening. Nothing but a sense that this had been inevitable. And that it was right.

For days this tension had been building between them. It was the reason he got under her skin so easily. The reason she'd instinctively turned to him when she'd finally admitted he might be right about the Inquisitor. Her intuitive recognition of his strength had played a role in that decision, as well, of course.

Whatever sparked the attraction that had so quickly flared between them, she wanted this. Wanted him to kiss her. To hold her. To make love to her.

If she had met him anywhere else, under any other circumstances, she would have been as fascinated as she was now by a man so different from the others she'd known. She might not have pursued that fascination, recognizing how dangerous for her peace of mind someone like Sean Murphy would be. Now that they'd been thrown together, in a situation fraught with a different kind of danger, it had become impossible to maintain that necessary distance.

He lifted his head, breaking the kiss. Bereft, she opened her eyes to look up into his.

"Not the smartest thing I've ever done."

What he'd just said had nothing to do with her and everything to do with what was going on around them. And she understood that.

In all honesty, she even agreed with his assessment. It wasn't the smartest thing she'd ever done, either. At the moment, she didn't care.

She stood on tiptoe, stretching until her mouth was again open just beneath his. Teasingly, she ran her tongue along his upper lip. Before she had completed the motion, his mouth closed over hers again. Their tongues melded, moving together as if this were the thousandth kiss they'd shared rather than the first.

His fingers began to work at the loose knot she'd tied in the belt of her robe. After a few seconds it parted, allowing him to slip one hand into the narrow opening, its warmth and roughness grazing her hip. His other hand was pressed into the small of her back, urging her body into a closer intimacy with his.

The fingers of the hand that had invaded her robe cupped under her breast. She could feel their callused hardness even through the silk of her gown. As his thumb moved back and forth across her nipple, causing it to grow hard, a sweet heat began to build low in her body.

His lips left hers to trace along the curve of her jaw. Her head tilted, allowing him access to the sensitive skin below her ear. As his mouth trailed down her neck, his hand deserted her breast to push her robe and then the strap of her gown to one side, exposing her shoulder.

When his lips replaced his fingers there, she leaned her cheek against the crisp thickness of his hair. It smelled of soap. Shampoo. Clean and totally masculine. Infinitely appealing.

His mouth, still opened, glided across her collarbone and then retraced its path, again encountering the intrusive barrier of her clothing. With the intent of alleviating that particular problem once and for all, she leaned back slightly.

The air of the room touched the dampness his tongue had left on her skin, cooling it. Another sensation to be added to all those destroying any possibility that they might not make love tonight.

She slipped the robe off her shoulders, allowing it to fall to the floor. Then, before he had time for second thoughts, she stepped back into Sean's arms.

As if there had been no interruption, his lips resumed their exploration, moving inexorably toward the shadowed V between her breasts. Her breath caught as his mouth followed the deep neckline of her gown, another obstruction to what she now desperately wanted—the sweet, wet heat of his tongue against her bare skin.

As she made that admission, Sean slipped his thumb under one broad lace strap, easing it over her shoulder. Before she could protest—if she had had the strength of will—his lips began to move over the top of the now exposed swell of her breast. The rush of desire turned her knees to water, so intense she was forced to put her hands on his shoulders for support.

Then his mouth closed around her sensitized nipple. He suckled it strongly enough to create an answering pull deep within her belly.

Her quick intake of breath caused him to release the pressure. With his tongue he gently laved the areola instead, circling with a surprising tenderness. That sensation, although completely different from the more demanding one that had come before, intensified the aching emptiness between her legs.

Unexpectedly, his teeth closed over the hardened bud of her nipple. Although the bite was light, almost playful, her fingers tightened over his shoulders, nails digging into his back as pleasure mingled with pain.

Her hips strained upward, trying to satisfy her growing need by pushing into his erection. Through the material of his jeans, she could feel its heat and hardness. And she wanted them. Just as she wanted him.

His thumb hooked under the remaining strap of her gown, preparing to sweep it off her shoulder. If he did, like her robe, it would fall away, removing the remaining barrier of her clothing. She wanted that, too.

To feel the heat of his skin against hers. Flesh to flesh. And to make that happen…

As he prepared to push the strap down her arm, her fingers moved to the waistband of his jeans. Trembling, they fumbled over the metal buttons of his fly.

"Here?" he asked.

A question that should have been answered long before they'd reached this point. Despite the near-mindless haze of need and desire, she knew that she didn't want him to make love to her here. Not surrounded by the mementos of her childhood.

"One of the other rooms."

Sean didn't argue with her decision. He released the strap and took her arm instead, drawing her with him toward the door.

The interruption allowed her time to think of all the reasons why this was a bad idea. She didn't want them in her head. All she wanted was to be held. To be kissed until she was conscious of nothing but his lips moving against hers. To be loved.

To be loved...

How many times had she warned patients about the dangers of equating sex with love? Or even with emotional intimacy. Companionship. Comfort. Any of the dozens of other fulfillments people believed they could find in what was—and would be tonight—a purely physical act.

Right now, however, she wasn't going to analyze why, against all the familiar and wise injunctions about safety and morality and self-esteem, she was about to make love with a stranger. Something that was foreign to the carefully logical person she'd always been.

She wasn't looking for commitment. And neither was he.

All she wanted was the warmth of Sean's living, breathing body against hers. His strength beside her through the night, keeping her safe.

She needed to celebrate the fact that she was alive. Still alive, despite everything. And she could think of no better way to affirm that than by spending these remaining hours of darkness with a man who had, during the last few days, made her feel more alive than she had in years.

What could be wrong with rejoicing in the fact that together they had managed to keep the darkness at bay for another day? Another night. Another hour.

Sean had stripped the satin coverlet back from the sheets of the bed in the guest suite, allowing it to slide to the floor at its foot. Then, laying his wallet on the bedside table, he had unfastened his jeans, peeling them and his briefs down over muscled thighs and calves with that same economy of motion.

He stepped out of them and turned to face her. Despite the dimness of the room, it was clear that he was totally, almost shockingly aroused. Again, that blatant masculinity seemed out of place. Almost frightening.

Unaware of the effect his nudity was having, he removed a condom from his billfold, unwrapping it with what appeared to be the ease of long practice. In the middle of putting it on, he glanced up.

"What's wrong?"

Only with his question did she realize that she had stopped perhaps three feet from the bed, arms crossed over her body as if she were chilled. She licked her lips, trying to find the right words to explain why something she'd been so eager for only seconds ago now seemed full of risk.

"I'm just not sure—"

"I am. Sure enough for both of us. Come here."

What he'd said made little sense. Yet even as she acknowledged that, she gave in to his certainty.

She had already taken a step toward him when she realized she was still wearing her nightgown. She lifted her hands to push first one strap and then the other off her shoulders. The silk slipped free, sliding down her body to pool around her feet.

When she looked up, she saw that Sean's eyes had followed its descent. Then they lifted, making a slow examination of her body before they met hers.

What was within them helped ease the sense of alienation she had felt almost as soon as she'd stepped out of his arms. She needed to recapture the feeling of rightness, of inevitability, with which this had begun. And maybe the only way to do that was to step back into them. When he held out his hand, she put hers into it.

He pulled her against his side, releasing her fingers to put his arm around her shoulder. Then he lowered his head, pressing his lips against her hair.

It was a surprising gesture, especially from a man who was so hard. Part reassurance and part comfort. And she had no idea how he could have known she so very badly needed both.

He held her a moment before, using the hand on her shoulder, he urged her toward the bed. He put his left knee on its edge, and then, bringing her with him, lay down on the lavender-scented sheets.

As his body began to lower over hers, she looked into his face, again slightly alien in the darkness of the room. With his hand, he parted her legs, guiding his erection into the wetness of her body. She hadn't realized until then how ready for him she was. Not until he'd begun to push inside.

She'd closed her eyes, mouth opening on a sigh as she tried to relax her sudden tension at his invasion. If he were aware of her anxiety, it didn't cause him to hesitate.

With one sure, hard thrust, he entered her, driving deeper inside her body than she thought she could bear. His hips ground against hers, straining for an even greater penetration.

She must have made a sound in response. There was a fractional pause and then a minute shift of his body, so that, although they were still joined in that most intimate of connections, her body no longer bore the full weight of his.

His lips brushed against her hair before he lowered his forehead to rest on hers. "Shh…" he whispered. "Shh…"

Since no one could possibly hear her, even if she had cried out, obviously that was meant to soothe. As if he were quieting a fearful child. And in comparison to his surety and control, that's how she felt.

As in her bedroom, his hand found her breast. His thumb began again that slow back-and-forth movement against its nipple. Despite the apprehension she'd experienced, she gradually began to relax.

His body made no more demands. And by now, she had become accustomed to the feeling of fullness, recognizing it was part of the masculine strength that had drawn her to him from the first.

There was another shift of weight, this time a withdrawal. Afraid that her attack of nerves was responsible, she had opened her mouth to protest when he pushed into her again— harder, stronger, more powerfully than before. Testing, it seemed, the very limits of her body.

From deep within her came a reaction that had nothing to do with fear or apprehension. Unconsciously she raised her hips, reacting to his downward thrust.

Joined as they were, it was impossible he wasn't aware of her response. Whatever doubts she'd had seemed to dissipate as he began again to make that slow, controlled withdrawal.

Her muscles, acting of their own volition, tightened around his arousal, sheathing it as if to prevent his desertion. Then, before she was prepared, he drove into her again. And then, without giving her time to breathe or to think, if she'd been capable of either, again.

He turned his cheek against the tender skin of her throat. His late-night stubble was abrasive, a sensation that warred with the other that had begun to grow within her body.

No longer discomfort, but something that had had been born from the friction of his driving caress. A heat that wouldn't be denied. And could no longer be contained.

It ran in molten streams, searing along nerve pathways throughout her lower body. Melting all resistance and restraint. Destroying inhibition until she was no longer conscious of anything but the motion of his body as it strained above hers.

A tremor began in the very core of the flame he'd ignited. And then another. Faster and faster, until there was no space and no time between them. A continual ecstasy that left her hips arching to meet his every stoke, mindlessly matching the rhythm he'd established.

Already he'd taken her beyond the boundaries of her experience. She clung to the unraveling edge of her control, afraid to let go. Afraid, too, that if she refused, he would leave her behind. Alone and again bereft.

She could tell from his frenzied, almost convulsive movements that he was close to his own release. She wanted that— for him as well as for her—and yet she feared it, too.

A step into the unknown. Or a leap of faith. Whichever it was, she realized, the moment to make it was at hand.

She could let him take her with him. Or she could retreat, refusing to surrender the last dregs of a control she hadn't dreamed, until this moment, she would resist giving up.

She had believed that was part of why she'd sought this To relinquish her control. To acknowledge his in this, as she had in the other.

His breath came in short, ragged exhalations. She could feel his heart against her breasts, pounding as if it would tear its way out of his chest. So near. So near.

She wanted that, too. To be swept away from a reality she longed to deny to a place where she would no longer have to think, but only to feel. The sweat-slick dampness of his skin sliding over hers. Hair-roughened legs against the smoothness of hers. The hard wall of his chest pressing her breasts.

As the pressure built, screaming for the release that waited now only for her capitulation, her fingers found the coarse aliveness of the midnight hair.

His head lifted, neck straining backward, as the cataclysm began. Her control spiraled away into the darkness, finally lost as wave after wave of sensation broke over them. They clung together, riding out the storm they'd created.

When it was over, they lay together, still one, still joined, in the oldest communion. Incapable of speech, almost incapable of coherent thought, she finally lifted her hand, allowing the tips of her fingers to move slowly through his hair. To express with their touch all the feelings for which she had no words.

After a moment, he raised his head, propping on his elbows to look down on her again in the darkness. With his thumb, he pushed a strand of damp hair off her cheek.

"Thank you," she whispered.

That single dark brow arched, questioning. "For…?"

"Being sure."

"Half of command is commanding."

"Meaning…you weren't sure?"

"I was sure I wanted you. And sure it would be like this. As for the rest… I told you at the start this wasn't the smartest thing I've ever done."

She had already acknowledged that was probably true for her as well. Despite that, she had no regrets. She had gotten what she'd wanted.

To forget, at least for the moment. And to have Sean beside her, keeping that reality at bay.

One more day. One more night. One more hour.

Twenty-Three

Not the smartest thing he'd ever done.

Understatement of the year. Yet knowing that, openly acknowledging it, he had still made love to her.

Dr. Jenna Kincaid. The last woman in the world he should have come on to. Especially now. Especially here.

He turned away from the breakfast room window overlooking the pool to check on the coffee he'd started. The pot was full, so the brewing cycle was obviously complete.

It had taken him longer to figure out how to operate the damn thing than it had for the coffee to brew. State of the art. Like the security system. Like everything else about this place. All of it as far removed from his world as she was.

His hand hesitated in the act of lifting the carafe. That distance hadn't seemed to exist last night. Not in any way that mattered. And this morning...

This morning they would have to deal with what had happened. A complication that, like it or not, had forever changed their relationship.

In the cold light of dawn, Sean had discovered that, as great as last night had been, he didn't know how to deal with that alteration. He had never meant to get involved with her. Not like this. Now that he had—

His cell rang, startling him out of the circling thoughts that had troubled him since he'd slipped out of bed before dawn. He realized he was still holding the handle of the carafe, his cup unfilled. He put it down, reaching into the pocket of his jeans to fish out his phone.

He flipped it open. "Murphy."

"We got ourselves a witness." Bingham's voice held a note of triumph, as if he'd been the one to come up with the scenario that had garnered this, the cops' first break.

"And?"

Sean told himself that whatever this was, it might not lead anywhere. Creeps came out of the woodwork in a murder investigation, especially one as high profile as this. Despite all those caveats, his heart began to pound as he waited.

"Gray car. Maybe silver. Sedan. She thinks it was an import. Something 'ridiculously expensive,' to use her words."

Far less than he'd hoped for, Sean acknowledged, considering the lieutenant's excitement. And he would have been more confident if the description of the car had come from a man. Maybe that was sexist, but he'd never met a woman who was good with identifying makes or models. Automobiles were too much alike these days to overcome what he'd always seen as an inherently feminine disinterest. Maybe Bingham's witness was the exception, but from the lack of detail, he doubted it. Still, it was more than they'd had yesterday.

"She saw Cummings get in?" he asked.

"She saw her talking to whoever was inside. Pouring down rain, and the girl's leaning in the window talking. That's why she remembers it. Right on Twentieth Street, maybe a block from the bar where Cummings left her friends."

"Where was your witness when she made the sighting?"

"Driving by. Going up the hill." Apparently Bingham realized that might not mean much to someone from out of town. "Opposite to the direction our boy was headed, which was away from the Points. She noticed the girl as she passed."

"Get a look at the driver?"

"Not enough for any kind of description. Said she thought it was a man because her impression at the time was that what was going on was a pickup."

Sadly, she'd been right.

"If you put out that information—the date, approximate time, weather, location, a description of the car, whatever she gave you—you might get somebody else who saw the same thing. Somebody who hasn't put what they saw together with the murder."

Sean guessed from the silence on the other end that the cops hadn't yet done that. He suspected, now that the idea had been broached, Bingham, who was nobody's fool, would get on the release of those details right away.

"I'm gonna put an officer out there, by the way. Just thought you should know," the detective said, rather than commenting on Sean's suggestion.

"At Five Points?" The non sequitur had thrown him. What good did Bingham think having a cop at the scene would do now?

"At Dr. Kincaid's parents' house. You *are* still there, aren't you?"

Fishing for information? If so, he'd made a very good guess. Which probably meant he hadn't been guessing.

"I don't understand," Sean hedged.

"I talked to Dr. Kincaid's employer this morning." Paper rattling in the background punctuated that information. "A Dr. Paul Carlisle. He's the one who told me where she is. Since you told me yesterday that you were still together…"

Sean stifled the profanity that was his immediate reaction. He'd warned Jenna about telling anyone where they were. He'd thought she understood what was riding on that.

Of course, just because Carlisle had given the information to the police didn't mean he'd passed it on to anyone else. Sean had to believe a man in his position wasn't a complete idiot. He just wasn't willing to bet Jenna's life on it.

She had. And it was up to him to deal with the fallout.

"I told you what would happen if you surround her with cops," he warned, working to control his anger.

"You also told me how the good citizens of this town would react to another murder. I got an earful from Dr. Carlisle this morning on the same subject. We got a lead now, Sergeant Murphy. Somebody came forward less than twelve hours after we put out the scenario you and Dr. Kincaid provided. And as you say, if one person saw something, maybe someone else did, too. This department isn't about to use Jenna Kincaid as bait to try and catch this bastard." The lieutenant's voice softened, his tone verging on threatening. "And no matter what your arrangement with her might have been before today, we aren't going to allow you to do that, either. You need to be real clear about that."

Sean didn't bother to deny the accusation. After what had happened last night, all the arguments he'd used to convince Jenna—as well as those with which he'd once convinced himself—didn't seem nearly as compelling.

Maybe it was time do what everyone had told him he should from the beginning. Get out of the way and let the authorities handle the hunt for the Inquisitor.

All he was obligated to do right now was keep Jenna safe. If his initial instinct had been right—and he had no reason to doubt it had been—that would be a full-time job.

"I got no objection to whatever deal the two of you got

worked out," Bingham continued into his silence, his accent thickening. "That's Dr. Kincaid's business. Mine's making sure our boy don't ever get 'lucky' again."

"Will you keep us informed?"

Another silence, longer than the previous one. "I'll stay in touch with Dr. Kincaid," the lieutenant conceded finally. "Maybe she'll think of something else that'll be helpful."

Before Sean could respond, the connection was broken. He closed his phone, pushing it back into his front pocket.

"Bingham?"

He turned to find Jenna standing in the kitchen doorway. She was wearing jeans and a gray sweatshirt over a white tee.

Her hair had been pulled back and tied with some kind of elasticized thing; her face was devoid of makeup. She looked about fifteen. Despite that, he wanted her. He wanted to make love to her. Right here. Right now. On her mother's table. On the goddamn floor if he had to.

He turned back to the coffeepot before she became aware of exactly how much he wanted her. He filled the mug he'd set out and then reached into the cabinet above his head to take down another. As he poured coffee into the second mug, he tried to occupy his mind with thoughts of anything other than how her body had felt moving under his last night.

Her responsiveness had been a surprise. For some asinine reason he'd thought she would carry that cool demeanor into bed. Nothing could have been further from the truth.

"Thanks," Jenna said.

While he'd been struggling to regain control, she had crossed the room. She was standing at his elbow, waiting for him to give her the mug.

In spite of the coffee's heady aroma, he was aware again of the dark, sensual fragrance that had filled his senses last night as they'd made love. The erection he'd been trying to deny was suddenly full blown. And with the thin denim of his aged jeans, there was no way in hell she wasn't going to be aware of it.

However, he'd never run away from a challenge in his life. He was a little old to start now.

He turned, holding the brimming cup out to her. She took it in both hands, lifting it to her lips to take a sip. As she lowered the mug, her eyes automatically tracked downward.

He hadn't bothered to search for his shirt in the predawn darkness of the bedroom. He'd simply pulled on the jeans that he'd discarded last night, not even bothering to fasten the top button. Then—barefoot and bare-chested—he had come downstairs where he could think without the temptation of Jenna's beautifully nude body curled at his side.

It was as if he could feel her gaze moving down his stomach, following the line of dark hair that would eventually disappear into the waistband of his jeans. The sensation was so real, his abdominal muscles tightened in response to it. And he knew the exact moment she became aware of the effect she was having.

Her eyes leaped up to meet his. For an instant there was something that looked like amusement in their dark depths. Before he could be sure that's what he was seeing, she lowered them, staring down again into the steaming mug.

The pretense that she hadn't noticed his arousal annoyed him. If she wanted to play games…

"They've got a witness."

The blunt statement accomplished what he'd intended. When she looked up, every trace of amusement had been wiped from her eyes. They were wide and dark, intently focused on his face.

"Someone *saw* him?"

"They saw the Cummings girl talking to a man in a car. Same day. Approximate time of her disappearance. *And* in the pouring rain. They've got a description of the car."

She took a breath, closing her mouth, which had opened as he talked. "Good enough to nail him?"

He shook his head. "Good enough to narrow the field."

She nodded. "That's something, I guess."

"Something they *didn't* have before you figured out why he broke his pattern. I suggested they put what they have out there in case it might jog someone else's memory."

"If they do, then…he'll know."

He didn't understand what had prompted the remark. It sounded as if she thought the bulletin might cause the killer to back off. To lie low for a while.

In her position she couldn't possibly be opposed to that. Sean was no longer sure he was. Considering what was at stake.

"Bingham's putting someone out here."

"*Someone?* You mean…an officer?"

"Apparently he's decided you need protection. Your boss has been on his case."

"Paul?" She shook her head. "I didn't think Paul even knew who was in charge of the task force."

"Bingham called him trying to locate you. It seems to have worked."

He didn't make the accusation overtly. She was smart enough to figure out that he was angry. And why. He could tell by the change in her face that she had.

"I'm sorry. Paul's my boss. I thought I should tell him what was going on. But…" She shook her head. "Believe me, I had no idea that he'd tell the police."

"You might want to think about making sure he doesn't tell anyone else."

Her eyes widened. "I told him when we talked not to tell

anyone. Why he would…" She shook her head again. "Look, I said I'm sorry. I just didn't think—"

"That's the problem," he interrupted harshly. "You didn't think."

"Paul Carlisle is a highly respected psychiatrist." The apologetic note in her voice had been replaced by anger. "He's been a force in this town for twenty years. He built the successful group practice I'm part of from scratch."

"And he didn't need to know where you are. Not if you want us to pretend to believe this location might still be safe."

"You've made your point," she said, her face tight. "I swear it won't happen again. I'll call Paul and tell him it's imperative that he not tell anyone else where I am."

"Yeah, you do that. While you're at it, try to remember what I told you yesterday. There are no second chances in this. No room for error. Carol Cummings probably thought the guy in the big gray car was a safe bet, too. Look where that got her."

Again, the long hours of the day had passed far too slowly. Jenna had avoided the downstairs den where Sean and the officer Bingham sent out kept the radio on, listening to the intermittent news broadcasts. As far as she could tell, there had been no further developments in the investigation.

The patrolman who showed up for the second shift turned out to be one of the men who'd escorted her home and searched her apartment two nights ago. Despite the fact that the other officer had been on the premises all day, the kid had insisted on doing the same thing here as soon as he'd arrived.

Faced with Sean's refusal to participate in what he clearly viewed as a farce, Jenna was again relegated to giving the grand tour. At the last second Sean had decided to join them.

His quietness as they moved through the rooms was in

marked contrast to Officer Daniels, who became increasingly verbal. He made no pretense of not being impressed by or envious of her parents' wealth, even to whistling when she opened the door to her father's extensive gym in the basement.

She found the entire exercise embarrassing. Especially in light of Sean's determined refusal to be impressed by anything. She ended up feeling as if she, as well as the house, had been judged and found wanting.

She again raided the freezer for dinner, thankful it was so well stocked. Although the three of them ate together at the breakfast room table, there was a marked strain between the men.

The young cop proudly showed off pictures of his wife and infant daughter, born the previous summer. Then he tried to engage Sean in conversation about his experiences in the military. He gave up in the face of the noncommittal responses. All in all, as uncomfortable a meal as she could remember.

She had loaded the dishwasher and cleaned up the kitchen, drawing out the tasks while the young patrolman made a final physical check of the grounds. She wasn't sure where Sean spent that hour. All she knew was that he was still furious about what he'd obviously viewed as her flaunting of his orders.

The chill that existed between them—especially in comparison to last night—made her regret having told Paul anything. It wasn't that she doubted her employer or his judgment—after all, telling the police where she was wasn't exactly a breech of security. But if she had dreamed Sean would see it as such, she would never have done it. And the sense of guilt that she'd betrayed his trust gnawed at her.

"If it's okay with you—" Daniels said, sticking his head in the kitchen "—I think I'll set up the command post in here."

The military terminology grated. As if he were playing soldier. "Wherever you think, of course."

"I might make a pot of coffee," he said, walking over to peer at her parents' Capresso machine. "Nights get long on a job like this."

"Of course. Do you want me to set it up for you?"

"You sound like my mom," he said cheerfully. "I'm pretty sure I can manage to brew coffee by myself."

He probably didn't mean anything derogatory by the comment. There were enough years between them that, ridiculously, it stung. Jenna discovered that she didn't give a damn whether he figured out the intricacies of the coffeemaker or not.

"Okay. Then…I guess I'll see you in the morning," she said, walking past him toward the door.

She wasn't sure of the exact protocol of having a cop staking out her kitchen, but she doubted he would want her wandering around downstairs once he started whatever he was here to do. In actuality, she wasn't entirely comfortable with the combination of the kid's inexperience and the fact that he possessed a powerful weapon.

The only good thing about the situation was that she was reassured by Bingham's choice for this assignment. Obviously he wasn't too worried that the Inquisitor might show up out here tonight. And since Sean had virtually disappeared after supper, apparently neither was he.

"You don't happen to know where Sergeant Murphy is, do you?" she asked before she stepped through the kitchen door.

Probably an exercise in futility. Since they were both persona non grata to Sean, she doubted he had been any more forthcoming with Daniels than he'd been with her.

"He went upstairs a little while ago. I'll guess I should tell you what I told him. You come wandering around down here in the dark, and I'm going to have to treat you just like you were an intruder. This may be your house, Dr. Kincaid, but tonight it's my territory."

A shoot-first-and-ask-questions-later mentality that might very well get someone hurt. Only it wouldn't be her.

"I don't think you have anything to worry about, Officer Daniels. I certainly don't intend to be wandering around in *your* territory. At least not before daylight."

Surprised at how annoyed she'd been by his comment, she walked out into the hall to keep from saying more than she should. She wondered how Sean had responded to that warning. Considering her own reaction, she could pretty much imagine his. Given the fact that he'd already been angry with her…

She had thought that last night would have changed their relationship in ways that were irreparable. Ways that would have destroyed the animosity with which it had begun. Now…

Now she had no idea what kind of reception she should expect from the man who'd made love to her throughout last night. And more troubling from her perspective, she couldn't decide what kind she wanted.

Given his attitude today, she wasn't feeling particularly romantic. Still, despite her annoyance, she couldn't deny the anticipation she felt at the thought of seeing him again. Alone. And without the intrusive presence of Bingham's patrolmen.

At the realization of what that might mean, the longing for his touch, which she'd denied all day, ached in her lower body again. From force of habit, she turned off the hall light as she passed the switch.

In the resulting darkness, she lifted her eyes, looking for light filtering down from the second floor. There was none. Maybe Sean had decided to take advantage of the policeman's vigil and catch up on the sleep he'd missed last night.

Somehow she didn't believe that. She would bet that his

assessment of Officer Daniels paralleled her own. Which meant he would probably be waiting for her in the sitting room attached to her mother's bedroom, planning to stand guard all night as she slept. Or...

She closed her mind to the other possibility. The one that set her pulse racing.

Whichever it was to be, there was no point in delaying the inevitable. She took one final look up the stairs before she put her hand on the banister. Then, aware for the first time of an exhaustion that seemed to have invaded every muscle, she began the ascent.

As she approached the first landing, she glanced up again. The darkness at the top of the stairs seemed total. If Sean was awake, she should be able to see a thread of light even if he'd closed his door.

She began to climb the remaining flight of stairs, choosing the one that led to her parents' wing. As she neared the top, she felt as if the silence of the house were closing around her. As if, despite her knowledge to the contrary, she were the only inhabitant. *The only living inhabitant.*

She had no idea why that phrase crept into her consciousness. She rejected it as she stepped onto the second-floor landing.

Officer Daniels was in the kitchen. She'd just seen him. Talked to him.

And Sean—

That thought shattered when an arm closed around her waist, pulling her back into a hard chest. A hand was pressed tightly over her mouth, preventing the intake of air that would have fueled her scream.

Twenty-Four

She knew who held her even before Sean put his lips against her ear. He had apparently spent the time she'd been cleaning the kitchen by taking a shower. The scent of soap surrounded her, replacing fear with a very different emotion.

"Shh…" he whispered against her ear. "You don't want Supercop to come storming up here, do you?"

Without thinking, she put her hand up to touch his cheek. Despite the lateness of the hour, it was perfectly smooth.

Even though it had seemed Sean hadn't looked her way all day, at some point he'd obviously noticed the beard burn on her throat, the result of last night's lovemaking. He'd taken steps to see that didn't happen tonight.

Anticipation created a release of moisture, her body already preparing for his entrance. Although he couldn't possibly be aware of it, she was embarrassed by her eagerness.

She turned, still enclosed in his embrace, to look up at him. They were close enough that, despite the darkness, she could see his eyes, their blue luminous against the shadowed planes and angles of his face.

"I thought you were still mad at me." As soon as the words

came out of her mouth, she felt childish. Ridiculous. All the things he could so easily reduce her to.

"I am." His mouth lowered to hers. His tongue teased along her parted lips, as his hand again found her breast.

Tonight he cut through the preliminaries, slipping his palm underneath the bottom band of her sweatshirt. His hand traced over her stomach on its journey to its ultimate destination. The abrasiveness of his palm and callused fingers against her bare skin sent chills along her spine.

He caught her nipple between his thumb and index finger, squeezing with enough force to cause it to harden. And with enough force, she acknowledged, to be painful as well.

"Can't you tell how angry?"

She was totally out of her depth. No one she'd ever had a relationship with would have admitted to being angry at the same time he was fondling her. Roughly fondling her, she amended.

Sean did it as if daring her to react. To refuse his touch. To do something.

She closed her eyes, instead, standing on tiptoe so that her mouth could make contact with his. This time he relented, allowing the kiss.

Influenced by the memory of how he could make her feel, every nerve ending responded. Heat shimmered through her body, rekindling the fires of desire that had, by necessity, been banked throughout the day.

His lips seemed to drug her, pushing all other thoughts from her mind, until there was room there only for him. And for this.

Eventually he broke the kiss by leaning back to look down at her. "This isn't any smarter than it was last night."

She didn't bother to answer. No matter what he felt about the passion that had flared between them, it wouldn't change what was about to happen. They had both known that from the instant he'd put his arm around her waist to pull her against his chest.

"The other wing." She stretched upward again to put her lips against his. As far as she was concerned, there had already been too much talk.

Without answering, he turned his head, looking down the stairs. She had actually forgotten that they weren't alone.

"What about Daniels?"

"He isn't coming up here." Sean's assertion was made with what sounded like absolute certainty.

"How can you be sure?"

The thought of their making love with the young policeman in the kitchen below wasn't appealing. The idea that he might at some point come up to check on them, one she hadn't entertained until Sean denied the possibility, didn't bear thinking about.

"Because when he warned me about wandering around down there during the night, I returned the favor."

It took her a second. When she understood what he'd done, she laughed out loud.

Sean put his palm over her mouth again, his hold light. Almost, as hard as that was to believe, playful. "Shh…"

She obeyed, but she couldn't help smiling at the thought of Sean warning Daniels about the dangers of straying into *his* territory. Not that the cocky young cop didn't deserve that.

Still, since the officer had the authority of his badge behind him, as well as Bingham's support, she was surprised Sean had crossed him. Maybe the result of all those years of being in charge of green troops coming to the fore.

As they should. Especially if local law enforcement was going to send a kid to do a man's job.

Especially when a man was already on it.

The word evoked memories of last night, as well as anticipation of what was to come. And she didn't want that to be delayed any longer by a discussion of Officer Daniels.

"Come on," she urged, taking his hand to draw him through the darkness toward the guest rooms.

She'd made the bed this morning in the one they'd used last night, but she hadn't changed the sheets. There would be time for that before her mother came home.

A wave of uneasiness swept over her as she thought about her parents' disapproval of what she was doing. Of course, other than the fact that she was in their home, she owed them no explanation or apologies for how she lived her life. She was, after all, thirty-four years old. An adult.

And compared to most women her age, her sex life had been pretty tame. Discreet. Smart. Safe.

Until last night. And tonight, she added.

And no matter what, she would have no regrets about either.

Jenna had probably been aware of the sound on some level long before she awoke. Still, when she opened her eyes to the near-total darkness of the bedroom, it took a moment to identify it.

Rain. Beating against the roof and windows with enough force to be audible, despite the house's solid construction.

For a moment the image of Carol Cummings leaning into the Inquisitor's car in just such a downpour was in her head. She destroyed it, refusing to allow those thoughts any place here.

She turned, burrowing closer to the strong, warm body of the man who slept at her side. Her momentary uneasiness dissipated, destroyed by the steadiness of his breathing.

She lay, listening to the unchanging rhythm of it. A slow

nasal intake followed by a sighing release. Not quite a snore, but still, completely and comfortingly masculine.

She closed her eyes, trying to return to the dreamless sleep she'd enjoyed before the storm awakened her. Instead, unbidden, her eyelids lifted again as she listened to another sound. One that intruded on the drumming rain and the pattern of Sean's steady breathing.

She held her breath, trying to decide what she was hearing. Low and regular, it lay like a pulse beneath the other noises.

A dripping faucet? Somehow, despite its regularity, the tone wasn't right. It sounded more like—

An alarm, she realized. As if someone had set a clock in one of the other bedrooms and then forgotten to turn it off.

She eased up on her elbow, taking care not to disturb Sean. Even then she was unable to determine the distance or direction from which the beep came. It might be something like a wristwatch alarm, she realized, leaning down to put her ear near the one Sean wore on his left wrist.

Assured it wasn't that, she straightened. At her urging, Sean had locked the door of the guest suite where they slept. It was clear now that the beeping was coming from somewhere beyond this room.

Whatever it was, it could beep all night as far as she was concerned. She lay back down, closing her eyes as she willed her body to relax into the solid warmth of Sean's.

Despite her intent, she was still aware of the sound, throbbing like a toothache. The rain had slackened, making the other seem louder now than it had before.

She opened her eyes again, focusing on the wall opposite the bed. She could see nothing other than some slight variation in its darkness, probably caused by the shadows of the trees outside the curtained windows.

Still the sound came and went with the regularity of her

heartbeat. Silently she released the sighing breath she hadn't realized she was holding.

Ridiculous, she told herself. It was. Still, she knew she wasn't going to be able to sleep with whatever that was going off and on all night.

She pushed up on her elbow again, looking down at Sean. He was turned on his side, his lips parted. One hand, wrist bent, was curled against his chin.

He looked at peace and, for the first time since she'd known him, vulnerable. She remembered the exhaustion she'd noticed in his eyes this morning. After the last few nights spent guarding her, he needed the kind of undisturbed sleep he was finally getting.

She hated to wake him up to check on what might turn out to be nothing. An alarm clock. Some kind of weather signal her dad had installed on his computer. Anything. Or nothing.

No room for error. And no second chances.

Sean had slipped the gun under his pillow. The smart thing to do would be to wake him and let him go outside the room to find whatever was beeping.

For all she knew, it might be his cell phone, set to alarm at a certain time. She couldn't remember seeing him take that out of the pocket of his jeans when he'd undressed. Of course by that time, she hadn't been paying much attention to things like that.

Maybe he'd used his phone while he'd waited for her in her mother's sitting room. The thought of her mom's domain, every item there dear and familiar, was strangely reassuring.

Of course, the same could be said of everything in this house. A house with a very expensive security system. And with a cop on guard duty below. Maybe she could just call down the stairs and asked Officer Daniels to check out the noise—

"What's wrong?"

Startled by the low question, she glanced down to find

Sean looking up at her. Trying to make a decision, she hadn't even realized he was awake.

"Something's beeping."

His gaze left her face, focusing on the ceiling. She held her breath as he listened. The rain had picked up, so that she wasn't sure he would be able to hear the sound.

She needn't have worried. He flung the covers back, leaping out of bed. In one motion, he bent, pulling on the jeans he'd dropped on the floor. Although she never saw him reach for it, the gun was suddenly in his hand.

"Get dressed," he barked.

He crossed to the door in a couple of long strides, leaning his ear against it. Then he bent, seeming to peer under it.

Fascinated, she watched him, believing that any minute he'd let her in on what he was thinking. He straightened instead, looking back at the bed where, on her knees, she'd been waiting.

"What the hell are you doing? Get your clothes on."

The command pushed her into action. She scrambled in the darkness to find the jeans and T-shirt she'd donned yesterday. All she could locate were the jeans and sweatshirt. She pulled them on and then hurried across the room, coming to a stop beside him.

The beep was louder here. "What *is* that?" she whispered.

"I'm not sure, but…it could be some kind of smoke detector. Automatic relay?"

He might as well have been speaking Greek. "What?"

"The security system. Does it automatically relay a breach or a fire to the authorities?"

She had no idea. When she had lived here, alarms had gone to the security company. Of course that had been more than ten years ago. "I don't know. We have to get out of here."

"I can't smell smoke—" Sean said, his voice sounding far too calm for her growing panic.

"It's downstairs." She had no idea why she was so sure of that. Maybe because of their obvious distance from whatever they were hearing.

"Stay behind me," Sean said. "No matter what happens, stay with me. This may be nothing."

Sean stepped to the other side of the door. Then he reached out and opened it with his left hand. He hesitated, nose raised slightly, obviously testing the air.

She did the same, taking a deep breath. She couldn't smell smoke. With the door open, however, the alarm was louder. More insistent.

"Come on." As Sean slipped out through the narrow opening, she followed.

He headed for the stairs, stopping to look back at her when he reached their head. When she arrived at that vantage point, she could see nothing frightening below. No flames. Not even the smell of smoke in the air. Still the alarm pulsed, seeming more frantic with each passing second.

"Daniels?" Sean called.

They waited, listening for a response. And hearing none.

"Is there another set of stairs?"

She shook her head, forgetting that he might not be able to see the gesture. "Only this one. There used to be a rope ladder—"

She stopped because she'd remembered what had happened to that. She'd taken it to college with her. It was probably packed away in one of the boxes in the garage.

"This is it."

"Okay. We're going down. Stay behind me. Hold on to my waistband so I'll know you're there."

She nodded, but he'd already turned to start down the stairs. He held on to the banister with one hand, the gun in the other.

At the first landing, he stopped and called again. "Daniels? You okay?"

The only response was the beeping.

She took another breath, again testing the air. This time, underlying the familiar scents of her parents' home, was the terrifying whiff of something burning.

Twenty-Five

Sean didn't like anything about this. Not the smoke, which had quickly grown thicker as they descended the stairs. Not the fact that the kid hadn't answered his call. And especially not the absolute certainty in his gut that what was happening right now had something to do with the Inquisitor.

Despite the reality that the cops were probably closer to the killer than they'd ever been before, Sean had never expected the bastard would just give up. But he also hadn't expected he would so radically change a methodology that had been successful for more than seven years.

This was no longer about stalking his next victim. It had become personal. Between the two of them. With Jenna as the pawn.

He had known he would have to be on his guard every second. He just hadn't believed that the maniac would try to burn the house down around them.

"I think it's coming from the kitchen." Jenna coughed, holding her hand over her mouth as, pulled by the natural ventilation created by the two stories, smoke now swirled up the staircase. "He was going to set up there."

"What?"

"Daniels. In the kitchen. He said he needed coffee to make it through the night."

That might explain why the cop hadn't answered. If he had been in the room where the fire broke out, it would have taken only a matter of seconds for him to be overcome by smoke. People always believed they had longer than they did before the oxygen ran out.

"Front door," Sean ordered, taking Jenna's arm to pull her down the remaining steps.

"What about—" The rest was lost as her lungs tried to expel the toxins she'd breathed in.

It didn't matter that she hadn't finished. He knew what she wanted him to do. Under any other circumstances, he would have agreed. Under these...

"He's on his own."

He managed to get the words out, but opening his mouth to do it let in enough of the choking fumes to set off his own coughing jag. Ignoring his need to breathe, he continued to pull her down the stairs.

They were almost to the bottom. On this level there seemed to be no air left inside the thick pall that obscured the front door. Its pale rectangle had been clearly visible from the top of the stairs. Whatever was on fire was creating an enormous amount of smoke, and it was filling the house very quickly.

Jenna's sudden stop pulled her elbow from his grip. "It's only been a couple of minutes. If you get him into fresh air—"

That was followed by more coughing. In the midst of it, he caught the words "fire department." Surely, given the house's vaunted security system, she was right about that.

His willingness to try to rescue Daniels wasn't the problem. Maybe it was better Jenna didn't realize what was.

Deciding not to waste breath arguing, Sean concentrated

on finding the door. When he had, he located the knob and turned it with his left hand. Nothing happened.

Night latch.

Fingers searching like a blind man's, he finally found the latch and threw it. This time the knob turned. He jerked the door open, but it caught hard after moving inward an inch or two. Still, the rush of night air that came in through the narrow opening was like an elixir.

He drew in deep draughts of it even as he reached up to dislodge the chain. Jenna's fingers were there before his.

She pushed the door closed again, shutting off the precious supply of air long enough to slip the end of the chain from the slot. Then, finding the knob with the ease of long familiarity, she got the door open.

He shoved her through, following her across the wide porch and down the brick steps. Coughing, eyes and throat burning, they ran a few feet out onto the lawn before they stopped almost simultaneously.

Jenna bent over, drawing in ratcheting lungfuls of the moisture-laden air between paroxysms of whooping. Although he ached to join her, that was a luxury Sean couldn't afford.

He held the Glock out in both hands, blinking to clear eyes blurred with tears. He scanned the manicured grass and the trees beyond. Nothing stirred in the darkness. There was no sound but rain, which fell with steady tranquility around them.

"Sean."

He turned and found that Jenna had straightened and was looking back at the house. In their haste to get out, they'd left the front door open. The outside air pouring through it would fuel the conflagration.

He looked to the left of the entrance, expecting to see

flames consuming the rooms beyond the glass of the windows. There were none. Nor was there the eerie glow normally associated with them.

Maybe, despite the thickness of the smoke, the fire itself was still confined to the kitchen. Or maybe Jenna had been mistaken about its location.

His gaze swept the entire length of the house. Wherever the blaze was, it wasn't visible from the exterior. And if it wasn't in the kitchen, then…

Then it was possible Daniels was alive. Maybe he'd been overcome by smoke before he could make it to the front door.

Sean glanced back at Jenna. She was looking at him as if she were waiting for him to do something. And the only thing he could do—

Where the hell were the fire engines? he thought, physically turning to look toward the road that fronted the property. And more importantly, the paramedics they would carry? It wouldn't do any good to get Daniels out if there was no one here to give him the treatment he would need immediately.

He glanced at Jenna again, her eyes dark in a too-pale face. She was still breathing as if she'd run a race.

They both had. One that had determined whether they lived or died. And this time they'd won.

Life and death. How many times had he thought that since this had begun. Decisions that hinged on a thread. Like Carol Cummings's decision to get into a car with a stranger.

Or going back inside that cloud of toxins to look for a fallen man? One who could be anywhere on the smoke-shrouded first floor?

The familiar words and the burden they had conveyed throughout his career echoed inside his head. *A fallen man…*

But not *his.* And not his responsibility. *Except that which every human being has for the life of another.*

Despite what he'd thought when he'd heard the alarm, there had been no indication that the killer had anything to do with this. If he were here, he'd missed his best opportunity to take Sean out when, blinded by the smoke, they'd come through the front door.

Jenna was safe. And the kid inside...

The image of the baby in the photograph Daniels had shown him would haunt him if he didn't try. He, as much as anyone, knew what this kind of loss would do to her.

"Here," he said, holding the Glock out to Jenna.

"What's that for?"

"Stand right here." He pulled her roughly over to the oak that centered the right side of the yard, positioning her so that her back was against its massive truck. "Don't move until I get back. If you see anybody out here besides me or Daniels or the firemen," he added, trying to cover his bases, "point this at them—" He thrust the gun into her hand, wrapping her fingers around the grip. "And squeeze the trigger. Don't try to aim. Hold it out in front of you like when you were a kid playing cowboys."

At the look on her face, he knew she'd never done that. She'd probably been the kind to play with dolls.

Then pray God she wouldn't need those hurried instructions, all he had time for if he had any chance of getting the cop out alive.

Suddenly he realized there were a dozen other things he needed to say. Some he hadn't known he felt until this moment. And because of that, it was probably better he *didn't* say them.

He turned and ran back across the lawn toward the open door. As he took the steps two at a time, he inhaled, filling his lungs with the clean night air. Then, without looking back, he plunged again into the swirling mass of smoke.

As he entered, he tried to remember the layout of the

house. Because he was unable to see anything to orient him, he couldn't even be certain he was headed in the right direction. The oxygen he'd taken in wouldn't last long enough to search the foyer and hall on his hands and knees, the only sure way to locate a body in this darkness.

All he could do was keep going in the direction he thought would lead to the kitchen on the off chance he might stumble over Daniels's body. And if he didn't—

He blocked the possibility of that outcome as he moved, hands outstretched in front of him. The fact that there was no light coming from the back of the house indicated the fire was advanced enough that it had gotten to the wiring. If that was the case, he didn't understand why he couldn't see or hear it.

Suddenly he broke into a clearing in the dense pall that had surrounded him since he'd come through the front door. The smoke seemed to eddy away, revealing the kitchen doorway.

He ran through it, forcing his burning eyes to search the room that seemed remarkably clear, considering the thickness of the fumes in the front of the house. White cabinets gleamed dimly in the darkness and across the room—

He sprinted toward the dark shape sprawled on the pale tiles. He bent, grabbing the cop's shoulder to turn him so he could see his face.

By that time he'd understood the significance of the black circle underneath the body. Although his eyes were opened wide, staring up at Sean with a silent entreaty, Daniels's throat had been cut from ear to ear.

Realization was instantaneous. Sean released his hold on the body, allowing it to fall back facedown on the floor.

He sprang to his feet and was in the act of turning back toward the kitchen doorway, when something exploded against the side of his head. He fought to remain conscious, reaching out to grab onto the figure that had materialized in front of him.

It moved, eluding his fingers. And then, unable to do anything else, Sean watched as whatever his assailant had hit him with the first time again connected with his skull.

Too long. Far too long.

Jenna wished she'd at least tried to look at her watch when Sean had gone back inside. That had been the last thing on her mind. Now, as more and more time went by, she wasn't sure whether her anxiety was turning seconds into minutes or whether he'd really been inside as long as she thought.

She'd still heard no sirens, she realized, glancing once more toward the highway. Surely by now the volunteer fire department that served this area had had time to respond.

She took a tentative step away from the oak, but Sean's words echoed in her brain. She raised the Glock, holding it in front of her as she had seen him do, while she scanned the area around her.

She understood Sean's fears. She even shared his suspicion that the fire was too coincidental.

But two lives were at stake. How could she continue to try to protect her own at the possible cost of theirs?

She took another step and then another until she was running toward the open door, only to slow as she approached it. The smoke that had been thick enough to obscure every object in the foyer seemed to have dissipated in the time she'd been outside.

Of course, fresh air had been pouring into the room. Since there seemed as yet to be no visible flames, maybe whatever had been on fire had literally burned itself out. Maybe Daniels had been cooking something and had fallen asleep.

Even as she postulated that, she knew there had been too much smoke for that. Whatever the reason for it, she had to find Sean and somehow get him out. Maybe by then the firemen would be here. Even if they were too late to help Daniels…

As she progressed down the hall toward the back of the house, the smoke thinned before her, so that by the time she reached the kitchen doorway she could see it. Obviously not the source of the fire as she'd thought.

She turned, looking back down the hall. From this point it seemed as if the whole house was continuing to clear. Although her throat was still raw, she discovered that she could take a breath without setting off that terrible coughing.

"Sean?"

There was no response. She took a step back toward the front door, pitching her voice in that direction.

"Sean? Where are you?"

Nothing.

The only thing she knew for certain was that, on her advice, he'd been headed to the kitchen when he'd entered. Without information to the contrary, that seemed to be the place to start looking.

There was a door there leading out to the pool. If Sean *had* found Daniels, it would make more sense to drag him out through that exit than back to the front of the house.

She turned and walked toward the kitchen doorway. Remembering Sean's warning, she raised the weapon he'd given her, holding it in front of her in hands that trembled.

"Sean?" she called as she stepped into the room.

She looked through the wide windows toward the pool area first, hoping to find the two of them outside. There was nothing out there except the chaises and her mother's plants, exactly as she'd last seen them after supper tonight.

Her gaze swept back, checking the door. It was still closed. And in the kitchen…

She heard some sound before she picked up movement in her peripheral vision. The force of the downward blow that struck her outstretched arms knocked the gun out of her hands.

For a few seconds her forearm, which had taken the brunt of that vicious hit, was blessedly numb. Then, as the shock to the nerve endings wore off, pain, worse than any she could remember in her life, sent her to her knees.

From that position she looked up, still stunned by that agony, so that the movement of her head happened almost in slow motion. Standing beside the doorway, where he'd obviously been waiting for her, was a figure from a nightmare.

Her nightmare.

A black ski mask, especially incongruous in this locale, obscured his features. Despite that, there was no doubt in her mind who he was.

And no doubt that, despite the promises everyone had made to her, it was her time to face the Inquisitor.

Twenty-Six

"We're still trying to work out how he got in," Bingham said. "The security company had no indication anything was wrong. Actually, it wasn't. A couple of army surplus smoke canisters. Some oily rags and rubber gaskets to give the stuff the right color and odor. The smoke detector he used to lure you downstairs wasn't connected to the security system, so ." The detective shrugged. "Until you called 911, nobody had any idea anything was wrong out here."

A few minutes after 3:00 a.m. If the severity of Sean's headache was any indication of the length of time he'd been unconscious, that could have been several minutes after he'd been hit. All he was sure of was that when he'd come to and stumbled outside, Jenna was gone.

During their preliminary search, the cops had found nothing useful, either in the house or on the grounds. As with all the other victims, they had no clue who'd taken Jenna. Or where. And right now, the latter was the only thing that mattered.

He wished to hell he could think. He'd refused whatever they'd tried to give him because he was familiar with the mind-numbing effects of anything powerful enough to work against this level of pain. And if ever he'd needed his faculties intact, it was now.

He'd also refused the paramedics' insistence that he go to the hospital for observation and to have the cut on his forehead sewn up. He had allowed them to bandage it, but nothing else.

Stitches weren't going to help the headache, and he knew from experience that the double vision he was also dealing with would eventually resolve itself. In the meantime—

"What about the lead you had on the car?" he asked.

"We're working it. But you have to understand that all we're doing with that is narrowing the pool of suspects to a few thousand people. In a city this size—"

"Anybody else come forward?"

"A couple of people. Frankly…" Bingham shook his head. "Frankly, we don't believe they're credible. Typical out-of-the-woodwork nutcases, if you ask me."

There had to be something else, Sean thought, struggling to contain his despair. Somewhere to begin to look. Someone to question. If there was, he couldn't think who or where.

That was the problem. He couldn't think. And the pain was bad enough that he was fighting an accompanying nausea.

He closed his eyes, forcing his mind away from it by remembering Makaela's face when they'd pulled out the morgue tray. Remembering the details of the autopsy it had taken him more than three days to read because he could only stomach a paragraph or two at a time of the coroner's detailed chronicling of what had been done to her.

So there *had* to be somewhere to start. Someone—

"Paul Carlisle." He opened his eyes as he said the name, bringing Bingham's face into focus by squinting.

"Dr. Carlisle? What about him?"

"Jenna told him where we were. He told you."

"Yeah?"

Obviously the lieutenant wasn't getting the connection. The only one Sean had right now. "Maybe he told somebody else."

The detective's eyes widened, before he nodded. "We can ask."

"Not we. *I* want to ask." Sean eased off the tailgate of the rescue truck where he'd been sitting.

Everything wavered as the air thinned around his head. He put his hand on the door to maintain a necessary contact with something unmoving.

"Let's get you to the hospital," Bingham said, taking his elbow. "You ain't gonna do her any good this way."

"Carlisle." Sean freed his arm, straightening his body through an act of will. "I want to know everybody that son of a bitch has talked to about Jenna in the past two days."

"If you're implying that I somehow—"

"This isn't about you, Dr. Carlisle," Sean broke in. "You *do* understand that a madman who cuts women to pieces has Jenna. And we have no idea where. All I'm asking from you are the names of the people you talked to about her in the past couple of days. Nothing that's confidential. Just some information that might help us find a woman you profess to care about."

The psychiatrist closed his mouth, looking at him a long moment. "Why don't you come into my study and sit down before you fall down? That isn't going to help find Jenna."

"Can *you?*"

Despite his mental acknowledgment that Carlisle was right, at least about the probability of him falling facedown onto the black marble floor, Sean refused to move. As a concession to the possibility, however, he leaned forward, placing the knuckles of his right hand on the long, narrow table that centered the right-hand side of Carlisle's foyer.

Unwilling to wait until daylight, Sean had made the detective drive him to the home of Jenna's boss. Although Carlisle lived more than twenty miles from the Kincaids, the houses were eerily similar. Both too big, ornately and expensively decorated.

They'd gotten the psychiatrist out of bed. Despite the hour and the presence of a police cruiser in his driveway, Carlisle had still taken time to throw a cashmere robe on over his silk pajamas.

When he'd discovered why they were here, he'd seemed shocked by the news of Jenna's abduction. His first question had been what he could do to help. Yet as soon as Sean asked who he might have told about where they'd been hiding, he'd taken the inquiry as a personal insult.

"I don't know that I can," Carlisle said. "Believe me, I would do anything in my power to help find Jenna. The problem here is that you're mistaken in your assumption—"

"Maybe you didn't do it deliberately. Maybe you said something that inadvertently gave her location away. Until you tell us the people you discussed Jenna with, we have no way of checking that out."

"You intend to question every person I mentioned Jenna to in the past few days? Do you really think that's the best method of finding her?" The psychiatrist's gaze shifted to Bingham. "Or is it simply the best *you* can come up with? If so, I'm afraid I have serious doubts about the efficiency of your investigative techniques."

"Let me be frank, Dr. Carlisle. We got nothing here."

The detective's voice was remarkably calm, considering the accusation that had been made. And although his answer was accurate, it was a truth Sean didn't need to hear again.

"We got a description of a car," Bingham went on. "One that fits thousands, maybe tens of thousands, of vehicles in the area. All of which we're checking out the only way we can. One vehicle at a time. In the meantime, we got no other clues. And no suspects."

Sean let the silence build a few seconds before he patiently said again, "All we're asking for—"

"I told Lieutenant Bingham where Jenna was because he asked," Carlisle broke in. "You know that. I didn't feel that was information I had a right to withhold from the police. Not in the middle of a homicide investigation. If you have a problem with that—"

"I don't. It's whoever else you may have told."

Sean put his other hand on the table, leaning forward. Although it was a matter of maintaining his somewhat precarious balance, the posture must have appeared threatening. Carlisle's eyes widened.

If you only knew how empty any threat coming from me right now would be…

"Several people on the staff," the psychiatrist said, "friends of Jenna's, asked me if I'd talked to her. I tried to reassure them that she was being adequately protected, but at no time did I tell *anyone* her location."

"A list, please." The economy of words was necessitated by the realization that any movement, even the minimal amount required for talking, would make the nausea start again.

"A list of our staff members?"

"Just the ones you talked to."

Carlisle's lips pursed as he thought about the request. "Beth Goldberg is the person who asked the original question. There were others in the room at the time. I'm not sure who was listening to the conversation. Actually, I'm not sure why any of this intrastaff communication is pertinent to your investigation. I've assured you I gave the information about Jenna's whereabouts to no one other than Lieutenant Bingham."

Sean wasn't going through that again. He wasn't up to it. "Then maybe the question we should be asking is where you were around 2:00 a.m. this morning."

"I beg your pardon?"

"We *know* that *you* knew Jenna was at her parents'. And you're the *only* person we *know* she told. So...where were you, Dr. Carlisle, when she disappeared?"

"I was here, of course. Asleep. Not that I acknowledge your authority to ask me for that information."

"Anybody who can verify that?" Bingham's intervention prevented Sean from having to come up with a response to the psychiatrist's challenge. No one could argue with the lead detective's right to ask where Carlisle had been tonight.

"Are you seriously suggesting that I could be a serial killer, Lieutenant? I'm flattered that you think I could work my ass off for twenty years in this town to build a practice of this size and reputation *and* at the same time manage to commit a series of apparently unsolvable murders in different parts of the country. Flattered, but still, I'm afraid I'm going to have to plead not guilty. I'm not Superman. Nor am I the Inquisitor."

"What makes it easy these days for someone to do what this guy has done is transportation," the detective said. "Last time I looked, we got plenty of planes flying out of the airport here. And you obviously got money to get on any of 'em you want to and fly wherever you want to go. So...I'm gonna ask you one more time, Dr. Carlisle. Is there anybody who can verify that you were here all night?"

Bingham's repetition of the question was controlled, but he'd made it clear he'd not been amused by the psychiatrist's sarcasm. Carlisle was intelligent enough to pick up on that. And smart enough to also know how unpleasant this could become.

"I live alone. I was alone tonight. Look, if I were planning to abduct Jenna, as ludicrous as the idea is, I certainly wouldn't have given away to you that I knew where she was hiding. I should be the *last* person you suspect of this."

"Unless you're just clever enough to figure out that by telling us her location, we'd consider you to be the last possible suspect."

"Lieutenant—"

"Provide us with the list of people you talked to about Dr. Kincaid," Sean demanded, carefully straightening away from the table. "All we want are those names."

Having recognized that he obviously had no choice, Carlisle complied. "Beth Goldberg. I mentioned her before. Gary Evers. Jeffrey Burrows. Ceil Rogers. One of the secretaries. Jenna's, perhaps. I really don't remember. She seemed highly interested in what I said, in any case. As for who else was in the room at the time... I'm sorry. I can't be more specific."

"And all those folks will be at your office this morning?" Bingham asked.

"As they are every weekday morning. We *do* all work for a living, despite common misconceptions to the contrary."

"We can't wait," Sean warned, turning to look at the cop over his shoulder.

Bingham glanced at his watch and then shook his head. "It's nearly five. In the long run it'll be quicker to meet them there. By the time we round up the addresses and roust these folks out of their beds..." He shrugged.

"Personnel files?" Sean turned back to shoot the question at Carlisle.

"Of the staff?" It was clear he wanted to protest, but one glance at the detective's face stopped him. "At the office, of course."

"We'll need to see those, too."

"If you're implying that one of Jenna's colleagues—"

"She swore to me you were the only person she told. I don't think she was lying. You say you had nothing to do with her disappearance, and we've taken you at your word, but someone must have given something away."

"You believe you'll discover who that was by going through the personnel records of my staff?"

"I believe that by examining their résumés we can eliminate any suspicion the police might have about your people being involved in these homicides. You can't possibly object to that."

There was a moment's hesitation, but the psychiatrist nodded. Maybe he figured that the quicker he gave them what they wanted, the quicker this would be done.

"And we'd like time to go over them before they arrive," Sean added.

"*Before* they arrive? You mean—"

"As soon as you're dressed, Doctor. If you don't mind."

Carlisle's expression said that he did. "I can meet you there. Shall we say in…an hour?"

"We'll wait," Sean said.

The hazel eyes were momentarily furious, but with an effort that was visible, the psychiatrist controlled the emotion. "I have to shower."

"Don't be long." Bingham's admonition seemed low key until he added, "After all, we have no idea how long Dr. Kincaid has before he begins."

Carlisle took a breath, deep enough to be visible. It was evident that, despite his doctor-as-God arrogance, Bingham's reminder had shaken him.

Maybe he did care about Jenna. Maybe he'd told the truth about the conversation he'd had with her colleagues. If he had…

They were right back where they'd started.

"Sergeant…Murphy, is it?" The psychiatrist had taken a few steps toward the staircase when he turned back to address Sean.

"That's right."

"Tell me something, if you don't mind. You said he killed the cop."

"Cut his throat," Bingham supplied bluntly.

Carlisle's eyes focused on the detective before they returned to Sean. "Then...why would he leave you alive?"

"He knew I couldn't identify him."

"You didn't see him?"

"Nothing more than a shape coming out of the darkness."

"Still... One would think he wouldn't be willing to take that chance. It seems like too big a risk. Especially since he so obviously has no qualms about killing."

The psychiatrist's question was only what everyone else involved in this had probably been thinking. Something Sean had already come to terms with.

"It's a game," he acknowledged.

"A game?"

"The kind with winners and losers."

Carlisle studied his face a moment. "And he wants you around so you can understand that *he's* won and *you've* lost."

"Something like that."

"I believe Jenna said your sister was one of his victims."

Sean nodded, unsure where the question about Makaela was going. Wherever it was, he probably wasn't going to like it.

"You know it's all about control, don't you? With the women, I mean. It isn't sexual. It's domination. It's just as obviously about control with you, too."

"Possibly."

"He wants you to do what you're doing right now. To try and find Jenna. To imagine what's happening to her. And to finally realize that you can't do anything to stop it."

"That's where he'd be wrong," Sean said softly. "If you're looking for someone to bet on in this, don't choose him."

For a dozen heartbeats, the psychiatrist held Sean's eyes. Then he nodded. "For what it's worth, I'm glad Jenna has someone like you on her side, Sergeant Murphy. And whether you believe it or not right now, I'm on her side, too. If any of my people are involved—" He stopped, obviously controlling the emotion that had crept into his voice. "That wouldn't be good for the practice. So...whatever records you need, you'll have access to. I promise you that."

Carlisle could couch the reason for his cooperation however he wanted. The important thing was that it seemed he was finally on board with what they needed him to do.

Believing that a slip of the tongue made by one of Jenna's co-workers had led to tonight's events was a reach. Still, it was the only thing Sean had right now.

He'd always believed you played the hand you were dealt. At least until it was time for the cards to be reshuffled. That's what he had to try to do. Otherwise, the Inquisitor still held all the aces.

Twenty-Seven

"Here you are." The psychiatrist held out the four folders they'd asked for, which he'd taken from a filing cabinet in his office. "Any preference?"

Without answering, Sean took all of them from his hands and laid them out on the edge of the desk. He flipped each open, then reordered them into two stacks. Those belonging to the men were on top, with a woman's folder beneath it.

"And the secretary?"

"I'll ask Dr. Goldberg when she comes in if she remembers who that was. These—" he said, nodding toward the file "—these are the people I'm sure of."

"Thanks."

Sean picked up the two belonging to Burrows and Rogers and handed them to Bingham. He took the others and sat down in one of the leather chairs on the visitor's side of the desk.

"If you'll excuse us, Dr. Carlisle," Bingham said, bringing Sean's eyes up from the file he'd already started to read.

He'd deliberately kept Evers's because of the visit he'd paid to Jenna's the night she discovered the box in her refrigerator. Coincidence, maybe, but considering the events at the motel later on that night, he was no longer sure.

"This *is* my office, Lieutenant," Carlisle said, sounding amused and resigned rather than annoyed.

"Maybe you could get some coffee or something. Give us half an hour to look at these."

"You know how to work an intercom?"

"I can probably figure it out. I have one of my own."

"Call me if you need anything. I'll be outside."

Bingham stood, clutching the two files he'd been handed until the door closed behind the psychiatrist.

"Exactly what the hell am I supposed to be looking for in these?" he said, lifting them. "These people are mental health professionals. You don't really believe that one of them—"

"He's smart. He's organized. He knows how to manipulate people. He knows how to get them to trust him. Not bad credentials for a 'mental health professional.'"

"So why the women? We know for sure he ain't female."

"Yeah, you're right. We'll learn more talking to them personally. See if they told anyone what Carlisle said about Jenna's location."

"Carlisle says he didn't say anything."

"Yet somebody knew where she was." It wasn't that Sean didn't know how thin this all was, but other than checking out every silver or gray sedan in town, he didn't have anything else. "And we need to know what kind of car these two drive."

"Burrows and Evers."

"Ask Carlisle. If he doesn't know, tell him to find out."

"Okay," Bingham said. "And the personnel stuff? What are we supposed to look for in these?"

"Their résumés will tell us where they've been for the last few years. We know everywhere this guy's operated. Read 'em and see if anything sets off alarms."

"That's assuming, of course, that a serial killer's gonna put down accurate information about where he's worked."

"Jenna says Carlisle's the kind who would check. Make sure how good they were before he hired them. You heard his 'it wouldn't be good for the practice.' He's not the kind of person who takes chances."

"Just like our boy. I wonder if the doc's got something in his garage other than the Porsche he drove this morning. 'Course, that could apply to the other two as well. Why don't I call motor vehicles and see what automobiles these gentlemen pay taxes on? All I need are their addresses."

That was the lieutenant's area of expertise. Sean was willing to let him handle it however he thought was best. He held out Evers's folder, waiting as Bingham jotted the information he needed on a notepad from Carlisle's desk.

When the detective handed the file back, he opened the personnel folder on Burrows and then picked up a business card from the holder on the psychiatrist's desk. "Want me to go somewhere else to make the call?"

"No need to let anyone else know we're checking. Even if nothing comes of it, suspicion in something like this lingers."

Sean looked down again at the file in his lap. He was aware when Bingham slid into Carlisle's chair and picked up the phone, but he refused to be distracted, concentrating instead on the information in front of him.

The first few pages were evaluations done since Evers had begun working for Carlisle, the initial one dated, as Jenna had said, almost two years ago. Which should probably eliminate the psychologist from serious consideration, despite what Bingham said about modern transportation. Something about Evers's visit to Jenna's that night bothered Sean enough that he kept reading.

Some psychiatrist could have a field day analyzing Carlisle's cramped printing, Sean thought, turning the page. What he said was far less interesting. Apparently he had found Dr. Evers to be an "exemplary" therapist and a "team player."

And the guy's résumé was impressive, as well, even to Sean's admittedly uninformed eyes. The list of awards, grants and other recognitions he'd received filled three pages.

Sean scanned them quickly and then turned to the information he'd been looking for—the listing of the schools the psychologist had attended and his previous employments. His Ph.D. was from UMass in Boston, with a clinical internship and post-doctoral fellowship at the National Crime and Victims Research and Treatment Center in Charleston. Convenient background for a serial killer, Sean thought, lifting the first page to reveal another, half full of training seminars Evers had attended.

Before he'd come to Carlisle, he'd worked briefly in private practices in Ohio and Spokane. Sean compared those years to the chronology of the murders that had, as of now, been identified as the work of the Inquisitor. There was no record of Evers being in San Diego during the relevant period. Nor in Detroit, where Makaela had been a victim. Nor Atlanta. Boston. None of the cities the murderer had terrorized before he'd moved on to Birmingham.

Frustrated, Sean went back to the first page of the résumé, studying the list of colleges again. Evers had lived in the Boston area when he'd been in grad school, but not at the time the Inquisitor had operated there. And four of the seminars he'd attended had taken place in San Diego. Other than those—

"They're gonna check 'em all and call me back."

Startled, Sean glanced up to see the lieutenant standing beside him, looking down at the folder spread across his lap. Obviously the phone call to motor vehicles had been completed. Some time ago, he realized, as Bingham put the folders he'd been given to read down on the edge of Carlisle's desk.

"Both of these are local," Bingham went on. "She attended UAB. Burrows got his Ph.D. in Fayetteville, Arkansas. The last time I looked that wasn't on the list we should be interested in. Other than that, this guy's homegrown. You got anything?"

"Somebody who's moved around a hell of a lot in the past dozen or so years."

"Yeah? Anywhere significant?"

Sean could hear the note of excitement the detective was trying to hide. They'd known this was a long shot, but since they had virtually nothing else, evidently they had both been hoping for something.

"The times are wrong. He lived in Boston, but long before the murders."

"That means he would have known the city. Somewhere familiar. Somewhere that makes him feel safe."

That was typical of serial killers. Especially in the beginning.

"He attended a few seminars in San Diego. No connection to Atlanta. Or Detroit. Not that I can see." Sean passed the résumé across to the other man.

Bingham looked at it, using his thumb to raise the first sheet so he could see the second. "Maybe his boss knows something about those two."

He stood, reaching across the desk to press the button on the intercom. "Dr. Carlisle? Could you come back in, please?"

The reply was immediate. As if the psychiatrist had been sitting in the outer office waiting to push that button in response. "Dr. Goldberg is here. Shall I bring her in, too?"

The detective looked at Sean, raising his brows.

Why not? They could ask her the same questions they needed to ask Carlisle. He nodded.

Bingham pressed the button again. "Bring her with you."

The lieutenant handed Evers's résumé back as the door to the office opened. They turned to watch Carlisle usher in a woman about Jenna's age, with the same dark hair and eyes. Reflected within them was disbelief. Anxiety. Concern.

Seeing them there, all the emotions Sean had fought since he'd awakened on the floor of the Kincaids' kitchen came roaring back. He wasn't sure whether it was Beth Goldberg's physical resemblance to Jenna or her obvious distress, but the images of what might be happening to Jenna—images he had denied for the past three hours—threatened his control.

"This is Jenna's friend and colleague, Dr. Beth Goldberg. Beth, Lieutenant Bingham. He's in charge of the local Inquisitor task force. Beth came in early to catch up on some things, so I asked her to come and talk to you."

"Is it true?" Despite Carlisle's introduction, for some reason she spoke directly to Sean. "What Paul said? You believe the killer has abducted Jenna?"

Bingham looked at him, waiting for Sean to answer. Unsure he could right now without his voice shaking, Sean said nothing.

After a moment the police lieutenant filled in the awkward silence. "We're relatively certain that's the case, Dr. Goldberg."

"Then if I may ask, respectfully, what the hell are you all doing here?" This time the question was addressed to the detective. "Why aren't you out looking for her?"

"Believe me, ma'am, we are. However—" Bingham stopped, turning toward Sean again.

He was right. The fact that they were here rather than anywhere else was because of his insistence. His instinct.

"Dr. Carlisle's the only person Jenna told where she would be last night. The fact that the killer showed up at that location meant we needed to ask him some questions."

"And who are you?" Beth asked.

"My name's Murphy. Sean Murphy."

"You're the man who threatened Jenna."

Not an unfair characterization, but the feelings that had provoked his visit seemed foreign to him now. "I tried to tell her she was in danger."

"Looks like you were right. So do you get a gold star or something?"

"Dr. Goldberg—"

"How the hell did this happen if you knew she might be a target? How could you have let it happen?"

"Beth."

Carlisle's admonition made the psychologist press her lips together tightly, but her eyes expressed her fury.

"You and Dr. Carlisle had a conversation about Jenna yesterday. Is that right?" Bingham asked.

"I asked if Jenna was okay. I hadn't wanted to call because I thought my worrying would cause her to worry even more. Give what you had told her credence. That sounds silly, I suppose…" She stopped, seeming to realize she'd gone off track. "Paul said he'd talked to her and that she was in a very secure place and that I shouldn't worry."

"Did he tell you where she was?"

"Not in so many words."

"What does *that* mean?" Sean demanded. "'Not in so many words.'"

The expressive eyes cut to his face. "It means I made an assumption based on what he'd said."

"Which was?"

Beth glanced at her boss, but in spite of the tightness in Carlisle's face, she told him. "I took what Paul said to mean Jenna was out at her parents' place."

"Why would you have thought that?"

"Because they were so proud of their damned security system. We went there for the retreat last year. The practice has one every year. Always informal. This one was a cookout around their pool. They'd just had the new system installed, and Jenna's father was extolling its virtues to anyone who would listen. Explaining all its bells and whistles."

"Like what?"

She looked surprised at Sean's question. "I don't know. I *didn't* listen. I wasn't interested. I remember Jenna rolling her eyes at the rigmarole her dad was going through. Some of the men seemed impressed."

"Was Dr. Evers there?"

"Gary? Yeah. I remember because he was overdressed, but then he's always been wound a little tight."

"You know him well?"

Despite his determination to maintain control, Sean could feel the sense of excitement he'd tried to tamp down before growing again. Now they knew that Evers had been to the Kincaid house. He'd seen the security system. Even Beth Goldberg's comment that he was "wound a little tight" seemed to play into his growing conviction that, against all odds, they just might be on to something.

"Only as a colleague," Beth said. "He… Frankly, I've found him difficult to get to know."

"In what way?"

"I don't know. Distant. Preoccupied, maybe. He seems an excellent therapist. Everyone says so. But…he isn't the kind of person you'd go out with after work for a drink."

"He ever talk about where he'd worked?"

"*Where* he'd worked?"

"Before he came here. Other cities."

"That should be in his résumé," Carlisle broke in, inclining his head toward the folders on the edge of the desk.

"He ever mention Detroit?" Sean went on, ignoring the psychiatrist's comments.

"Not that I remember," Carlisle said.

"He has relatives there." Beth Goldberg's statement was flat. And very confident.

"Relatives?"

"Cousins, maybe. I don't remember the details. It was… I don't know. Sometime last year. I was going to a training seminar there, and I asked a group of staffers about the location of the hotel they'd booked me into. How safe the area was. He seemed to know the city. I remember he explained it by saying he had family there."

"And Atlanta?" He didn't look at Bingham. He didn't want to see the same hope in the cop's face that crowded his chest.

"I don't remember him mentioning Atlanta," she said. "Paul?"

"Not to me. Not that I remember."

"Either of you know what kind of car Dr. Evers drives?"

"His car?" Beth Goldberg looked puzzled for a moment. And then, as she obviously remembered the repeated broadcasts of the witness's description of the car used in Carol Cummings's abduction. "You think Gary…" She shook her head, thoughts moving behind those dark eyes. "A Lexus, I think. Something big."

"Color?"

"White," Carlisle said softly. "That pearlized kind of finish."

A big sedan with the kind of paint job that might, in a twilight rain, gleam like silver.

Too many coincidences to ignore. The car. Evers's familiarity with the cities in which the Inquisitor had hunted.

And as for motive?

Maybe he'd been attracted to Jenna long before the interview. Maybe he'd even started planning how he was going to take her. And when Sean had shown up, it had sealed the deal, just as if he'd painted a target on Jenna's back.

"It's him," he said to Bingham, no longer concerned with hiding his excitement or protecting anyone's reputation. "Too much of this fits. It's got to be Evers."

Twenty-Eight

Jenna slowly opened her eyes and then shut them against the influx of light. It seemed to slice into her brain, pinpointing the pain that began in the center of her skull and radiated outward. Even with her eyelids closed, the throbbing behind them didn't lessen.

The ache in her right arm was almost as bad as the one in her head. She tried to raise her left in an attempt to reach across her body to discover what was wrong with it.

For some reason, she couldn't. For several seconds she puzzled over that inability before the events in the kitchen flooded back. All the things she didn't want to remember.

Searching for Sean. The blow that had knocked the gun from her hands. The man in the mask, who'd materialized out of the darkness. The cruelty of his grip on her injured arm as he'd jammed a needle into it.

The images appeared faster and faster, forcing their way into her fogged brain. At some point the realization of what they all meant was there as well.

Who had attacked her. The reason neither Sean nor Officer

Daniels had come to her aid during his assault. The fact that she couldn't move her arms.

She tried to lift her head to verify if she were right about the reason for that, only to discover that it, too, had been secured to whatever surface she was lying on.

She cut her eyes as far to the right as she could. She could see the edge of the strip of silver tape that had been used to immobilize her head, a couple of strings still hanging from when it had been ripped from the roll.

Panic bubbled inside her chest, tightening her throat so that she couldn't breathe. Frantic now, beyond reasoned thought, she fought to move her legs. And then, in desperation, her arms again, despite the shards of agony her efforts sent through the right one.

Only her hands had any range of motion and that was severely limited. She twisted and turned them, trying to pull free. The only result was that the duct tape chafed her wrists raw and the ache in her forearm became unbearable.

After endless minutes of that useless struggle, she allowed her head to fall back against the mattress the meager half inch she'd managed to raise it. She waited for the pain in her arm to subside, wondering for the first time if it might be broken. And then wondering what it would matter if it were.

He'd done this more than a dozen times. He had it down to a science. Even the police had admitted there were no flaws in his methodology.

And each of those victims must have struggled exactly like this. As desperate to escape as she was.

Not one of them had ever made it. He was far too careful to allow that to happen. Too good at what he did.

Screw that, she thought, furious at her own surrender. *And screw you, too, you bastard. If you think I'm going to lie here and let you make mincemeat out of me—*

Rage as well as fear fueled her renewed struggle. This time she didn't attempt to move the right arm, concentrating on freeing her left instead.

Her wrists had always been slender. If she could stretch the tape enough to slip her hand through...

Fiercely determined, she twisted and turned her wrist, putting as much pressure as she was capable of with her limited movement against the bindings. Sometime in the midst of her exertion, she realized that she'd been gasping aloud, almost panting, with the intensity of her efforts. If he heard her—

She froze, holding her breath as she strained to hear whether he was coming. At first she heard nothing. And then, almost in wonder, she realized there was some background noise that had been there since she'd awakened.

From somewhere nearby came the sound of water. It was distant, enough so that she believed what she was hearing came from outside rather than inside the structure. A creek or a stream, rather than a faucet? And God knew there were hundreds of those in the area.

Relegating her discovery to sensory background, she listened again, trying to identify any other sounds in her environment. There was nothing.

Other than the faint noise of the water, the place was as silent as a tomb. She closed her eyes, squeezing the lids tightly shut to stop the rush of tears the cliché had produced.

She didn't want to die. Most of all she didn't want to die like this. Strapped down like some terrified animal on a vivisection table. Aware of every slice. Every cut. Each precise mutilation—

She broke the chain of thought, refusing to give him that power. Not yet. Not until she was faced with the reality of what he would do and not simply with her terror of it.

The reality she had to face right now was that she had

no idea where he was or when he would return. All she knew for sure was that however long that might be, the time was finite.

He *would* come. And he would do to her what he had done to all the others.

She was under no delusion. There were no brilliant arguments to prevent what was going to happen. No psychological tricks. No plea that would deter him.

He had perfected what he did so that it was ritual. Unthinking. And unchanging.

And no one was going to stop him doing it. Not the police, who had been ineffective in stopping him for almost a decade now. It was even possible they didn't even know she was missing. Maybe if Sean or Daniels had still been alive—

She caught back her sobs. If the Inquisitor *was* here, she didn't want him to know she was awake. If he wasn't, then her only chance was to free herself before he came back. And she had no idea how long she had before that would happen.

"As far as Carlisle knows, he's coming in today," Bingham said, keeping pace with Sean's near run. "He hasn't called to cancel his patients. We wait for him here, with everything in place so that when he arrives—"

"You have any idea what he's doing right now?"

He glanced at the detective's face in time to watch the impact of his question. Although he'd visibly flinched, Bingham recovered quickly. He put out his hand, grabbing Sean's wrist hard enough to halt his progress and at the same time turn him around so they were almost face-to-face.

"You don't know that. Chances are he doesn't take them home."

"Chances *are?* That's the best you got? What kind of chance do you think those women had once they were in his hands?"

As Jenna was now. He jerked his arm out of the lieutenant's grasp, heading determinedly down the hall again.

"I can stop you, you know."

"You'll have to."

This time Sean didn't even look back. He hit the front door full force, pushing it open so that despite its weight, it slammed back against the side of the building. It was only then that he realized his SUV was back at the Kincaids'. He'd been in no condition to drive when they'd left the house.

And apparently in no condition to think, either.

He turned as Bingham came through the door that had not yet had time to close. "I need a car."

"You need to calm down and think this through. We don't want to scare him off. We do that and we lose him. Then he really can do anything he wants to her."

The first part of that argument didn't move him. The last, however— "He's not coming back here, Ray. This is over and done. He has to know that."

It was so clear to him Sean didn't understand why the detective didn't get it. Gary Evers wasn't going to come in to the office today and see patients. He wasn't stupid. He had to know that somebody was going to put Jenna's disappearance together with Carlisle's knowledge of where she'd been hiding with the description of the car that had picked up Carol Cummings, which was now public.

"You don't know that," Bingham said. "You go off half cocked and we lose any chance we have."

"Jenna to Carlisle and back to Evers. It's all there. He isn't stupid," Sean said again. "He has to know that once the threads start to unravel, everything is going to be discovered.

The connection to the places he's lived. The car he drives. He isn't going to get in that car and show up for work today like nothing's happened."

"As far as he knows, nothing has," Bingham argued. "There's been no media release about Jenna. He's got no reason to think we've made those connections."

"He wouldn't have taken the chances he took last night if he didn't know it was over."

"That makes no sense, Sean. You're the one who's been saying he was after Jenna all along."

"The risks he took—"

"Maybe he likes risks. Maybe what he got out of last night was worth taking risks *for.* And I'm not talking about Jenna."

"You think he cares that much about getting to me?"

"I think you're his antithesis. And he knows it."

"And I think we're wasting time. Who gives a fuck what he thinks? He's an animal. A mad dog. The only way to stop him is to kill him."

"I'm not arguing that. I just want to be sure that's what we do—stop him, I mean. This is the closest we've come—"

"Then get your head out of your ass and come with me. Let's take him down, once and for all."

Before he does to Jenna what he's done to the others. What he did to Makaela.

He could see indecision on the lieutenant's face. Bingham wanted this bastard, too. He just wasn't convinced this was the way. Sean was. But if they waited much longer—

"So what if he took her wherever he takes them and didn't go back to his house?" Bingham asked.

"He hasn't had time. I'm betting he's got her there with him now. And if he doesn't, what have we got to lose by checking it out?"

"He sees us and runs."

"He's not going to see us."

"You aren't thinking about— The two of us? Alone? Man, you're full of shit."

"*You're* the one who's afraid we'll scare him away. You go in there with a SWAT team, and you just might be right."

Bingham started shaking his head before Sean finished the sentence. "You had your chance last night. I'm *not* gonna let him walk away this time."

Sean could sense precious minutes ticking off as they argued. No one had ever been able to determine the sequence in which the bastard worked. No one knew where he began. The only thing that was certain was how it ended.

It had been nearly four hours since he'd taken Jenna. What he could do in that timeframe to the delicate skin of the woman Sean had made love to last night…

"You call in anybody you want," he capitulated. "I don't care. As long as I'm there, too."

Bingham's eyes fell to the bulge caused by the Glock Sean had recovered from the kitchen floor and shoved into the pocket of his jacket. When the detective looked up again, the brown eyes were hard.

"This isn't your mission, Sergeant Murphy. It's mine. I'm in charge here. I'm going to do everything in my power to make sure we bring this guy in alive. There are families out there who need information that'll give them closure—"

"Trust me. What those families *want* is him dead," Sean said, his voice equally cold. "Don't try to dress up what *you* want in any kind of reason supposedly coming from them. You want the credit for bringing him in, that's one thing, but don't you lecture me about what the families want."

He held Bingham's eyes as he made the ultimatum. The lieutenant was the first to look away.

"I'll get somebody out here."

"And the house?"

"We'll check it out. You, me *and* a SWAT team."

"And if he runs?"

"Then we'll catch him."

Twenty-Nine

Like the Kincaids' estate, Evers's house sat in the middle of several acres in a relatively rural area. Although not as large as that of Jenna's parents, it was impressive by any standard. And a setting that was perfect for the Inquisitor's purposes, Sean had thought as they'd driven up the curving drive.

At Bingham's insistence the SWAT team had made the initial approach. No one had answered the door, which they were then given permission to batter down while a couple of police helicopters hovered over the grounds.

The house had been empty. And according to the reports coming over Bingham's two-way, there were no signs that any violence, either past or present, had taken place there. They would do the standard tests for the presence of blood on every inch of the property, of course, hoping that the results might provide evidence when Evers was brought to trial.

If he was brought to trial, Sean thought bitterly. Somehow the bastard had managed to do what he'd always done before. He had eluded those who were searching for him.

"The Lexus is in the basement garage," Bingham said. "They're going over it now."

"He has another car. Something he uses to transport the victims."

"We can check with motor vehicle—"

"It won't be registered in his name. He may even have brought it with him." The same car he'd used in other places? If so, he wouldn't keep it here. Sean's surety about the odds against him doing that produced his next suggestion. "And check and see what other property Evers owns."

Mouth open as if he were about to complete the sentence Sean had interrupted, Bingham stared at him for a few seconds before he punched the button on his radio to do the things he'd been told.

"That may not be in his name, either," Sean warned.

"Then how the hell are they supposed to look for it?"

"He would have used a Realtor to find this place." The psychologist wouldn't have known about the house otherwise. It would have been listed only with someone who specialized in properties in this price range. "Find out who handled the transaction and then see if Evers mentioned he was looking for anything else. Something smaller. Secluded. Something for a relative or a friend, maybe."

It was a long shot. A chance Evers should never have taken. It was, however, a possibility. Working his hunches had gotten them this far. And those were still all he had.

Despite the chill in the air, Jenna's body was covered with sweat. Although she couldn't see the wrist she'd worked raw against the tape, she believed that part of the moisture she could feel on it was blood.

Undeterred, she continued to twist and turn her arm. The wetness, whatever its cause, should make it easier to slip her hand out of the bonds. The tape had already stretched enough to encourage her to redouble her efforts. If only—

There was another of those incremental relaxations of the plastic. Heartened by that success, she once more attempted to pull the widest part of her hand through the opening.

This time it moved. Not a lot, but enough to tell her that, despite his record of successes, the Inquisitor wasn't invincible. She used every remaining ounce of strength she possessed to try to pull her arm out of the grip of the tape.

Almost. Almost…

She folded her thumb against her palm, at the same time applying as much pressure as she could. Unbelievably, she felt her hand slip free.

In spite of her work and determination, she was stunned at the success. She lifted her arm, holding it in front of her face. Her wrist looked as if it had been through a meat grinder. Only when a drop of blood fell onto her chin did her sense of urgency replace her euphoria.

She reached up, trying to locate by feel the end of the tape that was wrapped around her head. Her fingers searched along every inch, moving from side to side as far as she could reach. Obviously that was not far enough.

She changed tactics, inserting her thumb under the tape to push it upward as she twisted her neck in an attempt to pull her head free. The maneuver was immediately effective at the cost of nothing more damaging than a few strands of hair entangled in the adhesive.

Elated, she started to sit up and was quickly reminded of the injury to her right arm. Moving gingerly, she propped herself on her right elbow, ignoring the pain as she tried to free her other hand. That necessitated reaching under the mattress to find and then unwrap the tape that secured it to the metal framework of the bed.

Now only her feet remained bound. Using her good arm, she pushed herself into a sitting position, cradling the right against her body. As she did, the bedsprings creaked. She froze once more, listening for a reaction.

After a moment—all she dared to wait—she began to struggle to untie her ankles, which had been bound by looping the tape around the wooden slats of the footboard. Working left-handed, she found the end and unwound it. Once that was done, she threw the sticky mess to the side.

Moving carefully in an attempt to keep the springs silent, she swung her legs off the bed, conscious of the soft noise she was making. Seated on its edge, she paused again. The sound of the water was still there, but she could hear nothing else.

As she eased herself off the bed, its metal springs made one last protest. High on the rush of adrenaline created by the fact that she was free, she didn't hesitate this time.

She ran to the window, pushing the limp curtain aside to see out. Firewood was stacked directly under the sill. Beyond it stretched a dense wood, mostly pines and other southern conifers.

Daylight, she realized. With the way the sun was filtered by the trees, however, she couldn't begin to guess how late it was.

She laid her cheek against the cold glass, trying to see if there was a driveway or road nearby. She could see nothing but forest, not even the water she could hear more distinctly now.

In this case, *any* unknown, no matter what, was infinitely better than the known. Nothing mattered except getting out of this cabin. And to do that—

She turned the latch at the top of lower part of the window and tried to push up the sash with her left hand. Even adding what little strength she had in her damaged right, she couldn't budge it. The wood was either swollen from the surrounding moisture or the window had been painted shut.

She turned to look for something to break out the glass. Instead, her eyes focused on the closed door of the bedroom

If the killer was inside the cabin, with the noise the bed had made, he would have come to investigate. Since he hadn't, it stood to reason that the house was empty, which meant she didn't have to go out through the window.

She examined the conclusion, looking for holes in her logic. If he were somewhere outside, but nearby, the sound of shattering glass might bring him back. Opening the door as carefully as she could, however...

As the thought had formed she started across the floor, bare feet making no sound on the rough-hewn planks. She stopped at the door, putting her ear against it.

For a moment she could hear nothing. Then, fainter even than the ever-present noise of running water, came the distant sound of a car's engine, straining as if to pull up a slope.

"It's still early. You can't expect—"

"The hell I can't," Sean said. "Somebody in this town sold that bastard a house. Or rented him a storage shed. Somebody knows where he takes them. They don't know it yet, but all they have to do is look at his picture and remember."

The local affiliates as well as the cable news stations had been flooding the airways with Evers's picture since Bingham had put out the APB. The cops were asking anyone who'd had any property dealings with the psychologist to come forward.

They were also searching the records of every real estate purchase between the time Carlisle had hired him and the first murder, betting that he would have had everything in place long before he'd taken Sandra Reynolds. So far, the media blitz hadn't produced the results they'd been hoping for.

"Something like this can take days," the detective warned.

"We don't have *days*."

"Every indication we have is that he keeps them alive—"

"Don't," Sean demanded harshly.

He didn't want to hear how long the sadist would keep Jenna alive. He wanted to know where the fuck he was. And when he did—

"They got a call you should hear."

They both looked up at the cop who'd stuck his head into the door of the lieutenant's office. Sean could read nothing from his expression, but then everybody on the local task force was aware of how grim the situation was.

"Whatcha got?" Bingham asked, straightening away from the desk he'd propped his hip on as they'd watched the media coverage of the search.

"Some lady thinks she remembers Evers. She says she may have sold him a cabin on the Warrior."

"That wasn't the name he used. I looked it up to be sure, but the news said he might have used an alias. I'm almost positive it was the same man."

"When was this, Ms. Clem?"

"July, summer before last. Hot as Hades. And I remember getting eaten alive by mosquitoes," the disembodied female voice on the other end of the phone line said. "He wanted something isolated. That was almost the only requirement. That there were no other places nearby. Peace and quiet, he kept saying. I tried to show him some mobile homes, but he was set on having a house. And he didn't quibble over the price."

"You're saying you found him a place?"

In the background papers rustled. "I thought you understood. I told the other gentleman I talked to. I don't remember his name, but—"

"You have the address?" Sean broke in, closing his eyes as the words to Hail Mary, something he hadn't uttered in years, slipped through his brain.

"I do, but I doubt you'll be able to locate the place from that. You know how river property is."

He didn't, but he'd be willing to bet that someone in the area's law enforcement community would. "Just give me what you have. We'll find it."

This time she didn't hesitate. Since she couldn't see a road from the window, whoever was approaching wouldn't be able to see her. As she ran across the room, she grabbed the rush-bottom ladderback that had been pulled to the side of the bedside table.

It was then that she saw the flat black leather case on top of the nightstand. The container for whatever he'd drugged her with? Or for something more sinister? The tools of his sick trade?

The thought lent strength to her swing. Despite that, the chair bounced off the glass, which refused to break. Panicked now, she grasped the rails on either side of the ladderback and, ignoring the jolt of pain through her forearm, brought the seat and the legs as far around as she could.

This time the window cracked, glass flying out onto the stack of wood. She dropped the chair, reaching through the opening to grab one of the split logs. She used it to knock out the larger pieces that clung to the frame.

As she worked, she listened, trying to hear the approaching car. She couldn't, but she knew that she hadn't been mistaken. Either the Inquisitor was returning or someone else was coming to the cabin. In either case, she needed to be outside.

She righted the chair and then climbed onto the seat to step across the sill. Holding on to the top of the lower frame, she stepped onto the woodpile, immediately feeling the log she was on shift beneath her foot. It rolled, setting off a chain reaction that sent others tumbling to the ground.

She fell with them, losing her left-handed grip on the frame. She hit hard, but she scrambled up immediately, stumbling over the scattered wood.

She still couldn't see the road, but out here the sound of the car engine was frighteningly close. She bolted toward the line of trees, perhaps ten feet away, trying to put as much distance as she could between herself and the cabin.

She was aware of the roughness of the ground she ran across, but there was nothing she could do about the toll it was taking on her bare feet. The terrain sloped slightly, the forest becoming denser the farther away she got from the clearing where the cabin had been erected.

Panting, she darted between the trunks. She threw a glance over her shoulder, trying to spot the vehicle she'd heard through the trees. As she did, her toe caught in an exposed root, sending her careening into a massive pine. The right side of her body slammed into the tree, eliciting an outcry, which she cut off by locking her teeth into her bottom lip.

Although she regained her balance without falling, the onslaught of pain was enough that her forward progress came to a halt. Body hunched, she cradled the injured arm against her stomach, left hand under its elbow. Sobbing, she tried to draw air into her aching lungs.

Some noise behind her brought her head up. She looked back in the direction from which she'd come. Something was moving along the forest floor, disturbing the pattern of dappled sunlight and shade.

That was enough to send her forward again. She used her good hand to push off against the trunk, no longer conscious of her injury. She ran, this time concentrating on the ground in front of her. She couldn't afford to fall again.

Behind her she could hear the sounds of pursuit. He was

crashing through the underbrush, obviously uncaring of how much noise he made.

She flew, sheer terror driving her flight. The loam under her feet was littered with pinecones, rocks and roots, but she was almost unconscious of her torn and battered feet. There had to be another cabin. A road. Some vestige of civilization.

She had no idea where she was. Or where she was going. All she knew…

The sound of the running water had gradually been getting stronger, but still, she was surprised when the woods ended abruptly. She skidded to a stop, the small rocks and dirt disturbed by her feet sliding down the two-foot drop into the water. The inlet was perhaps two hundred feet across. On the far side was the same dense growth of pine. She was a relatively good swimmer, but with a broken arm—

Now that she'd stopped, even above her gasping breaths, even above the sound of the water trickling over the beaver dam, she could hear him behind her. Decision made, she turned to her left, running along the relatively open riverbank. Although her progress was easier, she was too exposed.

She dared not look back to see how close he was. She knew by sound alone that he was gaining on her. She could hear his breathing, sawing in and out just like hers.

Her only chance was to cut back into the woods and try to find a house or the road he'd followed here. She'd begun to turn when her bare foot slipped on the layer of rotted vegetation that covered the bank. Thrown off balance, she went down on one knee, the fingers of her left hand scrabbling for purchase that would allow her to pull herself to her feet.

They didn't find it. Instead, her right arm was gripped above the elbow and pulled back. The force he applied was enough to turn her so that for an instant she was looking up into his face.

No longer covered by the ski mask he'd worn last night, his features were distorted by his efforts. Mouth open, stretched into a parody of the pleasant expression he'd always worn, Gary Evers looked down at her for perhaps two or three seconds before he brought his fist back to strike her.

She dodged so that the blow that would have broken her nose struck the side of her face instead. Ears ringing, she kicked out at him, but her bare toes had little impact. She began to backpedal, feet moving against the slippery slope in an attempt to get away.

"Stop it," he yelled, spittle showering her face as he attempted to jerk her upright by exerting an ever greater pressure on her arm.

She screamed, her eyes closing against the pain. Before she could open them again, another blow exploded under her chin.

Thirty

The chopper low-leveled, swooping down until the shallows and deeper barge channels were clearly distinguishable by shadings in the water below. The sound of the blades overhead had kept conversation to a minimum during their journey. The grizzled Jefferson County Sheriff's deputy, here because of his lifelong knowledge of the river, leaned across to put his mouth near Sean's ear.

"Getting close now." He glanced down at his watch. "The ground units should be approaching the turnoff."

The planned assault on Evers's cabin was two-pronged. Bingham was traveling with the SWAT teams, one of which had been borrowed from the same department as the guide on this particular helicopter unit. This section of the Warrior, which crossed numerous counties and jurisdictions, fell into theirs. Like all the agencies the task force had called on this morning, the sheriff's department had been more than willing to help.

"That's the slough up ahead," John Vines said, stretching his thin neck in an attempt to see out through the windscreen. "Look just beyond that stand of loblollies, and you should be able to see the road that'll give 'em access to the property."

Sean's gaze focused in the direction the deputy pointed, searching for the narrow two-lane. When he spotted it, he saw that a flotilla of police cruisers, their light bars flashing, followed its winding ribbon through the trees.

At this distance, and with the noise the chopper was making, it would have been impossible to hear sirens. He could only hope those units were obeying the orders to maintain radio silence as the rescue attempt was carried out. They'd found a police scanner in Evers's house and they weren't taking any chances on repeating the mistake Bingham had made in that earlier raid.

Evers had been there this morning, as evidenced by the smoke-saturated clothing in the bathroom hamper. That was something Sean had gotten wrong. Evers had apparently been planning to show up for work today. Arrogance or psychosis. And at this point, it hardly mattered.

The only thing that mattered now was reaching the isolated cabin where they believed Jenna was being held before the psychologist could. No one, not even the FBI profilers, would venture a guess as to how the killer would react to the knowledge that it was finally over.

"What the hell?"

Sean's eyes jerked from the line of cars back to Vines. The deputy was staring through the door on the left side of the helicopter, tension in every line of his body.

"What is it?"

"Down there," Vines shouted to be heard above the dual noises of turning blades and the jet engine.

Below them on the riverbank a man was struggling to subdue a kneeling woman. Sean's recognition of both was instantaneous, his relief so powerful that for a few seconds he couldn't think about anything other than the fact that Jenna was alive.

As the chopper began to roll in on them, Evers turned to

look up at it, mouth open in shock. Jenna wasted no time in taking advantage of his distraction.

She struck at his head with her fist. Despite the blow, Evers refused to let go of her other arm. Instead, he turned back to her and twisted it behind her back, using it to force her to her feet.

It quickly became obvious that she was injured. The hold rendered her incapable of resisting. She almost fell again as Evers began to drag her backward, careful to keep Jenna's body between his and the helicopter.

Sean leaned forward, tapping the pilot on the back. When the man glanced over his shoulder, Sean motioned toward the bank, trying to indicate he should set the helicopter down. The pilot shook his head, shouting words Sean didn't catch.

"Not enough room," Vines interpreted, again leaning close. "We can land on the road or in the clearing where the cabin—"

"Too late." He wasn't going to back off long enough to give the bastard a chance to finish what he'd started. The image of the blood pooled under Daniels's body was too fresh.

Holy Mother of God, please don't let him do that to Jenna. Don't let him kill her when I'm this close.

Evers was still dragging Jenna along in front of him, using her body as a shield in case they might be desperate enough to take what would be an impossible shot. Despite the season, the mostly conifer forest would be dense enough to provide cover once he reached it.

"I'm going in." Sean began to peel off his jacket as he pushed between the deputy and the back of the pilot's seat, heading toward the side of the chopper that was over the water.

Vines grabbed his arm, trying to pull him back. "That *ain't* the river, son. This time of year, that slough may not be more 'an a couple of feet deep."

"Then tell him to get me out over its center," Sean shouted, jerking his arm away to continue his drive toward the door. He dropped his jacket on the metal floor, stepping over it to grab onto the doorway, one hand on each side.

Wind buffeted his body. Behind him, he could hear the deputy yelling instructions. Poised in the opening, knees bent in jump position, Sean waited as the craft drifted toward the middle of the narrow stretch of water below.

Muscles tensed, he tried to judge its deepest part by color. Even as close as they were, it all appeared the same shade of dirty brown.

The Bell Ranger seemed to hang in place, perhaps ten feet above the middle of the slough. Sean glanced back, eyes questioning, and the deputy gave him a thumbs-up.

"I'm right behind you," Vines shouted, "so if I'm wrong about the water and you don't break your neck, you'd better start swimmin' before I land on your ass."

Sean nodded, his throat closing with an emotion he didn't quite understand. Maybe it was the fact that he'd always gone into combat as part of a team. With men he knew he could count on. It seemed that once again, unexpectedly, in a place as alien to him as any of the others where he'd fought, he had again found that.

Turning back to the open door, he took one last look at the water below, ruffled by their downdraft. He drew a breath and then jumped straight out. Better broken legs than a broken neck, he had time to think before he hit.

He'd gotten lucky. The water closed over his head, cold enough to take his breath. It was only a matter of seconds before his feet touched bottom.

He bent his knees, trying to absorb the shock as his boots sank into the mire. He brought both arms down, propelling himself upward. Even before he cleared the mud of the bottom, he began to kick.

When his head broke the surface, the noise of the chopper still hovering above him was deafening. Before he could orient himself and begin to stroke toward the place Evers had been seconds ago, John Vines hit the water beside him.

He waited until the deputy surfaced. As soon as he had, Vines waved him away. Sean began swimming in earnest as the helicopter above them lifted, easing the turbulence around him.

As he neared the low bank, he struggled to find footing in the slime secure enough to allow him to climb up. Using the exposed roots of a tree that had fallen victim to rising water, he was finally able to pull himself awkwardly onto the bank.

He glanced back once to check on the man who'd followed him through the chopper door. Vines was heading for the same spot where he'd managed to exit the river, swimming with a powerful if unpolished stroke.

Relieved, Sean turned back toward the woods, removing the Glock from the holster at the base of his spine. Although it had been immersed in the river, the weapon should still be operational. If it wasn't, he'd kill the bastard with his bare hands.

Faced with a seemingly impenetrable—and indistinguishable—wall of pine trees, he was no longer sure of the exact place where Evers had dragged Jenna into the woods. Crouching, he ran along the narrow bank, searching for something that would mark their entry. A disturbance of the black loam or broken bracken that would give him a trail to follow.

"Here."

He looked up to find Vines gesturing toward an area nearer the end of the slough. Before Sean could join him, the deputy disappeared into the forest.

Sean ran toward the spot, his breath a cloud of vapor before him. For the first time since he'd hit the water, he was conscious of the numbing cold.

As he plunged into the thicket, he could see Vines ahead

of him, his khaki-colored uniform blending into the pattern of light and shadow under the trees. Burdened as he was, Evers couldn't have much of a lead. Not unless—

Again Sean blocked the possibility of having this end in any way other than the one he wanted. Part of that was an outcome he'd dreamed of for almost three years. And the other…

…was now far more important than the vow that had brought him to Birmingham.

He pushed through a particularly dense patch of undergrowth and suddenly realized he could no longer see the deputy. He turned in a tight circle, Glock held out in front of him. His eyes searched the shadows under the trees as he listened, trying to hear any movement around him, but the noise of the choppers hovering overhead prevented that.

It was as if Vines—and Evers—had disappeared. Which meant he must somehow have veered off in the wrong direction. The woods here weren't thick enough to totally hide three people.

Somewhere to his left two shots rang out in rapid succession, followed after a few seconds by a third. It was the signal they'd agreed upon before the raid began. It notified the forces coming from the road that the suspect had been located so that the need for "silent running" was over. And it meant that John Vines, with his knowledge of the area and his tracking ability, had caught up with the killer.

Before the echoes of that gunfire faded, Sean was on the move, plowing through the tangled scrub in the direction from which the shots had originated. It had been only minutes since Evers disappeared. If the deputy had sighted him—

He stepped over a rotted trunk, pushing between two holly bushes. A small clearing opened up before him.

A shaft of winter sunlight poured into it through the break

in the canopy, seeming to spotlight the three people standing motionless in the center. Given the direction from which Sean approached, they were almost in profile. As unbelievable as it seemed, with the noise of the choppers overhead, they didn't seem to be aware he was here.

Evers held the blade of his knife against Jenna's throat. His other arm was now around her body, pinning her arms to her sides. Vines faced them, a big Smith & Wesson held out in front of him, his hands wrapped confidently around its grip.

There was no way the deputy could make the shot that would take Evers out. The killer was still being careful to keep Jenna in front of him so that very little of his head or body was exposed.

From this angle, however… Sean's hands began to rise of their own volition, carrying the Glock's muzzle upward until it was pointed at the psychologist's temple. All he had to do was squeeze off one round—

"You let the lady go, now, you hear? You do that, and I promise you ain't nobody gonna hurt you," Vines said. His voice didn't seem loud, but despite the growing noise of sirens and the hovering choppers, each word he spoke was distinct. "Just move the knife away from her neck slow and easy…."

Sean's finger tightened around the trigger, the southern accent of Vines's assurances background to its movement.

"They're bringing the dogs they use out at the prison, Dr. Evers. You shore don't want to go messing with them. You just put down the knife, and we'll have you out of here in no time. No press. No nothing. Just you and me in the back of a squad car, I promise."

Just you and me…

The moment Sean had dreamed about every day for the past three years. Squeezing the trigger. Putting a bullet deep into this sadistic bastard's brain. And then sleeping all night without his sister's screams echoing through his dreams.

All he had to do to accomplish it was allow his finger to complete its slow pull. Another fraction of an inch to send a lunatic to hell, where they would know how to make him pay for the pain he'd caused and the damage he'd done to those who had loved the women he'd tortured and killed.

Those who loved...

As Sean loved Cathy and Ryan, who were waiting for him to come home. Home for Christmas.

Can I have a puppy, Uncle Sean? Can I?

And who would again face the loss of the one person they had come to trust to love and care for them.

As he cared for the dark-haired woman standing in this sunlit clearing, chin lifted, eyes closed, as the man behind her slowly moved the knife forward until its blade was perhaps ten or twelve inches from her throat.

Someone who represented a new beginning. A chance for something in his life besides the hate that had driven him through the endless days and nights since he'd identified Makaela's body.

"That's good, Dr. Evers. *Real* good," Vines said. "Now, you just let it go and then you let her go and this'll all be over with. Ain't nobody gonna hurt you. You got my word on that. You just drop the knife, and nobody's gonna get hurt. Not you. Not that lady. I promise you."

Sean, too, had made promises. Whispered them over his sister's body. Offered them as prayers after he'd put her motherless children to bed at night. Breathed them as he'd pumped round after round into the man-shaped targets at the range.

Whatever it cost him, all he had to do now to fulfill all of those promises was to complete the motion he had already begun. Inexorably, as if it were no longer a part of his body, no longer under his control, his finger again began to tighten.

He would tell them he'd stumbled onto the clearing and hadn't known what was going on. That he had seen the knife at Jenna's throat and believed the only way to save her life—

Evers stepped back, releasing his hold. In the same motion he tossed the knife forward so that it landed on the ground midway between him and the deputy.

"Dr. Kincaid, you just step away from him now," Vines said, his tone almost hypnotic. Calm and controlled. "You come on over here and stand by me. You're okay. Everything's gonna be okay now, you hear?"

Jenna opened her eyes. Her mouth worked, as if she wanted to say something, but she didn't speak before she stepped forward, moving almost hesitantly. When nothing happened, she began to run, stumbling away from the man who had been both colleague and captor.

Before she'd reached him, in that same softly accented tone, Vines began to parrot the familiar phrases of Miranda. "You have the right to remain silent. You have the right…"

The rest faded from Sean's consciousness as he watched Jenna. She seemed to gain strength and confidence in her survival with each step she took.

He could hear the dogs now, baying through the woods as they followed the trail the killer had taken from his torture chamber. In minutes this small clearing would be full of law enforcement officials. The hunt for the Inquisitor would be over. Finished. Completed.

And the bastard would still be alive.

Like Jenna. Like Makaela's children. And like him.

I'm sorry. Sorry I wasn't there. Sorry that I didn't protect you. So sorry…

He took a breath. His hands, still holding the Glock out in

front of him, trembled as if the semiautomatic was suddenly too heavy. Then, in a conscious act of will, he slowly lowered the weapon until it was no longer pointed at the man he had traveled so far to kill.

Thirty-One

Jenna had been taken from the woods straight to the emergency room at UAB. They'd put a light cast on her arm to stabilize the fracture revealed by the X-rays. Other than that, she'd been given a clean bill of health and permission to go back to Bingham's office to give her statement, a process that had been far more difficult than she could ever have imagined.

Sean had been allowed to sit in on that, a concession that had apparently been made because he'd been instrumental in figuring out where to look for her. Until she'd glanced across the clearing this morning and seen him lowering his gun, she hadn't even known he was alive, much less that he'd been with the officers who'd rescued her.

As she'd told her story, always conscious of the watchful blue eyes focused intently on her face, it was brought home to her how close she'd come to being the last of the Inquisitor's victims. No one had been able to give a satisfactory explanation as to why Evers hadn't killed her during the time between her recapture and the deputy's arrival.

The closest to something that made sense was on a news bulletin she'd heard on the television in the emergency waiting room. One of the profilers had speculated that the ritual Evers always followed hadn't yet begun.

On some level, she had still been Jenna Kincaid to him. A colleague. A person in her own right rather than a substitute object of his rage against the woman who had raised and brutalized him.

That was something else she'd learned from watching those cable news interviews—what had driven the murderer. Since the search for information on Evers had begun as soon as the police identified him, quite a lot was already known about his background.

The grandmother into whose lap he'd been dumped as a toddler had eventually ended up in a state-run mental institution. Unfortunately, that hadn't happened before her insanity had created the monster who'd visited the same cycle of mutilation and humiliation he'd been subjected to on more than a dozen women. In this case, as in many others, no one would ever be able to separate the roles heredity and environment had played in that creation.

"I think that's everything," Bingham said finally. "Or everything that can't wait until the two of you get some rest."

"If you think of anything else," Sean said, rising and holding out his hand to the detective, "you have my number."

"And mine," Jenna added, although the last thing she wanted was to relive the terror recounting today's events had brought back with such force.

"Hopefully we won't have to get back to you until after the holidays. You going back to work, Dr. Kincaid?"

"Today?"

"I doubt anybody's that dedicated. I meant before Christmas."

"I haven't had a chance to think about it."

Now that she did, she realized how difficult that would be. She would contact the people she'd been told had played a role in her rescue, especially Paul and Beth. But walking back into the office where Evers's presence would haunt them all wasn't something she was in any hurry to do.

"Most people think they can shake off the effects of something like this and just will themselves back to normal," Bingham said. "I know I don't have to tell you that isn't the way it works. Give yourself some time. And my advice, if you want to hear it—" The detective paused to give her an opportunity to say if she didn't.

"I'd be grateful for anything you have to suggest."

"Then get some counseling. And do it right away. I don't know who treats psychologists, but…whoever it is, I think it's important that you talk to somebody."

"I will. And thank you." She held out her left hand, which was quickly enveloped in both of his.

"Thank *you*. I appreciate your willingness to do this today. With the press foaming at the mouth, I figured the sooner we could get the story out there, the sooner they'll leave you all alone."

Secluded here in the police station for the past two hours, Jenna had almost forgotten what a frenzy this would cause, nationally as well as locally. Another thing she wasn't ready to face. "You think they'll be waiting outside?"

"Since we put out the bulletin on Evers this morning."

"Is there another way—" She broke the sentence to look questioningly at Sean.

Because, she realized, she was still expecting him to protect her. Something that was no longer his job.

Actually, it never had been. It hadn't even been his intention.

"We can take you out through the underground garage where we brought you in," the lieutenant said. "Have a car pick you up there and take you wherever you want to go."

Wherever you want to go. Despite her acknowledgment

that Sean was no longer under any obligation to her, her eyes clung to his, hoping he'd provide an answer to that.

When he didn't, she turned back to Bingham. She could have sworn there was compassion in his black eyes.

"If you don't mind, I'd like a few minutes to make some repairs before I go anywhere." Right now her grip on her emotions was tenuous at best. She didn't want to break down in front of these two. Especially Sean. "I don't suppose there's a comb and a mirror and maybe even a washcloth around here."

"I think we can provide those." Bingham stepped back to his desk to push the button on his intercom. "Would you send Officer Dillon in? Ask her to bring her purse."

He turned to smile at Jenna. "Just tell Helen what you need. She'll get it for you."

"I don't want to put anyone to that much trouble."

"Trust me. She'll be more than ready for a foray outside. What about you, Sergeant? Anything you need?"

"Just to make a couple of phone calls. My cell doesn't seem to be working after the river."

"Be my guest," Bingham said, gesturing toward his phone.

"Long distance," Sean added, looking as if he expected to be turned down.

"I think we can cover that in the budget. After all, we owe you. Believe me, nobody around here is going to forget that."

"Nobody 'owes' me. My motivations were entirely selfish."

Jenna told herself there was no reason for the spurt of disappointment Sean's disclaimer evoked. He'd been up front about those from the first.

Bingham's eyes rested on her face again before he took her by the elbow. "Why don't I take Dr. Kincaid someplace she can freshen up and give you some privacy? Take as long as you want. Just open the door when you're through."

Too tired to even consider protesting, Jenna allowed the lieutenant to lead her out of his office. He reached back to close the door as soon as they were outside.

"I expect he wants to let his family know he's okay. And maybe to tell them the outcome of this. They aren't the only family that's gonna be real glad this is over."

Jenna nodded in agreement, although her gaze lingered briefly on the frosted-glass top half of his office door.

"You call *your* folks?" Bingham asked.

"Not yet. I doubt they even know what's gone on here. Much less that I was involved. I know I need to tell them before they hear it from someone else, and I will. Right now, I'm not sure what to say."

"Want me to get in touch with them for you?"

She shook her head. "Thank you, but I think that would scare them to death. I'll do it. I just need to... I don't know. Put it into perspective, I guess."

"The only perspective you need right now is that you're alive. Relatively unharmed. And that you got only one person to thank for that. No matter what anybody tells you, including him, I was right here for all of it. That man in there—" he tilted his head toward the door behind him "—wasn't huntin' a killer to get revenge for his sister. He was huntin' *you.* And without him—" The detective stopped, taking a quick breath and blowing it out before he finished. "I frankly don't know that we would have gotten there in time."

"Thank you for telling me that."

Bingham nodded, a quick, decisive motion of that well-shaped head. "Thought you should know. Now, let's go see what Helen can do about getting the stuff you need."

Bingham had escorted Jenna and Sean to the elevator that would deposit them to the basement garage. He hadn't gone downstairs with them, pleading the need to prepare the press statement detailing what had happened. He was already skating close to the deadline of the announced media conference.

The cop who'd ridden down with them had gone to find out what had happened to the car that was supposed to already be here. His suspicion, he'd told them, was that the driver had been held up by the traffic generated out front by the throng of reporters.

They watched him walk toward the exit to the street in silence. With Bingham's words echoing in her head, Jenna was conscious that this might be the last time they would be together—and alone. And she very much needed to know what came next in order to prepare for it.

She wasn't sure that right now she was in control enough not to react if this was it. If Sean was going to walk out of her life without anything other than the handshake he'd offered Bingham, she needed some kind of warning. And the only thing she could think of to solicit information about his plans...

"You think they'd be willing to stop and let us pick up something to eat on the way? The cupboard's pretty bare at my apartment."

She realized it was the wrong thing to say even before Sean turned to look at her. It brought back too many memories—all of which he would want to forget. The box tied with red ribbon. Gary's visit. All that had happened after it, culminating in his discovery of Carol Cummings's body.

"I imagine after they get us away from here, they'll be willing to take you anywhere you want to go."

You. Not *we.*

"And where will they be taking you?"

"To the airport." He glanced down at his watch. "There's

plenty of time to make a stop for food and deliver you to your apartment before I have to be there. If you're sure that's where you want to go."

Surely he wasn't about to suggest that she go to her parents' house. She would have to get someone out there before they returned from their trip, but that would have to wait until the police had processed the crime scene in the kitchen. She certainly didn't intend to stay there while that was going on. And maybe never again.

"You have a better suggestion?" She waited, hoping he would say the right thing.

"You'll be fine at your apartment." Maybe her eyes belied his confidence in that because he added, "It's really over, Jenna. He isn't going to hurt you—or anyone else—ever again. Bingham will make sure of that."

"I know. Intellectually, I know. It's just that somewhere inside—"

"Let it go. Let *him* go. Back to whatever pit of hell he crawled out of."

For a fraction of a second the therapist part of her remembered that Gary Evers had once been a terrified little boy, tormented by a woman who should never had been allowed to have contact with a child. In the next she remembered that something very similar could be said about the man at her side. One had become a monster, and the other had become...

Someone willing to protect, even at the cost of his own life. Just as he'd done for Makaela all those years ago. Just as he had done for her.

"Does it have to be tonight?"

"What?"

She strengthened her voice, determined, no matter the result, to ask him. "Why do you have to leave tonight?"

"Because I promised someone I'd be home for Christmas."

"Someone?" The tone of the question was as casual as she could make it under the circumstances.

"She's eight. Bright enough to have figured out what I was doing down here. He's four. And expecting a puppy."

Makaela's children. The ones Sean had become responsible for when his sister had been murdered.

"Then… It sounds as if you have some shopping to do when you get home."

"Know anything about dogs?"

She wasn't sure why the question made her heart jump into her throat. After all, he hadn't actually invited her to help him with the purchase, which would probably have to be made in Michigan.

"I always had one when I was growing up."

"What kind?"

She smiled at the memories, although the upward movement of her lips felt stiff. Unnatural. "Not any I can see you buying."

"Yeah? You had the yappy kind?"

"With papers."

"I was thinking about getting a mutt from the pound. It's not that I couldn't afford the kind with papers. It's just that I think there would be something…I don't know. Satisfying, maybe, about giving an abandoned dog a good home."

That word, too, resonated in her heart with far too much meaning. She seemed determined to read significance into everything he said. Maybe because she was afraid there wasn't any to any of it. After all, no promises had been made. On either side, she reassured her surge of insecurity.

It had been that way since she'd met him. More than any man she'd ever been involved with, Sean Murphy made her unsure of her own worth.

And she no longer bothered to deny that she *was* involved. Whether he was or not.

"Are you going to let the kids make the choice?" she asked, working to keep any trace of disappointment out of her voice.

"Not if I want to get out of the place with just one."

"I figured you'd be in complete command of the expedition."

"Which shows how much you know about kids."

That was another thing she hadn't had time to consider. If this did go anywhere—that was something she'd have to think about.

She knew enough about Sean Murphy to know that his niece and nephew weren't responsibilities he had undertaken lightly. He would be there for them as long as they needed him.

Maybe that was the key to his hurry to be gone. She no longer needed him to protect her. And she'd never bothered to tell him all the other ways she still needed him. Maybe because—until right now—she hadn't had to acknowledge them.

"I'd like to know more," she said. "At least about yours."

As admissions went, it wasn't particularly bold. She waited while the blue eyes examined her face.

"You got plans for Christmas?"

Her throat closed with the promise of that. And then she remembered all the seasonal things she was committed to, from Paul's annual party for the staff to the bread pudding she was supposed to deliver on Christmas morning to her mother's family gathering. Right now, none of them seemed nearly as important as Sean's question.

"Not really," she said.

"You like snow? I mean a lot of it?"

"I haven't seen 'a lot of it,' but…I've always liked the little we get."

She had. Despite the traffic snafus it invariably brought, even the predictions of snowfall were still exciting.

"Kids?"

"Do I *like* them?"

"You said you liked dogs. And snow. I figured I might as well go for a hat trick."

"Are you talking about… Are you by any chance asking me to go home with you?"

"You said you didn't have plans."

"Not any that can't be changed. How will your family feel about that?"

"That's why I asked if you like kids."

"I haven't really been around them a lot, but… I think I would."

"Yeah? Well, trust me, they'll be around. Especially since I've been away."

They would want him all to themselves. Just as she did.

"Then it's probably not a good idea to spring a visit from a stranger on them," she said, hoping against hope he'd refute the out she'd given him. "Especially this time of year."

"I figured they wouldn't notice as long as I brought the puppy home, too."

Her heart rate slowed to something approaching normal. "You plan to just sneak me in during the excitement."

"Something like that. If you're interested."

"I'm interested. I don't know if I could get a flight. Not this late. And especially this time of year."

He reached into the inside pocket of his leather jacket, pulling out a couple of sheets of paper. He unfolded them before he held them out to her.

Despite everything she could do, her eyes blurred as she read her name on the airline e-ticket receipt he'd printed out. Blinking, she slipped that page under the one for his seat, right next to the one he'd reserved for her.

She looked up, no longer worried about whether he would notice the tears. "Pretty damn sure of yourself."

"I prefer to think of it as being skilled at risk assessment."

"Is that how you see this? As a risk?"

"You don't?"

She did. She just hadn't expected him to be that open about it. "Maybe. But it's one I'm willing to take."

For a second, the blue eyes were suspiciously bright. By the time the long, dark lashes swept down to cover that gleam, it had cleared.

"Yeah, well, you'd better check the time on those," he advised, nodding toward the papers she still held in her hand.

She glanced down obediently, realizing that the tickets were for today. For a flight that would leave Birmingham in less than four hours.

"How fast can you pack?"

"Fast enough," she said with complete assurance.

Epilogue

"So what do you think?"

They were watching the children play with the eight-week
old mostly golden retriever they'd picked out of the Human
Society cages on their way home from the airport. Taking hi
cue from his new owners, the puppy seemed as wildly happy
to have been made a part of this small family as Jenna was

"I think you picked a winner."

Actually, Sean had left the choice up to her. With the littl
dog's outgoing personality, it hadn't been a difficult one.

"I think you're right."

Something in Sean's tone caused her to turn her head. H
was no longer watching the antics of the children. His eye
were focused on her. She had to resist the urge to read to
much into what was in them.

"Thank you for including me in your Christmas."

Her comment seemed noncommittal enough. It had th
added advantage of being absolutely sincere. After the horro
of the past few days, the love contained within this house ha
helped restore her faith in the essential goodness of life.

"Definitely my pleasure."

That, too, seemed sincere, despite the fact her visit here was obviously not going to include a resumption of the intimacy they'd shared only two nights ago. Given the circumstances, that would be impossible.

Sean had introduced her to the housekeeper when they'd first arrived. Although it was clear Maria Alvarez was deeply attached to the children, she'd seemed anxious to get home to her own family and preparations for the holidays.

Although Jenna had been prepared for, if not hostility, at least disapproval, Mrs. Alvarez had seemed nonjudgmental about her presence here. But maybe that was because Sean had put her suitcase on one of the twin beds in his niece's room.

At this point, he wasn't the one whose self-discipline Maria should be concerned about. Seeing him in this setting had made Jenna realize how powerful her attraction had become.

She'd met him first as a man determined to bring a killer to justice. Someone seeking to avenge the death of a loved one. She'd come to view him as a protector, someone skilled enough to keep her out of harm's way. And then as a lover, able to give her pleasure in ways she'd never even imagined.

Now, here with his family, she was seeing a completely different side of him. Whatever scars the past had left, they didn't seem to hamper his ability to love his niece and nephew wholeheartedly. And if he were capable of that...

"Jen? How about it?"

She looked up, realizing that she'd been so lost in thought she hadn't heard his question. "Sorry. I swear I'm half asleep. It's been a *very* long day."

Of course, that applied to Sean as well, and yet he seemed to be fully functional.

"I asked if you want to step outside with the dog while the kids get into their pajamas."

An opportunity to be alone. As alone as they could hope to be with a puppy and two children crowded together in these few rooms.

"I'd love to. Maybe the cold air will wake me up."

"I can guarantee that. There's probably a toboggan and spare pair of gloves in the front closet. They'll be either too big or too small, but we aren't going to stay out long enough for it to matter."

"Come on, Buddy. Time to get to work."

Ryan, the four-year-old, had been allowed to name the puppy. What his choice lacked in originality had been more than compensated for by his pleasure in making the decision. Although Buddy already seemed to recognize his name, he didn't appear to have the first clue about what they were doing outside.

"Maybe he doesn't have to go," Jenna suggested, crossing her arms over her body in an attempt to survive the frigid temperatures until Sean came to the same conclusion.

"My experience with the kids tells me something different. As soon as we get back inside, he'll decide he does."

"You're basing that on the *children?*"

"I figure this works the same way as snowsuits."

She hid the smile provoked by the image of Sean dressing and then undressing a newly potty-trained toddler by hunching her shoulders and tucking her chin into the upturned collar of her coat. Sean determinedly pulled the puppy along the scraggly evergreen foundation plantings again. Although Buddy seemed interested in how they smelled, apparently the scent didn't remind him of fire hydrants or tree trunks.

"Maybe if you let him off the leash," she suggested.

"You up for chasing him all over the neighborhood?"

"It might keep us warm."

"Why don't you go on back inside and check on the hooligans? No need for both of us to freeze our asses off."

"Actually..." She hesitated, deciding that whatever she'd been anticipating when she'd agreed to come out here had obviously not been what Sean had in mind. If that were the case, then she might as well go inside.

"What?" He looked up from maneuvering his boot out of the leash the puppy had wrapped around it.

"Nothing." She forced a smile, shaking her head at his expression.

"You mean you're not enjoying this?" The quirk at the corner of his mouth took the sting out of the question.

"Buddy? Frankly, not so much. The cold? Hardly at all. Being with you... Obviously enough to make up for the others."

"Are you by any chance flirting with me, Dr. Kincaid?" Sean closed the distance between them by dragging Buddy away from the bedraggled plant nearest the bottom step where she had stopped to watch him with the dog.

"I'm too old and much too tired to flirt. And if you really *don't* know what I'm doing, then you aren't nearly as smart as everybody back in Birmingham seems to think you are."

"I've always heard you southerners were easily impressed."

"Not tonight."

"If there's one thing I can't stand," he said, putting his gloved hand at the back of her neck to draw her to him, "it's a demanding woman."

He turned his head so that the last word was whispered against her parted lips. In spite of the cold, his mouth was warm as it closed over hers, claiming it with the same expertise with which he'd claimed her body the nights they'd made love.

At her response, he deepened the kiss, pulling her against his warmth. As his other arm went around her back, she relaxed into his strength.

She had wanted this all day. Despite what he and everyone else had told her, until she was here in his arms, she hadn't believed it was over. Or that she was safe.

Now she knew she was. And if she were lucky enough to get what she wanted for Christmas, she always would be.

He lifted his head, looking down into her eyes. "Something like this more what you had in mind?"

"Something like this." She brought her hands up to cup either side of his face.

She wished she wasn't wearing gloves so she could feel the texture of the stubble that darkened his cheeks. At least she could see it. Along with the color of his eyes, surrounded by their sweep of dark lashes. The slightly crooked nose. All the things she loved—

She stopped, acknowledging the magnitude of that realization. Something she must have known for days. Something she'd not yet admitted. Not even to herself.

"Another complaint? Damn, woman." Sean lowered his head again, finding her lips.

Still dazed by her self-discovery, she was slow in responding, so that he raised his head almost immediately to look down into her face. Reacting to what was undoubtedly revealed by her expression, his eyes narrowed.

She closed her mouth, moving her hand so that she could run its gloved thumb along his bottom lip. His head tilted slightly to the side, questioning.

She shook her head, smiling at him. It was enough now that *she* knew.

"Something wrong?"

"Absolutely not," she said. "Not in my world."

He studied her face for another heartbeat. "Why do I get the feeling you're keeping something from me, Dr. Kincaid?"

"I'm an open book."

Or she should be. After all, without notifying her parents or friends, she'd gotten on a plane with him and flown to Michigan to buy a puppy. And she hadn't even asked how long he intended for her to stay.

"Not quite, but…the first few chapters have certainly been interesting."

"Does that mean you'll keep reading?"

"You should know by now that I finish what I start."

"Finish? Is that a good thing or a bad thing?"

"It's whatever you want it to be."

"Then…I guess I want this to be more than a Christmas visit."

"Is that something like a summer romance?"

"I think it might be."

"You don't have to worry about that. We don't have many of those up here."

"Summer romances?"

"Summers. Actually—"

He stopped to look down at the puppy, who was sitting at their feet, soulful eyes staring up at the man he'd obviously picked out as the object of his deepest affections. The stern lines of Sean's face relaxed into the smile she was beginning to value for its rarity before he turned back to her. It faded as he looked straight into her eyes.

"I don't make commitments lightly, Jenna. Once made, I don't take them lightly. You should have figured that out by now."

She nodded when he paused, her heart crowding her throat again as it had at the precinct.

"I wouldn't have asked you up here if you weren't impor-tant to me. But…I come with a lot of baggage, including two kids who were traumatized by their mother's death before they were old enough to understand the concept of evil. I don't intend for that to ever happen to them again. Not if I can help it. That said—" He swallowed, the movement strong enough to be visible down the strong brown column of his throat. "That said, I still want something for me. I guess I believe, selfish bastard that I am, that I deserve it."

She waited again, but he didn't go on. "And the something you want…?"

"Is you. Whatever part of your life you'll let me have in mine."

Her eyes stung again, but she ignored the burn. This was too important to risk screwing it up. And despite all her training, she wasn't quite sure how to avoid that.

He hadn't asked any of the conventional questions. And he'd made no promises. No declaration other than that he wanted her. And for right now that was enough. More than enough.

"Yes," she said, stretching to put her cold lips against the warmth of his.

"Yes, what?" He whispered the words around her kiss.

"Whatever you want. Because that's what I want, too."

Buddy barked, somehow managing to imbue the sound with authority. A real dog's bark. The first he'd made since they'd picked him out of the cage.

They turned to look down at him. He was standing now, still staring up at them expectantly. Eyes shining in the light from the porch, tail wagging, he seemed to be celebrating that he once again had their full attention.

"Okay, dopey," Sean said. "You win. You can sleep in the bathroom. There's nothing you can hurt in there."

Buddy barked again, apparently in complete agreement with the plan. Sean laughed, the sound unexpected and, like the rare smile, incredibly appealing.

"Let's go get the kids, all three of them, to bed," he said, putting his arm around her waist to urge her toward the front door.

She leaned against his side as they walked up the low steps together, about to tuck Makaela's children in for the night. And although the feeling was almost as unexpected as Sean's laughter, Jenna discovered that there was something incredibly appealing about that prospect, too.

* * * * *

*Turn the page for
an exciting preview
of
multi-Rita Award winner
Gayle Wilson's
new novel of
Romantic Suspense*
BOGEYMAN
*coming in
December 2006
From MIRA Books*

Twenty-five years before...

She had known he would come tonight. In spite of the rain and the cold. In spite of her praying "Please, Jesus" over and over again since Rachel cut out the light.

She listened, but there was no sound now except her sister's breathing, slightly whistling on each slow intake of air. And the rain, of course, pelting down on the tin roof overhead.

It made enough noise to drown out anything else, she reassured herself. Whatever she thought she'd heard—

The sound came again, and this time there was no doubt what had caused it. She had anticipated this, dreaded it, too many nights not to recognize that soft tapping on the glass.

She opened her eyes to the darkness, staring up at the ceiling as if she could see through it to the storm above. Maybe if she waited—if she pretended to be asleep—maybe this time Rachel would hear him and wake up. Or maybe Mama would get up to check and see if they were warm.

The tapping came again. Louder. Demanding.

Her sister's breathing hesitated, a long pause during which she repeated her talisman phrase again. Then the sounds Rachel made settled back into the same pattern of wheezing inhalation followed by sibilant exhalation.

Mama always said Rachel slept like the dead.

Mama...

If she got out of bed and tiptoed across the floor to the door, surely with the noise of the rain, she could open it without him hearing. And if he didn't hear, then he would never know that she'd told.

If you ever tell anyone.

She denied the image his words had created. Denied them because she couldn't bear to think about that. And if she didn't go to the window...

She took a deep breath, squeezing her eyes shut to stop the burn of tears. *Please, dear Jesus.*

Except Jesus hadn't answered any of those other times. Somewhere inside her heart she knew he wasn't going to answer tonight.

Which meant nobody would. There was nobody she could turn to. Nobody who could do anything about what he'd told her he would do if she didn't mind him. Nobody but her.

She opened her eyes, raising her arm to scrub at them with the sleeve of her nightgown. He didn't like it when she cried. He said it spoiled everything. And that if she wasn't careful—

She drew another breath, fighting to keep it from turning into a sob. Then, moving as carefully as she could, she pushed back the sheet and the quilts and sat up, putting her bare feet on the cold floor.

By the time he tapped again, she was at the window. As she put her fingers around the metal handles on the sash to lift it, she couldn't find even enough hope left inside her heart to repeat the words she'd prayed all night. The ones they had told her at Sunday school would protect her from evil.

Now she knew that they had lied.

A Shenandoah Valley novel
by *USA TODAY* Bestselling Author

EMILIE RICHARDS

Sam Kinkade is finally feeling at home as a minister in rural
Toms Brook, Virginia, content with his life and Shenandoah
Valley congregation. But his plans to welcome the area's growing
Hispanic community are being met with resistance. Fortunately,
a stranger named Elisa Martinez walks through his door,
capable of building bridges.

But Elisa isn't looking to make connections. She's come to
Toms Brook to hide. But despite her fears of discovery and the
consequences for both of them, she finds herself powerfully drawn to
Sam, and to a generations-old love story rooted in the town's past.

ENDLESS CHAIN

"Richards seamlessly joins...an intriguing political mystery,
a long-forgotten local tragedy, and a contemporary love story
in an emotionally charged and transcendent tale of the ways
love and faith can triumph in the face of seemingly
overwhelming odds."—*Booklist* on *Endless Chain*

*Available the first week of July 2006
wherever paperbacks are sold!*

MER2316

A DR. MORGAN SNOW NOVEL
BY INTERNATIONAL BESTSELLING AUTHOR

M. J. ROSE

As one of New York's top sex therapists, Dr. Morgan Snow sees everything from the abused to the depraved. Morgan's newest patient is a powerful, influential man—secretly addicted to watching Internet Web cam pornography. He's not alone in his desires. She's also working with a group of high school teenagers equally and dangerously obsessed with these real-time fantasies.

Fantasies that are all too accessible.

Then the women start dying online, right in front of their eyes.

Now, it's all about murder.

"Rose writes erotic better than just about anyone... and does thrillers just as well as the big boys."
—*BookBitch.com*

THE VENUS FIX

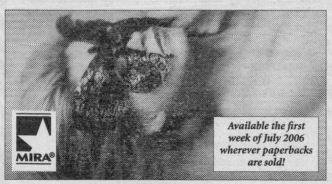

GAYLE WILSON

77073 DOUBLE BLIND   ___ $5.99 U.S. ___ $6.99 CAN.
77039 WEDNESDAY'S CHILD   ___ $5.99 U.S. ___ $6.99 CAN.
(limited quantities available)

TOTAL AMOUNT $ _____
POSTAGE & HANDLING $ _____
($1.00 FOR 1 BOOK, 50¢ for each additional)
APPLICABLE TAXES* $ _____
TOTAL PAYABLE $ _____
(check or money order—please do not send cash)

To order, complete this form and send it, along with a check or money order for the total above, payable to MIRA Books, to: **In the U.S.:** 3010 Walden Avenue, P.O. Box 9077, Buffalo, NY 14269-9077; **In Canada:** P.O. Box 636, Fort Erie, Ontario, L2A 5X3.

Name: _____
Address: _____ City: _____
State/Prov.: _____ Zip/Postal Code: _____
Account Number (if applicable): _____

075 CSAS

*New York residents remit applicable sales taxes.
*Canadian residents remit applicable GST and provincial taxes.